# JUICE

BOOKS BY TIM WINTON

NOVELS
*An Open Swimmer*
*Shallows*
*That Eye, the Sky*
*In the Winter Dark*
*Cloudstreet*
*The Riders*
*Dirt Music*
*Breath*
*Eyrie*
*The Shepherd's Hut*
*Juice*

STORIES
*Scission*
*Minimum of Two*
*The Turning*

FOR YOUNGER READERS
*Jesse*
*Lockie Leonard, Human Torpedo*
*The Bugalugs Bum Thief*
*Lockie Leonard, Scumbuster*
*Lockie Leonard, Legend*
*Blueback*
*The Deep*

NON-FICTION
*Land's Edge*
*Local Colour* (with Bill Bachman)
*Down to Earth* (with Richard Woldendorp)
*Smalltown* (with Martin Mischkulnig)
*Island Home*
*The Boy Behind the Curtain*

PLAYS
*Rising Water*
*Signs of Life*
*Shrine*

# JUICE

## TIM WINTON

PICADOR

First published 2024 by Hamish Hamilton,
part of Penguin Random House Australia Pty Ltd

First published in the UK 2024 by Picador
The Smithson, 6 Briset Street, London EC1M 5NR
*EU representative:* Macmillan Publishers Ireland Ltd, 1st Floor,
The Liffey Trust Centre, 117–126 Sheriff Street Upper,
Dublin 1, DO1 YC43
Associated companies throughout the world
www.panmacmillan.com

ISBN 978-1-0350-5059-8 HB
ISBN 978-1-0350-5081-9 TPB

'The Dream' words and music by Michael P. Franks, Russell Keith Ferrante,
James Haslip, Marc Russo. © Twenty Nine Palms Music, administered by
Universal Music Publishing Pty Ltd in Australia & New Zealand, Teeth Music,
La Viera Music, New Shoes Music, Kalabash Music. All rights reserved.
International copyright secured. Reprinted with permission.
Special thanks to Michael Franks.

3 5 7 9 8 6 4 2

A CIP catalogue record for this book is available from the British Library.

Printed and bound by CPI Group (UK) Ltd, Croydon, CR0 4YY

Visit **www.picador.com** to read more about all our books
and to buy them. You will also find features, author interviews and
news of any author events, and you can sign up for e-newsletters
so that you're always first to hear about our new releases.

To those who, from the beginning,
saw blood in the machine
tasted death in the air
and cried *enough*.

I had this dream
In which I swam with dolphins
In open sea a transparent blue
(Maybe you dreamt it too)

— MICHAEL FRANKS/YELLOWJACKETS,
'THE DREAM'


There was a world . . . or was it all a dream?

— HOMER, *THE ILIAD*

So I drive until first light and only stop when the plain turns black and there's nothing between us and the horizon but clinkers and ash.

I pull up. Drop the sidescreen. The southern air is mercifully still this morning, and that's the only stroke of luck we've had in days. I know what wind does to an old fireground. In a gale, the ash can fill your lungs in minutes. I've seen comrades drowning on their feet. Clambered over the windrows of their bodies.

I wrap the scarf over my nose and mouth. Hang the glasses from my neck. Crack the door. And step down. Testing the surface as gently as I can. Ankle-deep. To the shins at worst. No sound out here but the whine of our rig's motors.

Stay there, I call.

I know she's awake, but the child, slumped in the corner of the cab, does not move. I walk back gingerly to check the trailer. Everything is still cinched down as it should be – the maker, the water, pods and implements – although the days of hard running have left my greens in disarray. The leafier edibles are windburnt, but overall the losses seem manageable. I tap the reservoir to fill my flask. Then, with the glasses, I scan the western approaches. No plumes, no movement. We're clear.

I try to swipe the dust from the films and panels, but it's pointless. In a minute or so every generating surface will be furred with ash again. I just need the turbines to trickle in enough juice to get us across.

Back at the cab, I thump my boot heels on the step and climb in. She hasn't moved, and why that should be both a relief and vexation is beyond me.

We're okay, I tell her. We'll make this.

She gazes out across the scorched land.

This place, I say. It was all trees once. I flew across it. When I was young.

She blinks, inscrutable.

It went on and on. Trees beneath us for hours. The smell – you just wanted to eat the air.

She maintains her silence.

Have you flown?

Nothing.

I know you've been at sea. Just wondered if you'd been up in a stat.

She shifts and tilts her head against the sidescreen.

It's really something.

She offers no sign of interest. Sits back, leaves a smear of sun paste on the glass.

But just once, I say, I would've liked to fly for the sake of it, not because I was on my way to somewhere horrible.

The sun appears. Molten. Slumped at the edges. Liquifying before us like a burning blimp. Until it rises. Breaks free of all comparisons to become its unmistakable self. Something reassuring. And terrible.

I talk too much, I declare. And you? You never say a word. Once upon a time I never said enough. So I was told.

She gives me nothing.

I know you hear me. You follow my language.

She rubs at the glass and manages to spread more grease than she removes.

Listen, I say. Those men back there, we lost them. No one's coming for us. This morning we need to get across this ash. It won't be nice. But on the other side there'll be fresh country. We'll move and camp the way we did before. Okay? Until we find ourselves a situation. There'll be somewhere. We'll be alright.

The child cranks her head further away. When I take my scarf and tear a long hank from it, she turns back at the sound. I pull the rest of the fabric across my nose and mouth and bind it around the skirts of my hat. And although she flinches, she does not resist when I do the same for her. There's still dried blood on her brow where she beat herself against the dash. Her pale blue eyes seem more luminous above the mask.

There, I say. Cuts the stink a bit anyway. One day we'll scrub this cab out. And you won't just be watching, believe me. So. You set? There's water here. We'll eat on the other side.

I lift the sidescreen and set the rig into motion. Trundling just fast enough to make way, but slow enough to avoid stirring up a blizzard of ash.

On and on we go, hour after hour, over country as black as the night sky, across a fallen heaven starred with eruptions of white ash and smears of milky soot.

The vehicle staggers and wallows but keeps on until I'm down to reserve power. And then, as the midday sun drills in through the murk, I see new colours – tan, silver, khaki, bone – and the surge of relief that goes through me is almost deranging.

At the first solid ground I let the child out to privy. She seems energized by the freedom. Though when she's done, she baulks at being hustled back into the rig so soon. I don't manhandle her. But I do corral her. And I speak to her sharply. Because I'm tired. And still useless at this. And I really need to put some distance between us and that fireground. So when we finally get moving, the mood in the cab

3

is low, and I'm sorry for it, but soon I have reason to be glad because when the batts finally give out, a hard gust comes in from the south, and the whole rig shakes on its axles.

I climb down stiffly. The kid gets out. I point to the dirty pillars rising into the sky in the distance behind us.

Look, I say. We could have been in the middle of that. But we're out and upwind, see? That's not just a lucky escape. That's us being smart.

I crank out the shade. Set the array.

She watches the ash clouds twist northward. As the wind stiffens, they boil against one another. Then she follows me to the trailer. Watches as I dole out some mash. Accepts the dixy and the spoon. On her haunches, with her back to the wind, she swats away the skirts of her hat and eats. Avidly.

We can't just be lucky, I say. You and me, we have to stay sharp.

She's already licking her mess tin clean. I take it from her, give her mine, and while she eats I unlash my swag and roll it out beside the vehicle. Then I take down the bedroll I've improvised for her. Unfurl it next to mine. Not so close to make her worry, but near enough to keep an eye on her.

We're all out of push, I say. Machine and creatures alike. So let's sleep.

She shovels the last of the mash into her mouth, licks my dixy clean and the spoon also. Gets up, sets both back on the trailer and returns to sit, cross-legged, on her swag. She gazes east, the tail of her hat stirred by the wind.

Suit yourself, I say.

And then I'm gone. Out.

———

Sometime in the afternoon I wake to a faint keening. And for a moment I think I'm home. With an ailing hen downstairs. The whole flock at risk of contagion. Catastrophe in my compound. And I know I should get up, go straight to the growhouse, but when I open my eyes there's just the awning shimmying in the wind above me and I'm here, on the dirt, so far south from home. And it's the kid. Her face smeared with tears. Weeping. For the woman, I imagine, and God knows how much else besides. I reach for her, but she cringes away, so I leave her be and yield, once more, to sleep.

When I wake again the shadows of the vehicle and its trailer are long as safety ropes. The waif kips on. I clamber up, sore and creaky, to get us underway.

Before night falls, we're into the saltlands. Out on the hard crust, the going is smooth. I don't even need lights. Except for the dark islands of tree stumps, everything ahead is white.

Once the batts are low, I stop, roll out the swags again and carry the kid to bed. When I wake it's late and she's already out, setting pebbles in a circle on the salt. I sit up and look about. The glare is brutal.

You look busy, I say.

She primps her ring of stones.

We can talk about her. If it helps.

She scoops the pebbles up. Shoves them in her dungarees. Gets to her feet.

By day's end we're onto higher ground scattered with saltbush and thorny mulga. In the last light I pull up, shroud the rig in camo lattice and decant a quarter-cube for washing. It's well past time, especially for her, but I take the lead and step behind the rig to scrub down. When I return, my fresh fatigues peeled to the waist so I can air myself a little, I see the kid has assembled another halo of pebbles.

Your turn, I say. There's clean duds on the trailer gate.

She looks up. Stares at my chest. And I feel suddenly self-conscious. Shamed, even.

They're just scars, I say. Burns.

She gapes.

It's different for us, I say. Her skin wasn't like ours. This is just what happens when skin heals.

I hang the towel and cover up. Then I coil the scarf back around my neck.

You'll feel better if you wash. Use the soap. I'm going for a walk.

She goes back to her stones as if claimed by them. But when I return she's clean and her hair hangs damp against the shoulders of her tunic.

At last light, before we set off for the night, she catches me unawares. Just as I'm slipping the tool into the holster in the driver's door. I've finished charging the thing, almost have it secreted, and suddenly she's there. When she stiffens and steps back, it's clear she knows what it is.

You don't have to worry, I say. Don't think about this thing. And don't touch it. Ever. Okay?

She lingers a moment. Then she rounds the front of the rig and climbs up into her seat. The cab begins to smell of soap and scrubbed hemp.

Okay, I say, disquieted. Let's make some ground.

I catch the long, appraising glance she gives me before she settles into her corner. And, despite myself, I wonder at what else she's seen and endured. If not for the promise I made, I might have broken her neck out of kindness and pushed on alone. But here we are.

I put the rig in gear. We set off through the scrub, over pools of gravel and stands of bluebush, every frame and panel juddering.

In the middle of the night I come upon a track. Before long, I see a light in the distance. I kill the lamps and creep ahead until we're close enough to scope the place. Just some shanties. Still, promising. But the moment we stop, I hear screams. And laughter of the kind you don't want to be near. I give the place a wide berth, put a couple more hours behind us.

Next afternoon, another settlement comes into view. Gated compound. Battered shipping containers circled into a stockade. Inside, old hangars and mining habs are set out in rows. In the centre, a water tower. And that gets my hopes up. Until I clock the gallery midway up the tower where sentries are prowling.

We retreat to the cover of a gully to the west from where I can scope the place more thoroughly. Functioning places are rare, but this vill looks harshly governed. Safety never comes cheap.

Still, the prospect of sanctuary isn't easy to pass up. We lie there all afternoon, wedged into a crease at the lip of the storm gully. The kid never moves. She seems to understand the gravity of the moment, the choice before us.

In whispers, I catalogue every signal of collective enterprise. The food growing. The water bore. The reservoir and piping. I count the solar arrays. The motley assemblage of wind turbines. The harnesses distributing juice from structure to structure. All promising. And yet something about the place makes me uneasy. Sentries are no bad thing, but these blokes are not looking out – their gaze is downward, internal. And it's only when night falls and the lights come on that I see why. The white domes of the growhouses are bustling with shadows. Which should be a good sign. Folks raising food is an indication of order and co-operation. But even upright, the figures within look slumped. And I know what that means. Once you've seen the posture of forced labour, you never forget it.

So we withdraw once more. Blacked out entirely. And beat another careful detour.

We drive east. Keep going like this for two more days. Charging and sleeping under camo in daylight. Travelling slowly at night under the light of one beam.

Until, at the end of a faint and snaking pair of ruts, in stone country, we come into the wreckage of a prospecting camp. It looks deserted. I wheel around for a while. Sceptical, but open to the possibilities. If we're fated to go it alone for a stretch, we could do worse than a place like this. Yet I remain vigilant. Because threaded between the mine heads and spoil heaps, the trash-filled trenches, the snarls of rusty rebar and sheet metal, there's a maze of trails. And although I'd like to think that this far south there are still animals at large, I know it's hardly likely.

Again, I feel a treacherous spasm of hope. Hesitate. Kill the motors and crack the door to sniff the place and listen.

Nothing. Just the lowing of the breeze across the ruins.

I tell the child to stay in the cab. Then climb down to inspect the closest sign of a track. There's no animal scat. And no bootprints. But these trails are human.

I turn back, gesture to the kid, and she comes.

People dig stuff from the earth, I say. For trade. Or to make things with. This is a mine site. I used to look for places like this in the north. There was always something useful to score if you put the time in and had something to cart it away on. The stuff we uncovered in places like this. I couldn't begin to tell you.

We walk to a headless shaft. Stand at the raised rim. This hole's not rectangular like the others. It's circular. Like a well. We crane a little. Peer down. But it's too deep and dark to see much.

You know, I say. If it's not full of water, we could probably live here. Down one of these.

She scrunches her face.

If I could make it safe, that is. No guarantees. But it might be worth a thought. All we need is somewhere out of the weather, something remote and secret. I think this could work.

Which just goes to show, says a voice behind me, that there's no such thing as an original idea.

The girl starts so wildly she almost sends us both into the pit. I yank her back by the shoulder. She wheels away from the sight of the stranger and sets her face against my breastbone.

Stay where you are, says the bloke with the crossbow.

Mate, I say. You gave us a fright.

Looks that way.

He's smaller than me. Younger. His left eye is pearly. A greying beard covers much of his face and neck. His cheeks and hands bear the same white lesions you see on everyone, but the scars on his nose and around his eyes are not the work of weather.

We're just passing through, I tell him.

So you say.

He looks at the child.

She yours?

Yes.

You're a bloody liar.

She's not for trade, I say.

So that's how you got her?

No. Hell, no.

But she's not yours, is she.

She's with me. We're travelling together.

Doing what?

Doing what we can, comrade.

Don't fucking comrade me, he says. She real?

Would she flinch if she wasn't?

The hell should I know.

We're just looking for somewhere safe.

You and every other reffo.

We don't want to be a problem.

Well, you're here now. That makes you a problem.

But three's better than one, right?

Is it?

Of course it is.

Two more mouths to feed, the way I see it.

The crossbow, I say. Service issue.

He says nothing. I pull in a breath, preparing to move, but then I keep talking, buggering on to buy us a few more moments.

So, I ask. Were you any good? With that, I mean.

Standing here, aren't I?

*When an archer is shooting for nothing*, I say, *he has all his skill. If he shoots for a brass buckle, he's already nervous. If he shoots for a prize of gold, he goes blind or sees two targets.*

Well, smartarse, I already see two targets.

*The prize divides him. He cares. He thinks more of winning than shooting. And the need to win drains him of power.*

You're a scream.

Were they still using that when you went through?

What do you care?

We're both schooled, comrade. We both know what's right.

Fat lot of good that did us.

Both still here, though, aren't we? As you say.

For the moment.

Well, after what I've seen, I can settle for the moment. Reckon you're no different.

Reckon away, fella. It's no odds to me.

Seen any other operators down this way?

Why would I tell you?

Why wouldn't you?

You're living in a world that's gone.

You know that compound west of here?

I've seen it.

I don't want to live like that.

Might be the only way.

If you really thought that, you wouldn't be here. You'd have thrown your lot in with them.

He scowls. I'm still trying to get a read, looking to pick my moment to jump him.

What's on the rig? he asks.

A maker. Growpods.

You steal 'em?

Made them.

He grunts.

You got seeds?

I nod.

Where you from?

The peninsula.

Which peninsula?

North.

How far north?

North of Capricorn.

Jesus. What about her?

No idea. I think she's off a migrant boat. Maybe a slaver.

Those fuckers.

What about you?

What about me?

Where are you from?

Doesn't matter anymore.

And how do you live?

He sighs.

Really, I say. I'm interested.

Microbial protein, he says.

You can make powder?

He nods.

Why don't we consolidate?

I don't need you.

I don't see a vehicle, any kit.

Think I'd leave my assets in the open? Think I'm stupid?

No, mate. But I know neither of us will see home again.

Cheery bastard, aren't ya?

So this is either an ending or an opportunity.

Maybe both, he says, hefting the crossbow a little higher.

The child presses against me.

What the fuck're you doing with her, anyway?

Keeping her safe.

For what?

Jesus, man, to give her a life, why else? When's the last time you
saw a kid?

Are they farming them?

Brother, you've been out here on your own too long.

Show me she's real. Prove it, he says, jabbing the crossbow at her.

The child whimpers and clambers against me, and then, in a scalding rush that runs down the leg of my dungarees, she puts the question beyond doubt.

Okay, he says. Let's go.

Where?

Turn around.

Comrade, please. Don't touch her.

I said turn the fuck around.

The kid has her legs snagged in mine. It's no easy manoeuvre to gets us about-faced. But when I do there's nothing ahead but the dark maw of the shaft.

He hauls the top rungs up and locks them in place, but the child won't go down. Simply cannot make herself step over the lip and onto the ladder with her back to the darkness below. And though I feel the point of the bowman's bolt between my shoulder blades, I need no prompting. I take her in my arms, she latches on to me at the waist and the neck, and I hoist us over, clinging to the rails.

I know I should be using the long descent to frame a plan, to be ready to secure something – a hefty stone, a length of metal – but by the time I get us down, rung by rung, to solid ground I'm so knackered I can barely think and it's all I can do to lower the child to the compacted dirt and then drop down beside her, panting like a heat-struck fowl.

She peers along the tunnel into the distant darkness. Glances up the ladder at the bowman's silhouette on its way down. Then back at me. In expectation. As I lie there. Winded and helpless.

When I show her the palm of my hand, I'm not sure if I'm imploring her to wait or begging her forgiveness.

If she's disappointed, she doesn't show it. In any event, the bowman drops so quickly, hands and boots barely slowing his fall as he clamps against the verticals, sliding down without touching a single rung, that our chance is gone before I can get to my feet.

He hits the dirt with a thud. Before he's even turned to face us, he has the bow back in his hands.

Out of puff, old timer? he says, casting about as if he's seeing the place anew with us in it.

I get slowly to my feet. The child reaches, takes a fistful of my sodden pants leg.

You could've had me then, he says.

I don't want to fight.

Yet.

I'm tired of fighting.

Maybe you're just tired, full stop.

Both, I confess. Maybe you are too. Because if you wanted to see me off clean, you missed your best chance already.

Who says I want to do you clean?

It's a long climb up with a weight like mine on your back.

You don't think I have a block and tackle?

Seems like a lot of trouble.

I can manage a bit of trouble.

Me, I could do with less of it.

He shrugs. And yet here you are.

We don't have to be trouble.

Somehow I doubt that.

But, as you say, here we are. Still alive.

Maybe I'm just thorough.

Good for you. And for your training.

And maybe I'm a bit curious.

The pair of us? Showing up like this? Who wouldn't be?

I've met plenty who wouldn't.

Strange days, comrade.

Let's go, he says.

He palms a switch. A chain of tubes illuminates the chamber, a deep horizontal, high and wide, stacked with drums, coils of hose, some improvised domestic furniture. In the distance, maybe thirty metres yonder, a chain-link barrier.

It's hard to get a read on the extent of this bolthole, but it feels bigger than what I can see. Some of it looks hand-hewn, but the ceiling bears the broad sweeps of machine cuts. The shoring is steel, the braces hydraulic.

This is some find, I say.

Keep walking.

We do as we're told. At the wire enclosure, we stop to survey the stacked crates and drums on the other side. It takes a moment to notice the gate. And the lock. The hasp is open.

You want to lock us up?

Do I look like a fool?

You can trust us, comrade.

That's to be determined.

Fair enough, I say, shepherding the girl forward as casually as I can. In you go.

The child looks at me. I nod, open the gate and lead her in.

The bowman shuts the barrier behind us and sets the lock. He turns, lays the uncocked crossbow on the table behind him.

You need to know who we are.

That'd be a start.

You want my name?

No, he says.

But you want everything else.

Wouldn't you?

I would.

So, go for your life, he says. Explain yourself.

The child settles in a soft pool of dirt between some crates. I lower myself to a snap case that reminds me of a transport shell – field kit.

The bowman drags out a chair. He sits with his boots against the mesh, reefs off his hat and raises his eyebrows. And I see the situation plainly. If I can't get through to him, I'll need to kill him. But there's no guarantee I can manage either.

You sound like you're from the east, so you probably won't know the place, but I was born and raised on the Outer Cape. North of the twenty-third parallel. It's a peninsula. Two hundred klicks of rocks and red dirt. Only one settlement – a hamlet of five hundred souls on the furthermost shore, just inside the sheltered waters of the gulf. My people were homesteaders. We lived in the hinterland, out on the plain. In the days when you could still get by in that latitude if you knew what you were doing.

Those were better times, but even then it wasn't a place for the faint-hearted. The sun ate everything in sight and the salt air chewed through anything that wasn't. The winds came hard off the range and harder still out of the desert across the gulf.

My mother was widowed early. Raised me on her own. But she was a tough unit. Short. Wiry. Handsome in the way even a son will notice. Grey eyes and a bent-kneed stance that always made her look as if she'd just landed after a jump. Her hair was blonde and buzzed tight, so you only saw it indoors, once the hat and scarves came off. Mostly she went about in a wide-brimmer with neck-skirts and her face wrapped, so it was the steely eyes you saw most, the fierce gaze. Hamlet folks were careful around her.

She had heft, my mother. A gravitas I could sense as a child but not explain. She taught me everything. Not just how to behave and how to work and endure with honour. She gave me my letters and numbers and the stories of our people. Also the sagas. I was eligible for hamlet school and lived close enough to be driven in every day, but she never sent me, and I never asked to go.

We were self-reliant, the pair of us. In country as dry and remote as that, homesteaders had to be. We remained citizens in good standing with the Association, rendered our tithe to the Co-op every year without fail, but to hamlet folks homesteaders were a people apart. Aloof. Difficult to read. Hardarses, I guess.

Our compound was a big, dusty triangle buttressed on every side by a levee of compacted soil and rubble. The winterhouse, set toward the southern bund, was up on stilts and airy. We had good, storm-proof sheds and our growhouses had retractable cowls my parents had designed and perfected before I was born. Across the yard, a low parapet of sandbags and a simple A-frame portico marked the entrance to our summer hab. A cluster of cellars and underground cisterns. All interlinked.

The plain was mostly red dirt, spinifex and gibber. From the verandah of the winter place, you could see the distant sheen of the gulf in the east. Behind us, like some mummified leviathan, the long buttress of the range lay between us and the open sea.

This was all the world I knew. And for many years it was all I needed.

Like every good homesteader, I raised plants, to harvest seeds and sow them anew. I could manage egg birds and grind their shit and bones for the soil we brewed from dust. Alongside my mother, I learnt how to patch a circuit, mend a pump, rewind a motor. There were turbines to maintain and arrays to set and adjust and keep clean. I had to know how to nurse and pamper every species of battery, to capture, store and move water, and from the age of seven I drove vehicles – quads, fork-loaders, flatbeds – for the thrill of demonstrating my competence.

I felt like any ordinary plains child. I figured all of us could read a barometer and find our way home alone from the canyons at night. But the fact was, I didn't know any kids. Apart from the lame boy, that is, and I only saw him at the beginning of winter when his father, the filmlayer, drove out from the hamlet to resurface our grit-pitted walls and roofs. I was always discouraged from making comparisons with anyone else – my mother was strict about this – but with that crippled boy I didn't need to be told. And I liked him well enough. He taught me checkers. Beat me most years. But then he stopped coming, and I didn't ask about him.

I never really felt the lack of playmates or friends. On market days in the hamlet, or special days at the wharf, I'd sometimes encounter other children. I watched them. Carefully. They puzzled me. Disappointed me, really. And they seemed leery of me. Whenever I managed to engage them in conversation or to propose a game, they struck me as opaque. Hesitant. Even dull. They were always seeking consent or confirmation from those around them. They seemed unable to do anything on their own initiative. As I grew older, I saw their parents were no different. Not so much that their circuits were on the fritz. More that they were all set to power-reserve mode.

When I shared this thought with my mother she admonished me, but I detected a glint of amusement in her eyes.

There's nothing wrong with those kids, she said. And you're no better than any of them. Their parents are good factors and mechanicals. Sound citizens. And they will be too. Having common interest isn't the same as having interests in common.

I don't think they like me, I confessed.

Needing people to like you is vain. So is expecting people to *be* like you. You and I do what we know how to do, and they do what they can, and everyone's effort is useful. That's what keeps us all going.

Each of us needs a little something of what the other has – food, water, building materials, parts, doctoring, scholarship, labour. Even the bards and jokers have their place.

That's a trade?

Of course. Folks need to laugh sometimes. But whatever we do, wherever we live – in a hamlet, in the city or on the plain – no citizen is better than any other.

On this point I never questioned my mother, and yet over time I began to see we prospered in ways few others in our district seemed to. For one thing, my mother would never consent to trade for labour. But how could she refuse help unless we could afford to? My mother was an unstinting worker, almost relentless. She gave the very clear impression that the two of us worked harder than most in the district, and while such a notion was hard to verify, the ache in my bones and sinews at day's end seemed to confirm it.

We raised leaves and herbs of every kind. Our citrus was supreme. In mild years our hives rendered honey that tasted faintly of coriander. We grew rich crops of tomato, corn, okra, squash and eggplant, and no skin or rind of our fruit ever felt the scalding flush of direct sunlight. The first and only moment our produce saw the open sky was when we hefted crates from the trailer into the shade of the hamlet square.

On the plain, every citizen was the equal of their neighbour. And whether they'd made good trade, enjoyed a bumper season, or been blessed by the birth of a child, most maintained the sort of discretion that forestalls envy. There was gossip, of course, as in any small community, but the virtues of circumspection, modesty, generosity and hospitality were valued and rewarded. Not just by the Association, but by those who belonged to it. Which was all of us.

In the hamlet, as out on the homesteads, there was no talk of caste or rank. Civility was paramount. And while everyone understood that some tradesfolk and homesteaders might be more skilled or gifted than others, and some were wiser and probably more diligent, there was no tolerance for lording or vaunting. So much so that folks neither danced nor sang in public for fear of making a spectacle or appearing to put themselves forward.

There's no question that hard work was valued and laziness frowned upon, but there was no shame in availing yourself of help, whether you traded for it or were granted it freely by a neighbour. And the Co-op indemnified you from any misfortune that might lead to long-term hardship.

So, ours was a decent life. It was orderly. There was purpose in it. Honour, too. And self-respect.

But although the world was steady in the years of my boyhood, it was not always kind. In the hamlet or out on the homesteads, life was a struggle. Winters were hot. The summers lethal. Nearly every soul you met had white scab, and many suffered pink cankers that ate at them slowly. Locals were hardy and adaptable, but it was rare to see people of great age. And, for reasons nobody seemed to understand or discuss, the number of births had already begun to wane.

At the onset of winter, when folks finally came back up from underground, they were looser in their bearing, almost giddy with relief to be out in the open after so many months of languishing in stifling cellars. Within a few days they'd recover their decorum and go about their work. Come September we'd all be dreading the change of season and the return to life below ground.

As a kid, it's the big events that take up space in your head. The cataclysms of sudden presence – cyclones, locust plagues, lightning sieges, storm surges, flash floods. But as you get older it's the stuff that doesn't happen, the things that fail to arrive, that begin to preoccupy you. Cataclysms of absence, I guess you'd say. Like the years the monsoon failed to arrive. That was when you faced the horrors of running dry. Or worse – poaching in your own sweat, and when you couldn't sweat anymore, grilling from the inside out.

Most of the year we had desert heat. Hard, roasting, wind-driven. If the air is dry and you're careful, you can survive temps into the fifties. But when it's muggy, you're in real trouble. In the summer there were black-sky days without rain when tropical air rolled in from the north like a hostile force to occupy the peninsula for a week or more. No bunker and no fan could spare you that strangling humidity. Within a few days, even with temps down in the thirties, you'd fall prey to heat fever. The panic of the sickness sent folks out of their minds. Survivors were never the same afterwards. You won't need telling, comrade. You know it well enough. The ordeal – the indignity of it – robs you of something. Forever after, you're stalked by the shameful mewling thing you became.

So when March arrived, and the big cells rolled down from the death belt of the tropics, we ran the fans hard and prayed we had enough juice in the batts to keep ourselves alive. A day or two of that was tough. Nerve-racking. But a week might be catastrophic. In the middle of one of those events, if you could think at all, you knew there'd be folks coddling and stewing in bunkers and cellars the length of the peninsula. And some of them you'd never see again. Some died when their hearts gave out. Others destroyed themselves before it got that far. And there was no shame in that. Most folks understood the sensation of being possessed by that dread, those avalanches of panic.

Maybe it's different where you're from, but in our part of the world, suicide was frowned upon, though it wasn't censured by the Association. We were hardy folks, but not heartless. We had a firm conception of who we were, and maintained high social expectations, but we were realists. Or at least we thought we were.

Nobody pretended that plains life was easy. We were at the last margin, at the frontier of the tropics, with the desert at our back.

Year upon year we held out. And were proud of doing so. Things were less capricious then, so perhaps we could afford to be. We prized steadiness. Not just in people, but in our world. Because steadiness allowed us room enough to endure and make a life. The problem was, we believed this stability was of our own making. The fruit of self-restraint. And although there was some truth in this, it wasn't the whole story. We had our golden age in a lull, while the world was just dozing.

High on a ridge, at the spine of the range, stood a rock fig so large and sprawling it was as much thicket as tree. In its winter shade, twenty souls or more could work and rest out of sight. Children nested in its downswept boughs, and bowerbirds stole the buttons off their tunics as they slept. Between the tree's reptilian roots, their parents mended garments, honed blades and kept watch. At dawn and dusk, they went abroad to hunt and forage on the tops. In summer they followed the roots underground, for beneath the tree lay a cave whose deepest gallery brimmed with sweet water. They navigated the darkness by the feel of those rock-splitting roots, climbing from the light to the water and back. To survive the worst of the heat, they lived in the upper chamber, beneath an open roof and a canopy of limbs and leaves, subsisting on dried meats and fruits in the safety of the twilight.

These were my people. The children of the tree. And although that mighty fig and its water were long gone before my time, the cave remained. And I went to it, man and boy, to rappel into the darkness and feel the scars in the rock left by ancient roots. Their refuge was my refuge.

Hard to believe, isn't it? That there were harsher times than these, and folks hardy enough to survive them. But persist they did, right through the Terror. And when the madness subsided around them, they came up from the earth, children of the tree, to become the people of the plain.

This is who I'm from. That's what I'm made of. You need to know this.

Well, stranger, what I need to know is not for you to say.

Fair enough, I murmur. Better to say there are things I need to tell you.

To save your skin.

Improve our odds. All three of us.

So you say.

I need you to trust me.

Clearly.

I'm not a savage.

That remains to be seen. You're just another wayfarer. Taking your chances. I don't blame you for that. But you're nothing to me.

Not true, comrade. You know it's not.

You keep telling me what I know.

It's chaos out there.

True, he says. Things have gone to shit. But one thing I've learnt. Wringing your hands won't make water.

You're right, I tell him. But isolation doesn't produce order. Does it? Hiding alone in a bunker – doesn't the irony make your teeth hurt?

Jesus. Everything makes my teeth hurt.

Hear me out.

Do I have a choice?

Haven't you already made one?

I might already be regretting it, he says.

I see you, comrade. You see me. We both know already. We recognize each other.

Again with the assumptions.

Here, I say. My bona fides.

If you must.

My people were forged in the Terror. But we were never berserkers or barbarians.

This is what my mother told me. I can hear her now. She schooled me as we worked. And as we broke clumps of seedlings to separate and plant out in pods, I thought I could hear an echo of my father's voice in hers. In those words, I could almost feel him.

Before we were plainsfolk, she said, we were hill people, but not by choice. And prior to that, on your father's side, we were sea people – fisherfolk. In the days when the world was kinder. But eventually your father's people had to abandon their boats and retreat to higher ground.

So this is when?

A long time back. Many generations.

And what about your folk? I asked.

Oh. They were berry growers and scholars from the south.

And how did they come here?

Well, the way it was told to me, their soil turned sour and then it rained so long and hard everyone in their district got sick. And like everyone else, they fled to the city for shelter, but with so many people moving in all at once, civil order was lost and it was unsafe to stay, so they left again and pressed north. They travelled for months. A caravan of refugees on the road winding their way into hard dry country until they settled here on the peninsula, with the sea before and behind. Even then conditions were harsh, but these people were hardy. They knuckled down, fitted in, made a life. But then, as if it had been pursuing them all along, the weather overtook them. The sky itself seemed fickle, and this treachery turned people bad. In time, madness took hold on the plain. People believed the world was ending. They were consumed by panic and ugliness. They fell into savagery and magic. When my parents' people fled up into the range, it was more in blind desperation than hope. What could they possibly expect on the baked ridgetops but sun and starvation? But your father's people watched them come up, saw their distress, and took pity on them.

And that's how our clan was born?

Yes, she said. In extremis. Out of chaos. By necessity. With a compact of civility. Beneath the fig. They shared the skills each had brought to that place and those they'd learnt there. There were many crafts held in common, but the most prized of these was discipline.

She gestured to the long, tidy aisles of our growhouse, the bobbing heads of the birds, the rows of eggs.

But they were trekkers, I said. Scouts and foragers, right?

Yes, but there's no successful trekking and foraging without restraint. You don't survive up there or down here without self-control.

I went about my work a while, tamping soil around the root nubs of okra. I knew the old stories well enough. I only asked her for the pleasure of hearing them rehearsed again. They felt more intimate than the sagas because these were tales of kinfolk. It was good to hear how our people had held their own during the Terror when so many others lost their way. As you know, that age of turmoil was universal. Provinces and cantons that had once prospered from order and co-operation slowly lapsed into fiefdoms based on raiding and slavery.

It was said every hamlet square and city plaza sported a gibbet. Nights were lurid and raucous with public burnings.

Things were no different on the peninsula and on the plain, where the work of growing food and tending children and catching water was neglected. As provisions began to dwindle, any resources held in reserve were seized and hoarded by petty tyrants. Water became currency, then power itself. Many new bores and wells were dug to defend and consolidate that power, every one of them excavated manually, in all weather, by serfs worked to death.

During that time, secreted high in the ridge country, and safe beyond the barriers of superheated canyons, our people lay low in the shade of their tree, holding fast in the hope that they might outlive this blighted season.

To make a refuge, said my mother. And to live with water at your feet. That's the key. That's the rule. They never forgot this, the children of the tree. And afterwards, when they came down here to take up what was left when the plainsfolk had all died or fled, they lived this way. And that's how we live today.

People of the plain, I said.

Don't you forget it.

I promised her I wouldn't. And I haven't. Even if, as an old man, with the benefit of so much more information, I parse these origin stories a little differently.

As a youth, such tales of family lore did more than bind me to our homeplace – they helped make my father real. Because all I had of him were a few brief, interrupted years, fragments and memories I had to strain to keep hold of. If it hadn't been for the trek to the water cave we made each year as the winter waned, even these might have slipped away. His presence was closest and most vivid up there.

———

Our annual hike up into the range tops was a kind of pilgrimage, a ritual we fortified ourselves with before shuttering the house and retreating to the cellars.

Before dawn, we rode out to the range with ropes and harnesses and waterpacks lashed to the quad, and from the closest canyon mouth we clambered up spurs and terraces until we could feel the salt wind in our faces from the sea beyond. From that elevation it was a level but slow tramp along the fractured spine of the range to where the fig had once stood. There, at the broken rim of the hole the tree once hid, we shrugged off the rope and sat a moment to catch our breath and suck some water before anchoring off and harnessing up for the rappel.

My mother drilled rope work into me early. I was still a boy when I learnt to make the drop unassisted. But it never goes away, does it, that fizz of fear at the edge when you clip on, put your back to the abyss and step off. It was a vertical shaft, an open-throated swallet of thirty metres. The first descent I can remember, I was clipped to my father, my back against his chest, little boots bumping against his shins every time he kicked back off the wall. The sensations are still so clear: the rough stone wall up close; the dark fissures where massive roots once bit into the limestone; the scrape of his boots and the burr of rope through the pulleys; the leathery scent of him in the warm, sandy-tasting air into which we sank, as if into a tepid bath.

As a boy, descending alone, my mother already out of sight at the surface, I slipped back into those memories, and further still, imagining myself clambering down with my ancestors on the roots of that great tree, writhing through the fissure at the bottom, picking my way by touch to the pool deep underground. There I would kneel beside my father's people and lave up sweet water by the handful.

Of course, these old ones were my mother's people too. Generations of them had shared the place together. And yet I only ever thought of them as my father's line, and she never corrected me. I only thought about this later in life, how for my sake, in upholding tradition and keeping my father's memory alive, my mother rendered herself invisible. I went to the cave many times with her. But it was always him I was summoning. Clipping off. Standing at the swallet floor. Looking up at the almond eye of sunlight, catching the fire of it in his beard as he craned up to survey the scene beside me. When he drew himself upright and raised his hands to the sky, it seemed he was gazing in awe at the glory of the world in expectation that at any moment something even more wonderful would reveal itself.

Now, of course, I see the moment I invested with all the grandeur of antiquity, and the gravity of the sagas, was just an unremarkable instant. He probably wasn't standing there in anticipation of some miracle – he was simply catching his breath, freeing the line, and waiting for my mother to descend. But in my mind, and in that place, he belonged to a time of legend. And look, I'm old enough to know about myths, what happens to a stone if you spin it in a barrel with others long enough. But it still strikes me as impressive, the way those folks lived during the age of chaos.

Just imagine what it took to endure beneath that tree and in the guts of the earth while fires engulfed the plain, soil and ash taking to the sky, the wells of every compound turned so salty that folks went mad, peons and chieftains alike. There was no purpose on the lowland. Even the brutal order of the strongmen fell apart. Folks were possessed by nihilism, every kind of ugliness. The stink of death was everywhere. Until, finally, there was a great exodus. The plain grew deserted.

Still, it was a long time before our people came down off the tops. For years the soil was grey, the floodplain reeked, and the sky was dark with carrion birds. From the ridges above, the land looked scorched, haunted. So they stayed put. Life on the heights was all they knew.

Hadn't the tree and the cave kept them safe? Hadn't restraint and caution served them well?

But the water in the cave began to take on a worrisome taint. And for a while – too long – the people suffered doubt and denial. They delayed, telling themselves that the hint of brine in their spring was imaginary, just alarmism. They told themselves that the tree and the cave remained their best protectors. That all would be well while they hid and did nothing. These were years of shame and folly. They were so close to liberty, but unable to come out into the open to take it up. As the water turned brackish, their elders wasted away, and their newborns died. Their ways began to falter, and the young spoke against the old.

In the end, when it was rank seawater rising beneath them, the truth was unavoidable. But even then, some couldn't forsake the shelter of the cave. And by that stage many were too weak to make the descent, so only the hardiest and most determined came down off the tops.

Those who did inherited a field of bones. They ground them, and sowed them in the dirt. The bones of strangers. And, later, the bones of their own folk, which they carried down, season after season, from the ranges, until none was left behind. This is how my forebears made themselves anew. The people of the plain.

These stories never ceased to excite my imagination, and my mother seemed more than happy to tell them over and again. The day she gave me this iteration, in the growshed, as we planted out okra seedlings, she was brisk in the telling. Perhaps by then she knew she needn't bother with embellishments. She could tell from my rapt expression that I brought my own romance to the tale.

Was my father a good grower? I asked, pulling another punnet from the cart.

Oh, he was handy enough, my mother replied, flicking back the skirts of her hat. But he loved the sea more. He went back to it.

Because it was in his blood?

Maybe.

I don't feel it, I told her. The sea, I mean.

No, she said. Geography is destiny. But blood tells many stories.

Nobody talks about the Terror. No one in the hamlet, I mean.

Those were dark days, she said. Folks scrubbed it from memory. I guess they were afraid of being haunted forever. They wanted to forget.

So why don't we?

Because we're not ordinary people.

But I'm no better than hamlet folks. You said it.

Nevertheless.

As a boy I was proud of not being ordinary and careful to disguise it. Such studied humility was a family trait. I didn't look any different to hamlet folks. And if I made a little effort, I could sound the same, too. But in my secret self I didn't feel that way. I cleaved to the virtues — modesty, discretion, self-reliance, the greatest good for the greatest number — but I was schooled differently, and I suppose that made me more curious than the kids I met now and then at the wharf or in the market square.

Of course, I wasn't nearly as inquisitive as I thought I was. I learnt that later. And to say it came as a shock — well, I don't need to tell you, comrade.

For all that, I was a dogged little fellow. By the time I was twelve, I was pestering my mother about why our habits and routines were so fixed. I wanted to understand why we did things the way we did them. Beautiful as it was, the legend of the water cave had come to feel insufficient as explanation.

She was a woman of extraordinary patience, my mother. For the longest time she batted me off mildly with the same old tales. But eventually she cracked. Or came to a decision. Reached a point where she thought I was ready. I don't know if she was exasperated or relieved, but one morning, after I'd once again pressed and wheedled for an hour, she lifted a hand to shut me up. Then she kicked out a crate, sat me down on it abruptly and said: Look, there are things people simply don't know. Big stuff. Like why we exist at all. Then there are the things they won't allow themselves to know. Like when the water turned salty in the cave. It didn't suit our people to believe it.

So why *did* it go bad?

Same reason all the wells went sour down here on the plain. The sea rose. Pushed up through the limestone. See, under our feet, this entire peninsula is like a honeycomb. More holes than solid ground. Down here, for a while, wells would've turned into springs as the sweet water was forced up by the salty water. You know why?

Fresh water is lighter?

Yes, less dense. It forms a layer – a lens over the top of the brine. So, for a while, as the sea pressed in, there were days of plenty. And folks got complacent. They knew it, too. Deep down. They were simple folks but not ignorant. Yet even then they denied it. Until it was too late.

All salt.

Correct. The great mystery of people lies in the many ways in which they'll deceive themselves.

All people?

All the ones I've known. Everything you read in the sagas.

Even now?

Especially now. Like I said, there are lots of things we don't know. Stuff that's obscure. Even hidden from us. But there's plenty we prefer not to know. Things we don't dare remember. Sometimes that's a mercy. Other times it's a form of servitude.

Like what?

Well, like how the world is.

I know how the world is, I replied. It's round. Like an orange.

Okay, she said, passing me the shears. Go down and cut one.

They're not ripe, I protested. That'd be a waste.

Not if you learn from it.

Bridling a little, I got up and slunk past the furry-stemmed tomatoes, the blocks of bright-boy and crisp-leaf and mignonette, to where the trolleyed rows of citrus stood in their irrigated tubs. I searched for the readiest navel I could find, but it was green-gilled and hard, and it felt improper to snip it off, but I did as I was told, brought it back to where she sat with a bowl of basil heads in her lap.

She took the orange and pulled out her clasp knife. She set the fruit on its axis and passed the blade around the rind. Not quite at the middle, but a third of the way down. She turned it until the cut met itself. Then she set the knife a little lower and repeated the procedure. When she was finished, a curl of pithy rind came away and a whole band around the middle of the orange was naked.

She put the fruit in my hand.

That's how the world is, she said.

I don't get it.

Leave it here, on the bench. Come back tomorrow and look at it. And the day after that. That's the world, how it is. Most people know this. But not many understand why.

So, what's the answer?

That's for another time. Geography before history.

Why can't you say?

Everything in its time and season.

Talk like this unsettled me, but I was an obedient son. I left the orange where it was. Next morning, and several days thereafter, I returned to it and saw how the wounded orange scoured and struggled to heal itself.

Whenever my mother saw me examining it, her expression was impassive. On the third day, as she passed, she picked up the orange and dug the ragged nail of her index finger into the very centre of the sphere.

What's this part? Of the world, not the orange.

The equator, I said.

Correct.

Then she set her thumb against the lower band of skin.

See this? This is us. Just north of —

Capricorn, I said.

Yes, the Tropic of Capricorn. But all this, she said, fingering the dry band that ran around the middle, people used to live there — millions and millions of them. But not anymore. Only here. And here. Where there's still skin. North of Cancer, south of Capricorn.

That's where people are?

*That's* how the world is.

Since how long?

Before the Terror, she said. Just before.

In that moment, and for years afterwards, I lacked the wit to ask how she knew this. And while I sensed the promise of some form of arcane knowledge, I never pursued it. I was a plains boy after all. The notion of secret information frightened me. And part of me didn't quite believe her anyway. Because as far as I knew, my mother had never left the plain. I didn't see how she could know things our neighbours did not. This information was not in the sagas.

I stared at the orange — which would now never be fit for anything more than bird feed — and touched the hardening scar.

How will it mend? was all I could ask. The world.

How indeed, she said. That I can't tell you.

Because I'm not old enough?

No, she said, sending me back to work with a wave of her arm. Because I don't have the answer.

We lived eight months of the year above ground. You could still do that on the coast in those latitudes when I was a boy. And in winter, for up to three months, you could still be abroad in the afternoons if you had the kit and wits for it.

Life was manageable if you were competent. Better than that if you had the right mix of skill and discipline.

My mother and I kept bees and egg birds, grew figs and olives. In years of good water we propagated paw-paws and dragon fruit, and as cisterns emptied and more underground space became available, we raised mushrooms too. We pressed our own oil, built soil from plant waste, birdshit and chipped carcasses. Everything we couldn't grow or fabricate ourselves we traded for, like the cheese and milk hamlet folks made from the goats they raised in sheds. Or sun film, batteries, cabling and steel. We ran banks of vertical drum turbines to bolster our array. We cooled the place with fans and HiVap in the winter and AC in the summer, if we had the juice to run it.

As you know, comrade, it all comes down to how much you can fix and what you can forage. Half your mind is taken up with making stuff. And the rest goes into finding it. Our tech was patchy as hell, but we never went hungry. The only appetite we could never quench was the need for spare parts.

Knowing we had all summer underground ahead of us, we worked every winter hour we could. The tasks felt endless, but I could cop nearly anything so long as I was topside. Once the season turned, we were captives. As a boy I felt doubly constrained, because the cellar hab was also where I did all my lessons.

My mother was nothing like the young teachers sent up from the south by the Association. She had the build and posture of a labourer, but she was not a mechanical. Not even an ordinary grower. She retained the only bank of heritage seeds on the plain, of the same stock her ancestors had carried up from the south and those brought down by my father's people from the range tops. And her knowledge of plants and soil was unparalleled. She had a gift for appliances, too. She built the fork and the digger we used to keep our bund solid. She taught me to wire and weld and rivet, to cannibalize a motor and repurpose parts. But she was well versed in the sagas, too. Could reel them off at will. The choruses and adages. You'll know the stuff. *She who plants and she who waters are one, and each will eat according to her labours.* And: *virtue lies in our power, and so does vice; because where it is in our power to act, it is also in our power not to act.* Right?

She had hard, blunt hands. But her eyes were beautiful. When random bards or hawkers came calling, she gave them short shrift, and they seemed startled by how fierce she was. Local men knew better than to visit unannounced. Only the filmlayer came out now and then.

I rarely saw her laugh. She had no patience for frivolity. She'd known hard times. Behind those eyes and within those hands was a reservoir of experience she'd dammed and capped.

I'm also tempted to say that I never saw her afraid, though that's not strictly true. She wasn't scared of people – would back down to no man – but she had a fear of drowning, even if she couldn't admit it.

We lived on a peninsula, surrounded by water, but we never swam in the sea. I've seen it done in the south, but it never would have occurred to us. Because of my father, I guess, and because of what the ocean had done to every well and bore on the cape. For all that, though, I think my mother's preoccupation with drowning had less to do with the ocean and was more a matter of land and sky. She knew plenty about storm surge and coastal inundation. What she feared was deluge. With the deserts so close, rain was rare, but when it did arrive it came with monsoonal force. The bluffs of the range turned to cataracts. The canyons began to fill. Then it was only a matter of hours before the dry creeks and desert channels blew their banks and overran the plain. That's when we'd sandbag our summer hab, seal all hatches, open the cistern gutters and hope to hell our bund held.

These cataclysms were necessary. They kept us going. But they terrified us. Because cyclones came in summer, when we were living underground. In the sagas there are always beasts prowling the plain. They haunted the dreams of the ancients and kept them close in the cave. But what we dreaded was not some fanged creature or howling berserker. It was the patter of life turning into a murderous torrent.

So, every day before bed, she'd ask: have you checked the bund?

This wasn't just routine – it was sacred ritual. The earthen levee was the only thing that could save us from drowning in our beds.

I was content in my way. I knew that in days gone by the world was abominable, its people wild and treacherous. But now there was clemency, and we were steady. There would be better times ahead. If only we held fast. We had eight months of the year in the open. Food to hand, water at our feet and nothing to fear from our neighbours. We were confident we'd never again face the tribulation from which our ancestors had emerged.

Go ahead and laugh, comrade. Were you and yours any different? Life's always hard. But didn't you think you'd been born into the best of all possible worlds?

One winter morning, I woke early to thuds and clanks in the kitchen. It was still dark. I got up to find my mother stashing food and water into a pack. My breakfast was already on the table, the usual cake of nuts and berries, with a steaming bowl of tea beside it. She had her hard boots on. Her face was already white with sun paste. A scarf was coiled at her throat.

Eat up, she said. The quad's charged. We're out to the ranges in a minute.

What's happening? I asked, still dull from sleep.

I've done the feed, she said. We'll do the pick tonight. This morning I want to show you something.

As a boy some part of me was forever yearning for a break in routine. And yet, whenever a rupture finally arrived, it came so suddenly I needed time to adjust. For a moment or two I felt disabled by my mother's announcement, but I recovered enough to drink my tea off in one scalding draught. I stuffed the breakfast cake in the front pouch of my coveralls and went to the bathroom to slather my face.

Down in the yard, at the bottom of the stairs, my mother had the quad running. She handed me my hat and gloves and we rode out in the warm dark with the lights off, our scarves up against the dust.

How mild the air was that morning. The wind had no sting in it. A big moon was still up and, alongside us, the tapered wing of our shadow rippled across the silver pools of gibber. The darkling barrier of the range loomed larger the further we went, until at the foothills we parked, strapped our waterpacks on and began to climb.

I followed her up the lower spurs until we reached the chutes and clefts that led to the terraces. In the gloom we took no risks, went methodically, in stages, from level to level, until we crested out with nothing above us but the stars. Yes, comrade, a sky with stars.

I thought we were headed for the water cave, but instead we bore north, in the opposite direction. We hiked the riven tops a good while, and when the first light came up, the moon was setting over the pearly band of sea to the west.

I was glad of the light. Especially once we came to the razorback. Because I could see ahead that, as the ridge rose, it narrowed precipitously until its shale flanks were only an arm's length apart. And beneath those friable slopes, at either side, lay the canyon whose empty streambed was too dark and too deep to see.

My mother halted a moment. She turned my way.

You right?

I nodded.

Okay then.

She stepped out onto the spine of the ridge and began to climb. The incline was modest, but the footing was uncertain. I watched that squat figure, her sprung gait. It was a long traverse, but not once did she hesitate or stop to glance back for my sake, and I loved her for it. She left me to wrestle with the shame of my fear alone. I could taste the cake at the back of my throat. My legs trembled. But there was no possibility of turning back. I put one foot after the other and followed.

At the narrowest point, which was underhung by sandy slumps – awful to contemplate – I simply watched her boots and set my own in her wake.

Eventually, at the highest point of the incline, we reached the foot of an enormous limestone stack, a rock pile that teetered at the tip of the ridge. Atop the pile, against the pinkening sky, was a fortress of gnarled white sticks. It was so broad and strong, it looked as if a grown woman, if she were brave and crazy enough, could climb up and see the horizon in every direction.

From where we were, halted at the foot of this great stack, I could only see its leading edge and the foot of the wickerwork ramparts. Without warning, my mother dropped to a crouch. Then she prostrated herself. I stared a moment before following her lead. I watched the soles of her boots as she wriggled forward and I wormed along after her until we came to a marginally wider lintel. She twisted around, motioning me forward with one arm. I hesitated. At either side, the abyss was close. As the first sun hit the western wall, the rapidly heating air set off an updraft. It launched a churning pall of dust that hung just below us, beautiful and sinister. By noon the heat in that wadi would be lethal.

I looked ahead to my mother. She did not beckon me again.

I writhed up against her, tight to her side.

Good, she said. Good boy. Now watch.

Out of nowhere, a breeze swished by. A shadow ran over me and poppled across the rocks ahead. Then it disappeared. My mother seized my arm. When she hissed my name, it came hot and shocking against my ear. That's when I looked up. Saw a creature hanging in the air. Like something from a dream, it shone bronze and gold and umber. It was enormous.

Is it real? I asked.

Just watch, she whispered.

The bird alighted on the massive platform of sticks and waded in a half-circle, eyes glinting with every turn of its head.

I knew it, she whispered. Been seeing her all week.

What is it?

An eagle. That's a wedgetail.

Looks mean.

You think *we* work hard for our food. You should see what this gal will do, the country she has to cover to get a feed.

You've seen it before?

Not this same one, I don't think. But yes, we used to see them now and then, your father and me. They hunt lizards and snakes and mice – even small roos.

So it's a bird? Like a chook?

Yes, she said. It's a bird. But it's more like you and me than any chook. She doesn't just peck around between her feet. She's a worker. She'll fly the whole range and plain looking for food. If there's nothing alive or dead out here, she'll die looking. She's a traveller. And she's fierce.

Can she see us?

Oh, she knows we're here.

Doesn't look happy.

I wanted you to see her. It's important. Which is why I want you to stand up.

What? I asked, having heard her perfectly well.

I said stand up.

But. Why?

To see better.

I can see good right here.

Stand up, now, she said firmly. And watch.

I was terrified. But I obeyed. Because she was my mother, and that's how I was raised. And as I got to my feet, legs wobbling, the bird twitched, turned its head, and took me in. It hitched its elbows and set its wings back against its flanks. Its eye had the sheen of a polished stone.

Sometimes, said my mother behind me, you need to stand up and be seen. This bird will remember you. When we're gone, it'll remember you and wish you'd been small enough to eat. There you are, upright meat. Look! She's watching, wondering. Figuring the odds.

The eagle opened itself up in stages, as if assembling and enlarging itself moment to moment. It was a mighty thing to behold.

Then those wings cranked out, feathers fluttering five colours in the updraft, and the only noise I heard as it lifted into the sky was the rattle of dry sticks.

It's scared of me, I said exalted and relieved.

No, said my mother. She's discounted you. That bird's hungry. And you're not what she's after. She's got work to do. And so do we. Let's go.

I was never entirely sure what my mother was trying to show me that day. We never discussed it directly – then or later. Perhaps it was simply to show me how majestic an eagle was. And, of course, how exceptional it was that we should see one. Later that winter, I thought I saw it again, but it was probably nothing more than a mote of dust in my eye.

My mother said that when my father was a boy there were still emus on the plain – giant birds that couldn't fly – and quail, too, tiny ones that could. But apart from that single eagle and the fowls we kept for eggs, the only birds I ever saw were the finches. They arrived after rain once the sudden clouds of insects had dispersed, when the spinifex tussocks woke up and shed seeds like golden dust. They sounded like a million gleeful children. When the feed thinned out, the finches moved on, and for a day or two the plain felt lonely.

The loss of them stung. I can't imagine what it must have felt like to lose birds the size of people.

Emus, said my mother. They didn't just eat seeds – they spread them in their scat. But during the Terror they were hunted for meat. And when they dwindled, so did the plants of the plain. By the time your father was a boy, only a few stragglers held on this far north. Then came the ten-year dry. Those that didn't perish went south.

And what was there? More water?

Yes. And more hungry people.

The day of the eagle, it left its mark on me, comrade. I still think of it now and then, especially when I'm grasping for some sort of perspective. You see, like yourself, I've lived a life of watchful concealment. Yet for a while, and in its way, it was also a form of standing up. Despite my fear. Whatever the odds. To allow myself to see. But to act, too. When so few understood what taking action might mean. But remember, to serve was to remain secret. Nameless and invisible, right? Hiding in plain sight amongst our own. To most citizens, we didn't exist. We were inconceivable. Those who dreaded us, well, they only suspected our existence, wondering if perhaps we were anything more than a fever dream. The only time we revealed ourselves was to an object. At the moment of acquittal. When we did stand up to be seen, it was before those who, within a second or so, would cease to exist.

So yes, I think of that day of the eagle now and then. And puzzle over my mother's words. For once my childhood was over, it was never again possible for me to be properly known by those I loved. Perhaps, in the end, that was all I ever really wanted. To appear before them as I am. To see and be seen. But that's not how things went.

———

During the long, grinding summer after the eagle, while we were boxed in below ground, my mother came into the hab, sat on my bed and drew a book from a canvas slip cover. It was a small sketchpad. Every page was covered in drawings. Some were mere outlines, others finished likenesses of seeds and fruits and vegetables. But there were animals, too. Creatures whose names hung suspended above them in block letters. The wedgetail eagle was there. Also the emu and the black-flanked rock-wallaby and the desert hopping mouse.

This was his, she said. Your father's.

He saw all these? Here?

Some, I think, she said. When he was a boy. But most were those his parents and grandparents told him about. See this one?

Bowerbird, I read.

These were the birds that lived in the tree over the cave.

You remember all these?

Well, I remember the stories about them.

I thumbed through carefully.

Keep it, she said. Learn all the names.

In case I see them?

Yes, she said. In case you see them.

I looked up at her. There was a certain look on her face. Of course, being a kid, I read it as longing. For my father.

I've kept that book with me all these years. And in my travels I've seen some of those creatures a time or two. It's back in the vehicle, in the duffel behind the seat. If I live long enough I'll show it to the child. I never got the chance with my own. Or maybe I never made the time.

I can draw most of those creatures from memory. Knowing their names feels important. Even now. Which sounds a bit mad, I know. As if saying the names of things might bring them to life. And maybe me as well. You know there's no magic in it. It can't be done, can it.

But you do it anyway, because it's all you have in the face of extinction. Nattering, naming, uttering. Hot air, comrade. But haven't we both been borne aloft by exactly that? We've seen things we once thought were magic. So why shouldn't I tell stories and chant names?

Jesus, says the bowman, agitating his beard. Don't you ever shut up?

Am I boring you?

Fella, you're not the only one who's seen shit and done shit. We're all from somewhere better. We've all seen better days.

I thought you should know who we are. Figured you might appreciate some conversation, some intel. It must get lonely.

That's a lot of assumptions, there.

You're not interested? At all? You've been on your own how long?

You think I'm an idiot? You're pumping me. I'm not answering your fucking questions.

Well, maybe I read you wrong.

Maybe you did.

Somehow, I don't think so.

He scowls. But I can see his mind at work.

I think you need us, I tell him.

Bullshit.

How do I know your protein powder is real? Have I seen it? Have I watched you making it?

Listen to you, flapping your gums. You think I'm falling for that? You think I'm likely to show you?

Well, if you were making it down here, we'd smell it.

You think this is the only hole in the ground around here?

How many are you using?

Fuck you.

Maybe it's all just a story. You've got stories, I can see that. But this cache is temporary. What about down the track? Maybe you can see the end of it. You can feel it coming. And that's why you're keeping us. Unconventional sustenance.

Jesus God, he says. I should wash your mouth out. I should kill you just for that.

Comrade. Mate. I'm only thinking aloud. Speculating. If you were a barbarian, we'd have been dead an hour ago. Right?

You should be careful how you speak to me.

I understand.

I mean, Christ, man, you talk like that in front of a child?

She knows what's going on. She's seen what savages do. She's wondering the same thing as me. Who is this bloke? What's in his heart? What's his nature? Am I his guest or his prisoner? What will he do with me?

Fella, if talk was food, you'd be fatter than a week-old body bag.

Let's just lay it out. You've got plenty of secure space. Some water source, I assume. Stores and juice enough for one. Shelter for much more than one. I can add to that. Augment it. I can make water, grow food, generate juice, bank it with extra batts. Don't you see? We bring extra hands, more security. A vehicle, if you don't have one. Another if you do. You and me, we're both trained men. Doesn't all this shave down the odds? You've been in the field. Don't you want added capability?

Shut up! he bellows. For pity's sake, will you shut your fucking mouth or I'll stuff it with rags.

The child cowers against me.

The bowman limps away. The lights go out.

For a while it's black down here. The gallery, with its close fust of iron and earth, has taken on the old field reek of piss, sweat and nervous energy. But slowly the crepey light from the vertical shaft down the way begins to insinuate itself.

Hard to tell how long we sit in the dark. The girl settles, later she snores quietly. Then the lights come on again. And when the bowman returns, he's harder to read. And there's nowhere for me to go but onward.

When I was a kid, there was still a coral trade in our part of the world. In winter, folks from the hamlet rounded the tip of the cape to forage on the western shore, shovelling up the white rubble that lay piled in rows like abandoned fortifications. Citizens worked in gangs, tossing lumps onto trucks that carted them back to the wharf, where they were loaded onto scows headed south for trade. Down there the rubble was burnt to make quicklime for cesspits and slake to produce mortar and purify water supplies. There was plenty of limestone back up in the range, and for a time it had been quarried in some of the seaward canyons, but that was a far more laborious business and hardly worth the energy required.

My father crewed on one of those coastal traders, hauling loads a thousand klicks south, down to the harbour walls of Perth and even further afield, to the smaller ports of the cooler southern seaboard. To me it sounded like a life of grand adventure, but my mother never shared that view. She was careful to disguise it, but I think she fretted while he was away. Now and then she let slip a hint of the dangers he faced.

The sea's not like the land, she said. Nothing's solid. You can't depend on it. Ashore, you can retreat and find refuge. You can prepare for treachery. But at sea, there's nowhere to hole up.

You don't want him to go? I asked.

He's from sea-going people. It's what he wants.

It's brave work, I said defensively.

Yes. And important. They bring back stuff we need – machine parts, metal scrap, hemp, grain, solar film, zinc for sun paste.

But you want him home.

Well, I like it when he's home. And, to tell the truth, it makes me sad sometimes, to see the coral. All those bleached heads. It's like trafficking in skulls. Just to treat sewage.

I thought of our reeking long-drop and the slouching sack of lime inside the door. It wasn't an image I cared to associate with my father. I preferred to imagine him on deck at night, reading the stars, watching as the flares of all those abandoned grease rigs he used to speak of fell by. Navigating by the stars, comrade, can you imagine? That was probably getting harder even then, but I love to think of that time of the Long Peace – the steady years – when the stars came out like wildflowers.

They were long weeks when he was gone. Sometimes he'd be away for months. And when he did return, we'd never be at the dock to meet him. My mother said that, with no way for him to send news, it was impossible to know when he was due. But she seemed to have some preternatural sense of his proximity, because some mornings she'd excuse me from my chores and set me on the balcony as a lookout. She never gave a reason, and I was so glad to be free I never sought one. I was content to pace in the shade, watching the gulf glint and shimmer in the distance. The only things that moved out there were the willie-willies. They rose abruptly from the plain and twisted away to lumber across the landscape until they petered out in a welter of boiling grit. The novelty of the commission soon began to wear thin, but even so I kept a diligent watch until a pink column bloomed at the horizon and all my senses stirred.

That pillar of dust would reach up from the earth like a seedling and, minute by minute, grow larger, its stem canting, as if toward the light. Then, at last, I'd catch a glint of metal and glass. And in time – such a long, long time – a flatbed truck would turn in off the peninsula road and roll our way until the rattle of tyres and tin was audible. Then I'd be calling, running, scrambling downstairs, fumbling with my hat and scarf.

When the vehicle stopped in our compound, the train of dust overtook it, obscuring it entirely. And from that churning cloud, like a figure from legend, a solitary, wavering silhouette emerged to stride unhurriedly across the gibber, his face shadowed by a wide-brimmed hat. And when the truck was gone, and the grit had blown clear and there was nobody in the compound but the three of us, the skirts of his hat would flick back and there he'd be. My father.

We'd all clutch one another mutely a moment in the scalding sun. Nobody spoke until we got him inside. I watched, shy but avid, as he freed himself of the hat and stripped off his tunic to rinse the dirt away. He had white scab on his brow and hands. On his forearms, long, silvery lines. And low on his belly, a pulpy scar like a smashed fig.

During those homecomings I fizzed with excitement. But I was also conscious of my parents' uncanny restraint. The caution in their movements. The courtly quietness of their tone. And somehow I knew better than to violate that. It seemed to take days for them to become easy with one another, but even after they settled it was evident, once again, that my father had brought a great silence home with him.

With me he was solicitous, always discreetly relieving me of the worst jobs in the growhouse – whether it was feeding dead fowls through the chipper or scraping their shit into a scuttle – but at bedtime, as he sat by my cot and laid a callused hand on my arm, he told no tales of the sea or the southern cities. He seemed shy. Withdrawn, even. Looking back, knowing what I do now, I think he was cauterized, like the fearsome scar on his belly.

Some nights I'd watch them together out on the deck smoking choof, clearly having dipped into the summer rations, as if they needed the edges taken off things.

And this is really all I have of him. That and the expeditions to the cave. The rest is second-hand, almost mythical. I don't know how much of it's true in a literal sense, but I treasure it anyway. We need to believe in those who came before, the people from whom we spring. To know they had moments of nobility. Because nobody wants to feel they're the seed of monsters. This is something I don't need to tell *you*, comrade. You're not some dozing grafter. You've seen monsters. Not just savages – monsters. You've met their grand-children's grandchildren. Seen their faces as it dawns on them that they no longer have firm ground to stand on. As if they weren't all born of quicksand. Sump sludge, grease pits. Rivers of blood and fire. Christ, like me, you could almost pity them. But I know you don't. You can't. You won't.

I was not quite seven years old when my father died.

It's late winter. My mother and I. We're stooped in the grow-house. She draws herself suddenly upright. Sets her secateurs down beside the crate half-filled with the tomatoes we're picking. She winds the scarf about her pasted face and then reaches for her hat, binds the skirts at her neck. And only then do I turn to see what's caught her attention. A pillar of dust on the plain. But she doesn't send me upstairs to watch its progress. She instructs me to keep working, to stay *exactly* where I am. And, instinctively, I sense that this is not a homecoming but the arrival of something malign.

It's just a truck, no different from those that usually bring him. And I see her out in the compound. The vehicle pulls away. Leaves a moiling cloud to obscure her. And when it dissipates she's still standing under the blistering sun. Alone. Stranded.

Truth is, I don't really know if I genuinely remember this or if I've constructed it from spare parts after the fact. It *feels* real. Seems like the truth. Later, as a youth, I needed to fill that void. As a way of recovering. And I guess my mother understood that. She told me the story, like all the others. And you know how it is. These things become your own memories. I only really knew my father through her telling. And even with everything I learnt later, I think she did right by me in that regard. I'm not bitter about it. If she'd needed to invent him completely, she would have. And I'd forgive her for it still.

A storm, she told me. Off the Ninety Mile cliffs. His ship was lost. The entire crew gone.

We never got his body back. No part of him ever returned to the plain except the stories we told of him.

I took ill. I guess it was a confluence of things. The shock. Grief. And I think perhaps I tried to outrun it. Beat it with work. She suggested as much, anyway. Said she never forgave herself for allowing it. Confessed that she was so preoccupied by her own sorrow, she didn't notice the way my distress was compounding itself. I worked myself into a state of calenture.

Needless to say, a bout of heat fever is not the best way to begin a season underground. We were lucky the monsoon failed that summer. One decent low-pressure system – those doldrums, the humidity – would have killed me. My mother couldn't quite believe I pulled through. But it must have been bad, because it took me the best part of the new year to recover. And I don't remember any of it.

I think, if I'm honest, this was my chief vulnerability in the field. They knew I was a northerner, born sweating, breathing desert air from the get-go. But they didn't know my secret fear. You and me, comrade, we were trained to endure the heat. Think of the calefactions we've each seen and endured. Christ, it hardly bears thinking about. But I'll tell you now – I fear the heat sickness more than pain. Probably a mistake to tell you, to hand you my weakness like this, like victuals in a dixy. But I'm trying to get through here. I need you to see me.

I lost my father. Twice, as it happens. And both times I went a little mad. And look. This child. She's not like you and me. She fears our scars. You can see it in her eyes. But, dear God, be glad she can't see the keloid snakes inside us. Don't you think we owe her something better than terror?

So, yes, I lost a year. Recovered. And life went on.

But having been such a tractable child, I became a restless and irritable youth. I was never openly defiant, but I was mulish enough to test my mother's patience. By the summer of the year I turned fourteen, I was finding the night-time chores and morning lessons underground as oppressive as the cellar itself.

I was old enough to take choof by then. It helped in the afternoons to ease the sense of confinement, but once the season broke and it was safe to be topside again, I was agitated in ways I'd never felt before. I was smouldering, and it scared me. I was hopeless at hiding it.

But my mother was shrewd. The next winter she began releasing me from my early morning chores a couple of times a week. She encouraged me to roam a little. I think she figured if I was going to blow off some juice, I might as well learn a few things while I was at it.

So I began to comb the upper peninsula, to forage and explore unaccompanied. And instead of sending me feral, it served to rein me in, because I took this new freedom as a sign of confidence, and I wanted to prove this trust wasn't misplaced. To ensure the privilege wasn't withdrawn, I made sure I travelled safely. I needed to demonstrate my competence and show I was serious. I took careful note of every instruction. I was fastidious about equipment and meticulous in my preparation.

To the back of the quad I strapped a cube of water. Atop that I lashed my swag and a roll of foil. In the cargo box at the front I had supplies to sustain me a few days in case of emergency. I wore a bladder and oversoles, took a compass, barometer, and a tin of paste. Every time I set off – for the canyons and gorges, or the terraces of the western shore – I felt exhilarated. Proud of myself. As if this new freedom had been earnt, not granted.

That first season abroad I was callow enough to think I'd achieved this liberty despite my mother, not because of her, but the truth is she wanted me out there every bit as much as I felt the need to go. I guess it was an extension of my education. And a chance for her to get some respite.

I began with day trips. But once I'd proved I could plan and execute a day abroad solo and maintain sufficient discipline to take protective measures in the afternoon, I was allowed out overnight. In this way I became accustomed to the ascetic routine required by the conditions, always allowing time in the cooler hours, while I was still clear-headed, to search for shady hollows so that as the heat closed in I had a crevice to drag my bedroll into where I could set the foil blanket overhead and wait for the worst of the day to pass. Those were long hours. Despite the perilous urge to get on and do something, I learnt to hold my nerve. And it was this self-control and stillness that led me to see and feel things in the landscape I wouldn't have noticed otherwise.

I came home with papery snakeskins, petrified roo scat, the bleached bones of hopping mice, a fossilized tooth that filled the palm of my hand. But I saw live animals, too. Cave wasps that liked to sip at my sweat and sting me for the favour. Other creatures that conformed to certain drawings in my father's sketchbook. A thorny devil, once. And, now and then, rock wallabies or creatures so cryptic they seemed like visitations from another time. I knew they were real because I picked up their blocky scat and caught the meaty scent of them in tenebrous overhangs, but all I ever saw were shadows flitting past the fractures in gorge walls.

When I was fifteen, I crossed the spine of the range and picked my way down the western terraces with the salt wind in my face. I found a rock shelter. A long hollow in the limestone rampart with a wide ocean view. It was high enough to stand in, with sufficient space for twenty souls, maybe more. Here, fused into the ceiling, were large nubs of dead coral, like blurred faces looking down at me and past me to the sea. On the walls, strange patterns and marks were scratched or painted – I couldn't tell which. And underfoot, broken shells and bones lay strewn all about. When you scraped it up, the fine dust between these fragments was dark with soot, and mixed into it were shards and flakes of hard stone, black and orange, that looked alien in this country of pale and friable limestone.

I sat for hours to sketch all these things after the style of my father. And as the sun set in the sea and the salt breeze broke the back of the day's heat, I came out onto the threshold of the rock shelter and watched the last light on the rolling waves. That night, on my swag, with a pouch of keepsakes beside me, I lay under the stars on the terrace beneath the rock shelter, and although I was out in the open I felt enfolded, as if the oceanic roar, amplified by the cave behind me, was spilling back out to bear me up and float me in its ancient backwash.

Next morning, while it was still dark, I wrapped myself, pasted up, and hiked back east to the tops. I was home before the sun had time to kill me. I felt as if I'd broken through some barrier, as if childhood was behind me.

My mother didn't make a fuss when I rolled into the compound, but I could see the effort it took to disguise her relief. I was regaling her with details of my discovery before I'd even dismounted the quad. As she helped me unpack, she listened with a smile. Perhaps it was pride, or vindication – I don't know. We retreated to the shade, and after I'd doused myself and sat under the HiVap a while, we ate an early lunch and talked about the rock shelter. She knew the place. Of course she did. But that hardly dimmed my sense of discovery.

That's quite a trek, she said. And a hell of a spot. I'm glad you found it. Did you like the view?

Such a strange place, I told her. The sound of the sea, it filled the cave like a crowd. The old people, I could feel them there.

Yes?

You think I'm nuts?

Not at all.

But you've got that smile.

Well, she said. You may have felt *something*.

People. The old people.

Yes. But not our old people. Not there. Not that place.

But you can see it all around – bones, shells, old fires.

Yes, but those firepits and grinding stones – they're all from before.

You mean before the Terror?

Yes.

And before the people of the tree and the cave?

Long before.

So, they're not our kin?

The ancients of the rock shelter? No. And yes. But we're not of their people.

I don't understand.

They're the Countrymen, she said. Those who were here before. Actually, before there *was* a before.

I ran my hand over my sodden head, bewildered.

This is a very old place, she said. They came from forever ago.

Before there was a before, I said, weighing the idea.

Yes. And maybe they reckon they'll be around after there's an after.

Doing what?

I don't know, she said. Doing what people do to stay alive together, I suppose. Doing what they always did.

But they're gone.

That's what folks like to tell themselves. But some say they moved to the desert. To regroup, wait things out.

Like our people waiting in the cave. Waiting for the madness to stop.

Maybe. Perhaps something like that, yes.

Seems a long time to wait, though, doesn't it?

Maybe they're good at waiting things out.

But the sagas, I murmured. The sagas say there's more world behind us than ahead.

Yes, she said, beaming, and a little surprised that I should remember my lessons. But they also say this – that the world ahead is borne aloft by our dreams and works.

I don't know what that means.

Perhaps it means everything lives and dies at the mercy of our ideas.

Our ideas?

Yes. Every action is the fruit of an idea.

I don't get it.

You will. I hope you will. The world is older than you can imagine. And people have lived and done things and made things – and dreamt things – on a scale you can't imagine. The Countrymen will have their own sagas, stories older than any we know.

How?

Because they had world enough and time.

Right, I said, unsettled by the course this conversation had taken and needing to change tack before I foundered. So what about down south? Cityfolk, I mean.

Well, they share our sagas. Most of them.

What I mean is, do they live like us?

Well, yes. And no.

It's always yes and no, I said, unable to hide my exasperation.

She smiled. I got up to stand beneath the misters.

Cityfolk're just people like us, she said. They don't all look like us, but they speak and live like us, mostly. In association.

So they trade?

Yes. But not for water. Water's provided by the Association. Used to be from rivers. Now it's desal.

But what do they trade *with*?

Oh, lots of things. Many more people. More needs. More materials and produce coming in. So yes, they grow things, like us. And make things – much more than us – because they can. But they live close up. Like fowls in boxes. For ease. Efficiency, really. And safety. So the city's different, but its people aren't so different from you and me. But make no mistake, no city boy your age will be out on the tops to see the sun come up. He won't be sleeping alone under the stars. He wouldn't survive a day in the open down south, let alone north of Capricorn.

You're just saying that.

I'm saying it because it's true. Are you still hungry?

I am.

Well, let's see what we have.

I'll go there one day, I said, following her into the kitchen. The city.

No doubt.

I really thought I could feel them. Our old people.

Maybe you did, she said, pulling out some mash. Or maybe you were just feeling people.

Later that winter I was out on the deck, already sweated through from the morning's work and shucking my boots for breakfast, when I noticed a column of dust out in the distance. The sun was barely a smear on the eastern horizon but there was light enough to register the signs of a vehicle travelling north out on the peninsula road. I watched the plume of its progress idly. A rig passing by at this hour was hardly noteworthy. It was simply something moving in the landscape. What caught my fuller attention was the way the dust wake suddenly petered out. I waited, more alert now, expecting it to pass by or perhaps to turn in. But there was no more dust.

There's someone out there, my mother called from the kitchen.

I see it.

She stepped onto the deck beside me, her scarves unravelled, her head bare.

Take the quad, she said. And a spare batt.

I rode out along the drive, stirred by the diversion, enjoying the wind in my wet shirt and scarf.

Just south of our turnoff, I caught the flare of sun off a windscreen and headed for it. It was a flatbed. And behind that, a low-load trailer. As I approached, I saw someone sprawled on the track, trying to jack the lagger up in a welter of shredded rubber. I rolled in slowly, noting the load of steel pipe on the trailer, the crates of clamps and fixings lashed in beside it. On the tray of the truck was a furled swag wedged beneath a lift arm with a block and tackle. It wasn't premium kit, but it looked decent enough.

The kid dragged himself out and got to his feet as I drew level on the bike.

Morning, I said.

G'day.

All good?

He shrugged. I figured him about the same age as me. His teeth were bad, and I could smell the sour sweat on him.

Just the tyre?

He nodded.

Need some help?

Nah, he said, tilting at the water jerry lashed to the pillion behind me. But I could do with a slurp.

I switched off the quad, got down and poured him a pannikin.

I got me own somewhere, he said.

Don't worry, I replied. Saves you looking for it.

He took the pannikin and, as he drank, he chomped at the tin rim, like an infant. It gave me a queasy feeling, the idea of his rotten teeth in my water mug. He drank the lot and stood there with it dangling from one grimy finger.

Who'da thought, he said. Prince of the plain, givin me his cup.

What?

Nothin.

You're welcome, I said.

I held my hand out and he passed it back with a grin.

Been south?

He nodded.

Where'd you get the load?

Shit's where you find it, he said.

You trade for it?

Trade *with* it, mate.

So you find stuff?

Salvage, it's called.

I know the word.

Course you do.

You like it?

The word or the work?

The work, I said, struggling to make sense of his hostility.

Work's shit. And this place is fucked. Whole peninsula. Nothing I can do about it, but.

What d'you mean, it's fucked?

Not even the end of August, mate. It's fuckin hot already. Everything's hard. This is fucked. All of it.

End of the season, I said. That's just how the world is.

Says the prince.

Mate, what's your problem?

Change your own wheels, do you?

Yes, I said. Of course.

Show me.

What?

Show me you know how to change a tyre.

Who else'd change my wheels?

Thought you'd have help.

What, my mother?

You haven't got stiffs?

No, I said.

So it's true? Just the two of youse out here?

I shrugged. Irritated now, and wary.

You haven't showed me, he said, waving a hand at his mangled tyre.

Mate, you can change your own bloody wheel.

That's fuckin hospitable, eh.

You're not on our place. This is the public road. I've given you the help you need. I've done my duty.

Letter of the law! Mr Association! What a shiny-arse.

I've got work to do, I said, stowing the pannikin and mounting up.

I wheeled the quad around his rig and fanged it back to the house. I was hauling my boots off again when I saw his dust creep north toward the hamlet.

Who was it? asked my mother.

No one, I said. Just some hamlet kid with a flat.

My encounter with that surly grafter stayed with me. Not just because it rankled but because something about his salvage caper lit my imagination. Driving south, foraging for stuff we wouldn't have to trade for. Materials I could find and accumulate like water. Stuff we could trade *with*.

As the season waned, the romance of it grew, and by the time my mother and I made the move underground the idea of the open road had its hooks in me. I could think of nothing else. There was of course a perfectly practical argument for getting into the salvage trade. It gave us another avenue, more safety. But in truth the appeal for me was in what I imagined to be a life of rambling liberty, roaming the countryside, free and alone. The idea of taking a chance and seeing what could be found.

I was nervous about raising the prospect with my mother. I figured she needed to be approached gently. So I waited until the wee hours, when the night's work was done but it was still too hot to sleep, when we lay on our cots and smoked a bit of choof to ease the discomfort. Bit by bit, night by night, I introduced the notion to her. Initially I proposed it as if thinking aloud. Later, I began to make the case with more purpose and growing confidence. She resisted at first, as I knew she would. Then she said we'd need a second vehicle, which made sense. After that, she declared that I'd need to be older before

I could leave the homestead on a journey so long. Wasn't it likely I'd be away for weeks at a time? What about all the extra kit required – a second trailer, a bank of auxiliary batteries? Then there was the matter of how she was supposed to cover my chores in my absence. The impediments soon began to seem insurmountable and for a while that summer it felt as if the list of them would never end. And yet the season passed and, along with it, one by one, all my mother's reservations seemed to fall away.

It didn't happen immediately, not by a long shot, but I was on the road before I turned seventeen.

Even so, it wasn't a clean getaway. Because before I set out, my life took a turn. It was sudden. And huge. I guess you could say it was cataclysmic. It happened to all of us, I imagine. Each in our own way. In a matter of hours, the life you've known, the one you'd seen stretching out before you – it's over.

Me, I was too raw and isolated to imagine a disruption of such magnitude was even possible. Now, of course, I know it was inevitable. But it was a bloody long time before I copped on to that.

It was a market day, just after sun-up. I'd been sent to trade fertilizer for parts. Well, one part in particular. A summer storm had ripped our biggest barrel turbine from its mount. And once we'd cobbled it all back together in the hot fug, we found – well, we heard, really – that the central axle had warped. The unit was functional, if less efficient, but after a few months the wobble and clunk it made as the big drum turned was beginning to get on my mother's nerves. So, armed with bags of birdshit, I was tasked with sourcing a replacement in the hamlet.

I hadn't been long in the market square, casting about for likely prospects at the stalls and the long traders' benches under the rippling shades, when a bloke loomed at my side. A little too close for comfort.

He was a big fella. Took up more room than seemed reasonable. And there was something furtive about him. But also familiar.

The facial scars gave him a sinister look, especially the pulpy mess where his left eye had once been. It was puckered and cinched like a drawstring bag. He stepped in so close that when he uttered my name his breath scalded my ear.

It took me a couple of moments to place him. To get a proper look, I had to step back a little. But he took hold of my arm. Firmly. Drew me close again. It was the filmlayer. The one who used to come out now and then to visit my mother. The bloke with the feeble son. I'd never traded with him before. I hadn't spoken to him since I was a kid. Back then he'd had both his eyes.

I greeted him, as hamlet manners required, and tried to take another pace back. But he wouldn't let go. He smiled and showed his broken teeth. His hands were huge and workworn. I could feel the barbs of his calluses through the sleeve of my tunic.

Not easy to get, he said, hefting the warped axle from the public bench as if he had a right to my property and licence to be so close to my person.

No, I said. I was just hoping someone here would have something like it.

Well, good luck there, he said, turning it over, rolling it in his palm like a club. This is good gear.

If you don't look you won't find, I said.

What's that, the sagas?

No, I said. My mother.

Ha. Well, she knows where to look and where best not to.

Okay.

This is old kit, he said of the axle. But reliable.

Yeah.

Happens I know someone with a lathe. Might turn you a new one.

Oh, I demurred. We can't afford to trade for a new one.

Why don't we find out what she's asking?

He led me by the arm. His manner was not aggressive, but it brooked no resistance. He was my elder, from my own hamlet, so there was nothing for me to do but submit. I felt apprehended as much as guided.

He led me away from the shade sails and the growing crowd of locals, past the trestles and dropped tailgates of traders, toward the civil shelter.

With its hulking curves and storm roof, the municipal centre was unlike other buildings in the hamlet. While most local houses were up on stilts, this place was set at ground level, as if gripping the dirt at every angle. And it was not low and louvred like all the workshops in town, or the godowns beside the wharf, but wide and high. Its big, sleeved cyclone shutters were rarely cranked up, and there were no other windows, so the place always had a cowled and opaque aspect. The walls were ribbed steel, coated with film and, given how dusty the square could get, unusually clean. I couldn't imagine the water it must have cost to jet the place spotless every morning.

I'd never been in. My mother said there were meeting rooms inside for the Association and the Co-op. Also, a nursing station and a tribunal chamber for settling disputes. In the cellar, she said, there was a storm shelter with a vault full of emergency provisions held in trust on behalf of all citizens of the community. Not that our family had ever made use of it.

Since the age of fifteen I'd been eligible to cast a ballot, but my mother seemed happy to carry proxy while I stayed home and kept up the chores. I took no interest in hamlet affairs. Association candidates, traders, mechanicals, factors for procurers and suppliers from the south – I could hardly tell them apart. They struck me as uniformly old and dull. But they all deferred to my mother. And I figured that, like the filmlayer, they'd known and respected my father. It didn't strike me as odd that my mother never stood for the Association. The idea didn't even occur to me. She was a home-steader. People like us didn't want to be around the hamlet a moment longer than necessary.

Anyway, the filmlayer frogmarched me toward the hooded entrance of the civil shelter. And I'll admit that, along with a sense of alarm, I felt a flicker of excitement. I had time enough to think that this was an odd way to enter that edifice for the first time. But he steered me right past the doors. We rounded the corner, into the narrow shade beside the building, and that's when I came to my senses, felt something awry, and began to resist.

I lunged to retrieve our axle from him, but he fended me off with a laugh and ruffled my hair indulgently. Then he took me around the far corner and pressed me face-forward against the wall.

I pushed back, tried to twist free, but it was hopeless. I was a sturdy youth but clearly no match for this old coot. His easy skill and power rattled me.

He mashed my brow against the hot corrugations. Said I should remain calm and remember my manners. That he would only release me if I stayed exactly where I was and faced the wall. By this point I was more angry than afraid, but I wasn't stupid. The bloke had a big old lump of steel in his hands. I was always going to do as I was told.

This axle, he growled against my neck. I definitely know someone who can help you out.

Yes, came another, lighter voice behind us – a woman's voice. Yes, I can make that. Leave it with me, son.

Don't move, said the filmlayer. Don't turn around. And don't speak.

For several minutes I stood sweating in the early sun, too afraid and too stunned to turn around. I felt a firm prod. Something smooth and solid slid under my arm and rested gently against the glistening solar film that encased the metal sheet in front of me.

Here, hold this, said the woman. I think that's got you sorted.

And don't scratch my sunskin, said the filmlayer. That's the best coating this vill's ever likely to see.

I could only see the bearing end and a part of the shaft – less than half an arm's length – but it was a freshly-turned piece of steel.

Exact replacement, full spec, said the woman.

That's bloody quick, I said, knowing it was impossible to fabricate something like that in a few minutes.

*Momentum is key*, said the woman. *Everything turns on the axle.*

So what do I owe you? I stammered. What do you need?

Two hours of your time, she said.

Doing what, exactly?

Showing me what you're made of.

You need graft?

No, she said. What I'm after is your attention.

And this is how you trade?

Yes, she said. Today it is.

At that point I had a hot urge to tell her what I thought of the way she went about her business, but I thought better of it.

When do you need me? I asked.

Tonight, she said. Come back at sunset. Park out the front. When it's fully dark, come back here. The door there to your right will be ajar. Don't bring a light, don't bring anybody else. Tell your mother you're collecting an axle that's being turned for you. Tell her you'll be two hours.

*Will* I be two hours?

That's how long you'll be.

Okay.

We have your assent?

My assent?

You're not obliged to come.

I'm not?

Of course not.

So I can just take my old axle back and we're square?

Well, she said. I've gone to the trouble of making you a new one. And with that old battery sequence you've got out there, you need every turbine up and operational. What's going to pump your water at night? How'll you run your fans?

How do *you* know what we've got? I asked.

I notice things. And I work with people who pay attention. Do you know how to pay attention?

Do I know you?

No, she said. But we know you. And we know your mum.

Is that a threat?

No, son. You have nothing to fear from us. You can go in a minute. The old axle's round the corner there. If you don't want to proceed with our transaction, just take it and we'll call it evens. Otherwise, we'll see you at sunset. That minute starts now. Don't leave early.

I stood with my head pressed to the glossy surface of the wall and counted the sixty seconds. In all that time – and it felt like a very long time – nobody spoke. There were no footsteps, no sounds from which to take a cue. I hesitated a moment, then turned slowly to find myself alone. I scanned the nearest buildings, the sailmaker's loft, the sparky's shed. The eastern skins of those places shone fiercely in the morning light. Their shutters were down. No one was about.

When I stepped cautiously around the corner, I drew myself properly upright, stared across at the trading crowd beneath the sails, and strode out like a man who'd just taken a piss. The warped steel rod leant against the wall of the shelter, but I passed it as if it was a piece of kit I had no claim to.

To be honest, I don't really know why I went back that evening. Except that plains life was not exactly a festival of surprises. And the fact is, I'd been restless for months. I was still anxious to get sorted and head off on the road, try my hand at the foraging caper, but for all my misgivings, I was intrigued by these people. I was also impressed and a little overawed by their stealth, the boldness and competence they demonstrated. I knew they might be bandits, but surely no brigand would have access to the civil shelter. Besides, these folks had already had the chance to do me harm and I'd come to none. And they'd offered me a choice, hadn't they? I didn't like the reference to my mother, but it was hardly an insult. I was a rustic, I guess. A naive youth. And bored. I couldn't resist the mystery of it all.

So, at day's end, I headed in. Arrived in the hamlet in the grimy heat of dusk. The market square was stripped and empty. Lights were on in houses down the way. At the rear of the place, I strode to the door as instructed. As promised, it was ajar. I pressed it back and was instantly yanked into the darkness, and something was pulled over my head. I was held firmly, but without violence. The door was closed and locked behind me.

Then I was shunted forward with both arms pinned. We went down some metal stairs with high railings. Slowly. Carefully.

Everything resonated and clanged as we descended. I sensed at least two bodies with me. After two flights, we turned into what felt like a long corridor where sounds were dampened by something soft underfoot. Then we came to a doorway or gap of some kind and angled through it into a space that sounded and felt much smaller. I was wrangled into a chair and told that, when the hood came off, I was to face ahead and only ahead. The hood would only be removed if I promised to comply.

Confounded, I accepted their terms. The blindfold was swept off by someone behind me. And immediately I sensed there were others in the low-lit room. All of them out of view. Behind me.

Ahead lay a blank wall.

Eyes forward now, said a woman's voice, the same from earlier in the day. Now, just wait and watch.

The wall lit up harsh and white. A series of images rose and fell away without explanation. People, cities, homes, domestic fittings, forests, rivers of ice, throngs of wild-eyed fish, fields of grain to the horizon. This was not the world I knew. For one thing, the colours were wrong. Every picture had a cloying sheen that rendered it alien and disquieting.

This is weird, I said. What is this?

Just watch, said the woman.

I raddled my scalp and continued to sit, despite myself. Vast columns of grey smoke. Black lakes. Entire landscapes on fire. These were not images of a seer's paradise. But they seemed to suggest some sort of tale. I didn't know how they made these pictures move, where the sound came from. I got gooseflesh watching it all dance and dicker in front of me.

I saw throngs of people hurling themselves against walls. Kids with rags tied across their faces. Towers spewed flames that roared like nothing I'd ever heard before. Citizens milled and ran in their hundreds, maybe thousands — all of them coughing. I saw wide streets with made roads strewn with bodies. Piles of them. Then an angry sea the colour of bearing grease. Mountains of water crashing against a sea wall. Gaps between buildings filled with storm surge. Upturned vehicles. Floating trash. Bodies facedown — some clothed, some naked. It was awful. Sickening. And I let out a cry. Like a frightened kid.

I heard someone shift behind me and sigh. Somebody else cleared their throat. But no one spoke.

Then there was a pause. Just white wall. The only sound was me, panting.

Okay, I said when I got my breath. You're schooling me. This is the Terror, right?

Yes and no, said the woman. This is advanced educational material. But everything you'll see tonight precedes the Terror. This is the age that produced it.

No, no, I insisted, this must be the dark age. This is the Terror. Just watch.

A bunch of maps came up. Each one lingering only four or five seconds. The oceans. The continents. Progressing in some way I didn't catch by changes of colour. Then I felt a pang of recognition. My mother's pared orange.

Later came a series of diagrams and charts. They weren't so different to the ones my mother had drawn me for my lessons, but they piled onto one another so quickly I couldn't keep up.

After this, pictures again. Nothing that moved, just pictures of places. And kit — vehicles, machines, gleaming things I couldn't place. The houses. My God, the houses. And then places again, outdoor places — everything high and green and sticky-looking, as if it was all covered in cold sweat, or tall and jagged and covered in drifts of hail. Creeks with waterfalls and fish frozen mid-leap.

Suddenly, the unmistakable sea. Then we were *in* the sea, *under* the water. Where everything had crazy sunset colours. Vegetable colours. Fruit colours.

This is coral? I asked. Somebody made it like this? Painted this?

No, said the woman. This is real. It's alive.

I was huffing by then, beginning to hyperventilate.

There followed a procession of people. They were like us, coming in every colour and shape. Except bigger than us. Their faces plump and shiny as melons. Their arms meaty, with dimpled hands. The size of them took some getting used to, but soon I was more caught up in where they were, what they wore, the stuff they had around them. Sleek cars in wild colours. Huge, padded suits. Glass-faced helmets. Ships. Buildings that reached into the clouds. Beds the size of whole rooms. Devices that ripped green crops, sucked dirt, made women's hair dance. There were tables laden with food, bristling with ornaments and implements I didn't recognize. I felt a wave of awe. And then a kind of weight, like shame. As if these were things I should never see. I didn't really know what I was viewing. I only knew it was not for me. I would never have it – any of it – and I couldn't bear to watch another moment.

Stop this, I pleaded. This isn't real.

We understand you're agitated, said the woman behind me.

This is wrong, I said, writhing in my seat.

Don't turn around, said a man. His voice was unfamiliar. Older.

There's only another couple of minutes, said the woman. You need to see this.

No, I said. Enough. Stop it.

The wall went white.

What is this? I asked, abject and afraid. Why do I need to see this?

There was an uneasy silence. And then the woman spoke.

Thank you for coming. And thank you for not turning around.

I could muster nothing in reply.

You've been raised well, she said. Would you agree?

Yes, I answered, almost at a whisper. I think so.

Do you feel cursed?

Cursed?

Do you think the world's shit? asked the older man. The world's fucked and it's all you deserve – you ever think that?

No, I replied truthfully. Why would I think that?

But you've heard it said?

Sometimes, I said reluctantly. People say stuff when they're angry. Depressed. Some people get that way.

And you?

I have work to do.

You know some history, I gather, said the woman.

Yes.

That the world was once different?

Old, I said. It's old. And there used to be more people.

And they went where?

They died. Disease. Fever. The Terror. The weather went bad, and people went bad with it. Murder. Madness.

True enough, as it goes, said the older man. But why would all this happen?

I dunno, I said. The world makes its mind up and does what it does. The citizen submits.

Word for word, said the woman.

You can't do what can't be done.

So they say, she said.

You get the world you deserve.

Your *mother* told you that?

No. I heard it somewhere.

Well, it's defeatist nonsense. Slave talk.

Life's hard, said the old fella in a more conciliatory tone.

I shrugged.

You think you deserve it? he asked. You deserve a hard life?

I'm up to it.

I don't doubt that. But I'm asking if you believe hardship is what you're due. That the world's challenges are your fault.

I dunno, I said. I try not to think about it. There's jobs to do. I do them.

I hear you're keen to go on the road.

What? How could you know that? What the hell is this?

We understand that much of what you've been shown tonight is unpleasant and disorienting, said the woman. But these files are archival.

I don't know what that means.

Points for honesty, said the bloke.

It means they're real, said the woman. From the past.

How? How did you get them?

They were left for us. Deliberately. By our comrades.

And who're they?

Our ancestors, she said. The best of them, anyway.

My ancestors are from the hills.

And who were *their* ancestors?

Fishing people. Growers.

You're a grower, correct?

Yes.

And your ancestors brought seeds down to the plain.

That's right.

That was their archive. They kept the craft alive with stories and songs, right?

I guess.

And that's how you and your mum know how and when to plant.

Okay.

So there's all kinds of knowledge. All kinds of archives.

You're saying they left you stuff that shows how to make the old world?

Quite the opposite. Much of it's a record of the old world killing itself. Which is exactly what happened. That dispensation destroyed itself. And much of the world and many of its people along with it.

So, there was an old world and other people. Bigger people. And it's gone. Fine. What's the point of all this? Why bother me with it?

You're not curious? About why the world is like this? Thanks to these archives, we know.

And why should I care?

Because you're a victim.

I don't like the sound of that.

Of course, we don't know everything. But we have enough. Broadly, we understand how it happened. Why. And we even have the names. Who did this to us. To you.

No, that can't be right.

Please, just try to relax and follow along. Eyes front, understand?

No, I don't bloody understand.

You can leave at any moment.

Sure. Like *that's* gunna happen.

Believe it. It's true.

Really, who are you people?

We're just citizens like yourself, said the woman.

I don't think so.

Well, it's true.

We're the rearguard, said the old bloke. And the vanguard.

Whatever the hell that is.

We're offering you a chance to do something, said the woman. To be a part of something special. Something noble.

Some kind of religious thing?

No. No magic.

But it's secret.

Very.

And if I'm not interested?

You don't know us. No harm. You go on with your life. You embrace your fate like a good mechanical. You submit to the situation you're in.

There's nothing wrong with my situation.

Well, that's true, within its limits, she said. You certainly do better than most folks out here on the plain.

Me and my mum.

Yes, said the old bloke. Your mother is well known. But you live like desert frogs. Spend half your life underground, in the dark.

Course we do. We're not made of steel.

But you think that's normal? For a human? Living underground? You reckon that's right? You figure that's fair?

Buggered if I know – it's just how things are.

Spoken like a true plainsman, said the man, unable to hide his disgust.

No disrespect, said the woman more kindly. But that's the sort of thing a citizen says with his head down.

But it's true.

And yet it's no mystery, said the woman. And no accident.

What's not an accident?

The way the world is. How it came to be like this. Who was responsible.

The world makes itself, I said.

That's where you're wrong, said the man. Hopelessly, tragically wrong. It's what folks have been telling themselves since before our grandparents' grandparents were born. But it's simply not the truth.

Look, if I'm a buried frog, what are you?

We're the rain, son.

Poetry. Jesus, that's all I need.

Maybe you should see what else we have to show you, said the woman.

There's more?

I'm afraid you've only seen the preliminary material, said the old man.

Aw shit.

I think you're tough enough to handle it. What d'you say?

I can go now?

If you prefer. Or you could watch some moving images and keep talking a little longer. Up to you.

Is this allowed?

By the Association? Well, that's a complex question. We can discuss it later.

But it's not going to get me sanctioned?

No.

They know about it?

Again, we can discuss that later.

You have more moving pictures?

Lots.

Fuck it, I said.

Is that consent?

What?

We need your explicit consent, said the man.

Orright.

I'm sorry, said the woman. But we need you to formally give your consent. Before these witnesses.

What witnesses?

The comrades here behind you.

Eyes front, said the man.

Okay, I said. I give my consent.

Right, said the old man. This material is about what's been done to you. To you and to yours.

Nobody did anything to me.

Run the sequence, please.

When I got home that night, my mother was making her bed out on the deck with the awning cranked back for a full view of the stars. As I reached the top of the stairs, I brandished the new axle.

Well, that seems to have been quite the transaction, she said without looking up.

Yeah, I said. Not exactly what I was expecting.

You sure you don't have something else to tell me?

Sorry?

I wondered if you might have met someone new in there.

Like who? I croaked.

Well, like a girl, I imagine. Or a boy.

Oh, I said. No.

I see.

It was just a bit more complicated than I thought.

Looks like a good piece of gear, she said, tilting her head toward the axle.

Yeah, hardly used, by the looks.

And what did this person want for it?

Fertilizer.

That's a going to take lot of birdshit. How will we get that in a hurry?

I promised two more bags. He said he'd wait.

Who's this again?

Some bloke from down south.

And he'll be here next time we have two bags?

Says he will.

You catch his name?

Nah. Didn't say.

It isn't stolen, that thing?

I hope not, I said. How would we know?

Well, a bloke who doesn't give his name. Makes you wonder.

Fair enough, I said. To be fair, I didn't ask.

Huh, she said, tucking and straightening her sheets.

Still, I said awkwardly. It's good gear. And we need it.

This bloke, she said, sitting down on her cot and reefing the band from her hair. Don't spose that filmlayer fella put you on to him?

I stood there a moment as she unwrapped her headscarf and stretched.

No, I murmured. Like I said, he just bowled up to me at the market this morning.

Huh, she said again. I spose stranger things have happened.

I nodded lamely. Then I gathered the wit to stride across to present the axle. She took it from me, weighed it in her hands admiringly.

Yes, she said at last. Good gear.

I'm buggered, I said. And I need a wash.

Okay, she murmured. G'night.

As I walked away, I heard the small thud as she set the axle on the floor. I felt a dip in my gut. But I kept on toward my room at the other end of the deck. I felt a stranger to myself. I'd never lied to my mother before. Not about anything of substance. And I felt rotten about it. But that night I had bigger things to ponder.

It would be neater and so much prettier to say I left home one evening a boy and returned a man, but that would be a lie. Because after my encounter in the basement of the civil shelter, I lay awake on my bed with a shirt stuffed in my mouth. Weeping like an infant. And I was like that for some time.

Next morning, I went about my work like someone impersonating himself. It was as if the frame holding me upright had been compromised. Overnight, all pride and confidence had been knocked out of me. It wasn't just tiredness – I was bereft. I could feel my mother watching, wordlessly. And it went on like that for several days, this sense of solitary, shapeless grief. I couldn't digest this new information. Not even at the level of the prelims, which were only offering the crudest outline of where we stood and what had happened before our time. Not that I had much of a grasp on any of that yet. I didn't pretend to understand it. If my mother'd asked me what was wrong, I wouldn't have known what to tell her. Not about my state or the news that had caused it. Except to say that now it was me feeling like her wounded orange. I'd woken one morning charged with momentum, and by day's end I was lost.

That whole week, I felt paralysed by indecision. They'd invited me back, those shadowy presences in the civil shelter. Next market day, should I choose to come, they'd show me more, explain some things, and consider offering me an opportunity that would transform my life. They didn't say what this was. The air of conspiracy frightened me. And so did the gravity attached to this secret proposition. Because these were people of a different order to folks in the hamlet. Repelled as I was by what they'd shown me, I could feel myself leaning into them. Which excited me as much as it alarmed me. And I see this now, even if I couldn't then: I wanted to feel some of their brisk confidence. To be like them. These people I didn't know and hadn't even laid eyes on.

Of course, next market day, I went. Found myself once again in the bowels of the civil shelter.

I figured the second time around, the shock wouldn't be as intense, but I was wrong. The stuff they showed me. Well, it scrambled me completely.

After the way I'd been raised to think of my family and our forebears, it was a blow – no, a catastrophe – to learn that I was born of ashes and delivered into sorrow. And it was no consolation to learn that everyone else was in the same situation. I felt degraded. Debased. Don't get me wrong – I fought it. Every new picture, and each sordid assertion that accompanied it, I pushed back against. But what could the likes of me rely upon to resist the evidence these folks presented? Beyond a home education, all I had was my own stiff-necked prejudices, my habits of mind.

They strafed me with information. An endless parade of docs, motion clips. Thousands of images and charts. And then they started in on the voices – people's talk, captured and replayed. Testimony, they called it. Talk that made me grind my teeth. Dear God, the things these people said. Dead people. Ghosts, really. Strangers. That other strangers were making me listen to.

Are we near the end? I cried at some point, querulous.

Son, someone said, a woman whose voice I didn't recognize. There's no end of this material.

Where did it come from? How did you find it?

People warehoused it, said the woman. The way you store food and water. In their time, the period some once called the Hundred Years of Light, people seem to have archived facts, details, data. They did it all over the world. Sometimes in concert – in an organized way – but often independently. Mixture of motives, we gather. Apprehension. Outrage. Resistance, perhaps. They left caches of this material in lead-lined boxes, metal tubes, stone vaults. Deposited them in mineshafts, drilled them into the walls of cellars, buried them in mountain caves.

For what? I asked. Why?

Well, she said. For the future, presumably. For us. They wanted to bear witness.

To what?

You mean you can't see? said the man.

I don't know what I'm looking at.

I'm sorry, son, but I don't believe you.

It's difficult, said the woman. We understand.

Son, this is a crime. A billion crimes that make one crime against humanity. A crime against the world.

Okay, I said. Shit happened. I can see that now. But it's in the past.

Well, said the woman. That's where you're wrong, I'm afraid. Because it's still here with us. That past is shaping your life.

But knowledge is power, said the man.

You have adjustments to make, said the woman. It takes time. We've all experienced it. You will survive it.

No, I said, but in truth I was already shifting. I was not accustomed to being contradicted or bested by anyone except my mother. I understood that the citizenry, by way of the Association, could exercise certain powers over me. If I contravened community rules or shorted the Co-op they could find me wanting and punish me. But the only force I'd ever *really* been subject to was my mother's. And yet these people had a kind of knowledge and authority to which I was already submitting. I felt unmoored.

This briefing – it felt like a siege – went on for hours. And the details are largely a blur now. But the feelings it left me with, they're clear in my memory. Because by the time they were done, I was a sojourner adrift in my own world. From a position of such certainty they'd brought me to a place where I could no longer be sure of where I fitted in.

Like most of my neighbours, and the overwhelming majority of citizens across the land, I'd been taught from birth to submit to fate. And because we understood that our entire existence was preordained, we were free from anguish and absolved of any responsibility that didn't involve the practical dealings immediately before us. With our destiny written, we needed no rituals of abasement or appeasement to offset our own culpability and mitigate our suffering. Such primitive notions were the currency of the magic cults that sprang up in the Terror, and for them we had nothing but contempt.

We believed that the world was the way it was. That it did what it did. In the way it always would. Because that's how things were. Ever thus, right?

This idea that our travails were the result of others' actions had never occurred to me. Never could have. I was my mother's son. I couldn't imagine myself as a victim. The idea was obscene and absurd.

So, to be told that my trials were not random accidents but deliberate acts undertaken with the knowledge of their consequences? Jesus, the notion that my burdens were, in essence, other people's sins? It was infuriating to the point of derangement. It was impossible to imagine that humans had knowingly let this happen. And I fought it, out of instinct as much as loyalty, but the seed of it was within me now. The taint was in my water, all through my well.

We'll watch you, said the woman. The next few days and weeks.

I don't want to be watched.

Duty of care, said the bloke.

It's for your own good, she said. We can help you. With your consent, we *will* help you.

How? I asked, hating the idea of being surveilled.

To cope, you'll need training.

And I didn't understand it in the moment, but something wild and furious had already been unleashed within me. Without guidance and discipline, this new chaotic force would have consumed me. It was a dangerous game they were playing with us, comrade. What if I'd not consented? Without good counsel and firm direction, I could have lost my mind, become a terrorist, destroyed myself.


Recruitment and Induction were perilous processes. Not just for the recruit, but for the recruiters, too. Think of it, comrade, we were all volunteers. No one was pressed into service. Consent had to be given. But surely that was easier in principle than in practice. Imagine how things might have gone if you'd declined to serve. How could you unsee what you'd been shown? And, having refused to join, by what route could you return to innocence? How could you continue as you were? How could the Service safely allow it? How many reluctant men and women did they have to silently acquit for the security of the project?

I didn't think about any of that then. I was a doer, not a thinker. I wanted to act on this information.

By the age of ten, I knew how a cutter worked. My mother showed me the near magical power of the narrow flame. The meaner the taper, the hotter and more precise the cut. The year I turned seventeen, I began the process of becoming such a flame. Lighting me was only a matter of weeks. It took much longer for me to be straitened and tempered for the life that lay ahead.

I couldn't tell what my mother was noticing during those early days. But it was impossible to disguise the extraordinary success I began to have at market. Folks had always offered high-value goods in exchange for our produce. But the stuff they began to bring. And the quantity. People I didn't know handing over brake linings, rubber seals, plumbing fixtures, bolts of hemp. These out-of-towners traded furtively, never displaying their wares, and as they loaded cubes of our honey and crates of our tomatoes, they'd remark about the unexpected surpluses of certain items, especially in the south. Soon enough I figured these were prompts for the alibis I'd need to reassure my pleased but somewhat startled mother.

After my second visit to the civil shelter, I was never asked to return. I was directed to await further instructions. I still hankered for the open road, but the urgency of that impulse was muted by this new preoccupation.

In April, heading home from the hamlet, I saw a vehicle in the distance that was pulled over in the bulldust at the wayside. To avoid showering it with stones, I slowed. And when I noticed how heavily the truck was listing, I pulled over to see if help was required.

I failed to recognize the rig until the driver climbed out, wiping his face with a rag.

He jerked his head at my loaded trailer and gave a smirk.

Jesus, he said. Someone did orright at the market.

I looked at his deflated tyre.

What is it with you and tyres? I asked.

Bloody valves, he said. Cheap shit.

Yeah, I said. I spose that'll be it. I notice you're not changing it.

No spare.

Travelling without one – that's smart.

But you've got three.

I looked back at my rig.

I can't just give you a tyre and a rim.

Mate, you don't have a choice.

Says who?

I've got a message for ya.

Who from?

Fuck me. You really need to ask?

I said nothing.

Be ready to travel, he said. Before September.

Why would I travel?

Don't ask me. I'm just the pigeon. Head down the peninsula. You hit the mainland, go east. Look for the hills with their heads cut off.

That's it? That's all?

Yep. Oh, one other thing. This wheel, mate. You need to change it.

Bugger off.

That's the signal. You don't change it, you're not going. If I don't make my meet in two hours, that's you done.

Bullshit, I said, more in hope than confidence.

Thing is, you'll never know, will you? Hospitality of the road.

The little turd was right. I never did find out if he was bluffing. But I jacked up his truck, yanked off his tyre and replaced it with one of my spares. I never saw him again.

I spent every precious hour of my spare time that winter building my own vehicle and trailer, cobbling them together from parts, and by the end of August they looked ready to me. It had been a strange season with my mother. She could be in no doubt about what all this extracurricular activity was pointing to, but we never discussed it. Not until the moment I declared myself.

We were in the open-air workshop under the winterhouse. It was late in the morning, just as the heat was setting in. I was trying to extract the perished diaphragm from a submersible pump, and she was preparing to fashion a replacement.

My rig, I said apropos of nothing at all. It's finished.

For a moment, she didn't reply. She watched me crack the seal and set aside the twin hulls of the pump.

Oh, she said. I was wondering if it might be.

She set a stencil over the sheet of rubber she'd selected for the job and traced a circle on it in chalk. Then she took up the scalpel.

So, she said. When are you leaving?

Day after tomorrow. If it's okay with you.

And if it's not?

I shrugged.

Not exactly convenient, she said, setting the blade to the rubber and running a full circle without pause or hesitation.

I know. But I figure it never really will be.

That's true enough, she said, lifting the new diaphragm to examine it.

Her muted responses unnerved me.

You really want to try this salvage thing? she said.

I do, I said, telling myself it wasn't strictly a lie.

Maybe you just want to see the world.

I don't like leaving you on your own, I said.

That's just something you say to make yourself feel better.

It's the truth.

I can look after myself, she said. At your age, I was five weeks on the plain alone. It's how I ended up here. How I met your father.

I never knew that.

Well, she said. There are things you never ask about.

Despite the flippant tone, I felt the reproach in her voice. And the truth of her words. I'd always been hungry for details about my father, but I wasn't curious about her in the same way.

You'll miss your nice soft bed, she said, as if to spare us both further discussion.

I didn't respond.

And you haven't even properly road-tested that vehicle.

It'll be fine.

No.

No? You mean you'll try to stop me?

Not if you take the other truck.

But I wanted to take my own. I built it.

I understand. And it looks sound. But if you're going so soon, you need to take something we already know will get you there and back.

I took a breath. But saw that this was an argument I couldn't win. And knew she was right. My new vehicle was sturdy, but I'd only twice taken it to the hamlet and back. The home rig had proven itself over many years.

Hell, I said. I could've saved my energy. I could have gone in April.

And leave me without a vehicle? I don't think so.

You were waiting for me to finish it?

Let's just say I was wondering if you would. It's no small thing. If a boy can't build a rig at home in the cool of a workshop, what'll he be like trying to fix it by the roadside in the blazing sun?

I lifted my hands in surrender.

You're ahead of me.

I'm your mother. Being ahead of you is my job.

But you like it.

Nevertheless.

We looked at each other a moment. Each attempting to divine what it was that was happening between us – whether this was discord or affection. I looked at the pump, extracted the split diaphragm, set it aside and took the newly cut replacement she handed me.

Look for some decent batteries down there, she said. That's priority one.

Okay.

Nothing from repackers, though. After last summer, we need fresh units. And I want you to trade smart. It's not a holiday. Things don't work out, just come home. I know you're staunch. But there's no shame in being safe. And there's none in being a grower.

I nodded.

You better start prepping.

This was the last time we spoke about me going. From that morning until the day I left, she seemed remote and distracted. Resigned, I suppose. Perhaps a little conflicted. I like to think so.

I set four cubes and a reconditioned watermaker on the bed of the old rig. Beside them I lashed two metal trunks – one full of kit like wrenches and jacks and drivers, the other packed with dried food – and to those I strapped the cutter and the folded solar array. Because of the exceptional distances I was attempting to cover, I'd bolted three narrow turbines to my vehicle's push bar and wired them into the batt harness, so I'd be generating charge as I went. Now I pulled these off and remounted them on the old rig. I was pleased by this innovation, and still boy enough to hope it impressed my mother, but if she was impressed, she was careful not to let it show. Not once during that last day of prep did she come out to lend a hand.

During pauses in work – at breakfast, lunch and dinner – she was quiet. Once or twice she seemed on the verge of sharing some memory or observation, then thought better of it and kept her peace. And on the morning of my departure, she was up well before me. We ate bean mash and eggs for breakfast and stood out on the deck in the dark to drink our tea. The only conversation was about practical details. Charge times. Sun protection. Tyre pressure.

Down on the warm dirt, beside the loaded vehicle, she took me by the arms and hugged me with a ferocity that surprised me and mortified me a little. I hated deceiving her like this. I was proud of her. Proud to be her son. And some part of me wanted to declare myself, tell her what I knew, what I hoped to become. But that wasn't possible. From now on, I'd have to keep her in the dark. I needed to be ahead of her while pretending to be in her wake. And every part of that felt like a betrayal.

I bore south for two days on a road that alternated between stretches of red dirt and whitish capstone. I had the long wall of the range out to my right, and intermittent glimpses of the gulf to my left. I camped the first night in a field of pink termite mounds. On the morning of the second day, the gulf fell from view, and soon after midday the range tapered until there was just flat spinifex country to the horizon.

At the base of the peninsula, on the mainland proper, I met the gravel swathe of the Northern Highway. From there I turned south again until I came to a wayside stop near a dry river and the ruins of a bridge. There I rested in the shade to watch other travellers – traders, victuallers and folks who looked like rootless grafters – attempt the crossing. The old streambed was a gutter of soft, deep silt. Their trucks and vans yawed and wallowed, and one foundered and had to be dug out and towed across. I waited until the fuss died down before easing down the bank beside the ruined piers of the bridge. The rig was sure-footed. It trundled down, chuntered doggedly through the silt, and climbed the washouts on the far bank without missing a beat.

I kept on until I saw a track running east, just a pair of ruts in firm red dirt. I couldn't be sure if this was the correct turning, but I knew it was heading in the right direction, so I pulled in. Out ahead lay a patchwork of knee-high spinifex. In the distance, nothing moved but the slow-winding willie-willies that rose like waterspouts.

I drove east all day, peering through the smeary screen in search of the headless hills I'd been told about. By the time the light began to fail, there was still nothing to see but more spiky hummock grass, and I spent another night alone under the stars.

Next day, I figured I'd give it until noon and then turn back for the highway and try another tack. But halfway through the morning, a line of yellow buttes rose in the distance. Shortly thereafter, I was ambushed.

Back then, I was so green and gormless, I didn't see the signs. It was as if the hinterland stood up and walked. Within seconds I was surrounded by figures whose shoulders and backs bristled with spinifex. Every face was shrouded by mesh and scarves. I had time to count six of them before the door was yanked open. Then four more came up from behind the rig.

I got out because I didn't know what else to do.

A short, powerful man with dark skin and tattoos on his face greeted me gruffly. Someone taller, a woman, stepped in from the side and held out what looked like a pillowslip.

Put it on, she said.

Really?

Really.

I took it from her and hauled it over my head. At first all I heard was my own breathing. I tried to tune it out, to catch other sounds that might help me keep my bearings. Nobody spoke. I heard boots shifting on the gibber. The low whine of my vehicle's motors. Then tyres moving – the crunch and pop of gravel withdrawing, fading until there was only wind.

Don't speak, said the woman. And don't ask questions.

I felt a hand on one arm. On the opposite side, someone took a handful of tunic near my hip.

Right, let's go, said the woman to the company as much as to me. If this sucker tries to bolt, you know what to do.

Why would I run?

I said keep your mouth shut, she said.

At first, we walked into the breeze – that much I could tell. Which meant we were headed broadly east, further into the interior. The terrain felt stony, flat, wind-scraped. From the intermittent nipping at my shins, I knew we were still in spinifex country.

After a while the wind was at my right. Not long after that it was behind me, then on my left. I tried to keep track of these changes of direction but was soon bamboozled. I gave in and just listened to the creak and clomp of boots.

I expected to walk like this for a few minutes, but we travelled on for hours. When the stifling hood finally came off, I stood squinting in the harsh light until my eyes adjusted enough to reveal figures that resolved as a dozen men and women assembled before me. Most of them were dressed in the unfamiliar mosaic I came to know as camouflage fatigues. A few wore tactical field gear, which was even more alien. Some appeared to have paused amid tasks of various kinds. Behind them I saw benches, implements, mechanical and electrical parts, food preparation, a stack of water cubes. We were all under a skein of solar nets and lattice fabric in what seemed to be a long hollow between high yellow rocks.

Welcome, said a squat woman with a white furze of hair and long, puckered scars on her cheeks. I'm the senior of this camp. All these people here are your comrades. There's a lot going on right now, and most of it has nothing do with you, so it won't be discussed. Focus only on the work before you. We require rigour and discipline, and that includes discipline of gaze. Do you understand? Your comrades – this group before you – are here to help you adjust and learn. To some degree you'll understand the secrecy of our enterprise, but I'm here to remind you that we insist on total discretion. You should know that, even if you managed to calculate the co-ordinates of this site, it will never be used again. Nobody you meet and work with this month will ever make themselves known to you again. Is this clear?

I nodded, although I wasn't sure it was.

I know basically what you've seen during Induction, the woman continued. We're not always shown the same stuff in the same way. Each potential recruit is approached differently. You know the drill, I imagine. *From each according to her ability, to each according to her needs.* Regardless, I know how disorienting and upsetting the experience is. I won't pretend the adjustment is quick or easy. But we have specialists here to aid you in coming to terms. This company comprises experts and technicians in a range of fields you will need to draw on to become a safe, competent and effective operator. Use them, respect their knowledge, listen to them as if your life depends on it because the simple fact is it does. You'll need to hydrate immediately, and there's food supplied.

I'm fine, I said.

Not optional, she replied. Now, any questions before we begin?

That word you said. Operator. What's it mean?

One who acts. Without thanks. In secret. For the commons.

Like a spy?

Not really. Though it will involve subterfuge.

So, a warrior.

More of a champion. Liberator. Redeemer, even.

I still don't get it.

That's what this process is for. You're not really clear what you're agreeing to yet. Who we are, what we do.

No. But I want to do something.

Well, let's see about that, she said. Time for your handover.

She turned to the row of figures standing behind her.

These operators will be your trainers. They're wise folk. And busy people. They're seconded from Planning, Supply and Intel for your instruction. You're lucky to have them. I'll leave you all to it.

The senior strode away, and the rest of the company went back to what they'd been doing before I arrived.

I gazed along the row of instructors. There were seven. Some were not at all young.

Call me History, said a thin, dark woman. Although History is not my name.

Geography, said a man with tight brown curls. Not my name.

I'm Health, said a tufty-headed woman with brilliant green eyes.

Politics, said an older man with steel-rimmed specs.

Logistics, said a man of about thirty with an eyepatch.

I'm Awe, said a woman with silver braids and a patchwork of burn scars at her neck.

Kit, said the last of them in an accent I'd never heard before. I'm the tools, tech and tackle guy. Of course, everyone else over there except for the senior is kit, too, in a way. They all *do* kit, but I *am* Kit. And no one comes to the kit but by me.

I opened my mouth to reply, but History held up her hand.

We'll work you in rotation, she said. For every hour of education, you get an hour of training.

That's me, said Kit. These operators do the ed and I do the training. Trust me, you'll be glad to see me every time they get finished with you. I'm a harder taskmaster than them, but compared to what they'll be putting you through, training's almost easy.

Your name, for the moment, is Volunteer.

And right now, Volunteer, said Health, you'll hydrate, eat and rest. And as the senior has made plain already, that is an order.

Okay, I said. I get it.

Tell me, said Awe. When was the last time you were told to eat and sleep when you didn't want to?

I don't know, I said. I guess I was six, five?

Figured, she said with a grin. Your life is about to change. It'll feel more constrained, I'm sure, but the world'll soon be larger and more complex than you knew. It's normal to feel some distress in the transition. Health and I are here to help you through that. Don't try to hide it from us or from yourself.

You have secrets now, Health continued. You're soon to have many more. Everything here is confidential. And once you become operational, you'll have obligations and duties that set you apart for life. You will continue to belong to your family, but you'll also belong to the Service. Sometimes you'll belong to an action team, which is an operational group. That's a temporary cell only. For specific tasks or field missions.

These are small, tight units, said Kit. If you're deployed, you'll work closely with people you've never met before. Afterwards you'll never see them again.

Security, said Politics.

It's something to adjust to, said Awe. Not knowing people's names. But having to trust them with your life.

How does this work? I asked. Who runs all this?

The comrades, said Politics. The Service.

Which is what, who?

Everyone who's awake and organized, basically, he replied.

And how many are there?

More than you can imagine. Of course, even if I knew, I wouldn't say.

But where are they running all this from?

From everywhere, pretty much.

I don't see how.

Which works very well, said Awe. For all our sakes. Anyway, we're jumping ahead of ourselves. Time to feed up and put your head down. We'll give you to History in ninety minutes.

I hesitated a moment and then allowed Health to lead me to a trestle where there was water. She handed me the first tactical ration pack I ever saw. She took it back, opened it for me, then showed how I was to cook and eat the day meal. Disposal, she said, can wait until the logistics lesson this evening. She pointed out the cinched bedroll set into a rock niche behind the trestle.

Someone will wake you at 1700 hours.

What's this called? I asked as she prepared to take her leave.

The meal? It's honourable food, don't worry. Protein.

No, I said, gesturing to everyone around us. All this. The camp.

It's just temporary.

But what do you call it?

The whole bivouac is a muster point. People in, people out. Resupply, repat, that sort of thing. Most of that you won't see and you won't look for, as the senior said. But this niche here, the bit that involves you, is Basic. Basic Training.

Nobody told me.

If they'd told you, would you have come?

I'm a volunteer.

Believe me, Volunteer, if you knew what you're in for, you'd have been a no-show.


I woke with a bony hand shaking my arm. Shit, I thought. I've been drugged. I saw a woman's dark eyes first, then the shape of her face.

History? I said, remembering.

Well, she said. You have to start somewhere – let's go.

For a while it was one card after another. First a map, then a diagram like a family tree.

This is just a schematic, said Politics. To represent a network. Relationships, dependencies. Yes, worldwide. Trade, government. Right? And this next tangle of wires is a corporation. Like an association, I guess, except all the power is at the top and the drivers are conquest, profit, expansion, and ruthless defence. This bloke here is an oligarch, a corporate overlord. A king. This one, she's a flunky, like a factor, near the overlord but just below, abetting him. All these folks, well, they're aides and collaborators of every stripe. This poor soul is a serf. An empire feeds on serfs – bonded servants. And this fearsome fella here is a mercenary. A mercenary is just a serf with deadly kit. Like a serf, he's disposable.

This here is a grease rig. Only a little one. Three hundred metres high. You might've heard of these. This black mountain is coal. And these flames – that's a gas field. All this grease and gas and coal was how these overlords got their power. By burning this stuff. To generate juice. Every sort of juice. The stuff that drove engines, trade, empire. They had so much power, they could issue a directive, say, here in the Dallas tunnels – you understand geography, I take it – that would determine conditions over here inside the walls of the Benin Protectorate, or here, in the compounds of the Western Tiers.

A small cohort of people could lay down the law. They could dictate what was traded, and to whom. What could be uttered. What could be grown and eaten. What the water was like. How the air tasted. What was true and what wasn't. Even how communities were governed.

So, back to card one, here. This network. This is what shaped the era they loved to call the Hundred Years of Light. The dispensation before the Terror. We call it the Dirty World. Because this is the empire that poisoned the air and curdled the seas. This is the dispensation that wreaked the chaos our ancestors had to contend with. And even after the Terror, when the Long Peace emerged, the world you and I grew up in, these conditions largely stayed the same. The heat. The lost places. Lost people. The mass extinctions. Such is the legacy of this empire, these people. This is how they achieved immortality. Because even now they write our days and nights. Their works are in our blood, our lungs. And, in a way, most of us are still their servants. Yes, even you, Volunteer. So long as you live in ignorance, so long as you don't resist, you too are their serf.

Volunteer? Where are you going?

They worked me through the night, into the cooler hours, in a pattern of alternating lessons and exercises that had me deep in my head one minute and working with my hands or feet the next. And Kit was right. As if he'd known me before I even arrived. The reassurance of springs, bolts, webbing and latches really was relief from the panic that came with what the others were putting me through. By which I mean what they were telling me.

We worked till first light, when the rest of the company returned without my even having registered their departure. We ate a meal together. In silence. At the end of the meal my instructors left for another part of the camp on business I was not to inquire about. Then I was ordered to sleep until noon. At which point one of the instructors would return and escort me to the small ravine that served as my classroom. At the rear of the hollow, deep in the shade of the camo nets strung overhead, real operators worked on kit and snapped it into hard cases that were hauled off by others.

One night, in the middle of a long and dreary tutorial with Politics, I heard an uncanny whine in the air above us, the sort of ringing in the ears you get after beating the kinks from a sheet of metal.

There was a rustle of movement in the camp, lowered voices.

What is that? I asked. What's happening?

Head down, said Politics. Never mind that.

Is everything okay?

Standard procedure. Nothing to concern yourself with. Block it out. Stay with me. Your time will come.

The noise persisted. I heard it with Geography and with Health, though neither acknowledged it. And then after the midnight stand-to, during which I fell asleep, it was gone.

Basic was relentless. Just one thing after another without pause enough to draw breath or reflect, and the days were so full of ruptures and turns that there was no comfort in rhythm or routine. Early on, and for many days, I felt unusually sluggish. Weighed down with stuff I'd never had to contend with. Knowledge, I suppose. Whose chief effect was to render my world treacherous. And yet also larger. Enormous in a way it had never been before. Nothing was stable and fixed, the way I'd assumed. It was very discomforting, but also a little exhilarating, to be lured – often goaded – into contravening the provincial mantras and habits of a lifetime. Life was not simply a matter of knuckling down and making do. Because if you pushed, if you acted, things could shift. You could be a maker, a breaker, a doer, in ways I'd never contemplated.

I was accustomed to routine. My whole life had been shaped and governed by strict patterns, mores. Habits of mind. But I was shaped by the steadiness of my era as much as by my people. Out on the plain, people did what their parents did, and theirs before them. As if what we did had always been done because it had been proven worthy. Improvements or adaptations were rare. Almost suspect. As if change was unnecessary, even dangerous. Though to be fair, the way we lived *had* worked. It'd kept us alive for generations. And we were so much safer and happier than those who'd suffered through the Terror. Problem was, we hid behind this. That's what Basic taught me. That our shield was also our cage. In the way our refuge, in the days of the water cave, had become our prison.

I had some sense of history. I knew decent chunks of the sagas and understood that there had been a great passage of events and a long chain of lives before my own. If pressed, I could imagine people in antiquity, but these were never people like me; they were mythical figures in exotic tableaux.

Apart from my father, I had no great individuals to look to, no landmark events to memorialize. I'd lived through cyclones, fires, floods, dust storms, lightning sieges, but that was merely weather, and weather was just what happened to people. There were no heroic sagas being generated by the likes of us. Our world was hard but dependable. Dullness was a signal of safety, and few plainsmen were likely to jeopardize that safety for a bit of excitement.

In Basic, lessons were weighted heavily toward the past. And I hated this. I found it insulting to be told I'd been born into genera-tions of quietists, that the hardiness and competence I prided myself on, while genuine in their way, were just a veneer over a deep instinct for evasion.

This is nothing to be ashamed of, History told me. It's not per-sonal. Nor is it a slight on your family, or your district. We're all from similar stock – even those of us from the cities and collectives, those who went through academies. The habits of mind we're talk-ing about are not peculiar to your province. Remoteness *can* render a community's outlook a little more fixed than others, but that's no one's fault. The generations who came before us saw things that nobody wanted to experience again. Billions of people died in the century before the peace. Beaten down, enfeebled, starved, cooked, drowned. So many of them butchered in civil strife. Ground to meal in pointless wars. Most of which, in broad terms, you seem to know about already. Some brave few, whom you won't have learnt about, died resisting the overlords. Before the empire fell. But after the Terror that ensued, once things finally settled down, folks got used to better conditions. They didn't want to look back, and they certainly didn't want to talk about it.

But we know all this because some people remembered.

Yes, said History. They observed what was happening around them. Some saw things that others didn't. Some recorded stuff that others preferred to ignore.

What kind of person does that?

Every age and community has its outliers, Volunteer. You know — oddballs, rebels, folk who're a little —

Tapped?

I was thinking exceptional. Insightful. Courageous, even. Since the time of the sagas, there have always been people who left accounts of their era. Not all witnesses were saints, mind you. Some stored evidence by accident. Those mistakes have proven particularly useful to the Service.

But mostly they did it on purpose?

Correct. Far as we can tell. Scholars, resisters, ordinary grafters. Most of what these folks set down was widely known at the time. What was happening in the Dirty World, and what it meant for those coming after, none of that was secret. The science of it. The politics of it. The moral implications. They knew something obscene was taking place. And they captured it. Shared it if they could. And stored it anywhere and any way they could think of.

God, where'd they find the time to do all this?

Seems the way they lived, there was ample time available. In ways that aren't easy to grasp. In the age of empire, the elite had many opportunities for leisure. Generous intervals for rest and contemplation. I've even read accounts in which folks complain of an excess of leisure. They thought of it as an affliction! Can you credit that?

Well, I said. It's hard to swallow any of it. Look, all this stuff —

Evidence, yes.

You. I mean we. We have it all?

I doubt it. But we certainly have a lot. So much, it's taken generations to aggregate it, collate it, duplicate and store it. As you'll have seen – trade accounts, transcripts, images, voices, ledgers, journals, confessions, maps – there are docs of every kind imaginable. A vast reservoir of incriminating evidence.

And who else knows this?

Well, you do now. And your comrades.

And the Service. This thing happens throughout the whole western district?

No, she said with a grin. It's much bigger than that. Perth, Sydney, the Gippsland Concession. We're all over – here and beyond. The Tokyo Rim, Kyiv, the Stans, Santiago Heights, Montreal, High Buffalo. We're in all these places.

So let me get this straight, I said. Most folks don't know?

Perhaps some will have a kind of tacit apprehension. They know but don't know. But the details, they have no insight into. Even those of us in the Service have compartmentalized knowledge. For security's sake.

And we're the only ones who know for sure there's a resistance?

No, no, no, she said. There are some who know full well. They know what we are and why we exist. For some, we inhabit their dreams. They probably wish they didn't know. But we'll talk about them later.

———

I suppose at some level I already understood that people had once organized themselves very differently. My mother had been at pains to make this clear. And even in the sagas you got the sense that folks didn't always live in syndicates or district associations like ours. But neither my mother nor the great tales described the kind of monumental territorial arrangements that had been established in the age of empire. These were news to me. The nation-states, the faceless, far-reaching corporations. Neither did she explain that these arrangements were underpinned and sustained by so much violence, immiseration and coercion. Not just laws, codes, and the rest, but main force. The threat of death. Communities were stratified. There was predation and enslavement. And it wasn't just local – this was worldwide. From what I could glean those early days at Basic, there was during that century a brief interval in which there was a kind of federation among nation-states, a dispensation that held these associations together by threat of retribution or exclusion. The subjugation of one association at the hands of another was common. Which to a fella like you or me, born into a more civilized era, sounded like the stuff of nightmares.

And yet for all that, I couldn't help but think of the Dirty World as an age of wonders. Because humans then were capable of god-like feats. Some lived entirely unfettered. As restless and shapeless as liquid. They moved and parleyed and traded with a speed beyond comprehension. And they spoke that way, too. Recordings of their voices had been adapted – slowed, I guess – so the likes of us could keep up. It was not just that there were so many more humans in those days. There were also more kinds of them. More languages. More land. More good soil, more fresh water. In our north, now a mosaic of death zones, there were valleys dense with rainforests, great rivers, lush savannahs where creatures of all kinds roamed.

In that era, humans lived longer and in better health than at any time before or since. And some lived entirely without the burden of labour. Such a dispensation should have been a paradise. Don't you think it sounds golden? Did they do it to you, too, comrade? Spruik this age of ease and weightlessness, a time of lushness, softness, untold children, animals of every stripe, rivers you could walk into and drink from?

They set us up, of course. Those instructors. Well, they set me up, anyway. They let my mind run wild. And then they took my feet from under me. It was cruel. Humiliating. The way they allowed the miracles of the past to grow in me like a crazy vine, only to hack it back to a stub.

Of course, the Dirty World was rotten to the core. It seems too good to be true because it was. Every miracle came at a cost – a river poisoned, a people enslaved, a species or language expunged. It was a monster that devoured everything in its path, including its children. Then it gorged on the future, which is to say its children's children. Unwittingly, at first. Then by design. Some faked ignorance. Others pretended to care and promised to change course. But all along the most powerful knew what was coming, what it was costing. They hid that knowledge. Buried it. Confused it. Diluted it. To gain advantage, accrue more riches, and, finally, time enough to prepare themselves for flight.

And what really stung was this. All these fools and criminals? They're our ancestors. The future they ate was ours. The leftovers? Well, that's our world. Such was our inheritance. To be robbed. Of food, water, safety. We were robbed of memory, comrade, and of the courage to think.

You know, I'd never thought of myself as poor. At sixteen, I was a competent youth, proud that I could harvest water and grow food. Like my mother, I was independent, dutiful, honourable.

So it smarted to be told I lived by the lowered gaze, meekly accepting every adversity as inevitable, something to suck up and endure without complaint. What else was I, really, but a plodder, a hardy, dull mechanical? It left me reeling. Yes, laugh away. But my pride took a beating.

It took me some time to recover. To take note of others in the camp. To watch them go about their business. They had a self-possession I envied, and *there* was something I'd never felt before in my life – envy. And why did they seem so different to me? Well, it took a few days to understand, but I got there eventually. What distinguished these operators was the clear and unmistakable sense that they did not submit to how things were in the world. They did not accept it as the natural way of things. I wanted to be like them, like that. And I wanted it badly.

I told History and Health and the others. Declared my determination to be different.

Kit, to my surprise, was the clearest in explaining how this might be achieved. He said it was like making mud bricks. Which was, happily, something I understood. The other six instructors would render me liquid. They'd slash my world into chaff. And then he'd be the one to mix the mess they made, pour me into a new mould and let me cure. Once I was solid again, the heat of knowledge would fill me, the way the sun finds every space in the brick. What I needed, he said, was to feel knowledge as power in every limb and sinew. It sounded fanciful then, maybe kind of stupid now, but that's more or less how it happened.

I notice you're not laughing anymore. Well, okay.

Initially I came to the kinetic tools for respite, but as Kit had promised, they began to give expression to the feelings I was trying to process. It was a way of channelling thoughts that would have run wild and become dangerous to myself and others if I hadn't turned them into lightning that blew rocks into a million pieces.

I think it's fair to say that during Basic I didn't master much of history and politics. And, despite Awe's efforts, the snarls of philosophy were largely beyond me. These folks were scholars. I feel embarrassed they had to babysit me. In geography and logistics, I was more of a natural. But kit was the area I excelled in. And although by month's end I was deemed a sound operator with provisional standing, I only felt truly sound in the use and maintenance of tools. Not the wrenches and drivers and heat-cutters I'd grown up with. Kinetic tools. The killing kind.

And that was the thing. The slow dawning realization of where this was all headed. As ever, I blurted it, like the stripling I was.

This resistance, I said to Politics. All this training. It's about killing people?

Well, said the instructor. Sometimes. Interdiction, we call it. The process of acquitting objects. Criminals.

But hang on, I said. The Dirty World's long gone. These people are dust by now.

Okay, Volunteer. Here's the thing. The empire died, but its bloodlines and networks did not. Its culture endures. The scions and factors and collaborators persist in the shadows. It's our job to find them. To clean up. Rip out the roots forever.

Jesus.

What did you think this was? A bit of hijinks?

No, it's just —

Well, service is contribution. Offering our minds, our skills, our spirit, our fealty to the commons. To do the hard things that ensure something like the Dirty World and the dark age that followed can never happen again. We sacrifice ourselves, efface ourselves, for the sake of our people and those who come after us.

Remember that feeling, comrade, the moment the scales came off and you knew? My God, the bloody shock of it. Terrible, right? And yet precious. After being acted upon all your life, along comes the invitation to act. And once the horror and surprise recede a little, the surge of juice in your veins, that sudden fierce determination takes hold. Brother, don't you miss that?

At the end of my month of Basic, I pledged my allegiance to the Service and accepted a codename I must never write or utter, but answer to when summoned. Then I was spirited out of the ravine bivouac and marched to my vehicle. When the comrades yanked the hood from my head, I saw the new battery bank lashed to my trailer.

The journey home took several days. It was late in the season and already hot enough to turn the mind toward going below. When I arrived, my mother was so frantic I thought she might be ill. She hardly noticed the booty I'd returned with. She kept running her hands over me as if checking for breaks or flaws.

Too long, she said. I thought something must have happened.

I met some people on the road, I said. They needed help. Took longer than we expected.

That's when she saw the new L-packs.

Must have been some job.

Four weeks, I said.

But she knew as well as I did that gear of this quality was worth more than a month's labour. A man could trade his sweat for a year or more and still not hope to snag a bank of batts like that.

I thought I saw it in her face. Like a cloud passing over. The fear I'd been engaged in something improper.

It was honest graft, I said. I worked hard for it.

Well, she said, brightening. You do look fit.

Next morning, I woke early and crept downstairs in the gloom to where we parked the vehicles. I was keen to reacquaint myself with the rig I'd spent so much energy building. I didn't need sunlight to notice the modifications it had undergone. And there was no mistaking whose handiwork that was. I was overtaken by a boyish dismay, a fit of resentment that blinded me for a few moments to the ways in which she'd improved and strengthened both vehicle and trailer. I wanted to have it out with her, and right away, but I had enough presence of mind to know it was too risky. I had secrets to keep now. I couldn't afford a confrontation spiralling out of control. I'd been counselled on matters like these. So I let a week pass before mentioning the enhancements. By then, their merits and utility had supplanted my puerile indignation.

We worked together to hoist the old batts up from the cellars and lower the new L-packs into place. Over a fortnight, labouring methodically, we summerized the house, traded in the hamlet at the last market of the year, and decamped to the bunker with all our stores.

But it was an odd season underground. I guess Basic had altered me. I was in good health, fitter than ever, yet also excitable and unsettled. Training hadn't just lifted my gaze – it nearly wrenched my head off. And although my mother didn't mention the change in my disposition until late January, she was uncharacteristically liberal with the choof that summer. Probably more a matter of self-preservation than generosity. Trust me, it's no fun being trapped underground with someone who's got the jitters. No offence.

Anyway, she let it go a long stretch before she raised the matter.

Was there someone you met when you were away? she asked one hard afternoon as we lay prostrate on our cots with the AC running.

Why do you ask?

You seem to be pining.

No, I said. There's no one. It's nothing.

I guess I'm not very good company anymore. No youth wants to be stuck with an old lady.

You're fine, I said. And you're not old. It's just this heat.

No point fighting it, she said. We just have to outlast it.

Well, I'm sick of it.

You're seventeen, she said. You haven't seen many summers.

You're the expert.

Mind your tone, she said. I'm still your mother.

Yes, I said. Sorry.

Don't be sorry. Be staunch.

I did the best I could, but remaining steadfast had been easier before Induction. Now I was caught in a cycle of turmoil. I yearned to be deployed. And dreaded it all the while. I felt a compulsion to seek my mother's counsel. But I was sworn to secrecy. And I'd wanted so long to be abroad on my own, adventuring on the dusty byways. Yet now I felt alien, alone. On the cusp of being cast out. I was determined to serve, but still young enough to expect the kind of maternal ministrations I'd benefited from all my life without a thought.

After such a heady winter, the summer that followed was a chapter of doubt and anxiety.

I was raw. Clumsy. Conflicted. But already back then, in the first unsteady days of my service, I had a level of insight, and a mud map to navigate by.

The old crime clans knew what was coming. I don't mean us. For a long time, the Service wasn't even a possibility for them. But most oligarchs sensed the waning of their era. They were awake to what it meant, the kind of torment and chaos that would be visited on the future. The evidence was clear even then.

That's the perverse part. The end of the age, the misery to come – none of it was a surprise to them. They understood it. Saw it coming decades in advance. Their factors and lackey scholars predicted it with a level of precision that attests to their genius as much as their depravity. They buried that knowledge under an avalanche of lies. Later, even when they could taste it in the air, feel the scorch in their throats, they continued to lie. The commonfolk, the poor bastards who bore the brunt, were mired in confusion, and as the age waned the only ones who could prepare for it were the liars themselves.

Knowledge is power. But power decides who has access to knowledge. The overlords bought themselves time in which to prepare their long strategic withdrawal. They needed protection. From the weather, of course. But also from the people – the grafters and servants and artisans left in the open. They'd been wargaming it for years. *Managed retreat*, they called it.

It didn't happen suddenly, but I like to imagine it that way. Like a sea monster of old taking fright and pressing itself into a dark crevice. So many sucking tentacles retracting in a rush. And nothing left in its wake but clouds of black scum.

Accounts from the time suggest their flight was hardly noticeable at first. Yet somehow a class of oligarchs who'd ruled for nearly two hundred years managed to disappear entirely within the space of a single decade.

And once things turned indisputably to shit, the gangsters who endured longest were those who'd planned early. The clans who'd spent the most blood and treasure on secret strongholds. But only the very richest and the most ruthless could maintain their safety over the long haul. Access to outside assets was vital. The costs of concealment, procurement and defence were enormous and ongoing.

Years became decades and then generations. The survivors became an odd mix of the luckiest clans, the ones careful to the point of paranoia and those with the most means. It was inevitable that, in seclusion, they should turn inward. Many consoled themselves with memories. The truly deluded looked forward to some grand day of restoration, which would surely come if only they held out long enough. Maybe they'd anticipated the likes of us. But they could never have imagined how dogged we were, how often we'd replace and replenish ourselves, the way we'd pass on the sacred resistance to those who came after.

But it was startling to learn that not every overlord fled. Some hid in plain view. For decades. Fabricated new histories, purchased family trees without blemish, took new names and – as fantastical as it may seem – even bought new faces.

And it's a wonder they put themselves at such risk. Maybe for some the determination to press on and stick things out in the open was a matter of pride. Hadn't their empires been impregnable? In their heyday, these gangs didn't just survive – they prospered beyond all imagination. These creatures had remade the world in their own image. As if they were gods. And, protected by standover rackets, by blackmail, bribes and assassinations, they controlled the systems of trade and reservoirs of pressed labour, ruled nation-states by proxy or by decree, and were accustomed to personal and collective invulnerability. This is what they were bred to.

And for a time, many of these criminals *were* safe. Because even after their dispensation crumbled, its perverted logic lingered. Anguish had always kept the people addled. Convinced by propaganda that their servitude was freedom, they collaborated in their own entrapment. But when the world grew harsher and the culprits vanished, the victims turned on each other. And so the early days of the Terror served to enhance the safety of the clans who'd sown it.

It wasn't a season, that chain of horrors, it was an epoch. An age marked by ferocity of every imaginable sort. The world became capricious and its people followed suit.

You know why I'm saying this, comrade. I know you can hear me. We may yet live to see it again. You sense that. It's obvious. Look at this place. Consider why we're here. But we know better now. Right? We're better suited. More prepared. Less deluded. And that's the shame of it. It needn't go like this.

Anyway. Where was I? Oh. Yes. Telling you what you already know. Should I continue? Yes?

Well, the overlords and their princelings retained enormous households in their hidden citadels. That's the only way they knew how to live. Can you imagine the hundreds and thousands of bodies each of them required to keep them in the manner to which they were accustomed? They couldn't survive without cooks, gardeners, house servants, concubines, court cronies and advisors. They needed trade factors, secret victuallers, private armies. They had spies and proxies in every exposed jurisdiction. And yet, for quite a period they failed to understand what was happening out here in the open, what was brewing in the ranks of the unsheltered.

Mob violence wouldn't have concerned them. That was just the inferior classes feuding amongst themselves – family on family, village on village. Ordinary folks, fuelled by conspiracy talk and panic, butchering each other over scarce resources.

They seem to have ignored the first fitful uprisings. With security and supplies like theirs, a bit of motley rebellion, some amateurish sabotage of assets left in the public realm – these things probably felt like no big deal. Later, when they heard whispered reports of something more potent and organized, they would have brushed it off as fearmongering. Gossip about something as inconceivable as the Service probably sounded like little more than the fantasies of the suffering poor. Which, at some embryonic stage, it probably was. But resistance like ours was never really the province of serfs. Although it relied on the labour and co-operation of good unlettered men and women, it was, in the end, a project requiring more than just long memories and shared suffering. It needed great minds. And it isn't for me to know who its founding geniuses were. Or by what means the Service's trove of knowledge was husbanded through that dark age and into our time. But I know it was held in secret. And later it was tested – and enlarged and enriched – by scholarship and careful intelligence-gathering. Until it became an arsenal so vast and potent you and I could hardly imagine it. Knowledge. That's what we had, finally, at our disposal. It wasn't fury that sustained resistance – it was knowledge.

I don't really know where the story of the Service began and how it became such a highly organized and disciplined cadre of volunteers. But by the time I was recruited, it had been active a long time, so the traditions of the network, with its language and procedures, were mature. I was recruited locally, but always operated in other jurisdictions and provinces, and I'll bet my sorry back teeth you were too. Clearly they'd been doing it that way since the beginning and they'd stuck to it because it worked. It meant there was no chance of being exposed in the field to anyone who might know you, friend or foe. It's why the show ran so long. Discretion was our principal protection, and there was a kind of priestly pride in maintaining it.

But just imagine being on the other end! Think of the early days! A Service action must have felt like something falling from the sky, like unholy magic. Those oligarchs, they just couldn't have comprehended what was happening. And here's a thing. Did you know that in the earliest interdictions, an object had charges read to them before despatch? It was called Disclosed Procedure. Their crimes were *listed* for them. So they could digest what was happening to them. It's true! The senior had to read an indictment. The object's family tree was produced. All the proofs were put forward – yes, while all the other operators stood around like a makeshift jury – and then the object's fate was announced.

They were offered a chance to speak, by way of confession, but often as not they wasted it. Because, of course, they didn't want to confess – they wanted to bargain. And the strategies they used were pretty much the same shit they were still trying on the likes of you and me. As if in a hundred and fifty years they hadn't come up with a fresh idea. They'd offer a bribe and ask for a proxy. A vassal. If that didn't work they'd upscale to a factor or an acolyte. Failing that, an actual relative. And you can imagine how that went.

With us at their door, it was a rare object who understood the situation he was in. The moment operators penetrated a stronghold and apprehended the target, every member of that household shared the same fate. Simple matter of containment. Same as in our day. But back then, acquittal was delivered face to face. Out of a sense of fair play and humanity. But for all its idealism, this method generated a lot of extra distress and danger for operators. All that bargaining and denial – it was wearing. Soaked up precious time in the field. And it left the door ajar, quite literally, for leakage or escape. So after a while Disclosed Procedure was discontinued. Acquittals were delivered summarily. That's how we went about it in our time, right? Sudden. Unannounced. Wordless. I think it was more merciful on everybody.

If you were in an action team you were mustered separately, from all corners. The names and crimes of your object were never given to you. Most of the time they were nobody special. The sons of sons of sons. The spawn of a banker's line, maybe. Or a lawyer, or some other species of collaborator. The details didn't concern us. We were freer without that weight. We knew the sorts of criminals we were dealing with. Each action was obscure. A small event. But every one of them diluted the potential revival of the Dirty World.

Operators learnt to take the long view. Hell, we *were* the long view. We kept memory alive. Ensured it still meant something. So that what had happened before our time would not be forgotten. And when the time came that citizens could overcome their fear and know, and understand, they'd have a foundation from which they could build. But for the moment, amid such sorrow and forgetting, we were memory itself, awake and afoot. And we were relentless.

Here's the most curious element, though. I figured it out over time. Surely you did too. It was the only way we could have worked. Because while the Service was officially secret, it managed to operate successfully in almost every federated canton and province, at every latitude. So, clandestine, and never officially acknowledged, but tacitly sanctioned. Yet most communities were oblivious to the presence of an object's stronghold in their region. Let's face it, the everyday grafter would have no idea what a citadel was, and no way of knowing what sort of creature could build one. Let alone the kinds of crimes it took to amass that kind of wealth.

But an object always had assets on the outside. Some, inevitably, from the local elites. Many with divided loyalties. Certain citizens had to know about the proximity of a lair. Because they profited from it, were part of the racket. So when the Service came to root out the object, some municipal quisling might warn them, but no association or council would actively stand in the way of an interdiction.

Operators always deployed from abroad. The custom was to allow strangers to clean up your district. It minimized corruption, tip-offs, ambushes. But it also prevented friction between territories and jurisdictions. It preserved amity. And you have to credit the discipline of the arrangement, because it helped uphold the peace for a long time.

It used to puzzle me, this complex complicity, the knowing-and-yet-not-knowing. But that's why teams were shipped in from afar. Because if a job went awry, local authorities had plausible deniability. The resulting mess – the casualties and carnage – could be written off as banditry. Every field team was discrete and dispensable. As an operator, you knew nobody was coming for you if things went to shit.

And I was okay with that. Proud to serve. I wanted to be a part of the reckoning. To inoculate the future against the pestilence of the past.

But it was a tough thing to be broken in to. A hard thing to accept. The killing, I mean. We're damaged, you and me. For all our pride, all our achievements, tarnished. Don't you think? And caught between worlds. We can't go back to not knowing any better.

But we don't want to kill our way to safety anymore. Am I right? I know I am. I see it in your eyes. Ours was never meant to be a forever war. It wasn't even supposed to be a war, comrade. Because we weren't soldiers. We were janitors. I figured others had the long game in hand.

So, as I was saying, the summer after Basic, I was juiced up and twitchy. Convinced of the righteousness of our cause. But anxious I'd be found wanting in the field.

When the heat finally began to break, my mother and I went up before dawn to test the air, get a sense of how safe conditions were for moving around, even working. Those first forays were always cautious, tight, almost martial. We'd creep out for five minutes, then ten, then half an hour. Moving very slowly, for safety's sake. We'd check the compound. Uncover and unchain the vehicles. And once we acclimatized and felt the air gentling, we'd open the winterhouse. Dust it clean. Then, in increments, we packed the bedding, the kitchen gear, personal effects and moved them up from the hab.

Once it was safe enough to work a little longer into the morning, we slid the cowl back on the growhouse, tested the irrigation and cracked the cellar hatches. Then we started winching up the pods and hives and potted trees so they could be rolled or forked back into their rows. That was another week's work. It was physically harder to set up for winter than it was to break things down for summer, and yet you always seemed to have more energy for coming up than you did prepping to go below. The promise of winter, of freedom, made all the difference.

After summer, everything had to be jetted clean – screens, shutters, all the panels of our solar array. Whatever had been exposed to the sun the past few months had to be checked and replaced – perished seals, tyres, rope, cable sheaths. That process kicked off the new year stocktake. We made lists of items we'd need to trade for when the hamlet came out of shelter sometime in April. We wouldn't know the settlement was properly open until we began to see the dust of passing vehicles.

That year my mother sent me alone to the opening market day. In the hamlet, after their long confinement, folks were very low on staples. We grew produce under lights all summer and did it better than anybody, so fresh or processed, a load like ours had especially high value on opening day. I took water, of course, because it was always in demand. Also honey, oil and wax. But the crates of newly picked tomatoes, limes, okra and corn were the first to be traded. We always timed a run or two of lettuces and herbs for the opening day, but these were only for those with superior exchange.

Within the first hour of trading, our truck and trailer were stripped. In return for that I'd acquired a bolt of hemp, a reel of waxed thread, a bag of painkillers, a small tin of pencils, a bucket of zinc powder for sun paste and a carton of light tubes. There were tubs of seals and flanges, an assortment of circuits, a small crate of casters, ratchets and shackles, and for the leafy greens I traded two 50-centimetre tyres with fresh tread on good rims. I was strapping these to the flatbed when a woman stepped up to tell me I'd dropped something. She took me by surprise, and her face was wrapped, so I never got a proper look at her. She pressed something into my hand and was gone, quickly obscured by the stalls and the movement of the market.

In my palm lay a small metal disk. I turned it over, struggling to place it, and saw the instructions written on it. As soon as I read the message, I rubbed it off with my thumb and finished up.

———

I found the godown near the wharf. Stepped into its hot gloom as instructed. Heard a voice I knew.

You know the termite mounds? On the road south?

Yes, I said.

You have four days to get there. Set a landing pattern. And wait.

That's an all-day trip.

So, said the filmlayer, still deep in shadow. You have three days to get ready.

What am I doing?

I told you. Setting lights for a landing.

But my story.

You're a salvage jockey, right?

Yes.

So that's your story. Password is *carnival*.

I wanted to press him for details, but before I could summon the nerve he was gone, the sound of his boots already faint in the darkness of the warehouse.

My mother took the news of my departure with a strange sort of resignation. I couldn't tell if she was sad or angry.

Well, she said. We know which rig the new tyres will go on.

You keep them, I said.

Don't be wet, she said. You'll need all the spares you can carry.

Later that night, after a long, bruised silence on the verandah, she said: If you're really determined to go foraging, you should go to the mines.

I don't want to be a miner.

Of course not. But if you head east – well, a few points north of east – you'll find the ore fields, the ones the old miners abandoned.

They just left them? The Association?

This was before the Association. People were worked to death down there in the heat. As if they were machines. I guess they either ran out of people or ran out of ore. But there'll still be plenty there to salvage, I'd say. If you're careful. People used to talk.

You've thought about this.

Well, if I was going to be a forager, I'd want to be good at it. I wouldn't be rushing off without a plan.

I was thinking south by east.

Too many people. You'll just end up trading – one market day after another. What you want is an exclusive source and no transaction. That's the smart way.

Okay, I said. I'll try it.

How long will you be?

Hard to tell. I've never been out that way.

Work safe, you hear?

I will.

You'd better.

Four days later, as dusk approached, I pulled off the road and drove into the field of termite mounds. I found a safe clearing, set the diamond pattern of light cans out as per my training and sat on the push bar of my rig to wait. I'd brought a small pack and some water, but without a briefing I was clueless as to what else I should bring. I suspected this first outing might only be a milk run or training jaunt, the prospect of which helped stanch the queasy apprehension that'd been dogging me since November. An hour later, when I heard the sky begin to hum, I figured if this was just a drill, it was one hell of an elaborate affair.

I'd been briefed about aerostats at Basic, though I'd never seen one. But it didn't take me long to recognize that unearthly noise. The closer it got, the harder it became to stem the panic that rose within me. When the stars disappeared overhead, I made myself walk toward the landing pattern and there were boots on the ground around me before I even sensed the unlit mass of the gondola overhead. When challenged by some shadowy figure suddenly close beside me, I gave the password and within seconds torch beams lanced all around. Something fell to earth with a soft thud. I saw ropes trailing across the dirt, then bodies descending at speed.

Comrade, said someone from behind a headlamp. Drop your pack and get climbing.

In a beam of light, I saw a rope ladder. It yawed gently. I reached for it and began to clamber. As I went, I looked up into the blank field where the sky should have been. I glanced back down. Saw headlamped figures around my vehicle and trailer. They were rolling out camo lattice. Seconds later, I felt the jolt and sway of bodies on the ladder beneath me.

It was dim up there. And cool. Someone hauled me sideways and sat me on a hard deck. At the other end of the cabin, low rows of lights flickered as shadowy figures moved before them. The smells of sweat and metal and webbing were familiar, but everything else felt alien. It took a while for my eyes to adjust enough to make out the row of operators seated on the long bench across from me.

My ears popped as we rose and turned. Someone grabbed the straps of my dungarees and hauled me to my feet. When I looked down, I saw the dark blanket of the land and the shimmering strip of sea ahead. From the angle we were set at, with the sea as my reference point, I knew we were headed north by north-west. Within minutes I saw the southern approaches of the range, and for a moment it seemed possible we might pass over the very tip of the cape, even the hamlet itself, but before we got that far up the peninsula the blimp angled westward, and soon we were out over the sea at an altitude that caused my legs to tremble.

Here, said someone, pressing a pill into my hand. This'll take the edge off.

I swallowed it dry. Saw the string of flickering lights below. The ancient grease rigs still burning. At home, from the shore, those sinister beacons marked the western horizon, and the idea of being beyond this boundary dazzled me a moment. When I was a kid, there were many more of those lights. It was so eerie to pass over them, and then be beyond them. It was as if I'd crossed the edge of the known world. And then they were gone. Lost in our wake.

Around me, other operators seemed to be bedding down on benches and the lumpy contours of webbing and kit.

Get some rest, said the voice beside me. There's a way to go yet.

I was woken by someone yanking my sleeve. I heard movement in the cabin. My ears squeaked again. I got to my feet. Through the porthole I saw we were descending toward a dome of red light. After a minute or so, a dim outline began to resolve as the superstructure of a vessel. The red light glowed at the tip of the mooring mast.

This is you, said the voice as the stat was anchored.

When the hatch opened, I followed five others down the ladder. On the deck of the ship we stood in the gloom for a moment before being led down a companionway into the bright light of a hold full of kit and materiel. A crew of provisioners from Supply issued us full gear – rubber boots, tactical fatigues, body shells, hard hats, waterpacks. Three of us were given bows. The rest of us accepted noisier tools.

Then came the briefing. It was given by a tall fella from Planning with a grey beard and a red bandana.

The job, he said, is straightforward. Your senior will deliver you to the target. You all have climbing skills, and you'll need them. You'll rope up to the stronghold – it's a monopod – and you'll breach and clear. Intel anticipates minimal resistance – there's no discernible defensive posture – but don't be complacent. Your object is a woman. You'll know her when you see her. The entourage is entirely female – last reliable count is twelve. All to be acquitted. That includes the informant. Who, no doubt, will be seeking indemnity. Given the situation and sensitivity, this is not a job in which we can extract the source. Senior?

From our midst a woman stepped forward.

Questions? she asked.

No one had any.

Overhead, thuds on the deck. Chains rattling.

Right then, comrades, said the senior. Strap up. Let's go.

Up on deck, three foils were cranked out and lowered to the water. Once they were secured, we rappelled down in pairs and started them.

I rode pillion. I'd never even seen a foil before.

We pushed away, got up to speed until we rose on our blades, clear of the smooth sea, and skated toward the tiny white light ahead. Eventually that single glow blossomed to become a series of lights high over the water. Closer in, they spilled a glittering slick on the sea. We paused at its outer rim, cleaving to the safety of the dark, while the bowmasters loaded their bolts and set coils. Then we idled on into the glare, down on our hulls, hunched instinctively against exposure, until we reached the foot of the towering steel monopod.

As per the briefing, there was no ladder. The bowmasters sent graps up with ropes in their train. We gained entry as directed. And the acquittals themselves were the work of a minute or two. It was one of the simplest, cleanest jobs I ever did. But being my first, it took some digesting.

At Basic, the List was discussed in fairly abstract terms. As if it were an historical outcome rather than a literal roster consisting of actual people with names and faces. Operators like us would never know those names, of course. But we did have to confront the faces. There was no hiding that. Still, nothing could prepare you for the reality of the moment. What an object was. And exactly what the job entailed.

———

But the biggest shock of that first job was not the killing. Awful as it was. No, what disturbed me most was the object herself. She was very short and yet she had the body mass of two operators in full kit. Her skin was sleek and unblemished, as if she'd never stood under the sun. And her glittering green eyes were so close to her nose she looked deformed. She wore slippers with flecks of shiny stone in them, and her manner was bizarre. Back then, I wouldn't have had words for it. But she was grandiose. And yet ethereal. Managing to seem both childlike and preposterously high-handed.

When we broached the hatch and poured up into the great wide hab, she hoisted herself from a throne-like chair and regarded us with an eerie, fey smile. She spoke to us as if we were naughty children, so wild and messy, with our sodden boots and silly toys. She treated our intrusion as if it was some sort of prank. She'd hardly got out a few words in her lispy accent when the senior cut her down.

After she fell, and the chamber filled with the ozone reek of lightning and the stench of burnt flesh, the rest of her entourage got to their feet, staring at us in disbelief. They uttered no expressions of outrage, no shrieks of terror. Offered only an awed, puzzled silence. As if they couldn't credit our sudden appearance, what had just occurred, the very existence of us, even as we stood before them real as death. I don't know if they were drugged. Or maybe just simple. It was the most peculiar thing to witness. None of them came forward seeking clemency. I didn't even discharge my tool. I just watched as the more experienced operators despatched them, each in turn. All watched the others die with a stupefied curiosity I'd never seen before and did not yet understand.

Then the senior kicked us into the second phase of the job, which was the search and secure. The stronghold ranged over three levels. The lowest, where we'd entered, was mostly common space with kitchen facilities and included a massive, refrigerated chamber for perishables and a freezer room the size of a domestic storm shelter. The deck above seemed to be the quarters of the entourage, which was more comfortable than anything I'd ever seen before – soft furnishings, rugs on the deck, appliances I didn't recognize. Above that, with its own sealed companionway, and another degree of lavishness altogether, the top deck was clearly the object's domain. The bed was enormous and overhung with a tasselled canopy. The coverlet was heavy and shot through with glittering thread. The air temp was so cold it made me shiver. I watched as the senior took up a small device from a tabletop and bagged it.

A pole in the ocean, I said. Imagine looking out there all day, nothing but sea. No wonder they went mad.

I'm just trying to imagine the bodies and blood it took to make this place, she replied. What it took to keep these crooks out here so long. Them, and the generations that preceded them.

What's that device she had?

She gave me the kind of look my mother offered whenever I overstepped. I lifted a hand to acknowledge my error.

First job?

I nodded.

You did well enough.

I hesitated, I said.

It's normal. And better to wait than to overdo it. If you're too keen, you put your comrades at risk. Especially in an enclosed space.

This is so weird, I said.

Does your head in, doesn't it. Seeing all this shit.

Yes, I said. It's —

Disorienting, she said.

Yes.

Box it off, she said. Don't let it distract you.

We set the charges now?

Correct.

And the bodies?

They've been logged.

We don't bury them? They don't go back to the soil?

I guess they feed the sea, she said.

Why didn't they resist?

It's time to signal the stat, she said. Here's the beacon. That's the hatch there, I think. To the gyro pad. You go up, set the signal. The rest of us will join you in a minute.

Up in the warm, salty air on the platform whose edges lacked guardrails, or safety barriers of any kind, I set the flashing beacon and had a minute or two alone to regain some composure before the rest of the team came up the gangway.

Jesus Christ, said someone slumping to the deck in a clatter of kit. These people.

Can it, said the senior. Check your gear. Charge tools down, safeties on.

The stat came in low. It illuminated us and the pad and dropped its tethers for the extraction.

I was home inside three days. Everything about that first job was unexpected and shocking. It all happened so fast, it didn't seem real.

There was so much to process. So much to keep secret.

I'd never seen a gangster before. She wasn't what I'd expected.

Good God, says the bowman, stepping back into the light. Are you still talking?

I thought you were here.

Well, I wasn't.

You went somewhere?

Figured I'd case your rig. While it's still light.

Oh, I say, my mind going straight to the tool secreted in the door lining on the driver's side.

Not so shabby. Actually impressive. Looks like you know what you're doing.

Well, I should hope so.

Where'd you get kit like that?

Like I said. I built it. Most of it.

But the materials, he said. Aluminium. H-packs. The watermaker. How does a grub-grower get hold of premium shit like that?

You really haven't been listening?

Shit, fella, you grind on like a dry bearing. A man needs a break.

So how d'you imagine I got that stuff? If I didn't steal it. Which I didn't.

You're saying you're connected.

Look at me. You know what I am. What I was. Foraging was my cover.

Big noting yourself now? You want me to think you were that valuable?

Comrade, I served for a long time. I saw some major action. Not something to flaunt. Just a fact.

So, where's your tool?

There is no tool, I say, catching the flash of the child's turning face. You know they never let us bring that sort of kit back.

That a fact? he says, running a hand down his bow.

I glance at the waif, who's studying me in a way that kicks my pulse along. I'm hoping she's not about to choose this moment to finally pipe up. Her expressions are difficult to read, but after these weeks on the road with her I think I'm safe in guessing she's weighing my lie against every other consideration. And I think I see her features set. Like a landscape suddenly dulled by cloud.

Oh, there'll be a tool, says the bowman. Has to be. You've been thinking about it all day. Beating yourself up you were so sloppy. Imagine getting this far, finding a spot like this, and getting out of the vehicle empty-handed. Fuck me, how's that for a blunder?

Might've been if that's how things are. But it's not. Anyway, that rig's a giveaway if you leave it out in the open like that.

Don't worry, pal. I've moved it. If you have others coming behind you, they won't find it.

There's no one coming. It's just us.

I guess we'll see.

We're it. There were three of us, but —

You misplaced one.

We lost a friend. I'll get to that. But I wanted to ask you. What did they dig for here?

Gold, he says. Best I can tell.

And you've had people come through here before?

Once or twice.

What did you do?

Sat tight. Scoped 'em. Cityfolk. Clueless. They never knew I was here.

What, they just faffed about and moved on?

More or less. One lot stayed an hour. The others slept a night in one of the sheds.

And you didn't kill them?

Why would I do that? Unless I had to. Why would I expend the energy, give away my position, if there was no need?

I shrug, masking my relief, knowing it mightn't stand for much.

I could do with some water, I say.

Not surprised. The gob on you.

He walks away, returns with a pannikin.

Don't get comfortable.

Thank you, comrade.

I pass the tin to the child, and she drinks greedily.

More folks will be coming through here, though, don't you think?

Stands to reason, he says. The dumb ones – the scared ones – will settle for one of those gated vills.

Yes. But there'll be others on the road. Smarter folks. Resourceful. Decent. A bunch of us, we could do something here.

Fuck that, he says. I'm done with people.

I don't believe you.

I don't give a shit what you believe.

I take the empty pannikin from the child. She settles back into the grit, curls up with her head on her hands.

So, what's your plan? I ask.

For you?

No, for you. You're gunna hole up here alone for good?

While it lasts.

I nod sceptically.

She drank it all, I say.

You should learn to control her.

You ever have a family?

Don't even go there.

Okay, I say. But she'll need a feed soon. And a wash.

I can smell it. And you.

And I just got her cleaned up.

Not my problem.

There's food on the trailer, some duds in the rig.

Not interested.

For her, I mean. It's not much to ask.

You know what you sound like?

Like a comrade, brother. That's what I am.

You ever get one who wanted to bargain?

I peer at him a moment or two.

An object, you mean?

He nods.

Yes, I say. Yeah. A time or two.

The fuckers'd say anything. Just keep it coming, strafing you with talk until you could hardly think.

But they trained us to resist all that.

Now you're catching on. *Comrade.*

I'm not bargaining with you, I say. I'm just explaining myself.

He pulls up a crate, grunts as he sits to haul off a boot, unwind the rag and flex his pale foot. When he sets it flat, I see the angry pink weal. A gel burn.

That would've hurt, I say.

No shit.

Still?

He nods again. Some days.

How long ago?

Ten years.

Ah.

First job.

I never copped one.

You were that good, right?

No, I said. Just lucky. Plenty of other burns though.

Where'd you go?

It's supposed to be secret, isn't it?

Like it makes any fucking difference now.

Well, I said. That's fair. I went all over.

Like where?

Petersburg, I say.

Gazprom.

I guess. They never said. I was in Houston, too. Dallas. Otago. Rio. Utah. Plenty other places. You?

Oslo. The Steppe. London. We did a job in Dallas, too – a clusterfuck.

Ever get into the Hermit Kingdom?

What d'you reckon? he says scornfully.

I never knew anyone who did.

They say they ate their own, over there. You believe that?

Sounds like the sort of thing people'd say.

Yeah, when they know jackshit.

What about the Equatorial Belt?

Manila, he says. Malaysian Heights.

Bareback, or suited?

We had suits, thank God. You were in Utah? You were on that show? For real?

I'm sure there was more than one job in Utah. Over the years.

Yeah, he says. But they only ever talked about one.

Man, I said. Crazy, isn't it. How unnerving it still is. To be talking about this stuff.

You don't seem all that bashful about it.

Did you never sing the songs?

Yeah, he said. Late in the piece. Sure, we sang them.

That part, I miss. You?

Maybe, says the bowman, cocking one leg over the other to air his foot. A little.

Comrade, are you not gunna feed us?

You won't starve overnight.

How about some water, then? I'm parched, mate.

I gave you water.

Seriously.

Tell me about Utah, I'll give you water.

What, specifically, about Utah?

I want to hear it all, go to whoa.

I dunno, I say. *Now* you want me to talk?

I need to know who I'm dealing with here.

That's why I was yacking like a maniac before.

But now I'm interested.

Why you interested in Utah?

You know exactly why. And you do look old enough to have been on that job.

Like I say. Had to be plenty of jobs in Utah.

I want to hear you say the name.

Which name you have in mind?

You know which fucking one. The name above all names. Quit pissing about and tell me the story.

But why?

Maybe I just need the entertainment.

It's a long one. I'll need a drink.

Tell me first. Then you get water. We'll see how staunch you really are.

So. My first show. The nutjobs in the monopod.

When I got home, dragging a load of salvage that once again pressed the bounds of plausibility, I told my mother I'd never made it to mine country. Hell, I'd only been gone three days. I told her what I'd been instructed to tell her. That I'd discovered an old homestead at the bottom of the gulf.

I know it, she said. Wrecked in a cyclone, I think. I'm surprised you even got in there.

Wasn't easy, I said, vamping haplessly. I spent most of the time winching myself out of the mudflats.

Might be worth going back, she said.

Maybe I will.

You're good at this salvage caper.

I got lucky, I replied, looking up from my bean stew and fresh-picked corn.

It's given you itchy feet.

A little, I said, putting my fork down. We could trade for some help. If it's making it too hard for you.

Not necessary, she said. I just miss having you round, that's all.

I'll stop going if you want me to.

You know I'd never stand in your way.

I watched her take a cob from the bowl and set it on her plate. She turned it slowly, as if checking a machine part for faults.

Besides, she said with a smile. Think of all the extra trade we can do.

I nodded, sensing something awry, a closing off. Perhaps she was hurt. Maybe this was what mothers did when sons outgrew them.

You know I'll always come back, I said.

Yes, she murmured. You'll always have a home here.

Well, I said. This is me. This is where I'm from.

All that mud, she said. You did a good job getting it off the rig.

Found an old well on my way out, I said. Couldn't drink from it, but it was clean enough to run through the jet.

Saves wasting our reserves. Good thinking.

I watched her face. She looked more amused than pleased. It made me uneasy.

In the days that followed, I struggled to find my place at home. After the monopod job, the cycle of homesteading work seemed to lose its gravity. I didn't feel the same pride in it. The hypnotic reassurance I'd once found in the endless repetition of tasks — that was gone. All my daily jobs felt dull. Safety itself felt dreary. I did what I could to hide this change in attitude from my mother, but I think she saw it. I worked longer and harder than I needed to, but the stoic look on her face was plain enough.

A few weeks later, our birds grew feeble and began to die.

At first it was just a handful, and the outbreak felt manageable. We lifted each fowl from its cell in the rank to nurse it by hand. Those that died, I put through the chipper as usual. We hadn't suffered a major infestation of sticky flea for years, so it was a surprise when the whole flock began to falter. Almost overnight the birds' combs and wattles were black with them. Those tiny blood suckers got under their wings and darkened their vents. The birds scratched their own feathers out and got the staggers. Eventually, and reluctantly, my mother drove to the hamlet to fetch the vet. And that's how I met the girl who became my wife.

The vet arrived next day, just after dawn. My mother was annoyed it took that long. She did not enjoy seeking help. And she hated to be kept waiting.

I was pushing a barrow full of dead birds to the chipper when the little van swept into the compound.

Two strangers got out, both women. The older one was tall and slightly stooped. Her offsider, the driver, was small and nuggety. She had a bounce in her step that caught my eye.

I dumped the birds and hurried back to the growhouse. My mother was all business as she walked the visitors into the shade. When they wheeled around to take me in, she looked pained. I guess I'd arrived with a little too much enthusiasm.

The older woman was pale. With her hat and scarf off, I could see that her boiled-looking face was freckled with white scab and a couple of darker lesions. She looked at me dismissively. The young one had almond eyes. Her skin was darker, and unblemished. The expression she offered, flapping her hat in her hands, was one of wry amusement, and the way she scanned the compound irritated me. It was as if she'd never seen a homestead before. But she was handsome. So beguiling, it almost hurt to look at her.

It was rare to have a girl visit the compound. I'd met the dirty-kneed daughters of travelling egg candlers, and the addled little sisters of panelbeaters or grease collectors who sometimes turned in from the peninsula road. This young woman was not at all like them. And not just because she was beautiful. She gave off an antic energy that was infectious. She was curious, impish. Clearly intelligent. I was enchanted from the get-go.

In the growhouse, the vet took one look at our sorry flock and sent her assistant back to the vehicle. And the way she did it rubbed me wrong. She was imperious, putting on a show, vaunting her authority, and I expected my mother to correct her, but to my dismay she hardly seemed to notice.

Through the mesh-skin wall, I watched the vet's offsider wrestle sacks out of the van and onto a trolley. The ground out there was already hot. In a couple of hours, we'd need oversoles just to cross the compound. I left the older women and went to offer help, but the girl rebuffed me cheerfully. All I could do was yank the skirts of my hat down and watch as she tilted the loaded trolley and began hauling it gamely across the dirt.

So what's this stuff? I asked.

Diatom mix, she said. But I think your birds are past saving.

Damn.

Sorry. I'm probably not supposed to say that.

Sure you don't want a hand?

Nah, she said. I got it.

Up here, you gotta pace yourself. Otherwise you get crook.

That'll explain a few things, she said, cheeks shining with sweat.

What things?

Doesn't matter.

What things?

Oh, she said. The way people are.

What d'you mean?

Well, she said brightly. Let's just say folks are uniquely adapted.

You mean a bit slow.

That was rude, she said, without seeming apologetic.

How long have you been up here?

Six weeks. It's a secondment. For my prac.

You're from in the city?

From *in* it? Yeah, kind of.

She gave me a look of frank appraisal.

We moved around, she said. My parents and me.

What do they do?

Teachers.

For their association?

They were. Now they freelance.

Is there good trade in it?

I guess, she said. They do alright.

Huh, I said.

You were home schooled? she asked.

You can tell?

Just a guess. And you're a grower?

I do salvage, too.

I watched as the hopelessly narrow wheels of her trolley became bogged in the bulldust.

You need sand wheels on that thing, I told her.

Tell me about it.

I could trade you some.

Tell the boss, she said. And soon!

Here, let me.

Because you're a bloke?

Because you'll blow an O-ring and cook your windings.

She laughed winningly. But she didn't relent. By the time we came into the safety of the shade, she was so hot my mother insisted she lave herself and go upstairs to sit under the fans awhile.

The vet was not pleased. Made some snarky quip about the softness of cityfolk. The kind of joke I'd usually laugh at but which struck me, this morning, as uncalled for. And then, while her stricken assistant cooled off, she told us our birds couldn't be saved. She said not to grind them for fertilizer, that everything should be incinerated, litter and all. So while she and my mother broke every neck in the flock, I went out and cut a trench with the digger. I bedded the hole with dry spinifex and piled the birds in, tipped dirty kitchen grease over them and lit them up. It was miserable work. I didn't understand why a job like this couldn't wait until the cool of night, but my mother deferred to the vet. And having my mother submit to someone – *that* was something to see.

Back at the house, while black smoke tumbled away in the southerly, the women drank tea under the misters and settled the account.

Sun here mentioned you have some sand wheels, said the vet.

I do, I said, wiping myself with the skirts of my hat.

He travels for salvage, said my mother.

I imagine it's honourable work, said the vet doubtfully.

Is it dangerous? asked the girl called Sun. I hear there are bandits.

That's mostly talk, I said.

You're new here, said my mother to the girl.

From Perth, yes.

Contracted by our co-op?

And the Association, said Sun. Regional support.

And very welcome you are, said my mother without warmth.

I'll get the wheels, I said.

I'll give you a hand, said Sun.

My mother gave her a look I couldn't read.

If nobody minds, said Sun.

The vet waved her away. My mother poured more tea.

Geez, I said when Sun and I were out in the compound. Your boss is a bit of a dragon.

True, she said with a laugh. But she might have met her match in your mother.

Could be.

The hills look beautiful, she said, accepting the little tub of sun paste and daubing it down the low bridge of her nose.

Yeah, I said.

You ever go up there?

All the time. When it's cool.

Dear God, when is it ever cool?

Early morning.

Maybe we could go sometime, she said, handing back the tub and wrapping up.

Up there? I said, my heart jumping. Sure.

By the time we returned with the salvaged wheels, the women were already coming down the stairs with their hats and visors on. I showed the vet the condition of the rims and tyres. Carried them over to the vehicle for her.

Very handy, said the vet. You're a resourceful young man.

Well, said my mother. He's a plainsman.

I can put them on now, I said. If you like.

No need, said Sun. I'll do it when we get back to town.

Suit yourself, said the vet.

A single, baking backdraft rifled through the compound to raise a welter of dust and smoke. For a long moment we had to contend with the reek of burning fowls.

Wow, said Sun, now there's a pong. How'd they do it, the old folks?

Do what? asked my mother.

All the meat eating. The animals. Imagine. Folks in the olden days, they even ate birds. I mean, apart from everything else, how could they tolerate the stink?

Perhaps, said my mother, they removed the feathers first.

Ah, said Sun tartly. Perhaps that was it.

I really would've settled for tomatoes, said the vet to my mother, as if this little exchange hadn't occurred. But I thank you for the wheels.

Yes, said Sun. You've made *my* life easier.

Good, I said.

The vet shook my mother's hand and got in the van. Sun offered her hand likewise, and shook mine as well.

You're in the hamlet? I said quietly, following her to the passenger side.

She nodded.

Guess I'll find you, then.

Resourceful young man, I hear.

That's me.

When the vehicle pulled away, I watched for a bit, oblivious of the scorching sun, until I noticed my mother. She was staring at me as if she knew already, as if she was seeing it in her mind, figuring how things would change here, for both of us.

A week later, I went searching for Sun in the hamlet, as I'd promised. She was down in a shed by the wharf, holding a listless goat while her boss tried to treat it. The dairywomen were tipping out milk and hauling a jet cleaner in through the rear doors. The looks on their faces were grim. The vap fans blasted overhead, but those women looked fit to burn.

The vet was not pleased to see me. She was even less happy about the prospect of her junior stepping out for a minute, but she consented with a grunt, and Sun and I had long enough to make an arrangement to meet on her next day off.

I only had to wait a few days, but I was skittish and fractious the whole time. And while my mother made a show of her great forbearance, she seemed almost pleased to see me in such a state.

When the day finally came, I rose at three, drove into the hamlet and brought Sun back to the homestead. From the compound we rode the quad out across the plain in the moonlight, to the foot of the ranges, where the tepid air felt almost cool.

What happened to the goats? I asked as we got down and pulled on our packs.

Destroyed, she said. Fever.

Bugger. That's the last dairy in the hamlet. Back to powder for us lot, then.

You'll survive, said Sun. I gather you're a hardy crew.

This is a waterpack, I said, cinching the heavy bladder to her back.

I switched on my headlamp, drew out the hose to show her how it worked and wound the nozzle end through the front strap of the pack.

It'll get lighter as you go.

Good news, she said.

You sure you're up for this?

Are you kidding? An actual civilian outing. Come on, plainsman. Let's go!

God, what a fool I made of myself that day. I was busting my freckle to demonstrate the charms and virtues of our homeplace and its folk-ways. And for some reason I figured the best way to show Sun all that was by goading her into idiot levels of exertion. I should have known better. Because I wasn't just a simple plains boy anymore. I'd been recruited and lit nearly six months before this. I'd been on active service. I was a fledged operator. I'd flown, seen people killed, witnessed a stronghold being blown out of the sea. And yet in front of this lively, lovely young woman, I reverted to being a yokel.

But Sun indulged me. She was amused, I think. And although I ran her ragged that morning, as if my sole mission was to prove the pitiful softness of all cityfolk, she was game enough to keep up.

In the gloom before sunrise, we traversed the wadis and wash-aways of the foothills. Then we worked up the lower slopes and spinifex-stippled ridges, scouting for marvels, and talking all the while. When we reached the canyon tops, I steered us west with the gulf behind and the smell of sea ahead.

This is amazing, said Sun as the first light hit the rocks underfoot and sent our shadows rippling out ahead.

Not bad, eh? They say we're people of the plain. But my father's people were from here. The uplands.

He's . . . gone?

Yes, I said. He died when I was a kid.

I'm sorry.

Well, I said lamely. Nothing's forever.

Oh, she said. Don't say that. I hate that old saw.

But it's true, isn't it?

Maybe. But it's so conventional. So . . . lazy.

Right, I said, stung.

The sort of thing people will say to avoid having to think.

About what?

About losing things, losing people.

It's just a thing to say.

Hm, she said, sounding unimpressed. No offence.

Sure.

I've put my foot in it, haven't I?

No, I said. It's fine.

Look, it's not just you, she said. City people say it too. All the time. Ah, nothing's forever. Like, oh well, too bad, what do you expect, everything's crap. Nothing we can do about it. No point using our brains or doing anything.

I laughed nervously and stole a glimpse of her. Sweat shone on her brow. Her eyes glittered.

Seriously, she said. That attitude really shits me. Nihilism. I've got no time for it.

Okay, I said. Good to know.

Truly, people can be pathetic.

You're right, I said.

Of course I'm right!

We both laughed and the sound of it felt strange out there on the ridgetops.

But what if some things just can't be changed? I asked.

I don't know, she said. I just think people are too quick to give up and absolve themselves of responsibility.

Only a few months previously, a remark like this would have meant nothing to me. I'd have dismissed it out of hand.

To be fair, I said. Most people are just trying to settle for what they've got.

I understand. It's no different in the city. But there's no curiosity. It's depressing. Things get paler and thinner and meaner. And everyone just accepts it.

You really think that? I asked, surprised. That things are getting worse?

I don't know, she said. Maybe I don't have the clearest picture.

But you sound pessimistic.

Frustrated, maybe. But no, not pessimistic. We need to live as though things can change. Isn't that the only way?

Well, I said. I was raised not to kid myself.

Hell, we're all brought up that way. Realism, common sense, modesty. All the dreary proverbs and platitudes.

What's wrong with that?

Nothing, I guess. Except that it feels as if we're trained to suck it up and carry on.

But being staunch, I said. That's not something to be embarrassed about, is it?

No. Not at all. But don't you think there's something bigger and better to aspire to than a capacity to endure? Isn't there more to courage than suffering?

I don't know, I said in a fog of awe and trepidation. Like what?

How about boldness? Audacity.

Jesus, I said, breaking off before I got myself into any more trouble. Where did you come from?

I guess I've been locked up with that dragon too long.

As the sun rose over the gulf behind us, I led Sun out to the lip of the biggest canyon on the cape. It was quite a hike to get that far, but the morning's conversation had addled me somewhat, and I needed the time to settle, to gather my wits and reset. This girl was dazzling. But in my new circumstances, with their novel and onerous obligations, I knew she was impossible for me.

At the edge of the precipice we looked down into the gut of the canyon where, far below, a pale and winding ribbon marked the course of the streambed.

Can you imagine this gorge full of water? I asked.

No, said Sun. I don't think I even want to.

How come?

There'd be no people. That much water — it'd be the end of the world.

True.

Still, I guess the world has ended before. In its way.

You think?

Well, yeah.

It's hard to think of a world without people, I said.

This country existed a long time before people arrived here. Before humans even evolved. You know that, right?

From the sagas, yeah. *From all points, one point, suddenly and forever expanding. Such is the first new idea.*

And the first thought was not a gradual event. It was a cataclysm.

If you say so.

It's science.

Right. So the world's old, I get that.

So old that every era might as well have been a world unto itself. If you and I were suddenly sent back, we wouldn't know where we were. We'd lose our minds.

There's only so much of the world we can see, I said carefully. And know.

Yes. *We saw as through a glass darkly.*

I don't know that one.

*And the days were rendered dim by the deeds of the dead and the living.*

Right, I said sheepishly. Well, this is home for me. I reckon I see it pretty clearly.

You love it, she said.

Lost for words, I watched as an updraft sent veils of dust skyward.

You do, she said. I can see that.

Again, I had nothing safe to say.

I've met people who don't, she said.

Love their home?

Yes. See it. Love it.

Cityfolk?

Not just them. Some folks go dry. Flat.

Like, lose their juice?

In a way, yeah. They fall out of love. With their home. With the world. They end up destroying themselves. And everything around them. You're not like that.

No, I said. Well, I hope not.

It happens, she said. I'm sorry. I've shocked you.

No, I said, with the image of another girl suddenly in my mind. It's just I remembered something.

I felt stranded a moment. Sun waited.

Do you want to tell me?

Yes, I said. But it's so weird to remember it right now. Something that happened when I was young, maybe twelve. There was this kid who came to our place. A girl. Arrived with her mother. She was skinny. Kind of pale. And floppy, you know. Like a sick hen. I reckon she was about my age. I didn't see girls much. I was trying to get her attention, trying to impress her, I guess. Who'da thought, eh? Yeah, laugh. Anyway, she's sitting in this truck, and her mother gets out – this scrawny woman, face like a cauliflower – and she's trying to trade something to my mother. Some kind of tonic in a bottle. Which my mother doesn't want. I mean, *really* doesn't want. Meanwhile, I'm doing everything I can think of to get that girl's attention. I'm making faces, jumping up and down. But she just looks through me. Like I'm not there. Like she can't even see me. And then my mum sends me to the sheds for a box of food. Some trade we've prepped for someone else. She's angry, my mother. Angry at *me*, it feels like. And I run back with the box, nearly falling over myself, embarrassed and confused, and my mother grabs it and shoves it at the woman and pushes her back to the truck until she climbs up and drives away. And I'm left standing there, nearly in tears, wondering what I did. I mean, there was no trade. My mother gave them food. Gifted it, see? But she was so furious, she didn't speak to me the rest of the day. That night, finally, she tells me what that woman was hawking. It was some kind of suicide potion.

God, said Sun. That's . . .

Yeah. After that, I got the message *that* subject was off limits. Not to be discussed.

She's fierce, your mum.

Aw, yeah.

She must've had her reasons.

I shrugged.

I hadn't thought about it that way before, I said. Falling out of love. With the world.

Well. People suffer.

They have a right to be sad, I said, wishing immediately that I hadn't.

How do you mean?

I don't even know what I mean. Forget it, I said.

I kept us out in the open way too long that morning. Both of us were blistered before we even got back to the quad. My mother was not pleased, and nor was Sun's boss, because neither of us was fit to work for some days afterwards.

I'd met southerners and cityfolk before. New nurses or teachers were sent to our hamlet every other year. Tailors and cobblers came through now and then. And engineers would arrive in the wake of a bad storm. But although she seemed to have been seconded in much the same way as all the others, Sun was not like them.

It wasn't just her confidence and machine-cut clothes that marked her out. She was curious. In a way that was unexpected and disarming. The superiority of her education was evident. I was simultaneously fascinated and intimidated. And though she seemed watchful and was clearly bemused by plains life, she was never haughty.

I wasn't the only one who noticed how distinctive she was. The girl had stamina. Even in those early days, before things really developed between us, I think hamlet folks rated her. When we were in the market together, or on the wharf, locals nudged each other knowingly. They deferred to her, which pleased me. But it bothered me a little, too. For there was something about Sun that felt just beyond reach. And I guess that's what drove me to keep pursuing her. I wanted to match her, in order to be with her.

In the wake of that first outing, I tried to see her at every possible opportunity. And the best times were those we got to spend alone, hiking in the ranges. We'd set out in the dark like bandits. Every trek an expedition of discovery.

Before Sun arrived, I'd never felt isolated or lonely at home. But now, in the gaps between our encounters, I was desolate. Tormented. This species of turmoil was different to the kind I'd felt in the wake of my first contact with the Service, but it was every bit as destabilizing. And although I was thrilled to be with Sun, her company left me conscious of how limited my knowledge was. It was good for me to be wrong-footed now and then. To have my certainties challenged. Locally, I knew *where* things were, but Sun could often tell me *what* they were.

For example, I knew all the rills and coulees of the high range country. I could find every wadi and rock shelter. And I understood this was limestone country, but until Sun put me straight, I didn't really know what limestone terrain was, or how it was formed.

Just imagine, she said. All these countless plants and animals from the sea – they don't exist anymore. But they're still present. In these rocks. This was sea floor, all of it. So this range you see every morning and evening, it's not one solid mass but layers of billions and trillions of creatures, the traces of all their lives and bodies accumulated right here on your doorstep.

In layers?

Yes, she said. Sedimentation. All the skeletons of creatures so small you can barely see them —

Piling up like dust.

More or less. Calcium carbonate. Fossil dust. The afterlife of sea creatures. Think of that – your ranges are the work of ghosts!

She laughed, and I chuckled along with her, but talk like that put me on edge and Sun could see it.

Relax, she said. I'm not talking about magic. But everything has an afterglow. Look at all these canyons and wadis. Aren't they the ghosts of water?

Results, you mean.

Consequences.

But erosion isn't from ghosts. Water and wind aren't ghosts.

Have it your way, she said. But things linger.

I gave a sceptical squint.

You know what coral was, right?

Yes, I said. My father used to ship it south.

But you know what it looked like alive, right? All the colours?

I've got an idea, I said cautiously. Well, I guess I do. What I mean is, I spose I could imagine the colours. Did each one look different?

A coral wasn't an individual. It was a community of animals called polyps.

Really? Huh. I figured them as plants.

No. Definitely animals, said Sun. Each polyp was soft. Like jelly. And every one of them was a builder, laying foundations, leaving a hard crust in its wake. Or actually, out ahead of its body. Coral reef. The terraces out on the west side? They were reefs too. All those bodies working away, doing their bit. When you see them, you just think, well, rocks, right? But they're the afterlife of corals. So they're not gone. Those lives and all that labour? They're still present. Ghosts.

I see, I murmured nervously. I was wonderstruck, a little cowed – but also perturbed – that she should know such things.

Polyps are like us, she said. They're makers. And the best stuff we do is the stuff we make together.

You really think that?

I do.

And you're stuck on this ghost idea.

I am. And I have a better example. Your father.

What?

Hear me out. You still feel him sometimes, don't you? And, sure, that's just sentimental attachment – no offence. But it's more material than that. Because he's in your bones, isn't he? In your blood.

I bridled at the sudden intimacy. Her boldness. But I could hardly deny the truth of it. And once I'd had a moment to absorb the notion, I found some comfort in it. The longer I thought about it, in the years immediately after this conversation, the more strength I drew from it. Yes, I carried him in my own bones and blood. His presence did linger in me. And I took him forward with me. I liked the idea. Very much. And I wished my mother could have offered me an insight so consoling while I was a boy.

Sun brought such joy and revelation – it was intoxicating. And perilous. Because for me this was already a precarious season. I was still adjusting to my new and much more complex life. One I could never share. Not with my neighbours. Not even with my mother. So, if by some miracle Sun stuck around, I had secrets now that she could never be privy to. And that seemed suddenly cruel and unfair. Which made me wish – half-heartedly, I'll admit – that we'd never met. If only we'd discovered each other six months earlier, I told myself, my life could be different. Maybe I wouldn't have consented to being recruited. How could I? Why would I?

I was lovesick. Unquestionably. Sun was a miracle. She understood me. It was as if she already knew me. Still, I saw this season with her could only be temporary. I told myself to enjoy it while it lasted. And I did what I could to bear that bittersweet weight and draw whatever pleasure I could from being in her company. Which makes my behaviour sound more calculated than it was. Because, in truth, I was clinging to Sun in a way that put my service in jeopardy.

I was so desperate to impress her, to make myself understood, I took her up to the old eagle nest and recounted the boyhood story. After that, we climbed to the westerly crests where the ocean lay glittering and treacherous below. We picked our way down onto the seaward terraces. I longed to take her to the rock shelter to rifle through cherts and bones and shell fragments. But something in me wouldn't allow it. That and the water cave – these were places that merited more than a season.

Cuntstruck, says the bowman, still burrowing at his toe jam.

Comrade, I say. The child.

She's asleep.

Even so.

This girl. What did she look like, again?

Does it matter?

Sounds like it mattered to you.

She was beautiful. I told you.

Indulge me. I'm down in a hole on me own. Can't you entertain a fella?

You said you weren't interested.

A bloke says all kinds of things.

How about that water?

Incentive. That's what you need.

Sun had a scar. Inside her mouth, in the meat of her lip. Puffy. Half the length of my thumb. And she didn't like me taking an interest in it or touching it.

An accident, she said. A car hit me. When I was a kid. It's not like here where the roads are unmade. In the city, you can't hear a vehicle coming.

I can't imagine.

What? she said, almost irritable.

Any of it. The city. Being hit by a car.

I'm sorry, she said. I can't talk about it. Not a happy memory.

Do you miss the city?

Not really. To be honest, I'm looking for an excuse to stay away.

And you haven't found one yet?

Maybe, she said, stony-faced.

I put my hands around her waist, and she wriggled a little.

Sorry, I said. Rough hands.

Doesn't matter.

How old were you?

Twelve, she said.

That's a hell of a scar.

It's ugly.

Nah, it's impressive.

I've finally impressed you. With my scar.

Everything about you impresses me.

She gave a wry and momentary smile. But in its wake, there was something sad in her face. We lay in the shade of a wadi wall as the hot wind luffed about us.

I mean it, I said.

I know.

Is that a problem?

Probably.

I don't understand.

Maybe that's why it's a problem.

As the season wore on, I sensed my mother's patience ebbing. And I understood why. Well, I thought I did. I was no longer the dependable son and helpmeet I'd been before. My long absences from the homestead were disruptive and burdensome, given she had to shoulder the load alone. But that wasn't the worst of it. Because even when I was home, and doing my share of the work, I was distracted. My efforts had become slapdash. I knew it. My life was suddenly so complicated. I felt perilously unsettled, riven with mad hopes that were instantly undercut by dread. My mind was lurching madly from one thing to another, on the edge of disorder. In the growshed or the undercroft workshop, my mother was shooting me looks. It was only a matter of time before she called me on it, and to tell the truth I was surprised she left it so long.

After dinner one night, as I was getting to my feet to clear the table, she reached across and took my arm.

We need to talk, she said.

I know, I replied, settling back into my seat. I'm sorry.

Time you made some decisions.

I'll sharpen up, I said, fidgeting with cutlery.

I'm not talking about work.

You're not?

I'm concerned about your future.

I'm staying here, I said. I'll always be here.

Perhaps, she said. But this isn't about the homestead. I'm talking about Sun.

Oh, I said, confused, and suddenly more alert. You don't like her?

That's beside the point.

Ah, I grunted, hopelessly thrown. So what *is* the point?

You should consider her feelings.

In . . . what way?

I think she's waiting for you.

To do what?

To bestir yourself.

*Bestir* myself?

To give her some indication of your interest.

Oh. Right, I said, writhing. Okay.

And what *is* your interest?

I dunno, I said evasively. She's great.

And when she leaves?

I sat there beneath the fans, turning my plate one way and then the other.

When she leaves? she asked again.

Well, to be honest, I don't want her to leave.

There you have it.

I guess I was wondering if *you* like her.

She's a smart girl.

So, you like her?

It doesn't matter what I think. You just need to decide what *you* think. And then you need to act.

I love her, I blurted, seeing immediately the way my mother turned her head, as if struck, or perhaps embarrassed for me.

Don't waste it on me, she said, getting to her feet. Tell it to the girl.

With that, my mother stepped out onto the deck, glanced into the warm night a moment, and went downstairs.

For a minute or so I just sat where I was, thrilled and appalled. The idea of being with Sun was delicious. But also utterly absurd. Given my obligation to the Service, the prudent and honourable thing to do was to stop this before it went any further. That's what I decided as I went about the business of washing the dishes. Yes, I thought, this is the only loyal and responsible course of action.

But by the time I'd set every dried pan and plate in its place my resolve had weakened. And when my mother returned, it was gone altogether.

Come morning, I was determined to take my chance and tell Sun how I felt.

Two days later, at four in the morning, I pulled up outside Sun's billet in the hamlet. She stepped quickly from the dark, yanked the door open and climbed in without a word of greeting.

It's warm already, I said, steering through the rutted alleys and out onto the peninsula road. We'll need to be sharp. It's a bit of a trek today.

Sun sat slumped. In the murky glow of the instruments, she was hard to read. Her nutty scent filled the cab.

There's a special place I want to show you.

Okay.

Involves a bit of climbing.

Uh-huh.

You ever been on a rope before?

I'll figure it.

Sure, I said, rattled by her mood.

Hoping it was just the hour, or the effects of a restless night, I let her be in case she needed to nap. But she showed no sign of dropping off, and by the time we bumped up the track into the homestead compound my jitters had graduated to foreboding.

The growshed was already lit. I could see my mother's silhouette moving behind the sheer cowl. Was relieved she elected not to come out to greet us. Because this venture had begun to feel doomed already.

We got out, mounted the quad I'd packed and prepped hours before, and still Sun said nothing. She felt limp on the pillion. Her singular verve was gone, and I guess my alarm at this sudden change got the better of me. I aimed the bike at the bund and hit the ramp at such a clip we got airborne at the crest and landed on the other side with a bone-rattling thud.

Jesus! yelled Sun in my ear. Take it easy, will you?

Chastened, I backed off the throttle and we rode across the plain in the warm darkness until I found the canyon spur I wanted.

Up there, the rocks still radiated the previous day's heat and the spinifex was already sweating its musky oil.

What's up? I asked, pulling rope and harnesses from the carrier crate. Something's wrong.

I got sacked, she said.

What?

The old dragon put in an adverse report. Tomorrow's my last day. After that, there's no job, no accommodation. I'm on the next truck out.

That's bullshit, I said. She can do that?

Apparently.

I switched on my headlamp. She winced and turned away.

Sorry, I said. You should've said. Listen, we don't have to do any of this today.

But I want to, she replied flatly, switching on her own lamp.

What'll you do?

Well, what can I do? she said, taking the harnesses from me. Anyway, I'll figure that out later. Today I'm going climbing, okay?

Sure. If that's what you want.

It's what I want.

I tried to hug her, but she shrugged me off, so I gathered my wits, best I could, draped the cinched coil, secured my pack's straps and set off up the first incline, feeling the day curdling before it had even begun.

There was none of our usual banter. I wasn't game to offer anything beyond the odd caution about blind crevices or soft edges. And Sun just hiked in my wake without speaking. When we reached the tops, and the site I'd been aiming for, it was light enough to see without the lamps. Soon enough, the sun smeared the horizon behind us. The sea still lay in the shadow of the range.

This is such a peculiar place, Sun said, suddenly beside me. Don't you think?

Not really. Not to me.

Peculiar sounds wrong, she said. Sea behind, sea ahead. I guess I mean distinctive. I'll miss it.

You think?

Yes. And I guess I can say I saw it – the north's last stand. Most folks wouldn't have a clue. What it's like on the frontier, I mean. I guess they imagine an outpost – bunkers and wild-eyed holdouts, not an actual settlement.

Is that what you imagined?

Pretty much.

So why'd you come?

It was a posting. You don't get a choice.

Well, I'm glad you came.

She looked at me a moment. Appraising. Amused.

You said you had something special to show me?

I did. I do.

Are we close?

Very.

Great, she said, hoisting the jingling harnesses back across her shoulder.

As she made to press on across the lumpy ridge, I took her arm and drew her back.

What? she said, more puzzled than irritated.

Best not to go any further, I said, unclipping my pack and shrugging the coil off. Sit for a minute. Have a drink. We're here.

Where? I thought you said we were climbing.

We are.

Up what?

Oh, I said, finally beginning to enjoy myself as I anchored the rope. The up bit comes later. First we gotta climb down.

I heaved the coil across the rock and Sun gasped as it fell from view.

Oh my God.

Yes.

That's . . . that's a very big hole.

And that's not the half of it. Here, let's get you strapped up.

How far down is it? she asked as I clipped her to the line.

Pretty far, I said. But you just go down slow, push off the wall, simple.

I showed her how to belay using the block and how to unclip at the bottom.

You won't be coming with me?

There's only one rope. I'll come after you.

I'm going first?

Well, you could come down after me if you prefer. But you'll need to talk yourself off the edge.

Not much of a choice, is it?

Not really.

I showed her the braking technique again, switched her headlamp back on for later and coached her gently over the rim.

As she made her first cautious descent, creeping backwards into the abyss, our eyes met. I'd expected terror, but her expression of concentration was almost bellicose.

To urge her on and bolster her nerves, I said the kinds of things my mother had crooned from the hole's lip when I was a boy.

To her face. Then to the crown of her head. And once she was lost to view, I hollered into the darkness until her whoop rang out and the tension came off the line, and I knew she'd made the full thirty metres.

When the rope was slack, I clipped on and paused a few moments to dampen my excitement. Last thing I needed was to rush this descent and make a mess. I went down briskly, but nothing showy.

As I reached the floor of the chamber, Sun stood in a brightening shaft of light. Her gleeful smile suggested this day might be salvaged yet.

I pointed to the deep vertical scars from the long-lost tree.

Folks used to climb down freehand, I said. On the roots. Can you believe that?

Sun craned to take in the long and slightly crooked shaft above us.

*The world made by water*, she said. *Unpathed waters, undreamed shores.*

I don't know it, I confessed.

*And the earth standing out of the water, and in the water*, she said. Sorry, I think it's the rush!

This is just the entrance. There's more.

We're going further?

Only if you're interested.

Well, hell, she said, grinning. I've come this far.

We shed our harnesses and I led her to the vent in the chamber floor. I explained the nature of the chute below and how best to negotiate it.

What if I fall? she asked. There's no rope.

No room.

For rope, or for falling?

Both, I said, setting myself into the crack and working my way down, one shoulder after the other.

Just turn your body when you feel the ledge, I called up. Turn ninety degrees right on your bum. You'll feel the foothold and the step down.

Dear God, she said.

You'll be right, I said, my voice muted by the narrow passage.

Sun came through slowly, but without a hitch. Once she was set beside me, squatting in the lateral, I explained the long crawl and the second drop-and-squeeze awaiting us at the other end.

In the lamplight, she shone with sweat, and her coveralls were soaked through.

What is this place?

We're nearly there. Just follow me.

On hands and knees, with the ceiling clawing at our backs, we worked our way to the niche at the farthest end, and there I lowered myself feet-first and twisted through into the dank, briny atmosphere of the grotto. Once I was on the sill, I talked Sun down through the squeeze, and while she was still finding her feet I found a loose stone and dropped it into the pool. The sound of it reverberated around us.

Fuck, she said. What was that?

Here. Turn around.

She gasped. In our lamp beams, every surface of the chamber danced with reflections.

Is this fresh water?

Used to be.

I helped her down off the sill and showed her the long duct that filled the narrow floor of the cave, stretching back into the darkness. We sat. Shucked off our boots. Soaked our feet as the ripples scintillated every surface. That's when I told Sun the story of my father's people. The living water they found here. How they carried it up, day after day – men, women, and children – to the broad chamber above, where somehow, despite every hardship and danger, they endured in seclusion, under the baleful eye of the sky.

Seriously? she asked. They lived here? How long?

I don't really know. A long time, I think. Through most of the Terror.

This is sea water.

Yeah.

So they were forced out.

Came down onto the plain.

She reached in. Ran a hand through the water. Licked her fingers. And was quiet a while.

What? I asked in the end.

I envy you.

Really?

Yes. All your family stories, they start here, don't they. In a real place you can come to. Like – I don't know – like, a sanctuary.

You don't have stories? Your family?

Refugees.

My people were refugees too, I guess.

Internal refugees. Mine were from the Hermit Kingdom.

Well, they must have stories.

No. Nothing. Nothing before arriving. Like a wound sealed by scar tissue. If my family had stories, they wouldn't tell them.

They were afraid?

Of course. They left it all behind. Even the language. The only honest story we have is the one our faces tell. And maybe that was interesting once, when faces like ours weren't so common. But these days, really, who cares?

I wonder what happened there.

Who knows, said Sun. They were always careful about food. Not just prudent – a bit obsessive. I used to hear them whispering some nights. About hunger. Or starvation. When we had no shortage of food. Best I can figure, their ancestors fled a famine, or maybe a series of famines, and I get the strong sense they had to do hard things, terrible stuff, to get out. But none of this was ever spoken of, not to me. All these generations later, the Kingdom's this big blank.

*Undreamed shore.*

Oh no, she demurred. I think it's dreamt of. One way or another. But those dreams are unspoken. Never shared. And the place? Well, it's no place now. Not for us. Nothing to see, nothing to touch. So, yeah, I envy you.

That's . . . hard, I said.

Sun sighed.

Trauma, I said. That's the word, right?

This is where you come, isn't it. When you're not actually here. In your head. This is your secret place.

Yes, I said, flustered at being understood.

I took her hand. It was still wet from the sea welling beneath us.

Listen, I said. Don't go back to the city. Stay here.

How? she asked. What will I do?

I don't know, I said. We'll figure it out.

We?

Why not?

We, she said experimentally.

I know you could do better. Than here. Me.

Yes, she said. Possibly. But you have me at something of a disadvantage. I'm deep underground and you're my ticket out.

You can think about it.

Yes, she said. I'll do that.

Sun and I made a life together out on the plain. And although it was considered irregular, we were happy. Hamlet folks seemed uneasy about the absence of a ceremony, but my mother wasn't troubled, and nobody dared raise it with her. Sun said formalities were of no interest to her, but should she ever manage to track down her parents, a wedding might be something we could entertain, for the sake of tidiness. I didn't care either way. Conscious that I could be deployed at any moment, I was too busy savouring what we had then and there. I was as contented as I'd ever been.

Sun had only been with us a few weeks, and had barely adjusted to our routines, when my mother suggested I take her on a foraging trip. So the two of us could have time together. And so that Sun could learn the salvage trade. I felt guilty leaving my mother by herself again, and so soon, but I needed no encouragement to hit the road, and Sun was curious to see the hinterland, so we packed my vehicle and trailer and headed off.

I guess that was our grace period. A gift from my mother. But it wasn't all largesse. Being suddenly three in the house was taking some getting used to.

By that stage, my rig was well tested. It was sturdy and comfortable. We had plenty of provisions. The days were still relatively mild. We drove south, camping along the peninsula, prospecting for abandoned homesteads. Further east, on the mainland, in the back country, the red, stony terrain was interspersed with forsaken hamlets and old mine sites. The most accessible ruins were already well picked over, but out in the badlands, especially to the north-east, as my mother had suggested, there were places only the hardiest and best-provisioned prospector could reach. Here it was warmer, but there was plenty to be salvaged. Mines had been abandoned so hurriedly, workers had left clothes and personal effects in the habs. In mess huts, you'd find tables encrusted with petrified food.

After a few days in that region, collecting steel, timber, function-ing panels and fixings of every kind, I realized there was such a rich lode of trade material, I could stockpile it for later. So, working back from the remotest sites, where we could feel the proximity of the desert but never quite see it, we headed west toward the coast, establishing depots as we went, filling underground storm shelters with rolls of solar film, crates of wrenches, drums of drill bits, sheets of rubber, lengths of pipe, stacks of insulated wall panel, coils of wire. It wasn't hard to shroud these caches. I'd learnt the craft of camouflage at Basic and, once I'd hacked the filtration stacks off the roofs of these shelters, there was plenty of junk with which to obscure their hatches. But the ground out there was stony and jagged. I spent many hours changing and repairing tyres. It was easy to see why few citizens ventured out so far.

Sun was as game as ever. She was a staunch labourer and unexpectedly handy with the hot-cutter. But I could see she didn't enjoy the thrill of the hunt and the taking of the spoils the way I did. For her, the work was something of a grind, a means to an end. What she appreciated about the trip was the freedom and privacy it afforded. Being able to lie out under the night sky. To make love without the risk of being overheard. And to strike camp on a whim without having to consult a third party.

She never actually said so – she was always circumspect about her past – but I sensed her new lightness on that first salvage sortie was about more than the strain of living with my mother. I had the impression that before she'd come north, Sun had been living a life considerably more constrained than the one she had with us. Even in the compound, some mornings I'd seen her standing a moment to drink in the open spaces. As if physically relishing her freedom. Of course, to me this was hardly surprising, given she'd traded city living for life on the plain. Back then I lacked the imagination to consider what other forms of duress or bondage she might have known before.

For both of us, these were precious weeks. We got grafting before first light. In the afternoons we dozed in the hot shade. And after dark we sprawled on our swags to watch the stars and explore each other's bodies.

When you look up there, she said one night. And you realize that every dot and blink is another place, a different world, does it make you feel lonely? Or is it comforting, somehow?

I don't know, I said. Sometimes, when I was a kid, I used to lie on the deck looking up and wonder if some other kid in some other place was seeing the same stars.

Well, they probably weren't. Unless they were at the same latitude, at the same time.

Yeah, well I guess I figured that out later. Not comforting.

We laughed.

But I guess, when *you* were a kid, you already knew that.

Yes, she admitted. But in the city, you can't even see the stars, so what's the use in knowing?

You sure you don't miss it?

The city? No. I'm here. I'm happy.

The rest of that winter, we shared the house with my mother. And although we all got along equably, Sun and I soon decided to build our own place. We planned a series of trips to source materials. But before we could set out, the season turned, and Sun had her first taste of packing down and retreating to life underground.

It was a shock for her, our summer routine. We did our chores at night, after the worst of the heat had broken. We hadn't replaced the hens yet, so it was mostly a matter of keeping the lamps up to the plants and checking pumps and moisture levels. We picked twice weekly, brining and bottling whatever we couldn't dry or press. The hives required coolers and regular checking. During the day we slept as much as we could, and the rest of the time we lay in bed huffing choof, talking and daydreaming.

In summer, I'd always slept in the same room as my mother. But that season Sun and I set up a nook of our own. We altered the hab, knocking up a couple of partitions so there were separate quarters either side of a central chamber where we all cooked and ate. It rendered every living space even more snug, and our sanctuaries were hardly more than alcoves into which you could squeeze a bed, desk and chair, with a couple of shelves bolted to the wall. But with the vent fans running throughout the hab, and the pipes humming day and night, we could speak in bed with a measure of privacy.

Anything more intimate had to wait until the irrigation pumps kicked in.

We fantasized about travelling to new places. Bold expeditions into the desert. Treks to the far north in search of marvels – refuges, remnant creatures, human survivors. It was mostly just choof-talk to pass the hours, but it was nice to imagine ourselves in the open, discovering strange frontiers and novel situations.

Sun liked to quiz me about my childhood, and I was happy to oblige, but she'd only speak of her own upbringing when pressed. She told me her parents were scholars. That for a long time they'd worked as Association teachers. It was steady work in the city, but they grew restless and quit to travel, and as a child Sun roamed with them as they trekked right through the south. She saw residual patches of hardwood forest, open-sky farms, some rivers, and many small children. She said there was good trade in knowledge, but that it was uncertain work and sometimes dangerous. Association teachers were safe because they kept to the curriculum. But to avoid conflict, an independent scholar, especially one with ideas alien to a smaller settlement, was forced to keep moving. So it was a peripatetic existence, and for Sun a lonely one.

What about your parents? I asked. Didn't they ever get lonely?

They were doing their own thing, she said. They're very self-sufficient people. But when you're a kid, you're a passenger, not a driver. I was miserable, and in the end they sent me back to the city. To an academy. I was eleven.

How long has it been since you've seen them?

Two years. Maybe three.

Can you imagine them here?

They're mentally staunch, she said. Fierce, really. But they're not robust people. They're intellectuals. They'd get bored pretty quickly. Besides, I'm not sure I'd want them here.

They put you in an academy!

They're serious people. They were doing what they felt was important.

See, this is what I don't understand. Are they in trouble? I asked. Have they been disassociated?

No, she said. They have full protection. They're citizens. Co-ops recognize them wherever they go. The truth is, maybe it really was kinder for them to leave me. I was happier in the academy. People need to make hard choices. What's best for the greater good.

When Sun spoke like that, of hard choices and the greater good, I felt myself recoil. From apprehension. And remorse. Because I knew I had a reckoning due. Just didn't know when it would arrive.

The hours before sunset were the cruellest. Sometimes it was an effort even to talk, and much too hot to smoke. The only way to endure it was to pack a wad of choof, lie back, and chew yourself into a stupor. Trouble was, a dose like that slowed you down for the night's work, setting you back even further, so as summer wore on your body felt as if it were leaking charge. You started every night with less juice than the evening before.

Just before dawn, despite how drained we felt, one of us would prepare food while the others went up to secure the compound. In the roasting darkness, one checked the bund and oiled the turbines while the other dusted the array and made sure the shutters and films on the house were still cinched tight. We'd all meet at the bunker hatch to set the ventilators. And before going below we'd scan the sky for weather and sniff the wind for any sign of change.

Have you checked the bund? my mother would ask.

I have, I'd reply, running with sweat.

We don't want to drown in our beds.

No.

So the bund is solid?

The bund is good.

As first light came up, we'd file down and the last inside would secure the hatch. Then, after dinner and the clean-up, we'd retire to our separate quarters.

Once we were abed, Sun would whisper: Have you checked the bund?

There's a bund?

Apparently.

Bugger me! Is it big?

Huge.

What's it look like?

You can't miss it, she'd say. You could play chess on it. Lots of checks.

We'd lie giggling until we broke out in the slimy sweats.


We never argued, Sun and me. And there were no harsh words with my mother. Or from her. But by season's end there were days and nights when not a word was spoken in the hab or in the connected cellars and empty cisterns. We laboured in silence. It was as if each of us carried a load we were no longer certain we could bear. It was all we could do to complete our tasks and keep out of one another's way. The prospect of some outburst or explosion down there felt catastrophic.

In those years, no southerner could imagine the feats of self-control that kept plainsfolk from running amok in summer. Given she wasn't born to such hardship, Sun's fortitude was impressive. That year, the heat broke in the middle of April. And when we came up into the withering twilight and felt the southerly breeze on our faces, she fell to her knees and wept.

A week later, I was headed to the hamlet when I came upon a truck pulled up in the middle of the road. As I eased off the juice, the driver got down. A stranger. Not from the district.

It's not as if I hadn't been anticipating deployment. But I'd convinced myself the Service would give me longer. They'd been watching me since my induction. They knew about my changed circumstances. And yet they called me up anyway.

Within ten days I was gone.

That was my first true long-haul job. First time north of the equator. And the first op I was on that involved children. There was tactical resistance.

That's all I want to say about it.

Afterwards, in the debrief, before repat, a medic from Planning pulled me aside. She set me down in a corner, put a light in my eyes, took my blood pressure.

Your misgivings, she said. They're perfectly normal.

I did my job, I said.

Nobody's suggesting anything to the contrary, she said. But I know what I'm seeing.

I understand the policy.

The children bear no responsibility. Let's be very clear.

I'm straight on that.

But you must understand that all the alternatives have been tried previously.

I know, I said. Live extraction. Redemption.

At the time it was thought to be the morally correct course of action. But —

Added logistical burden, I said. Higher losses.

True, she said. But that's not the half of it.

Maybe I looked off in some way. I don't know what she was seeing, what she was looking for, but she took a breath, stared at me a long moment, as if hesitating. Then she rolled out a stream of stuff I already knew.

When these kids were spared, she said, the Service was essentially kidnapping them. Like it or not. Think about that. Having just eliminated their parents, we were seizing them by force. Traumatic for the kids. Obviously. But horrible for the operators as well. And lots of kids didn't survive the initial extraction. Particularly if there was an arduous transit and repatriation. And even if they made it, the challenge of living as citizens in the outside world – well, it was often beyond them, beyond what could reasonably be expected of them. Think of it, comrade: all they've known is being indoors, locked away with plenty and luxury. And suddenly they're out. Dragged off to be re-educated. We integrated them secretly into hamlets and cities all over the world. But there was no way to disguise their oddness. Their behaviour was utterly mystifying. They presented as defective, insane. Perverse. Diseased. Even the best of them sowed disquiet in their communities. The citizens who adopted them were bewildered by them. Even afraid. And the kids themselves? Well, a life out in the open – as an equal – it must have been terrifying. Most were depressed. Many destroyed themselves.

Yes, I said as evenly as I could. I was told all this.

The project post-Terror was to foster harmony. Calm. Civility. After the trauma of those bad years, the survival of every compound, hamlet and city has depended on it. So our policy of child redemption, honourable and painstaking as it was, became a threat to peace everywhere. It cost the lives of many good operators. And citizens. And overlord children. It was tragically misguided.

Yes, I said. Mistakes were made. Lessons learnt.

No child should bear responsibility for the crimes of her parents. Or her parents' great-great-grandparents. And I know it will never feel that way in the moment. But it's kinder to acquit them along with the object. It saves lives and spares suffering. The gravity of that choice is part of our shared burden.

Understood.

I'm sure you remember the words of the sagas in this regard.

*It is not your duty to finish the work. But neither are you free to neglect it.*

You'll be repatriated separately.

Can I ask why?

You need some rest and reflection. You've earnt it. At the end of that period, you have the option to withdraw with an honourable discharge. No stigma attached. No disgrace in that.

I'm fine, I said. I'm solid.

Yes, she said. And right now, you may even believe that. But you need to rest and consider. We'll see how solid you are.

All I'll say is this: I never liked killing the kids. But I always knew it was the decent thing to do.

I dreamt I was still there. Stranded on the Steppe. The snow turning to slush where the fires had raged. Through the mask and balaclava, the smell of cooked flesh was inescapable. The sky was nacreous. In every direction, the land lay white and featureless. I looked for any sign of my unit. Found the dirty gutter of our tracks. Followed them until they petered out. Saw the scourings where anchors had secured the stat. And then I knew. They'd left me behind.

I woke, shivering. The medic was there with a hypo. And as I sank back into sleep, I felt the gondola deck vibrating in my shoulder, my hip.

———

Strange thing to be cold. Isn't it? Stranger still to be dangerously cold. But there's no panic in it, and after a while, no pain. I think it would be a good death. But I doubt that'll be the way I go.

Back home, the compound was in good shape. Winter conditions were fair. And our produce was healthy. The trailer-load of steel purlins I'd returned with was better than anything Sun and I had brought back or cached in our underground depots, but neither she nor my mother was particularly curious about its provenance. They were more focused on what this material could do for us. Having steel of this quality and length meant Sun and I could begin work on our own place, a second winterhouse. My mother seemed every bit as happy about this as Sun. Relations between the women were still cordial, but the care required to maintain amity was evident.

Aside from making occasional suggestions about the design of our new place, my mother left the job of building it to us. We took this as a sign of trust, and of letting go, not as a failure to lend a hand.

It took three weeks just to set the footings. The red earth was baked so hard it was like chipping stone. Our concrete was hand-mixed. Each hole required an entire day to fill. The stirrups were the size of trailer hitches. We got up at two every morning. Finished our chores by five and worked on the house until the heat sent us indoors.

By the time the frame was up and fully secured, we were out of good steel. The Service had gauged it perfectly. We didn't have to leave a half-built skeleton wallowing in the wind while we paused for the rest of the season or went off in search of fresh materials. We debated the pros and cons of waiting, but the prospect of a bit of independence was too hard to resist, and my mother didn't object. If anything, she encouraged us to press on, told us she'd happily cover for us.

It was only after we hit the road that it occurred to me she was as keen for some privacy as we were. There was nothing we could do about the summers. Unless Sun and I dug ourselves a new bunker, we'd all be forced to share the shelter hab indefinitely. But at least there'd be respite during the longer winter season. The promise of that was enough.

It was late June when we took off down the peninsula, to the mainland. And the journey was like a glorious intermission. A break from routine and hard labour. Not to mention from what I'd seen and done at the other end of the world. The days on the road provided long stretches of companionable, restorative idleness, and we treasured it. It was a chance to be ourselves without being observed, indulged, even managed.

But travelling the roads is not a solitary business. There were often strangers by the wayside. I avoided encounters wherever possible, and this baffled Sun. She was less guarded than me, more willing to engage with unfamiliar folks. She was curious about people, interested in their stories. Where they were from, where they were headed, and how they were faring. Occasionally – for her sake, and to make myself seem less of a fogey – I'd relent. But I remained reserved and alert.

The truth is, there wasn't much to fear on the road in those days. The industrial press-gangs were no longer a factor, and although there was always talk of bandits and chancers, most tales of brigandry were just folklore, the sorts of myths people used to make themselves – and each other – knuckle down and stay home. They were stories told to keep hamlets and compounds stable. But despite knowing all that, I was acutely vigilant on the road that season. If Sun noticed it, she never let on.

Most travellers were just tradesfolk or prospectors, sojourners or immigrants, roaming in search of a bit of luck or at least a new situation. Some were fugitives or religious seekers, but they were easy enough to spot and evade. Sometimes, at water points or roadside camps, Sun would approach citizens in family groups and, from a distance, I'd watch her move among them. Strangers responded to her without hesitation. She took a special interest in their children. I never gave this fascination much thought.

Before we headed north-east toward the caches we'd laid down in our previous expedition, we heard news of rain further inland. Nobody seemed to know exactly where it had fallen, or for how long. Some folks reported seeing lightning on the horizon. I wondered if it could be a training camp and not a storm at all. But it seemed too reckless for the Service to set a bivouac that close to public byways, so I discounted that notion.

There were no signs of fire inland. Rain seemed plausible. I was keen to crack on and secure our materials as soon as practicable, but the prospect of mud gave me pause. I didn't fancy getting bogged in the hinterland, so far from help. We could end up stranded out there for weeks.

That night, camped at a prudent distance from a roadstead where the lamps of other travellers were still visible, a north-easterly breeze came up and with it came the rich, foetid smell of wet earth.

That's it, I said. We either go home and come back when it's dried out, or we wait.

Here?

No, I said. Not here.

We'll be a week just getting home and back, said Sun.

I know. It's mad. Listen. There's a place I know. South-east. It's interesting. No one goes there. We'll try that. Wait there a day or two, then cut back north and see how firm the ground is.

Sounds like a plan.

We were like children. On an adventure. Making our story up as we went. Hell, comrade. We *were* children. Think of that.

It took half a day to reach the abandoned hamlet I had in mind. The country down there was dry, but the going was hard. There was no road or track except in tiny remnant stretches. It was easy to see the route had been deliberately obliterated. When we came down into the narrow valley, it took Sun only a few seconds to see what distinguished this place.

Is that a graveyard?

Yes.

God. It's twice the size of the town.

Bigger, I said.

What kind of settlement was this?

I think it's a plague town.

How do you know?

The gravestones. The stuff written there.

Epitaphs.

Huh, I said, savouring the sound of the unfamiliar word. Epitaphs.

I drove her down to the ramshackle perimeter and we got out to wander among the rows of fallen tablets and memorials.

I don't understand, said Sun. Were they sent here to die, or did they all live here?

Hard to tell, I answered.

I wonder who buried the last of them.

Nobody, I guess.

Oh.

Yeah.

This reminds me, she said. Something I noticed but sort of didn't notice. About the peninsula. I've never seen a cemetery.

Ah. True.

What happens, she asked. Do you send people south to be buried?

No.

You cremate them?

No, I said.

But if you don't bury them —

Well, we do. We bury them. But we do it differently.

O-kay, she said carefully.

It's a plains thing. In the old days, before the Terror, growers fertilized the dirt with fish. Animal shit, too. But everything changed. When my father's folks came down off the tops, they had to adapt. No fish or animals. But they needed fertilizer. I guess they figured, if you're from the soil, and you live by the soil, you return to the soil.

But these people here, she said gesturing at the graves. Haven't they been returned to the earth?

You see anything growing here?

Not really.

I think we only started keeping fowls in my father's time. Once people came up from the south to trade. Before that, there was no other source of blood and bone.

Dear God, she said, incredulous, shocked enough to laugh. You put your people through a *chipper*?

Well, it's not pretty. But up our way, soil's everything. Right? You gotta have it. *Make* it, half the time. Mix dead birds with green waste. Chaff. Food scraps. Guano.

Compost, you mean.

Well, yeah. Dirt's dirt. Dirt with compost is soil.

Of course. But, my God.

And people, I said self-consciously. They want to be useful. *The most benefit for the most citizens.*

Well, she said ruefully. They did warn me. They told me you people were different.

It stung a little, but there was just enough mordant amusement in her voice to save me from feeling too offended.

It's a cultural thing. Nobody would expect it of *you*. I mean, I'd drive your body south, if that's what you wanted.

Sun looked at me as if I were defective.

You want to talk about my funeral?

No.

Well, let's stop there, then.

Okay. I'm sorry. I didn't —

Listen, she said, interrupting me. How many times have you been here?

Before this? Just once.

Why would you come back?

Why d'you think? I replied. Salvage.

But there's nothing standing. It's all rust and rubbish.

Not the hamlet, I said, wishing I'd thought of a different place to wait out the rain.

She looked around at the graves.

You're joking.

No.

You took headstones.

Slabs, mostly. Granite, marble. But yeah, a couple of the headstones.

And that's all.

These folks. They were buried with all kinds of stuff. I figure I'm not robbing anyone. There's no one here.

You take these people's belongings?

Well, stuff they once had, yeah. It doesn't belong to them anymore. Doesn't belong to anybody. Remember I break up houses, sheds, machines, too. It's salvage, Sun. All this material. It was all somebody's once. And then it's not. What d'you think our house will be made of?

She was silent.

Don't we take dead people's words? I said. Their stories? Skills? Ideas?

Yes, yes, I get it, she said. There's no life without dead people, no future that doesn't rely on the past. I understand the concepts. It's just the . . . brute reality. At this level.

It's not pretty.

No.

I don't know what to say.

It's getting hot, she said. I'm going to lie down a while.

Sure, I said, uneasy.

Sun retreated to the vehicle, cranked out the awning and lay in the shade with her water flask. I lingered a while among the graves to give her space. I walked until I was sweated through and feeling light-headed. Eventually I had no choice but to return to the rig, fill a jug at the watermaker and sit in the shade beside her.

They must have buried whole clans here, she said after a nerve-jangling pause.

Maybe they just had big families.

Whole names would have become extinct.

Possibly. Probably.

Doesn't that seem like the saddest thing you could imagine – a family name, wiped out forever?

Yes, I said, delivering the lie as evenly as I could manage.

She was quiet for a while.

What? I said.

Sometimes I feel you're hiding from me. But then other times I wish you wouldn't show yourself.

Okay, I said. That's confusing.

Show me how you do it, she said.

Do what?

Open the graves.

Why? This was clearly a mistake. Why make it worse?

Maybe it's better to see it, she said. To know, not just imagine.

Maybe tomorrow, I answered miserably. When it's cooler.

You want to camp down here, with all these graves?

We don't have to.

We will, she said.

Better if we don't.

We'll camp here, she said.

And we did.

In the morning, after we'd eaten and it was light enough, I went to the tray of the rig, cracked open the kit locker and lifted out a pinchbar and hammer. I brandished them dolefully, hoping Sun had changed her mind, but she had not.

She followed me deep into the haphazard rows until I stopped before a stone child with furled wings. Its face was gouged blank. The plinth on which it stood was canted back so that the effigy seemed to be falling slowly away from the vault at its feet. On the marble slab, chiselled deep into the stone, were five names. I broached the seal and worked the lid back on itself.

The ground around the grave had subsided. The interior was

surprisingly shallow. Like mushrooms growing in the dark, the brows of two skulls rose proud of the dust. Endeavouring to ignore Sun's sorrowful gaze, I raked through the silt. Found three smaller skulls and a femur, but no treasure.

*We stand on the bones of those who came before*, she said tartly.

Funny. But I don't take any bones. It's not like that.

What is it you look for?

Rings, chains. Stones.

These poor bastards.

Don't pity the dead, I told her. They stand on us, too.

What could you possibly mean by that?

Nothing, I said. Forget it. C'mon. Let's get moving.

For Sun's sake, I went to the pointless trouble of coaxing the lid of the vault back into square. We walked back to our rig with a bruised disquiet between us. That mood didn't lift for hours. Not until we were long clear of the place.

I drove north into the rising wind. We camped on a stony plateau and suffered a restless night.

Next day we kept on in the same direction and slowly came into the old mining badlands. The ground up there was still tacky, but firm enough to drive on. The first new shoots already speckled the edges of the trail.

At the first of my depots we soon realised there was more useful material here than we could cart back in a single trip. The iron cladding alone filled the trailer. It was half a day's work just loading and lashing it. By noon we lay in the shade, spent.

Next day the country around us was transformed. Tiny flowers – red, yellow, purple, blue – had bloomed as far as the eye could see.

Trundling west and bouncing through this endless field of colours, we were beset by clouds of dragonflies.

I told Sun of the time locusts had descended upon the plain in the wake of a cyclone. How at first we'd rushed to secure the growhouse and then spent the next two days running around to catch them. I'd never eaten locusts before. They were fine food. We stuffed barrels with them but sadly didn't know how to preserve them properly.

Don't tell me, she said. They ended up as mulch.

I waggled my brows.

She gave a rueful but indulgent laugh.

You people.

Are we that weird?

I'll get used to it.

I hope so.

For a while Sun said nothing. She looked out at the sea of flowers and the tsunami of dragonflies that billowed from it. When she rolled down the window, the cab filled with wings.

Crazy, isn't it? I said, batting them away.

Bonkers.

We're stuck with them now.

I don't mind. Look at these things.

The dragonflies battered themselves against the screen. They were in our scarves. Our clothes bristled with them.

You think the world is good? Sun asked.

What?

Do you believe the world is good?

Good enough, I said with a laugh.

Benign, I mean. I'm serious.

As opposed to what – evil?

Well, malign, I guess. Some folks say it's trying to shake us off. Rid itself.

And what are we, vermin? Like the fleas on a chicken?

She shrugged, picking dragonflies from her hair.

Who says that, I asked. Your parents?

She shrugged again.

You believe that?

No. I think the world's good. And the world made us. That's what I think.

But that's not what your parents believe.

Family's not everything.

You serious?

It can't be. Nothing works if family trumps every other consideration. Isn't that the point of the peace? Isn't that how we've survived all this time? Association, co-operation, regardless of tribe and clan? Nothing changes, nothing improves, until you can see past family. Without disinterest, there's just partisan chaos.

That's what they taught you at the academy?

Uh-huh.

You're having second thoughts, I said. About us. Me and my mum.

No, she said. Just thoughts.

How can I help?

You can't.

But you're family now. You know that.

Yes, she said brushing the last dragonflies from the cab. I understand.


By September, our house was finished. It was plumbed and wired, and I'd made a start on a new growshed, but before long we were out of materials. I figured there was just enough time for one more sortie south, but things had come to feel a little unsettled in our compound, so I was hesitant about leaving again.

It was hard to pinpoint the source of our agitation. Sun and I lived separately to my mother now. The space between the old place and ours was just beyond shouting distance. For the moment, we all still worked together in the old shed and continued to take the evening meal at my mother's, but we hadn't yet settled into equilibrium. Both women were bright, accommodating, courtly, but also watchful in a way that came to seem chilly. Amid all this, I felt a bit lost.

Sun was eager to have our new shed finished, but the heat had begun to knock her around and she wasn't keen to go back on the road so late in the season. She didn't think I should go either. My mother refrained from expressing a view. She said I should do what I thought best. At that, Sun flushed but said nothing. She didn't seem surprised. But neither could she hide her displeasure. I had a suspicion this matter had been discussed before.

I couldn't bear the idea of being trapped in that vortex for the foreseeable future, so I decided to make one more dash south.

It was an uncomfortable leave-taking. Sun could barely speak to me. It was the only time I ever left her for a genuine salvage expedition. The only time I wasn't lying about my intentions. But it was the worst way to set off on a trip.

I didn't get far. And that was the irony.

I was making camp at the pinnacles for the night when a vehicle jounced up behind me.

You've led me a merry chase, said the filmlayer.

I had no idea, I said. What are you doing here?

You have to ask?

So, this was the houseboat job.

They flew us the whole way. And it was a long trip. Time enough to be grateful we were high above the stifling blanket of dirty cloud that obscured any glimpse of the islands and waters of the Equatorial Belt. I thought of my mother's wounded orange. And what it must be like for those still trapped down there.

Once we descended and broke the cloud cover, I saw – ahead of us, to the east – a lake of light. Beneath us lay a vast swathe of shimmering darkness. The Yellow Sea. I guess there's no harm in saying that now. Hell, I might be dead by morning. So, I figure the vast murky blank falling behind as we turned was the Hermit Kingdom. That's as close as I ever got to it. Not a light to be seen. Granted, we'd lost altitude and were a long way out, but it was unsettling to see no lights at all in a land mass of such magnitude.

We transferred, after dark, to a ship anchored outside a mighty harbour. Rain beat on the deck. We were led below to be supplied and briefed.

The kit was light. I noted the crossbows.

The planner who briefed us was matter of fact. This would be, she said, a tough job. Six operators only. Two foils. We'd be deploying at close quarters in a densely populated site. Our object was a 76-year-old male. He lived on a houseboat in a busy quarter upstream from the main harbour. Five years previously, having somehow been tipped off to an impending action, he'd abandoned his remote and fortified villa in the highlands. Since then, he'd moved assets in the open, using citizens as both camouflage and shield. He lived surrounded by family and servants, hemmed in by neighbours who were ordinary foragers, grafters, boatmen. He was unknown in that canton, but remained alert and wily, careful to never show himself. His middle-aged son and daughter-in-law seemed to feel more secure. They were often on deck, and his two adolescent grandchildren appeared several times a week in the markets in the company of vassals and guards.

Our job was to acquit all hands with minimal noise and fuss. And no collateral damage. It was important to leave no one alive.

According to the intel, the object's houseboat had two guards. One posted forward, the other aft. Although they didn't carry kinetic tools openly, it was reasonable to assume they'd have them close at hand. Both had to be neutralized silently. Hence our archers.

The planner ran us through the route and penetration procedure three times, then stood us down to sleep until dark.

But it was hot down there in the hold. And the rain drummed unceasingly on the deck overhead. I suppose I should have been excited at the prospect of seeing my first great city, but the humidity was punishing. I was breathless. The air felt too fat and wet to inhale.

Early in the afternoon, the operator across from me, a woman with short red hair, began to claw at her tunic. They gave her oxygen and let the rest of us stand in shifts in the rain under the half-opened hatch.

After sunset we checked our kit again and, once the recap was done, the senior, a stocky, dark-skinned woman, distributed pills and motioned for the oxygen kits to be brought out for all.

You know the drill, she said. If we're captured, the Service can't help. We'll be detained as bandits – if we're lucky. So keep your pill handy. Now have a good suck and get sharp.

With our pills stashed, we huffed oxygen until an hour after dark. Then we strapped up, primed our tools, and filed out on deck to stand in the steady downpour. Even through the curtains of rain, the rim of light onshore and the penumbra above it were dazzling. I felt clean and ready.

The foils were lowered.

I climbed down, settling into position between the senior at the helm and the archer behind. We were still well offshore, but the smells of cooking and welding and the exotic reek of rot were unmistakable.

Once the second unit was ready, the senior signalled night visors down and we peeled away, soon at sufficient speed to rise from our hulls to the faster, more efficient blades of our foils. After the slow tedium of the outbound journey, the sudden rush of momentum felt glorious. I clamped my thighs to the long seat and looped a hand through the senior's webbing to secure myself. Sea and rain hissed as we cut through them. Wind fluttered in my helmet.

It was dark and flat out there. Between us and the land lay a chain of lights. As we closed, this chain resolved as dozens of anchored freighters. The senior steered us through the gauntlet, hunting shadows until we were past. Once we were inside the harbour, though, there was nothing to be done except put the hammer down.

Ships, cranes, lights – everything flashed by high and fast. And then we were on to the river beyond, where the current was sluggish, the banks low and the city's towers loomed against the sky.

I'd seen images and clips of places as densely populated as this, but nothing could have prepared me for the reality. Thousands upon thousands of people lived there, pressed in cheek-by-jowl as far as the eye could see. Their dwellings came down to the water's edge and onto the river itself, which smelt sulphurous and was clotted with refuse. At every bend and bank, the river was festooned with stilt houses, jetties, floating docks and barrages to which a bewildering variety of dwellings was moored. Some appeared to be iron hulks or decommissioned trawlers. Many were hardly more than canoes rafted alongside one another and bound together by films and canopies strung overhead. Others were just sheds – simple boxes with skillion roofs of tin or bamboo thatch, patched with panels and sheets of film. The largest were well-appointed house-boats with verandahs and wide decks and privacy screens. These hummed with fans and clattering AC, and their hulls spewed bilge water in sudden gouts.

The clamour of the river was a surprise to me. But it was obvious our planners had been relying on the noise and rain to give us cover. The waterway echoed with clanks, cries, moans. Every finger jetty was busy with glugs and coughs. Wherever we passed, things were being hammered, sawn, ground and pounded under whatever shelter could be gained. Over that racket, the whine of our jets and the fizz of our foil blades would have hardly registered.

When we came to the designated cove, the senior slowed up and set our hull down on the greasy water. The second boat eased in alongside us, and the senior gave the signal for readiness.

There were very few people out in the open, but those who saw us quickly withdrew. Shutters came down, blinds were drawn. I knew we'd probably have assets on this waterway, but it was unnerving to be observed like that. With our visors and tactical kit, we'd have looked a sinister outfit to ordinary locals.

We angled into the narrow cove and idled along the finger jetties until we found the houseboat that matched the briefing docs. The senior signalled for confirmation from the other foil and immediately got a thumbs up.

It was a larger-than-average houseboat, but not ostentatious. It was low-roofed and looked to be clad in woven matting, but according to the intel the underlying structure was steel. The shutters were closed. Two rattlebox ACs rumbled on the near-side bulkhead. The guards we'd been warned about were not in view.

A motorized canoe was tethered to the transom step facing the main channel of the river. As we eased in between the houseboat and the reeking boardwalk, the senior motioned for me to cut the canoe loose. I sent it clear, and the current took it out of sight.

When the other team slid into position abeam of us, and we confirmed there was nobody on deck for the archers to target, the senior signalled go and we scrambled aboard as quietly as we could. The second team went forward, and we braced for kick-off near the stern.

The place seemed very still, as if the occupants were all asleep, but after a few moments I felt vibrations through the soles of my boots. Not a motor. Bodies moving. I shifted forward to press my head to the aft door to hear better. But there was nothing. Then a viewing slot opened right beside me, not a handspan from my helmet. A blade of cold air jetted out, fogging the edges of my goggles. And before I could even move, a bolt from one of the archers flashed past my head and a man began screaming behind the wall. As doors slammed and feet pounded inside, the senior called it, set the puck charge, and a few seconds later the door blew in.

I was first through, and as I stumbled over the smoking door and the writhing guard with the bolt in his eye, someone came at me from the left and I took them down with a short burst. The injured guard kept wailing until the senior killed him. Then we heard the forward door blow and suddenly we were all in, going room to room in silent pairs.

We left the lights off and used our night vision, taking in the empty, rumpled beds, the strewn towels, the mats askew underfoot.

There were two living spaces, four bedrooms, a bathroom, a kitchen. The layout matched our intel in every aspect, and yet, for the moment, there was no one else to be seen.

We scoured the ceilings and floors for hidden escape hatches, to no avail. Nothing was said, but I could feel the dismay passing through the company. We assembled in the kitchen. The senior signalled for the archers to cover the decks, fore and aft. They hadn't even made it through the doors when we heard the sob.

It was a woman. Or perhaps a child. And the sound seemed to be coming from back toward the bathroom. The senior beckoned for me to accompany her while the others stood to.

The bathroom was empty. It took the senior only seconds to find the hatch in the bulkhead between the toilet and the sink. Still kneeling, she turned to me, pointing out the hinge along the left side. It looked like a utilities hatch. Except there was no exterior handle. And it was large enough to crawl through.

The senior got to her feet, ran her gloved hands across the rest of the bulkheads, then took out her clasp knife and scraped some paint away. She set the point of the blade against the naked metal and scored it deeply. Aluminium panel. A false wall.

She drew me back out to the kitchen. Signalled someone to fetch the archers. They arrived within moments. She pointed to the far wall, gave the sign to shoot, and after their first bolts had pierced the wall she ordered more. When she unclipped two gas canisters, I understood the plan. The archers kept loosing, reloading, and loosing again, until they'd thoroughly perforated the soft panelling.

She signalled masks on. Pulled the plugs from both canisters. Rolled them into the bathroom and shut the door.

In less than a minute, the door swung open again. I took out the first comer, the senior got the second. The next four were half dead before they even got to us.

We found the two juveniles in the hidey-hole. When we dragged them out through the hatch, they felt broken, as if they'd been trampled.

We laid the bodies out for processing. It was a brisk business, but the senior lingered a while over the old man, the one I'd taken down, confirming his ID against the image. His chest was scorched and imploded. But his features were clear enough. She gave the thumbs up and left the picture sheet on him.

Except for their smooth skin, good teeth and soft hands, the object and his family looked no different to ordinary folk. Their clothes were indistinguishable from those of their vassals. None of them wore ornaments or jewels, though one of the strongboxes was full of stuff that glistened and shone. Another was full of documents that I helped the senior pack into satchels.

It puzzled me that so many of these clans persisted in keeping records. It was as if they imagined things would blow over eventually, and when that day finally arrived they'd need their bona fides, their promissory notes and deeds of title.

There was no opportunity and no time to dispose of the bodies. Burning the houseboat would put the homes of surrounding citizens at risk, so everything was left in situ. Most locals would figure it for robbery. The rest, whether they were with us or not, would know what had transpired.

Seventy-six years old, I thought, looking at the body of our object. So that's what it looks like.

We got back to the ship without incident. It had weighed anchor and was already running south when we came alongside. Just before dawn, a stat met us to take us the rest of the way.

———

There's plenty to like about flying. But the best thing about it is being high enough to get cool. Don't you think? The mild air. It renders the world gentle, softens your thoughts.

That first night out, I looked at the sleeping senior. She was crusted in salt. There was blood on her tunic. She was shivering. And I thought, how peaceful she looks.

When I got home, it was too hot to finish the second growhouse. Sun and my mother had already begun the move underground. They granted the spoils of my bogus salvage trip cursory acknowledgement, but neither was interested in my tales of misadventure. Sun didn't hide her distress. It would have been hard for her. Shuttering the house she'd only just moved into. I was left feeling feckless and secondary, the subject of shared glances as I scurried to catch up.

It was a hard summer. One night I came in from the pump room to find Sun weeping silently on our bed. She lay curled on her side and when I asked what was wrong, she didn't answer.

I know it's not easy, I told her. I know it's not this tough in the south.

You don't know anything about the south.

Okay.

You don't know what you're talking about.

You miss the trees, the green grass.

That's just bloody nostalgia, she spat. The country's burning half the year. People still talk it up, as if it's some kind of paradise. Doesn't matter how miserable it's got, to them it's the best it's ever been.

I laid a hand on her hip, but her skin was hot and damp. I withdrew before she brushed me off. I knew how intolerable it could be to be touched during the hot season.

You're like a ghost, she said.

Oh, I murmured.

You come back all charged and full of yourself. For a few days you're all earnest consideration. And then you go flat and faint.

I'm sorry, I said. I guess the road takes it out of me. It only catches up with me once I stop.

I can feel it. When you're planning to go. I know it before you even say you're going. You're transparent.

Like a ghost, I said haplessly.

Sun ignored me.

Is it my mother?

At least with her, I know where I stand.

I won't go again.

You have to. I know how this works. I just need you to spare me the humiliation.

What's happened? What's she said?

It's not her. It's you. You run off and have yourself a big adventure, and when you get back I'm a problem to manage, a let-down.

No.

Bullshit. I can see your mind racing. Your life was simpler before I came along.

Not simpler. Different. Look, I shouldn't have gone. It's the shed. I thought we wanted to be independent.

Not if it means we're never together.

It won't be like this forever, I said with more hope than conviction.

You know it will.

I said nothing. She stayed silent. And at that moment I felt myself close to a precipice. Sun was perceptive enough to know that something was fundamentally amiss. But she didn't press further. Whether it was from fear, or loyalty, I couldn't tell. I hated that I'd done this to her.

That was the night she miscarried. It was years before I knew. And even that was only half the story.

As it was, the next evening my mother contrived to get me alone topside, ostensibly to check the array, which I'd already cleaned. She walked me across the dark, baking compound to the stilts of her winterhouse and suddenly seized me by the arm.

This is hard, she hissed. Competing obligations are painful.

We're fine, I said.

You're not. That's beyond dispute. All this having and holding. It's tough. It can feel impossible. No one knows how to do anything this difficult until they've actually done it.

What're you saying?

I'm saying work harder. Try harder. Sometimes you have to perform a role until you inhabit the part naturally, instinctively. That's how every new and difficult task is mastered.

That's just ridiculous.

No, she said. You're ridiculous. Your behaviour is ridiculous. And you're making this girl miserable. So, if you don't shape up, you can take your self-indulgent mess elsewhere.

You'd kick me off my own land?

This is family land. If you shame this family, I'll remove you. You can be sure of that.

I was shaken by this conversation. Even if, as it turned out, it was not quite the conversation I thought we were having. But my mother's intervention had a potent effect. The rift it opened between us served to intensify my allegiance to Sun. In the wake of that evening, I did everything in my power to be more attentive, to demonstrate my loyalty to Sun, to make it clear she was the most important person in my life.

My mother must have known what this would cost her. She understood all the ways in which a young man like me would show fealty to his wife. During our long incarceration underground, where the spaces were so close and the distractions so few, there could be no subtlety in it. I guess she figured it was for the best. She surrendered me for the greater good.

And Sun? There was no triumph in her. Only a kind of sad, depleted recognition.

When we came up into the open next April, Sun's reaction to being released was muted. She looked relieved, but showed none of the elation of the previous year. She seemed diminished by the season she'd endured. My attention was immediately consumed by the challenges of establishing our winter household and cracking on with building the new growhouse.

Then I got a message from a pigeon in the market. I didn't know how to break it to Sun. As it turned out, she took the news mildly, with an air of resignation. She seemed preoccupied. And there was something perfunctory about the way she saw me off.

This turned out to be a brief job. But it didn't go well. There were intel failures. Which meant we'd been betrayed. Only two of us survived. And both of us were lucky to make it out. I'd been warned at Basic. Told to expect depravity. But it was deeply shocking to see what this looked like up close. It didn't seem possible that a man would use his children as instruments. But it's true. He'll deploy them for his own survival. Not just as decoys. But as killing devices. Walking bombs.

The debrief on that show was longer than the job itself.

I came home hardened. With a new shell of armour. I thought I was okay. I gave a good account of how I'd come upon a full-length sheath for the growhouse as well as the necessary hoop frames and hoses.

Sun seemed relieved to see me. It was as if she'd recovered something of herself in my absence.

You look different, she said that night, in the privacy of our own bedroom.

Tired, I said.

Was it hot out there? You looked a bit cooked.

Maybe I overdid it a little.

She was tender. Solicitous. We made love. And, afterwards, I had the most beautiful dream of my life.

I was deep in the sea, and it was alive, with a million fish – bronze and silver and gold – pressed against me in one shimmering, quivering phalanx. And I was just like them, one of them, swimming effortlessly. The water was cold and clear. I felt safe, one of many, and we were all turning, turning, weaving and twitching as one, like a single creature, at one purpose, banking and diving through the soup of increase and possibility in which we were all suspended. And we swam together, angling, spearing, hurtling up toward the lucid pale surface. Shining like a complete and unified thought.

I woke in a kind of rapture. But as the dream receded, I felt wistful. No, it was more than that; I was grief-stricken. Because the dream had felt so real, so precious. It was something I wished I could return to. To summon up again. But afterwards, I never could. Try as I might, I couldn't conjure the thing itself. And it would not return to me unbidden.

I had other dreams, though. From those I woke in a sweat to find Sun watching me. When she asked what was wrong, what I'd been dreaming, I told her I couldn't recall. Often this was true. But the bits I did remember, these could never be shared.

I worked hard that winter. And so did Sun. We finished the growhouse, and I helped her install the new water-only system she'd designed using the reservoirs and pipe we'd plundered. Together we stocked the aisles with cuttings and seedlings propagated over summer. But although by day's end I was utterly spent, I found myself resisting sleep, resting only at short intervals, like a parched man gulping.

You look ragged, Sun would say.

I'm fine.

I think you're pushing yourself too hard. You're working right until noon most days. You're going to get sick. And I can't keep it up.

I didn't realize, I said.

You know better.

Okay. Yes. I'll ease up.

Inside by ten-thirty.

Yes, I said. It's for the best.

Are you worried about something? Not having enough? Not being able to make this work?

No, I lied. I'm fine.

You know if we shut the whole thing down, we could still make ends meet with your mother.

No need. But you're right. I need to wind things back a bit. More to life than work, right?

She nodded. Smiled faintly. But she seemed watchful. That winter I caught my mother observing me too. And more than once. Her gaze was cooler. Untroubled.

I wondered if they'd been talking. I hated deceiving them both like this. Hated the creep of my paranoia even more.

I kept bracing for another deployment. Dreading it, really. But for months nothing disturbed our routine. Then, one morning at the market, the filmlayer eased up alongside me as I sorted my trades before leaving.

Ship wants victualling, he said. She'll be docking tomorrow. Go to the blue boat at four. Don't wait for anyone to come down for you. Just go up the gangway and say you're there to arrange the provisions. Bring what victuals you can spare.

Should I be ready to leave?

What am I? he said. Your mother?

The next day, having decided it was better not to try to hide this transaction, I drove into the hamlet with four crates of fresh produce. At the dock stood a small freighter I'd never seen before. I carried a crate up the gangway and was met by a stocky seaman with half an ear missing.

Thank you, comrade, he said, taking the crate from me. Any more?

Back of the vehicle, I said.

This way, he said, leading me to a cabin door.

After knocking, he let me in, then stepped back out onto the deck again. I found myself in a spartan wardroom. A woman entered from another door.

Comrade, she said.

Provisions?

Please, she said. Sit down.

Am I going somewhere?

No, she said. This is just a chat. Please, she said, indicating a chair fixed to the deck.

I sat uneasily.

She was a wiry woman, perhaps in her thirties. She wore light coveralls without sleeves. She hadn't seen much sun. I figured she was no mariner.

How's your health?

You're a doctor?

She nodded.

I'm fit, I said. Good to go.

Have you ever been told you talk in your sleep?

What? No.

Somniloquy, it's called.

Okay. Never had it.

Not even when you were a child?

Not that I know of.

I see.

What's this about?

It's been brought to our notice.

Me? Really? I don't even snore.

She smiled.

Someone's said something?

She nodded sorrowfully.

In the field?

Only repat, at this stage.

I tried to take this in.

How was the job? she asked.

They haven't told you?

I'm asking *you*, comrade.

Well, it wasn't good.

The use of children.

Yes, I said after a long hesitation.

And how do you feel about that?

I dunno, I said. Disgusted. Upset.

Angry?

Well, yeah.

Understandably. It's barbaric.

These people, I said. Sometimes I've wondered if we exaggerate a bit. Because they're them and we're us. Like it's useful, even necessary. To keep the comrades at it.

You really think that?

I'm just saying I've wondered. I mean, I've seen some things. Stuff I couldn't believe anyone would do. So, there's that, yeah. But mostly they do what anyone would do to stay alive, protect their families.

And this?

I looked away from her. I had to stop a moment. To rearrange myself, catch my breath. To wipe it away. But when I thought of it, when it was there with me again, I had the panicky feeling I would have it all adhering like spilled tar forever.

Comrade?

Yes?

Everything okay?

When do I go back out?

Well, she said. I don't have operational input.

But I'm good to go.

I applaud your zeal. But whether you're good to go is not really your call.

Honestly, I'm fine.

Actually, I doubt that.

What's this about? I said, suddenly agitated. Talking in my sleep? What was I saying?

I don't have details.

I'm not sure I believe that.

Best not to contradict me.

I dipped my head to indicate submission.

The details of what you're saying in your sleep may or may not be critical. But your propensity to be doing this – to be having such a thing happen to you – may very well be. I'm sure you understand the risks.

I understand my obligations. I understand the importance of security. You honestly think I'm going to shoot my mouth off? Betray my comrades?

No one is doubting your discipline or your integrity. This is probably just a symptom of stress. If this phenomenon is new, as you suggest, then that seems likely.

This is bullshit.

Excuse me? she said, sitting back demonstratively.

Sorry, I stammered. I'm sorry. I apologize. I withdraw the remark.

I should hope so. There's no need to take this as an affront. We need to keep you and everyone who depends on you safe. That includes your family. You had a very challenging deployment. You need some time to recover.

I've had some time.

We think you need more.

So there's nothing you can give me? Like drugs?

I gather ganja is widely used in these parts, correct?

Yes. In summer. For the heat. We call it choof.

Ah. And it aids sleep?

Normally, yes.

But it hasn't helped since the repat?

I haven't had any. Want to stay sharp, you know? In case of another show.

She smiled kindly.

You can't give me something stronger?

Nothing that wouldn't risk a more depressive effect. Nothing that's operationally safe.

I gave a curt nod, seething. You're standing me down.

You're owed a rest, comrade. You have family.

Yes, I said, as if this were an impediment and not a blessing.

We'll keep tabs on your recovery. Bring you in when the time's right. Not me personally, of course.

I nodded again, defeated.

You're disappointed. I understand. But this is just temporary. And our struggle, as you know, is a long game. Thank you for the produce, by the way. Your family's reputation in that regard is well earnt.

I went home humiliated. And furious that one of my own, some nameless comrade on the repat leg, had informed on me. I was a loyal and competent operator. To be summarily declared unsound – well, it was stupid, but it stung. I didn't believe the allegation for a moment. Didn't understand how this could have happened. But I knew the only way back to operational duty was by submitting.

We grew good choof, Sun and me. Especially once her water system was established. That season I smoked as if summer had yet to leave us and might never end. It blunted my frustration. And helped me sleep. And increased my anxiety.

The dreams persisted. And they became more frequent.

One night I woke to find Sun standing by the window, watching me.

What is it? I asked, scrambling up onto one elbow.

Something's wrong, she said. You have to tell me.

There's nothing wrong.

Do you ever feel a sense of dread?

Dread?

Like, doom.

Me? No.

Are you afraid to go to sleep?

No, I lied.

You're wearing yourself out. You're losing weight. I'm worried.

Don't be. I'm fine.

She looked at me as if deliberating. Hesitating. Or just taking stock. Of me, I assumed. Which goes to show how trapped I was in my own mess.

The next night my mother came across the compound to join us for dinner. Afterwards, the three of us sat outside with the awning cranked back so we could see the stars.

This could be a good winter, said my mother. If our luck holds. I was sceptical, I admit it, but Sun's new system has been a triumph.

She's brilliant, I said.

She is.

Well, it's nice of you to say, said Sun. It's nice to have the support.

You're family, said my mother, gazing out across the moonlit plain to the rumpled mass of the range.

It can't be easy to give up a son.

My mother sighed. Children leave. Eventually they divide themselves from us. It's natural.

I am still sitting here, you know, I interjected with as much good humour as I could summon.

They're not ours to keep, said my mother. And our children are not our keepers either.

No, said Sun. I understand that well enough.

Where's this coming from? I asked.

Sun's right, said my mother. It's hard to give up a child. But it's inevitable. You only have them a short time. It's as if, from the moment they truly become themselves, they're leaving you. You give them up to the world, to the greater good. Despite yourself. However much it hurts.

Maybe we should talk about something else, said Sun, glancing sideways at me.

Again, I'm sitting right here, I said. And, Mum, I live across the compound. I haven't gone anywhere.

You'll see. Both of you.

Sun got up abruptly and left the deck.

What is this? I hissed at my mother. What's got into you?

I'm perfectly fine, she said, her gaze averted.

You sound bitter. Are you jealous?

I don't have the luxury of feeling jealous.

I don't understand you, I said.

You're a very young man, she said. I've lived longer and seen so much more than you.

Oh, I doubt *that,* I said.

Son, a few excursions don't make you worldly. Nor do they make you wise.

Time for bed, I said, getting to my feet.

You shouldn't be angry, she said, remaining in her seat.

No? What should I be?

Careful, she said. Staunch, yes. But always careful.

I gestured toward the stairs, and she went meekly, as if she'd yielded.

But she hadn't yielded. Not in the way I thought. And that year, because of the state I was in, I was not careful. Not in the way she meant. Probably not even in the way I thought she had meant.

I took them both for granted – Sun and my mother. I underestimated them. Misread them entirely. And I've had a long time to regret it.

The child stirs. I see the bowman peering at her.

It's something, isn't it?

He stiffens, suddenly self-conscious. Then he sniffs. And attempts to regain his tactical demeanour.

You ever have kids? I ask.

He shakes his head. I draw a breath to speak but realize I have no idea what to say. The bowman notices the hesitation.

So what's this, then? he says. Some sort of do-over?

What?

You had 'em. You lost 'em. Now you want to redeem yourself?

How do you know I lost them?

Well, for one thing they're not with you, are they. And this yarn you're spinning – I can feel it coming.

This is not about making up for my mistakes. I'm just trying to do the right thing.

I don't believe you.

I made a promise.

To who?

A woman.

What's her name?

She's dead. I never knew her name.

You took in a stray for a woman you didn't even know?

I knew her.

But not her name. Jesus, I figured you for a bullshitter. But maybe you're just soft in the head.

I'm just trying to be decent.

He offers only a scowl.

The kid deserves somewhere safe, with honourable people. Some kind of future.

Good luck with that.

I don't need luck, brother. I need help.

He snorts.

That's funny? Seriously?

Listen to yourself, he says. You're like some wild-eyed pilgrim looking for paradise.

No. Not me. They're searching for the end, those folks. I'm looking to start something.

Grind me down, more like.

I'm trying to show you who I am.

You're just buying time. I'm starting to think your story's full of shit. All this talk and somehow you never get around to Utah. You were never on that job. Probably weren't even one of us.

I shake my head. Close my eyes. Draw a ragged breath. And begin to sing in a dry croak. Fitful at first. Stuttering, almost. Because my gullet burns. And my gums are pasted to my cheeks. But once I find my stride and get my wind, the song fills me, lifts me, bears me forward. And out they pour, the forbidden names.

Shut up with that! he yells, waking the child.

But I can't. I won't. My blood is up, and my spirit stirs. It has me now, and all I can do is submit until I'm the song, not the singer. So on we roll, the song and me, the song and my comrades, down through the descant of secret victories, until it returns me to myself, and I open my eyes to see the waif startled, and the bowman weeping.

I never saw the List. And neither did anyone else. Such a prospect was impossible, the idea absurd. Even if, by some miracle, you gained access to the catalogue, you'd never get through a roll of names as massive as that. It was so large and dynamic, no single human could read it, let alone retain it. Before you could run your eye all the way down the myriad columns, names would have multiplied, metastasized. From its earliest days, in the era of the pioneers, when the List was but a primitive inventory, the register was constantly growing. Every acquittal and interdiction, rather than reducing the number of names, brought more and better intel. New networks and bloodlines came to light. Fresh objects found their way onto the roll. There was no single cache or dossier capable of accommodating such an endlessly branching web.

It's said that in the old world, as late as the first years of the Terror, data machines could contain information at that sort of scale and transmit it across vast distances. But by our time, this was the stuff of fancy. At its best, the tech we had was patchy, and with transfer systems so localized and intermittent, something like the List could only exist and move in fragments. Which was safer anyway. And just another way in which smallness, like citizen syndicates and loose federations, helped keep the peace.

Some criminal clans still had tech and comms from the old

days, stuff we'd log and destroy after an acquittal, or sometimes confiscate. But their superior kit didn't keep us from their door. Wherever they were, and from whatever part of the world we came to find them, we got there in the end. No matter how archaic and gruelling the means.

The List was never the property or the project of any single tribe, province or association. It was the secret we shared across frontiers. In shards and slivers. To protect the security of the enterprise, and the lives and sanity of the individuals who gave themselves to it. Me, I never wanted to see every name. Just hearing one said aloud could turn my blood to copper wire. It was enough to know the List existed. That it was something I could act upon in concert with others. This was a mighty idea. It was liberating. Enlarging. And in its scope and implications, a little terrifying. Right? The List shaped the life we gave ourselves to. This was the vessel in which all our aspirations were set afloat.

You know all this. But no harm in comparing notes, right?

After Basic, I never discussed the List. Not explicitly. We were sworn not to. But it was ever-present. We knew its grand and secret hope had been nurtured and handed on for generations. And that gave us power. Remember? Power beyond the sum of our parts. Power despite our inferior kit. Strangers, all of us. And yet at one purpose. That's what the promise of agency feels like when you've never known it before. That's what every child should inherit.

So, no, we never saw the roll and we never uttered the few names that fell our way in the field. And yet, over time, we came to sing them. Together. On the march, or after dark. This, I think, was a late-stage phenomenon. It arrived organically, unheralded, and without discussion. It happened in our time, comrade, during our years of active duty. What does that tell us, you think? A cultural elaboration like that? Was it a signal of vigour, or evidence of decay?

Maybe we'll never know. But I do think about it. Because, originally, the singing was forbidden. And in my early days it was still frowned upon by Planning and Intel. But over time the practice seemed to establish itself as worthy. Because it *was* bracing, wasn't it? Singing built solidarity. Kept us on our feet. And somehow, without us really noticing, I suspect, it became integral to culture in the field. It was like the letter home you could never write. The explanation you were forbidden to give to family and community. We sang it from pride. And fear. For the blessed relief of utterance. We sang it for the dead and for those who'd come after us.

Of course we could never sing the full List itself. No march would be long enough. No, we just sang of it, from it. Because all we ever had were fragments. The names of the acquitted. Clans extinguished by operators before us. Successes old enough to be safe to utter. But then, as years passed, as the work progressed and their collapse became wholesale, fresh names arrived – more and more all the time – and we sensed we might be singing our own deeds, the achievements of our moment, and that, brother, that was intoxicating.

But I never expected to live long enough to chant the most dread name of all.

I think this might be what you want to hear but don't dare ask of me. All your talk of Utah. I note the tactical face on you. I see it.

Well, I was a scarred old stager by the time I uttered that name, but I sang it with special fervour, secret pride. Because, as you'll know, and I can see it in your eyes, only one vanquished name retained power enough to inspire our weary limbs on its own. You should know that, in the field, I could sing it with the authority of experience. With the faces of men and women in my mind. People I knew, who'd given their life to wipe it from the face of the earth. By what authority could I claim this? Well, because I'd been there.

You want me to tell you, I know. But I need to work my way there. You need to be patient. The path wasn't direct. Hell, I didn't even know it was a path.

Comrade? Where are you going?

The bowman's gone a while. Time enough for me to cool off and gather my wits. But also long enough for me to wonder if he's gone in search of something to beat me with. But when he returns, he has a fresh canteen.

You didn't need to do that, he says.

The singing? I don't know, brother. Feels to me I did. I needed the knees-up anyway.

You're taking the piss.

I'm telling you the story.

You sing the song and you leave the name off. You're dicking with me, aren't you?

No, I say. I just don't want to get ahead of things. Jumping ahead – it'd be cheap. It wouldn't be honest.

Fuck you, he says, shoving the canteen through a gap in the wire.

I accept it silently. It takes all my self-control to palm it, then examine it appreciatively, as if it's a keg of pure plains honey. I twist the cap. Sniff the contents. It smells like caught water, not made water. Useful to know. And so much more enticing to drink. But I stop. For effect.

Like I said. It's a long story. I'm getting there.

Dear God, he says. You're doing my head in.

Then I drink. I drain the whole thing in one long draught.

So, I was relegated. Didn't like it one bit. And for a while, wasn't very smart about it. Made things strained at home. Worried Sun. But in time I mastered myself. Trained myself to rest. Or to appear, when awake, as if I were at rest.

The fear of sleep was harder to manage. I couldn't simply smoke myself into a stupor every night. No matter how I got to sleep, the dreams would be lying in wait, so I had to find ways of yielding to the darkness and embracing – or at least facing – what lurked there. Which is, I guess, just a fancy way of saying I learnt to put a kind of spell on myself.

I convinced myself I was doing it for Sun's sake. To relieve her of the nightly turmoil and the day of brooding absence that followed. But I also did it for myself. I know that. With the hope of getting back to active duty. Look, I loved Sun. Needed her. That was real. Fierce. But I loved and needed the cause, too. And I enchanted myself into believing I could be faithful to both. How? By sheer willpower, I suppose. And quality of performance. That doesn't mean my loyalty to either was bogus. You know what it was like, having to play a role for those we knew and loved. But divided fealty – it has consequences. Collateral damage. You know, for a while I thought things could have been different if I'd had someone close I trusted. Some mentor, maybe. I mean a comrade. Not some random medico from Planning. A friend who really knew me and understood my predicament, who could pull me aside, confront me, show me I was kidding myself. Perhaps they could've gotten through to me. Helped me draw a line, make the hard choice.

But even if I'd had all that, I can't honestly tell you what – or who – I'd have chosen. My own happiness, or the common good? Sun, or the cause? They were both selfish choices. False choices, as it turned out. And there was never a friend, anyway. Never could be. Besides, I wasn't the only one ensnared in a performance. Ugly choices were being made all around me.

Now, of course, for you and me, options are narrower. Makes that earlier time look golden. Even so, opportunities to shape the present and future still exist, surely. Aren't we facing them right now? Another place, another moment? The fresh torment of another decision? But I'm game to take a chance if you are.

Anyway, that winter furlough was rough. Still, for all the deceptions and delusions of that season, we had good days, and the more I got myself in order, the better they became. Sun was closer to her old self again – bright, sharp, funny. She seemed glad to have me within reach. After the initial weeks of turmoil, things gradually grew equable, and we enjoyed long intervals of contentment, moments of great tenderness. Yeah, there were still times when I caught her watching me. That searching gaze. And between Sun and my mother there was a coolness now. But although things were not truly as they were before the April job and the thing with the kids, the three of us managed to work together. Peaceably. Without strain. And our holdings prospered.

I think what finally broke me free of my funk was our excursion to the rock shelter. It was something I'd been meaning to show Sun all along, a trip that had been so often postponed or supplanted by other obligations. But I saw her peering at the little scatter of bone fragments and stone flakes on the sill of the kitchen window, arte-facts I'd collected and kept over the years, and I sensed this could be something to bind us.

We left in the dark, took the long way around the cape in my rig, and as the light came up we hiked out into the western terraces. Compared to the eastern approach, across the range and the canyons, it was an easy walk. We had the sea breeze and the roar of the surf at our backs.

There's coral everywhere, she said.

Yeah, I replied. I think all these terraces are coral.

You didn't bring climbing gear. Is that a good sign?

I angled us up to the jumble of broken slabs at the threshold of the cave.

It's just here, I said. I found it when I was a kid.

We clambered to the lip where a lintel overhung the dim recess. I beckoned Sun in, and we stooped to crab across the jangly bed of the shelter.

Crouching, I ran my fingers through the shards of shell and bone. Showed her the charcoal stain on my fingertips.

God, she said. This is ancient. Is this your family?

No. Before us. Before anyone.

The Countrymen.

You know about that?

Only a little. Some say they go back a thousand generations. That they'll outlast us all. Look! That's a mammal bone. This one is fish.

My mother says these bits of stone are blades.

Whatever they are, said Sun, they're not from here.

Of course they're from here.

No, she said. Look around you. Everything's limestone. But this fiery-looking chunk here – there's iron in it. This is from the desert. Or at least mine country. There's nothing hard enough on the cape to make a blade from, or a hammer. See? This black one. That orange piece. Look how smooth they are. Feel the edge!

They were brought here?

Yeah. I think so. Like steel. Solar film. They must have traded for it. With folks from the desert.

Sun held up a nub of jasper. Rubbed it with her thumb. Set it into the pocket of her dungarees. We stayed a while, caught up in our mutual wonder, until we became conscious of the mounting heat of morning. We chattered excitedly all the way home. It was a blessing to have something other than our domestic predicament with which to occupy our minds for a little while.

Weeks later, one morning in the growhouse, as we swept the cuttings into the mulch hopper and Sun's ingenious system trickled and dripped all around us, she asked, apropos of nothing, whether I had regrets.

Regrets? I said, knocking the stems from my broom.

I mean, would you do it all again?

You and me? Here? Of course. In a heartbeat.

You could've had a different life, she said.

I doubt it. You think?

I don't know, she said. Sometimes I suspect we lack imagination. That we could have tried different things.

You mean live in the city?

No, she said. I've done that. Maybe we could have just lived like nomads on the road.

We can go back out for a while. There's always stuff to trade.

I don't mean that, she said. I mean just travelling place to place, seeing the world. Living as we go.

Like your parents?

No. Just being in the world, not trying to . . . shape it.

You think that's what we're doing, the two of us?

Yeah.

Huh, I said. And what about family?

You can have a family on the move.

We'd, what, just live hand to mouth, day to day?

Follow the seasons, the food, the stars. Life's been lived like that for longer than we can imagine.

Sounds romantic.

I know it's just a fantasy, she admitted. But sometimes I wonder why we don't live like that. Is it because we don't know how? Or because we're too small and scared to dare?

It's a nice thought. I like the road. I'd like to see places. The southern sea.

Sun pushed a matted snarl of corn silk into a pile with a listless twitch.

What is it?

Nothing. Really.

I see.

Do you want a family?

I have a family, I said.

I mean children.

Yes. Of course. Do you think it's possible?

I'm not sure your mother would approve.

Why would anyone not want grandchildren?

Well, said Sun. She's very focused on all this. The work.

But all this is for family, I said. Otherwise, what's the point?

Good answer, she said, stepping in to kiss me.

The solstice was barely a memory when I got notification of my next deployment. I was given a script to memorize, and at home I delivered it, word for word, as instructed. Some needlessly complex fib about a citrus disease rife in Perth and a trading opportunity we couldn't pass up.

Sun received the news of my imminent departure soberly, without surprise. As if she'd been steeling herself for it. I struggled to hide my exhilaration. I felt vindicated. I didn't really understand how the Service could have gauged my recovery, but I was galvanized by the prospect of seeing action again, and in the days leading up to my departure I worked ever harder to manage myself.

The night before I left, my mother crossed the compound on foot and hugged me with surprising ferocity. Be careful, she said. I'll take care of things here.

That night, I didn't sleep at all. And from the way she lay, motionless and silent beside me, I was sure Sun was awake as well. But when I went downstairs two hours before dawn to lash my load of grafted citrus stock to the trailer, she stayed in bed. It was only in the hot minutes before first light that I sensed her standing beside me as I worked.

We built a good house here, she said.

We did.

I finished stowing perishables on the rear tray of the vehicle and then stood with her wordlessly a moment. I felt queasy. Couldn't tell if it was from excitement, dread, or guilt.

Sun pressed something small into my palm.

Here, she said.

In the beam of my headlamp I saw the lozenge of jasper from the midden in the rock shelter.

Something to hold, she said. Something to remind yourself.

Of home.

No, she said. Work.

Confused, I pocketed the stone and hugged her.

I'll always come back, I said.

Yes, she said. You'll try. I know.

When I flipped the lamp off, the darkness was so complete that if not for Sun's cashew scent I wouldn't have known she was still there.

Life, I said. It needn't be just work.

*To everything a season.*

What's that one about passion again?

*Without passion, a soul is just latent force and possibility. Like the flint waiting for the shock of the iron.*

Maybe that's you, then?

Made of iron? I doubt it, she said.

We'll get our time.

Yes. And the passion?

Don't worry, I said. You still shock me. Every day.

We reached for each other in the dark. My mother never showed.

We only got the briefing once we made landfall. That was six days after the initial muster. The planners didn't sugarcoat the show for us. It presented, they said, a high degree of difficulty. But from the orders and intel they laid out, there was nothing to suggest the job would be anything out of the ordinary. It sounded like a standard long-haul interdiction.

The country below was parched and riven. It looked like a smashed plate. High desert. Canyon country. It was eerie. To be on the other side of the world and feel such a sense of familiarity.

Two hours before set-down, I was told I'd be the senior for the ground team. That's how tight they were about security. I certainly hadn't expected to lead the show. But the plan and the orders were straightforward. I knew I was capable. It felt like a reward for faithfulness and persistence. Vindication.

The set-down was tidy. But the stat was already gone before we logged what was missing. The drones and the thermal wraps were listed on the manifest clipped into each cargo shell, but they were not in our kit.

They'll be out over the Pacific already, I said, as we took stock of the sun-blasted plateau.

Fucking Supply, said the dark comrade, a woman with a face full of silver teeth.

At least the makers arrived, said another operator, also a woman, in an accent that sounded Spanish.

Saves drinking our own piss, said one of the young blokes.

That never works anyway, said Silver Teeth in the clipped inflections of the Highveld.

*Coño*, said Spanish, I bet the *joven* never tried.

Well, I've tried, said Silver Teeth. *No recomendada.*

Me too, she said. *Joder eso.*

Okay, you piss drinkers, I said. Let's bury these cases and strap up.

There were six in the ground team. Good operators, all of us. This was the America job. Former Republic of Utah. Okay?

Discipline shapes and protects our enterprise, they told me in Basic. But its core must be personal as well as collective. To preserve and maintain honour, discipline has to hold at every level. Our cause is not a crusade of vengeance. Actions in the field should be executed dispassionately. Our role is to prevent, not to cure. To purify, not to conquer.

So what's the end point? I remember asking. What do we do when the slate is finally clean?

Then we stand down, they said. We become civilians. As if the Service never existed.

So we're gardeners, not janitors.

Yes, they said. We water. And we weed. And allow growth. Whatever emerges will be organic.

You don't think this plan is a little trusting, a bit hopeful?

How do you think this mosaic of associations and syndicates arose? they asked. How do you think the Long Peace has been achieved and maintained? By husbandry. Benign and impartial.

You mean that was us?

Those who came before. And those who'll succeed us. This is no airy daydream. The Long Peace is real. And we'll tend it for the sake of the common good. In obscurity. And when the end comes, we'll stand down and rejoice.

The trek in was a thirty-hour traverse. We did it nonstop. Keeping to schedule. As ordered.

That was a tough trip, no question. You wouldn't survive it today, not even in a suit. Back then, a hike like that, at pace, in country so hot, it was no jolly jaunt.

As it fell away from the plateau, the lower plain was an eerie prospect. Dune fields of ash. With stretches of hard, glazed earth between. Lucky for us, there was no wind, but I still ordered breathers on while we crossed the drifts.

All day and all night, there was nothing to see out there. No infrastructure, no tracks, no indications at all. Once we got to the critical zone, where a gentle gibber slope suggested a draw, I watered and rested the crew. We dozed under camo in the filthy-hot morning and, when we'd fed and strapped up again, we went down in patrol formation. Found the canyon mouth, then retreated to reconnoitre the hinterland around it. This work took the rest of the day, as expected. And as per our intel, there was nothing to see. Nothing human, anyway. And we were thorough. You wouldn't have found a crew more scrupulous. As ever, none of us had met before embarkation. But everything about the bearing and conduct of the team suggested Planning had assembled a top-shelf crew. And that gave me confidence.

We scoured every secondary ravine and overhang for tunnel exits, refuse pits, swarf, rubble – anything. There were no birds. Very few insects. We didn't expect to see animals. Intel had the nearest formal settlement a week's march south.

Once we'd circled back to the wide, gibber-strewn draw at the mouth of the canyon, I watered the team again, had the maker secreted where we could find it easily on the return trip, and stood us to. There was no expectation of surveillance – this detail was explicit in the briefing. But given the nature of the stronghold, an assertion like that was hard for an experienced operator to accept, so I was determined, for safety's sake, to act as if we were being watched at every turn.

I gave it six hours. And nothing happened. No one showed. Everything was aligning as anticipated.

So, under cover of darkness, we entered the canyon. Moving with painstaking care. Literally one ponderous step at a time. So slowly, it felt we were hardly travelling at all. And yet in time the canyon began to narrow. Its towering walls pressed in closer until we were forced to forsake the relative luxury of the open floor, with its river of sand and islands of cobbles, and press ourselves against the base of the stone ramparts. Here the footing was uncertain, the ground a jumble of fallen shale. By the time we reached the blind end of the canyon it was almost daybreak, but I was confident we'd reached our destination.

I signalled for daylight posture. Everyone sought some kind of overhang or cleft in which to wait things out. And then, in tantalizing increments, the light came up. The first sun struck the brow of the bluff. Then, with a languor that messed with my thoughts, it painted the buttress beneath it, creeping down its tawny face until, toward midday, the canyon floor brightened treacherously, and hour by hour we pressed back deeper into any shadow or cover that remained. Not just to escape detection but to avoid being roasted alive.

I hoped to hell our intel was sound. There was plenty of time to wonder.

It's no sport lying on your belly or your back for twelve hours in the grinding heat. Sucking protein stems. Shitting where you are. In a diaper. Making a motionless ghost of yourself. By mid-afternoon, in those conditions, even your thoughts sound noisy enough to give you away.

Dusk fell with cruel torpor. Once it was finally dark, I signalled the stand to and night glasses on. And then, an hour later, at full darkness, I gave the order to move up into offensive posture.

Our two climbers picked their way across the cobbles and sand to the base of the canyon wall. The rest of us hauled up slowly to our firing positions. The sweat began to freeze on me before I was even settled. The desert sky was blank. The air tasted metallic.

Out before us stood the towering rock face. Without night vision, just a silent vertical slab, a field of grey against the black beyond. With the thermal down, it was a grainy, pale void with the swimmy texture of sleep.

The heat plumes were there as promised. It took a while to adjust sufficiently to find them, but they were unmistakable. High on the bluff, just short of the crest. Two of them. Both were nicely baffled and well disguised, but under night-viz they were exactly what we needed to see. Something incontrovertibly discordant. In the middle of nothing and nowhere, two beautiful, shimmering green columns. My blood jumped at the sight. For the confirmation. And the pride of having made it to the right spot despite everything.

Exhaust plumes. As a signal of human occupation, this was a major tell. Because every bolthole, however well hidden, needs ventilation. And keeping a large household in a sealed fortress depends on circulating air, filtration, cooling. Every bit of that effort produces heat. And that must be vented somewhere. So a pair of industrial-scale heat plumes made it nearly certain that a fearsome citadel lay within this canyon wall.

I scoped our flanks. Saw the higher team to my right vigorously signalling confirmation. The sight of those plumes had clearly buoyed morale.

I checked my piece. Fourteen minutes to spare. Meaning we'd barely gotten ourselves set in time for kick-off.

But there was no kick-off.

Nineteen-forty-five hours came. And went. And nothing happened.

The colder the desert air got, the clearer those vent plumes became. Long and wavering. Green as the ponderosa pines in the old clips. Whose ashes we'd waded through the day before.

Our vigil ground on. And despite myself, I could feel the sense of vindication beginning to decay.

We stood to. All night. In the bitter cold. Our camo lattice was as effective for insulation as it was for shade. Which meant we froze. Those green wands danced and wavered above us. And our eyes went dry and grainy from staring at them.

We held position. Stayed staunch. Because that was our way, not just our job.

An hour before dawn, seething but still calm, I ordered the stand down, and we withdrew to the canyon floor and daylight posture.

We did the same thing again the next day. The day after that. And the night that followed.

The nights were bad. But the days were worse. Not just because of the heat and the fact we were wedged into gaps and holes too small and too twisted or jagged to allow a moment's comfort. And not simply because we couldn't move except to suck blood-warm water from our bladder packs. It was the passivity of it. The helplessness. The understanding that during daylight hours there was no prospect of offensive action. At night, freezing as it was, we had the spark of anticipation to keep us sharp. In the dark there was, at least, the possibility of action. But by day, especially since our early certainty had been eroded, there was only endurance. Of one moment after another. And the dread feeling that everything might be turning to shit.

We were schooled not to speculate on mission detail. For the sake of security. And because overthinking saps energy and morale. We were drilled to keep a hard body and a clean slate. But a man's not a machine.

After the second day in that box canyon, I began to question everything we'd been told about this mission. And by the next night, the intel had begun to feel fatally soft.

I still believed we were at the correct site. Geographically, everything aligned. The distances, the dimensions of the canyon. But in all this time, the only other confirmation had been the exhaust. Which had seemed convincing initially. But this whole scenario. Was it real? Was there really a citadel here? Was our object really bunkered within all that stone? And was he still none the wiser to our presence? Or was all this just an elaborate decoy?

You know this already, comrade: a single no-show could be explained away. But two consecutive failures to conform? That was red-flag territory.

I determined that if nothing happened by zero-hundred hours of that third night of standing to, we'd withdraw and bolt back to the uplift point. But this was not a pretty option. People – hundreds of them, for all I knew – had probably worked on this job for years. The groundwork for an op this big was astronomical. No senior liked to come in from a job empty-handed. We were not the kind to die wondering. But I had the lives of five good operators to consider.

It was all well and good to have these vent plumes, but we'd seen no movement, sound, smell. Not a single corroborating sign of habitation. If this wasn't a dummy location to begin with, then there was every chance our object and his company had already scarpered. Which meant that a ground force, or something worse, could soon be upon us. The longer we held on here without shelter or resupply, the more vulnerable we became. We were weatherworn already, and a long way from the watermaker at the canyon mouth. So I was resolved: tonight was it.

Darkness fell. And we did it all again. Glasses down. Night posture.

The climbers creeping out with coils on their backs, cartridges in hand. The rest of us crawling up to best vantage either side.

According to Intel, our object emerged once every evening. At 1945 hours, he came up through an airlock and stepped out onto a long parapet cut into the bluff. Above this terrace lookout was a landing pad which had once been, but perhaps no longer was, remotely defended. Without confirmation, we had to take this on trust. It wasn't my business to know how this information had been obtained. But neither the parapet nor the gyro pad was fully visible from our positions. The terrace *seemed* to be distinguishable, if only partially. But the landing pad was still unsighted from these angles. Without drones, we were guessing.

I accepted there was a decent chance that lofty balcony was broad and deep enough to mask the flare generated by body heat. The parapet wall around it would be high, and probably a metre thick. Whichever clan had built this stronghold would surely have had the means to do it right. There was no point going to the trouble unless they could guarantee themselves total discretion, optimal strength, maximum security. And with their sort of history, they'd be highly motivated. They'd have seven billion reasons to be careful. Objects like this one hadn't held out so long by accident. By and large, these types were as ruthless in defending themselves as they'd been in the pursuit of their fortunes and the conduct of their empires.

Maybe that's why we hadn't seen him. For all we knew he'd come out both nights. Been out and back, undetected. Because he was canny, and his fortress well designed. Not a thought I wanted to entertain. And yet, there it was, heavy in my mind. Bloody Supply.

I'd been trained to trust our intel. You'd go mad if you didn't. But the days and nights had eaten into me. And I was thinking, seriously now, about whether any of what we'd been told was credible. Like the reported absence of mercenaries. In the briefing, that detail was jarring. No mercenaries? No confirmed defences at all? It could have been misdirection on the part of the object. Maybe the Intel assets had fed us bullshit to set a trap. But our planners were adamant. And it was true, no force had slipped in behind us. No airborne assault had arrived to take us by surprise. As yet, there'd been no defensive action from the citadel of any kind.

Although I was still a young operator, I was by then well-acquainted with depravity. I began to wonder if this joker could be one of those inbred nutjobs you encountered now and then. Because, by all accounts, not only was he going undefended, he'd reportedly discharged his entourage. Eighteen months back. Apart from kin, he had no household to speak of.

The prospect of eccentricity rattled me. In this entire complex, behind that cliff face, there were, supposedly, only four individuals. The object. His wife. And two children. Nobody else. I'd seen it there in the docs, but I struggled to believe it. I just couldn't see how it was possible. As a longstanding arrangement, it simply couldn't be. Bastions and bloodlines like these didn't hold for generations without layers of personnel. These creatures required servants, mercenaries, technicians. But according to our assets, this peculiar divergence was recent. And personal. Like some sort of whim, or a burst of innovation. Which, of course, explained the sudden flow of information to the Service and its assets; the fact that *we* were there at all.

To prosecute these jobs, the Service usually relied on information from a recent escapee or a traitor in situ. But in this instance, our sources were said to be emancipated servants. And that was unheard of. Unnerving, really. Because criminal clans didn't release slaves from bondage – they murdered them. Which meant we were dealing here with either a momentary lapse of rigour or some sort of idiosyncrasy. There was a whiff of madness in it. Slaying redundant staff and vassals – this wasn't just a matter of security and economy for these people. It was culture. Tradition.

Evil bastards are predictable, in their way. Not all of them, I admit, and not always. But *crazy* evil bastards? They're worse than weather.

I waited. In a funk of disgust and anxiety. And did what I could to hold my nerve. But by then I was convinced that we'd been sent into a situation that was beyond ordinary. Turns out I was right. But it was years before I understood how extraordinary it was.

That third night, as I stared up at those crenellated slabs near the canyon rim, I concentrated on what a lair on such a scale really meant. What it might have taken to build. The genius behind it. But also, the suffering it embodied.

A fortress like this. Yes, it was something to despise. But if it was real, you had to acknowledge the prowess of such an accomplishment. The idea of it was daunting. The technical expertise, the engineering required. An entire rock wall – a hundred and fifty metres of it – hollowed out, honeycombed, reinforced, heated, cooled, furnished, victualled. Its existence was almost beyond comprehension. But the means of achieving it – that was even harder to come to terms with. Not just what it must have cost to fuel the great, belching machines that dug this lofty bunker, but the expenditure of bodies that would have toiled, stumbling and coughing in their wake, to get it done.

And to construct all this in strictest secrecy? To make it self-sufficient? And then to maintain total discretion afterwards? Every bondservant and labourer would need to be slain. If they weren't incinerated, their bones would have been mortared into the walls. All the talk of *blood and treasure* we heard about in Basic. This is what it meant. People ground to smuts, unknown, unseen, unremembered. And here is where it went. Into the luxury and safety of criminals. Slavers, poisoners, mass murderers, accomplices, collaborators.

Once we penetrated this place, if we ever did, I knew it would take grit to contend with what lay within that wall. The endurance required to get here and to wait it out like this was no small matter. But that was just physical courage. What we'd need on the inside was moral discipline. Self-governance. Something of a different order. Because there'd be sights in there that'd rattle us. Not even the most hardened operator was immune to the awe and dread the interior of a stronghold could trigger.

I'd already cautioned the crew about this. I couldn't know for certain, but for some it might be a new experience. This object, I told them. He's a man, not a god. Remember that. No matter what you see in there, remind yourself that there's no magic in him. For all his marvels and riches, he's no better than you. What is he but a creature hiding in a hole? He's not free. He's bound. By rock, by his past, by fear of the people, by terror at the prospect of justice.

I told them: *you*, comrades, you're still abroad, under the sky. With your crew, on behalf of free citizens. You've crossed lands and seas to reach him. You did it willingly, on principle, for the common good, for the honour of it. And once this job is done and he's mush, you'll be leaving for home. Free women and men. With your heads up. Compared to you, this poor bastard's nothing. And his trinkets are nothing. Okay?

I tell you now, I was sincere. I believed every word of it. And yet I was secretly spooked. Not by this prick's wealth and power. Or even his odious ancestry – at which I could only guess. No, what made me uneasy was the fearful enigma of his eccentricity. The weirdness he was giving off.

And yet, for all that, I admit that something about this idiot made me smile. Because if the intel *was* correct, we were promised a moment of comedy.

According to the brief, this gangster was addicted to tobacco. His weakness had been an open secret in the household for decades. And for years he'd promised his wife he'd quit – for the children's sake, for the health of the family. Everyone knows that stuff gives you cankers in the lung. Any peon could have told him that. Maybe some had. Not that they should care if he lived or died. Anyhow, by all accounts he'd given quitting the fags a red-hot go. Managed to taper down to almost nothing. And he'd declared to his wife that he'd conquered the habit altogether. But every evening, at 1945 hours, while the missus was occupied with putting the children to bed, he came up through the airlock and the blast door to step out onto his terrace. For a single durrie. As if, for all his need to prove himself a good father and a civilized man, he still couldn't let go of his last private vice. His secret manly power.

And *this*, comrade, was the detail upon which everything hung. The entire operation! The reason we'd crossed continents and seas to be there. And it was funny, afterwards, to think of him. Tangled up in his performance of virtue. For here was a man whose clan and trade and prodigious inheritance had helped asphyxiate half of life on earth. And now, for the sake of love, and clean air for his kids, he'd resolved to give up smoking. Nearly. Mostly. Almost! I mean, fuck me, brother. You don't find that funny?

No word of a lie, I was thinking exactly that when, bang on time – *finally* – he emerged. We all caught his heat signature in our scopes at the same moment. And incredibly, for a second or two, we all hesitated.

Because his flare was too big. The green flame of him was improbably wide. We all held for a few moments, waiting for the secondary flash of his cigarette, but that never came.

Then the heat signature split in two. Literally broke in half down the middle. So, now we had two discrete bodies up there. I was nonplussed. I hadn't anticipated a deviation.

The green plumes fused again. Jesus, I thought. Are they fighting or making love? Has she caught him out, or is she feeling frisky? Either way, they'd plainly forgotten themselves because they moved out, scuffling or maybe dancing, right to the parapet wall, where they were entirely exposed. Head and shoulders. Hot and clear. Crisp as you like. Looking out over our heads at God knows what. The world they'd left us with, I presume. Or maybe just their own deaths. Which were waiting for them, closer than they could know.

It was as if we were all mesmerized, even me. But the spell couldn't hold.

Our first salvo came in from the right flank, one of the women – Silver Teeth, I think – and that probably did the job on its own. The rest was just noise and mess, to be honest. Noise I hoped only we could hear. And a mess I knew we'd have to clean up in a hurry.

After about four seconds of engagement, there was silence and the rolling stink of ozone. We followed up with the gas immediately, cartridge after cartridge pooting away. After that I gave the order to secure the place. Two archers sent the graps up, ropes snaking behind them. The vanguard climbers put their masks on and got to work, and once the air cleared we followed to help process the bodies.

We bagged them, the object and his wife, and humped them down the hewn stone stairs into their lair. At the end of a narrow, blank-walled concourse was a blast door that stood ajar, and beyond that lay the shining halls of the bunker.

The first level of the installation – the living space – was a series of large, interconnected chambers. No windows or skylights, of course, and yet it didn't feel like a bunker. The floors gleamed. The furniture was plush, heavy, majestic. And despite the eggy taint of our gas, a characteristic citadel smell persisted. Remember that shiny scent? The otherworldly fug of perfumes, scorched meat and cleaning chemicals?

Looming from every wall, like views onto a fantastical realm, were enormous pictures. All bore the same peculiar sheen. The colours were fatty. Calorific. The contours soft. Redolent of impossible plenty.

In every frame, the human faces were pink and pillowy. Most prominent, initially, were the portraits of our object and his family. These were unsettling to walk past. Especially with their disarticulated bodies hanging from our shoulders in bags. Both adults were sleek and fair. Well fed, but not heavy. And very handsome. Startlingly so. With an expression you don't see much anymore, except in the faces of those whose minds are broken. Satisfied? Content?

Serene, I suppose, is the word. The children were rosy, wide-eyed, and fair like their parents. No sun scars, no white scab, no lesions. Teeth like milky, polished quartz.

Eerie to behold, naturally, but not nearly as discomfiting as the views of waterfalls, forests and corals that followed. These were dangerously discombobulating. Huge gleaming sea creatures. Beasts of the savannah with enormous, glistening eyes. Everything in view was prodigious or so close you felt as if you'd fallen into the image by some dark magic. Gigantic insects spread their many legs over foliage so intensely green it made you queasy. There was an image of a plant with leaves as big as dinner plates, and from those convex pads hung glistening pendants of moisture that brimmed with gentle light. All these stood in glass sheaths three or four metres tall. I hadn't seen stuff of that order since Induction and Basic. And never at such scale and proximity. It made my head swim and my feet heavy. And I wasn't the only one. The whole crew had come to a gawking, blinking standstill.

Enough! I barked at myself as much as the others. Clock's running!

I sent four operators ahead to find the sleeping quarters while the fifth helped me survey the office space, the library, kitchen, dining hall and a freezer full of meat, documenting the tech and collecting docs. I found two comms devices, but they were beyond my ken, so I bagged them out of precaution and pressed on. It would have been faster work – and safer – with a set of blueprints, or even a basic floor plan, but our intel had not extended that far.

By the time I got to the sleeping quarters the children had already been located and bagged. They'd died in their beds. The gas. Their rooms were bristling with toys whose polymers were bright and glossy. Their walls were covered in images of legendary creatures and windswept beaches. To prevent anyone getting moony, I hustled the crew out in search of the installation's disposal facilities. But I needn't have worried. Compared to the fixtures and devices, the kids were of small interest to them. As they left in search of access to the lower levels, I reminded them of the standing orders on looting.

I stood alone for a moment in the opulence of a bathroom. I didn't feel the impulse to take anything for myself. But I'd have forsaken all the swag on offer in that place for half an hour in one of those black marble tubs. To lather up with the soaps that smelt of my growhouse. To lie back in hot water. Or pick blisters off my feet in peace. But there wasn't even time for a change of diaper.

When I caught up with them, the crew had found the inner concourse. At the stairwell, we surveyed the level below. The physical exercise facilities, the provisioning cells and the enormous growhouse which used a soil-free system like Sun's, only on a scale and a level of sophistication beyond anything I'd encountered before.

Then, still humping the body bags, we were down to a third level – the service spaces – in search of the disposal facility.

I'm sure you were in remote outposts like that. There was always a compactor, right? And sometimes an incinerator. Thankfully, this place had both. As you know, the Service required some objects to be expunged entirely so that nothing – no relic or fetish – could be made of their remains. This case was one of those. On this point, our orders were insistent. And I guess that should have alerted me to the high likelihood that this was no ordinary job. But by then I didn't care who we were turning into bricks of ash that day. I just wanted to get it done and get out.

It was quick work. The easiest part of the job. Four hot, mealy ingots. Two large, two small. Which we dumped onto the floor like failed loaves. And left.

From there we fanned out to scope the rest of the services level as ordered. We needed to confirm the absence of subterranean egress, though by that stage it seemed to me there was little point in having such information. We moved through ventilation. Water supply. Power.

And then we found a hatch in the floor the size of a bed. My hackles went up. I ordered full readiness. And we stood back as two operators slowly, carefully, prised it open.

I didn't know what to expect. And we had to be prepared for anything. But gas is heavier than air. It sinks. And that hatch had no better seal than any other in the facility. So it hardly seemed possible anyone could be holding out down there. But this installation was a labyrinth. And although it was only home to four, it was large enough to shelter eighty souls. If there were others holding out, this was where they'd be. But surely they'd be dead too. Wouldn't they?

We tilted the trapdoor back. Peered down carefully into the cavernous vault. It was lit. We called out. Heard nothing. I considered dropping in more gas. But waiting for it to disperse would cost us time we couldn't afford. So I sent Silver Teeth in. And Spanish to back her up. Within seconds they gave the all-clear. There was no one down there, dead or alive.

This is how we finally confirmed the lack of escape routes. And how we found the ancient generators and boilers entombed like forgotten hostages. They were enormous. The size of small houses. Surrounded by gangways and ladders. All their joints and moving parts still gleaming with grease. Rivet heads like fists. Cables as thick as an operator's arm. They were sinister looking. Also breathtaking. To stand beneath them in that great crypt was menacing. The whole place stank of something noxious and oily. In a separate bunker, through a blast door, we found the reservoirs. Steel cisterns marked DIESEL. Others stamped LPG.

I wanted to document all this, but we couldn't linger. Heading out, I thought of the tech that had replaced these behemoths. The batteries upstairs were magnificent. Massive H-packs. Beyond anything available to us. It seemed a shame, almost a crime, to destroy them. There wasn't time now to go up and inspect the size and quality of the solar array, or even the landing pad, but it was clear the kit here could have powered thousands of hamlets and cooled countless compounds.

On the way up, passing back through the services level at a jog, we almost missed the piggery. Whose existence explained the vast store of meat preserved in the freezer room on the floor above. The door to the animals' chamber was sealed against odour and noise. Nevertheless, the pigs had not survived the gas. They were heaped in a pyramid at one end of the room. None of my operators had ever seen a pig before.

So there was plenty to think about as we worked our way back to the habitation level. This was a citadel of great age. And what we'd seen confirmed our intel. The place and its denizens had undergone a recent change in circumstance. An innovation of some sort had taken hold.

The piggery suggested an unusual degree of self-reliance. And confirmed what Intel had told us. In recent months there'd been no resupply to this place. No provisioning by air. And no defensive posture at all. Every bit of which was hard to credit. And yet the evidence was right here before us.

This place – I was only guessing, but it seemed possible it had been built before the Terror. Perhaps long before. Clearly, it had stood for many generations. And over that time hundreds of cartel types and vassals – probably thousands – had lived and been born and died here, in safety or in servitude, all of them in seclusion. The clan could only have survived because of its vast wealth, its far-reaching networks, and a culture of unyielding ruthlessness. And this is what was so confounding. Within these adamantine walls, someone had changed course. It was as if this object and his wife had spurned the succour of their own bloodlines and tribal webs to go it alone. Was this a kind of moral surrender? A symptom of exhaustion? After all, liberty of this sort was hardly different to incarceration. Or had this bloke decided he was immortal? Maybe he'd simply lost his mind.

I was fascinated – troubled, really – but I didn't have time to think it through, because, level by level, I had to oversee the laying of charges and keep the crew moving upward toward our exit point.

Back in the living quarters, we provisioned as we could, taking only food and water. With a thirty-hour hike ahead of us, we were down to just a handful of protein stems. Needless to say, no meat was taken, nor any other edibles we couldn't safely identify.

Then, with the last mines set, I mustered everyone back up on the terrace for the rappel down the cliff face.

The exit went smoothly.

It was dark out there. The rock face was cooling rapidly.

Once we set down and broke clear, unburdened by ropes and climbing kit, we were lighter across the ground. We ran as hard and straight as we could but, even with night glasses on, the footing was unstable and getting clear quickly was no easy matter.

We were halfway across the canyon floor when the charges went live. The shockwave scraped us off our feet. I went skidding forward like a tumbleweed. Bounced once, twice – slammed into boulders, other bodies. Picked myself up. And as a hail of grit rained down in the dark around us, I counted heads. All good. We set out for the canyon mouth, the watermaker, and hopefully a clean extraction.

By night's end we were away from the canyons and out in gibber country. Tired, slowing a little, though still working our evasion patterns with discipline. I felt we were sound. Was glad we were moving. But knew we were basically unsafe. Bad enough to be out in the open, without cover or air support. But the ground we were traversing was low. The sky was muddy. I worried about weather. I didn't want to drown out there.

When the light came up, it looked bad. Sullen sky. The creepy feeling of being watched. And the knowledge that our extraction window was closing.

As the morning progressed, the heat intensified. And just before noon, everything got much worse. Spanish put her leg down a sinkhole. To her great credit, she never made a sound. All we heard was the snap of bone. So the rest of us dug in and covered up long enough to splint her. She was one hardy operator. At the worst moment, as we closed the ragged hinge of her tibia, she whispered something fierce I didn't understand.

Silver Teeth winced.

You don't wanna know, she said, glancing away.

I clasped Spanish's arm to show my respect, stiffen her resolve, but she was out.

I called a two-hour halt. Issued water and food. Set the maker going for the next stop.

We resumed in the full heat of afternoon. I wouldn't normally try it, but by then we had no alternative. Porting our casualty was costing us twice the effort for half the speed. Spanish was mercifully small, but it was still two hours after nightfall before we reached the ash field. That put us just short of halfway. I called a rest there and watered the company again. I could feel our chances fading with every hour, but if the weather held, I thought there was still a possibility I could get us all past that powder ground and set the beacon at the uplift point.

When the first rumble of thunder rolled in across the plain, we were up on our feet again, still rolling up lattice web and savouring our last sips of water. I ordered masks on. And we ran. But I already knew there was no hope now of getting six of us to the outpoint alive.

As we lurched along, the ash billowed up from beneath our feet. There was higher and harder ground ahead. Reaching it was a long shot, but if this system turned to rain, we'd be swept away and drowned. What we needed was some elevation. Even if it didn't rain we were in desperate trouble. On an ash field this big, with drifts so deep, a decent squall would suffocate us, gas masks or not. Still, I wasn't about to let us lie down and take it.

As the dark contusion of the storm bore down, we took turns hustling Spanish across the powder dunes, grunting, heaving, grabbing at loose kit, stumbling, staggering on. She was staunch, but also often unconscious. Which was a mercy for her, no doubt, if not for her comrades.

We didn't make the plateau.

Once the first slamming gusts were upon us, I called a halt. And as we phalanxed hurriedly, the sky looked and sounded like it was tearing itself apart. With only groundsheets, camo nets and gas masks, we covered up best we could and lashed ourselves together.

It was a dry storm. But those katabatic winds were mighty. Hours of them. Hours we couldn't afford. The noise was unearthly. The sound of pure suffering. As if something were unwinding, prolapsing catastrophically around us. That's all I could think of. While I was still capable of thinking. The world is pushing itself through its own arsehole. It's angry. And afraid. And here I am, in its path.

When I came to, I was in a grey fog, as if my night glasses had failed. I was pressed into a snarl of limbs and kit, my head cocooned within a pocket formed by what was left of my groundsheet. And as soon as I moved, I dislodged an avalanche of ash that set me gagging and flailing. I remembered to unstrap myself from the others, and eventually fought free. When I surfaced, I saw it was morning. I ripped the mask off, and the glasses with them. In every direction, a stippled field of grey. Moguls of ash whose new peaks were gilded by sunlight. I coughed until I thought my ribs would break. And once I had the strength and the presence of mind, I hoisted the others out of the drift and did what I could to clear their airways. But only Spanish responded. I gave her the last of the water. She passed out again. The maker was nowhere to be seen. I strapped her on. Left the rest of the company where they lay.

It took me the rest of the day to haul her up onto the plateau. The going was better on hard ground, but I was quickly juicing out. I think, best I can tell, I managed to make it another five klicks or so. It was hot, and I had neither films nor blankets to shade us. The signal beacon was gone. Likewise my helmet and goggles. When I finally fell, I knew there'd be no getting up again. I was facedown in scalding dirt. And when I unlashed myself and crawled out from under Spanish, I had nothing left. I felt a peculiar equanimity. No distress. Just acceptance. The young woman's face was blistered already. She was delirious. I shaded her, as best I could, with my own body. But there wasn't much I could do. For either of us. We were a long way short of our uplift point. And without water or shelter, I didn't expect to see the sunset. I think I stopped caring.

We were out there for hours. That's the consensus. But I don't recall much of it. Except the very end.

The uncanny shadow. That's all I have. The only clear shred of memory that's stayed with me. Something enormous, some animal, perhaps. Suddenly present. Rippling over the contours ahead of us.

Some vast boneless beast carpeting over the land, truffling in sediment, like the legendary sea creatures my father had tried to draw.

It was mesmerizing. For a while – a few moments or maybe minutes – I was convinced that this was my own death arriving. I lifted my head. To greet it. With relief, I think. And yes, I see the joke. Because at that moment I elevated my gaze. Quite literally. To see the stat looming above us. Impossibly, unaccountably there. Where, strictly speaking, it should not be. For despite the directive, the comrades had come looking for us. Into territory over which they were not meant to fly. And I stared in wonder. Like a man who'd never beheld such a marvel. The stat was sleek, clean, glinting, growing ever larger, humming and yawing, drawing close until it manifested faces, hatches, tumbling tethers. And when it finally spilled its shade across me, I felt the holy chill of deliverance.

I was aloft before they even got to me.


Spanish lost that leg in the end. Sepsis. Killed herself in a field hospital. And I was angry about that for a while. But I understand why she did it.

I was five weeks getting home. Hospital. Debrief. Repat.

I had no idea what we'd done. Who we'd acquitted. And at the time, given the shape I was in, I couldn't have cared less. Not even if they'd told me. As far as I was concerned, I'd done my bit. Removed our object. And now I was going home.

That's some show, says the bowman.

Yeah, I murmur.

Fucking weather. I think it killed more good people than all their bastard mercenaries and machines.

Probably.

I saw some horrible deaths in my time. People gassed, stabbed, set on fire. But the weather deaths. They were the worst.

Please, I say. The kid.

She's asleep. Anyway, you think your little yarn's any sort of bed-time story?

I don't want her frightened. She's been through enough.

He grunts.

Heat's the worst way to go.

I nod, letting him talk.

But suffocation. Jesus, that's no fun. Bloody common, though, eh? Smoke. Crushed by rubble. And drowning – that's just another form of suffocation. Am I right?

I nod again and sigh inwardly. He's one of those. A type so familiar at muster points and on long repatriations. The old stager who catalogues death the way others talk about food. But I let him rattle on, glad of the chance to rest and get my breath.

But not all wet deaths involve drowning, right? he says, not pausing for an answer. I've seen people lost to torrents. Beaten to death by flood debris before they even had a chance to drown. But that's nothing. You and me, we've seen humans destroyed in ways ordinary folk wouldn't understand, wouldn't credit. Average citizen had no idea. But now it's every man for himself.

To this I say nothing.

Lightning, he says. That'd be quick at least. Gone in one mighty crack. They say bleeding out isn't so bad. Watched plenty go that way. Better than screaming and wailing like a baby from the fucking heat.

Yes, I say despite myself.

But every man wants to die in his bed surrounded by his children, right? That's what you're dreaming up, by the looks. It's a fucking pipedream.

I don't see why it should be, I murmur. A decent life. I'm not finished hoping for that.

He smiles scornfully and surveys me for a long while. I return his gaze as evenly as I can. Long enough to see his mind working.

So that job, he says. You really didn't know?

No, I say. Not for a long time.

But you could tell it was big.

Yes. I sensed it was a major caper. But I had no idea how big until later.

He gets up, stretches, sits down again.

We could make something here, I say.

Fly the flag for decency, eh?

Something like that. I've still got the juice for it. I'm hoping you do too.

I don't know you, he says.

And I know nothing about you either. But I'm game if you are.

He sniffs. Still bent on doing the work, eh?

*The task changes. Do not be daunted.*

Ah. A bard *and* a scholar.

No, I say. Just a grower.

From the plains of Capricorn. Yeah, quite the story. Or maybe you're a bullshit artist trying to make it through the night.

If I was, would you blame me?

Well, he said. It passes the time.

There's more, I say.

Of course there is.

It's always a strange thing, to see your country from the air. In a sense it's just like the way you imagined it might be. When you were a kid dreaming of being a bird. And yet it manages to look like somewhere you've never been. Coming back, seeing it after a long absence, this mixture of recognition and bewilderment is intensified. As you finally outlast the inexhaustible expanse of the sea, lose altitude, and feel the heat of rocks and sand buffeting the deck beneath your feet, the country below looks familiar in a way that's alienating, almost upsetting. I never felt it more keenly than in those last hours of the repat flight from the Utah job. Because for all the anticipation and relief at finally seeing it tilt into view, my homeland looked no different to the Alberta Badlands, or the blighted wastes of what used to be Federated Russia. And it jangled. How hard it was to distinguish from Utah.

When I was finally delivered to a muster point at the far western edge of the desert, I'd been gone nearly eight weeks. Someone – only hours before, judging by the tracks in the sand – had driven my rig to the rim of a dried-up well. Beside the ancient watering point, in a scatter of gibber, stood the ossified stump of a date palm. There was nothing on the trailer. No booty to bring home.

The trip back took three days. The going was hard, and even after the weeks of convalescence, I was still washed-out and jittery.

It takes a lot of juice to perform. For your comrades in the field, for the medicos in repat, and then for your loved ones in the aftermath. On a show, or for your handlers, you play the part of the hardy, anonymous operator. Capable, fearless. Your true self – your personality, memory, homeplace – all of it withheld. To keep that up, you're whirring like a dynamo day and night, awake and asleep. And when you get home there's a different role to play and other things to withhold. That's how you keep things safe. Safe for them. Safe from them. But the dissembling, comrade. Doesn't it burn you up.

On the road home I got the yips. Suddenly afraid of how I'd look, what I might say. And I was right to be worried. Sun and my mother seemed to register the state I was in before I even climbed down from the rig.

Sun just stared. She held me as if I were a cracked urn.

We were getting desperate, said my mother.

Malaria, I said. The city's rife with it.

But your face, said Sun. Your hands.

I was sick for a day or two before anyone found me.

In the open? In the street?

I'm a stranger, I guess.

But someone found you?

I don't remember. It's what they told me. At the clinic.

Malaria? said Sun.

Twenty days of rain. Before I got there. The streets were like open drains.

And the trees? Our grafts?

They barely covered the clinic.

Here, said my mother. Get him out of the sun.

They took an arm each and walked me into the shade at the foot of the stairs. From there we turned to mutely acknowledge the empty trailer. All I'd returned with was the tiny wedge of jasper Sun had sent me away with.

No matter, said my mother. You're home.

It took me the rest of that season to regain my strength. And although the remainder of the winter had its challenges, it was the beginning of a good period for me and Sun. She'd traded for a new flock of fowls in my absence and her hydro methods had increased our crop production substantially. The vet in town had moved away and now, on market days, hamlet folks sought Sun out for advice on their animals' ailments, and this brought extra trade. It was a while before I could work properly again. But gradually I took up my end of the labour. Even without my contribution, the combined output of the homestead had us prospering.

I revelled in Sun's company. Some cooler mornings, once I was strong enough, we hiked. A couple of times we drove back around the tip of the peninsula to explore the west coast and the hillocks of coral on the shore. We walked up through them into the rock shelter again, and sat in the shade to run our fingers through the midden like children hunting for gewgaws and trinkets. We brought home shells, cherts and the bones of animals, and spent many hours trying to identify them.

Sometimes at night, Sun would hold my face and peer into my eyes. Tender, but also diffident. Even sceptical.

One morning, when the air was thick and still, and my tunic was heavy with sweat, I grew dizzy. There was a roar in my head like the sound of battle. And I found myself on the floor of the growshed. Sun said it happened quickly. Without warning. I went down like something dumped off a truck. When she brought me inside, I was shivering and feverish. A feeling of dread overtook me, and then I knew exactly what it was. Sun laid me down, stripped me and bathed me. She cranked up the fans and bound me in wet towels. She packed a pipe, lit it, and set it to my lips.

As if she'd sensed something amiss, my mother appeared. She registered the pipe in my mouth with a frown. It was the middle of a workday.

A relapse? she whispered.

Perhaps, said Sun. But I don't think it's malaria. It's heat sickness.

The smoke was hot in my throat and the fatness of the heat set off tremors of foreboding that bordered on panic, until the feeling was blunted by the choof.

He's never had malaria, said Sun. Look at him. He's been cooked.

Well, said my mother evenly. Neither of us is a doctor.

I'm fine, I said. I'm better now.

Listen to him, said my mother with a chuckle as she left the house.

What is it? I said to Sun. You look angry.

I am. How could they let this happen to you?

I was a stranger there. Maybe they were afraid. Thought I was a madman or a drunk.

Not acceptable, she said, her lips quivering with emotion. Not remotely.

I'm sorry.

It's not you who should be sorry.

They're just people.

People are disappointing, she said, taking the pipe from me and stepping to the window to compose herself.

When summer came, we were in good shape to make the move below ground. Our spirits were high and supplies were sound, even if water margins were tighter than usual. In the two empty cisterns we'd established staggered crops of corn.

But there were many days of low wind and heavy cloud, so it was a challenge to maintain steady charge. By the end of December, after a long chain of tropical low-pressure systems, we were nursing our batteries, rationing the use of lights and pumps, saving whatever we could for a single fan. Now and then a dust storm rolled through to get the turbines turning, but these soon petered out to leave a barrage of dry lightning in their wake. For a few days a fire ignited by a ground strike burnt across the spinifex to the north of us, and we cracked the hatch at night to watch the glow with mounting apprehension, until at last a rainstorm arrived to extinguish it. And it's odd, but that reprieve caused us to let our guard down.

It rained again next day. Without force or drama. But long enough to top up our collecting cisterns. And the day after that, when a real dump arrived, we didn't recognize it for what it was. Because the build-up was so beautiful. The clouds looming in the north-eastern sky were like a troop of towering black figures, rootless, nomadic, seething, with faceless anvil-shaped heads. The spectacle left us more entranced than alarmed. We wasted a lot of time watching from the shelter hatch instead of preparing to defend ourselves against what was coming. Turned out we weren't the only ones.

Luckily, most of the hard work had been done already. At my mother's relentless insistence, we never went below at the beginning of summer without reinforcing the bund around the compound. We shuttered the winterhouses and drove the vehicles and trailers up onto loading ramps to spare them from being inundated. But with a cyclonic storm bearing down, we had barely enough time to dash out to ratchet everything down, lock off all awnings and reinforce the sandbag ramparts around our bunker.

The first new flickers of lightning were kicking off in the canyons as we raced back to set the vents and double-check our pumps and auxiliary batts.

In a way, that cyclone let us off lightly. The eye of the storm glanced off the tip of the peninsula, found hot water again and ploughed back out to sea. It made landfall again further south with wind speeds that were catastrophic. No, it wasn't the wind that did the damage locally. It was the tidal surge that ploughed in from the sea, pressed into the gulf and spilled through the seaward alleys of the hamlet. The wharf was badly damaged, and several houses were undermined and swept off their footings. People drowned in their cellars. Dozens of survivors lost their summer stores, and many reservoirs were tainted with seawater. But that was not the end of it. Because while the swell and wind and lightning moderated, the rain did not. It fell hard and unceasing for three days and nights.

It was hot below ground. We sat in the entry shaft to catch whatever cooling draughts rifled down, and once the wind abated we took turns to go up into the hatchway to watch the endless rain squalls barrel in. After the first day, glints of silver showed against the bluffs and crags of the range as water began to cascade from the heights. Then the wind died and the rain kept on. By the second day, the canyon mouths were gushing like dirty bores, spewing boulders and bones, scraping the dust of the plain up in a welter of mud as pink as melon juice. On day three, several homestead families drowned in their own bunkers, their plant and equipment swept away entirely. We only learnt this later, of course. But that same afternoon, once our storage cisterns had filled, including the two we'd reserved for growing corn, our bund gave way and the channels blew out. In a cataract of mud and stones, we got the hatch locked down and retreated from the streaming shaft.

In the hab we listened to the hum of the pumps and willed the batteries to hold out long enough to keep our heads above water. To save power, we sat in the dark. We only used our headlamps to check kit or prepare food. Most of the time there was nothing to be done but listen to the ominous rumble of water and the grind and crash of debris overhead.

Have you checked the bund? asked Sun mordantly during that first night as my mother slept in a far corner.

What bund would that be? I replied.

The one that just washed into the sea.

Oh, I said, *that* bund.

Look at you, she said, switching on her lamp.

What?

You're different.

Different in what way?

You're all sparked up. Your eyes are glittering.

You're a riot.

I'm serious.

You are? I said, alert.

This is what you're like before you go away.

Like what?

Sparky, she said. Jumpy, excited.

Oh? Really?

Something crashed against the hatch and both of us flinched as a shower of mud came down the shaft.

You come back home all shut down. As if you're going into hibernation.

I glanced at the dirty puddle forming in the shaft.

I'm not whining, she said. Just making an observation.

I need to check that, I said, getting up.

You don't need to hide from me.

Something's up, I said, rushing to the shaft.

The pumps were faltering. Moment to moment, I could hear their pitch change. And then, as I stood there, they fell quiet, one after the other.

Losing power! I yelled, pushing through to the battery locker where there was silence, but at least no smoke. Sun came after me to help switch over to the auxiliary bank. I got two pumps going again – the third was cooked. So now if the hatch seals blew out, or if it rained for another whole day, there was no guarantee we could keep ourselves from drowning. Without a break in the rain, or a big stretch of wind to stir the turbines, the reserve bank would not be sufficient.

You're worried, she said.

Not really.

I don't want to drown in here.

You won't.

I'd rather drown up there.

That's a plan, I said, glad to hear her laugh.

We stood there a moment, suspended, it seemed, as the pumps hummed and the canyon cobbles thudded against the hatches overhead. And then my mother appeared in the shaft, casting about with her lamp as if to find a shortfall for which she could offer a directive.

Everything's fine, I said.

We're holding?

Yes, said Sun. Holding.


The wind returned. The batts and pumps kicked on. And eventually the rain subsided.

As I said, we were lucky. But that storm left an unholy mess in its wake. We laboured for weeks in the steaming heat to restore the bund and reset our gates and posts. The houses and sheds held strong. One turbine was on its face, undermined, but all the panels of our array had stood the test. We wallowed in mud and debris to square things away, working slowly, in brief bursts, to save getting sick, and once we'd finished, the only enduring sign of the deluge was the buttress of canyon cobbles piled high against the loading ramp on which our vehicles and trailers had ridden out the flood.

After our labours in the perilous humidity, we lay depleted and somnolent in our bunker until the summer finally broke. And when it came time to emerge and prep the houses for the season up top, we were lethargic and low on stamina. I couldn't remember beginning a winter in such a diminished state.

For all that, and the lost corn and the work ahead to rebuild the levee, the homestead was still sound. Out beyond the winter quarters, parallel to the bunker, we had five cisterns. Each with a 50,000-litre capacity. And now every one of them was full. Whatever else happened, we had enough to drink and plenty to trade.

Not long after we moved upstairs, the plain burst into colour. Everywhere you looked was a puzzle of pink and yellow, blue and white. Tiny brown frogs emerged from the sodden earth. Broad puddles on the plain teemed with weird wrigglers, creatures with domes on their backs and scores of legs. And then mosquitoes descended on us, a storm of their own. Despite every tincture and ointment we made to keep them at bay, all three of us were left pocked with rashes and scabby sores, and my mother developed ulcers on her arms that Sun had to scrape and pack with mustard. Eventually, very slowly – and then quite abruptly – everything dried out, including our weals and wounds. The puddle crawlers desiccated and blew away. The frogs disappeared. And the plain returned to dust and silence.

For a while, in the wake of the flood, Sun seemed distant. More contained. Newly cautious at work and at large. At first I thought this inwardness was a form of resignation. I wondered if life with me had dimmed her flame, or whether the watchful presence of my mother had finally crushed her spirit. But it was something else.

Have you ever seen a child born? No? Dear God, comrade, you have no idea.

My mother must have known about the pregnancy before me. If Sun hadn't confided in her, I'm sure she would have sensed it. She had to have known. But in the surprise and joy of the revelation and the months of consuming excitement that led to the birth, and of course the momentous event itself, for which nothing on earth could have prepared me, all that seemed irrelevant.

We had a child. Delivered by my mother. Born under a full moon. On the deck. Sun was magnificent, a champion – staunch beyond all reckoning. The child emerged like a glistening marrow. And after my mother put a finger into her mouth and hooked out a plug of mucus, the little girl gave a cough and mewled for a moment with an expression of indignation. And so began the best years of my life.

We called her Ester. For the smell of sweet fruit. And for the warrior queen of the sagas. The name was Sun's idea. A child conceived underground and born under an open sky.

Before she'd even taken the breast, I held Ester to the heavens. Like a trophy. For reasons I still don't understand. Was it to show her the stars? Or to let the celestial bodies know she was here among us? This atavistic moment – I still can't tell if it was an act of homage, vanity or defiance. The women laughed at me, and I laughed with them, feeling sheepish, ridiculous, but incandescent.

Ester changed the atmosphere of the homestead. With her in our lives, the way we worked – all three of us – was different. I don't know how to explain it except to say we were all less dutiful. We were lighter in spirit. At times even frivolous. Everything she did, every sound and look she produced, brought delight. She seemed to blossom before our eyes. I loved the smell of her breath, the silkiness of her skin, her cross-eyed sobriety, the boundless novelty of her movements. She was our shared treasure.

Of course we were discreet about her advent in the hamlet. In the early months we rarely took her in. But we could hardly keep her a secret. Eventually she made appearances in the market, strapped to Sun like a wallaby in its pouch, another family face at the stall.

I could only assume the Service was observing all this. Because no pigeon came with a message for me all year. And I didn't miss field action for a moment. Never even thought about it much. I just grew comfortable with the way things were. As if this was my life now.

Ester was blessed with Sun's complexion, her smooth skin, dark hair, half-moon eyes and inky irises. As a babe, she was placid, sober, observant. Many times I sat to watch her feed and she'd survey me carefully with one eye while still busy at the nipple. Low on her back, and across her tiny buttocks, she had blue blotches, the Mongolian spot common to those whose heritage goes back to the Hermit Kingdom. Her cries were like the bleating of a hungry goat.

She grew teeth. Learnt to sit. In the shade of the house or the cool of the sandbox in the bunker, she'd run her fingers through the dirt and sieve up glinting stones and shells like plunder.

Her first season underground was a challenge. For all of us. But by the following winter, with the summer jaundice behind her, she was crawling. In the coolest mornings we let her play in the shade, and she loved the feel of the yielding dust and the grit between her fingers. Ester was enchanted by the world. I'd watch her from the stairs as she beetled along, scraping up loose mounds of dirt into caches, as if provisioning. And she ate the soil – perhaps all children do this – shovelling fistfuls into her mouth, expecting this paprika-red stuff to taste as sweet as it looked. What a picture she was, with her cap of black hair and those chubby limbs, her face running pink with drool.

She was a curious and strangely patient child. Once she was walking, she was stoic when she fell, which was often. In the grow-house, she'd follow us down the aisles, smelling and touching everything in its turn. Tasting, too. Anything red seemed irresist-ible. She loved the look of hot peppers – all those witchy fingers, glossy and wrinkled – and she quickly learnt the difference between a tomato and a chilli.

I can still see her shaking the moisture from columns of corn, fingering the thistle stumps and smooth ribs of okra. Collecting eggs alongside us, she was clumsy in her great displays of care. But she lingered most often amongst the tomatoes, seemed to luxuriate in the strange, hairy texture of their stems, stroking each plant in turn as if it were some furry creature redeemed from extinction. Later, up in the house, I'd catch her sniffing her fingers in astonishment that she'd somehow brought that green scent with her.

The growhouse was a work hall for all of us, but also a sanctuary. And I think Ester understood this instinctively, as if she'd been born with that secret apprehension, knowing somehow, in her body, that growing and feeding and blossoming and fruiting were sacred.

We took Ester to the canyons. We hiked on cool mornings to fossick in creekbeds and gullies in search of feathers, bones, signs of movement. I carried her on my shoulders as the chalky winter breeze raddled our hair and our hats and chilled the sweat in our tunics.

We shouted to hear our voices bounce and chime from wall to wall and laughed at the noise that rolled back over us.

My mother was at pains to leave Ester to Sun and me. But she watched her hungrily. And I felt for her. Such, I thought, was the nature of her sacrifice: to step back and give us this.

Ester was born into the last steady years. That's something to celebrate, not to mourn. Anyone who lives is lucky. But some are luckier than others. It's strange, you know, comrade, but despite all the hard things I've done, and those done to me, I don't feel cursed. I don't mean to sound like a skiting windbag, but the truth of it is, I feel blessed.

Would I feel different if Ester hadn't come along? I honestly couldn't tell you.

The summer that followed was milder than the one before. But it was not an easy season underground. By then, Ester was bridling at the confinement, and once she was mobile and beginning to talk, she was much harder to please and manage. It took the wiles and energies of all three adults to keep her occupied and safe. And for all our efforts to keep her cool and away from the killing sun, the lack of sunlight affected her mood as much as ours. What made everything worse was knowing the darkness was a threat to her growth. The hamlet was full of folks with bones like chalk and legs like hoops. The sun ate them in winter and the lack of it sapped them in summer.

When we came up out of the cellars for the new year and settled into a fresh season, it soon became evident we were working harder for less. Our seedlings were leggy and our birds listless. In the hamlet, fowls sickened. At the same time, an outbreak of scabies took hold amongst the people. Sun managed to help with the itching plague, but when she failed to cure their animals, folks gave up seeking her counsel at the market. Some of them began to politely shun her. She took this hard. Sun was a person of strong will. She wasn't used to defeat. Or the ways in which country folks react to the defeats of others. Trust is as fickle as weather. She seemed bewildered by the way people withdrew from her.

At home, we killed and chipped all our ailing birds. Ours and my mother's. The horrified child watching on at a distance. Without our surplus of water, oil and preserves, we would have fared badly that year.

It was a lean period. And this was when Sun began to grow distant again. At times she seemed to struggle with Ester's curiosity and her own impatience. The child had so many questions. And perhaps she could feel our disquiet. The undercurrents of anxiety we must have given off. Sun remained as competent as ever, but sometimes she looked as if she were in mourning. I wasn't sure of the loss, whether it was the regard of others or just her sense of self, the loss of power over her situation. I asked her about this. Repeatedly. Initially, she deflected, made light of her moods, or insisted there was no problem. Until, in the end, she refused to discuss it, cut me off before I could raise it again.

By the time the solstice came, I knew it was time to drive south and draw on our caches of salvage. Our water stores would keep us safe, but we needed other materials to trade. Yet I was reluctant to leave the homestead. I broached the idea of a foraging mission with Sun. Suggested she and Ester come along. But she demurred with a look of resignation that bordered on grief. She seemed depressed. I couldn't understand it.

And of course it occurred to me it might be best if I stayed. But I worried how things might stand come October. The idea of going back underground short of supplies – it frightened me. Sun refused to discuss it. And I couldn't bring myself to enlist my mother to help convince her I needed to go. In the end, I left in vexed silence.

Half a day down the highway, I came upon a roadtrain jackknifed in a scour off the shoulder of the road. My spirits were already low, but the sight of this set-up made my heart sink. I almost didn't pull over. But a woman jumped down from the cab and stood in the road and waved me in. Then she stepped up onto my running board.

Pull around behind, she called through the window.

I can't tow that rig, I said, smelling her sweat.

Not expecting you to. Look at the rear trailer.

I reversed a little way and saw what she meant. The third trailer was a low-loader.

I'll winch you on, she said.

Seriously?

I'm just the pigeon. I don't issue the orders.

Where are we going?

Elsewhere, she said flatly.

She got down while I manoeuvred into position. She dropped the ramp and, when I eased onto it, she hooked my bar and cranked me up. By the time I climbed out, she'd chained my truck and trailer to the anchor points. And while I watched from the roadside, she ran the shrouds around.

Climb up, she said, pointing to her cab.

An hour after sunset, I was in the air.

The job was a milk run. A delivery of materiel deep in the desert. I was back within two days, but the site we landed at wasn't the one I'd been mustered to. A few hours later, we lifted off again and flew south. We set down in the dark in the wilds beyond a port town on the southern coast. There I was transferred to another stat with a full action team that flew east, high over the deserts, all night, and the following day.

We ended up on an island in the Pacific. A mucksweat job in full suits. It was hellish hot out there. A highland stronghold. Straightforward, at least. No losses.

The whole time, I sensed I was being watched. And I was torn. Because I knew that if I acquitted myself well, my seasons at home would be fractured again. I'd be away from Sun and Ester much more than I wanted to be. But if I came up short, my days of active service might be done. And I didn't know how I could accept that.

On the repat run back from the islands, as we made landfall on the eastern coast, we came over low enough that I could see the field of light behind the walls of Sydney. The air stank of rotting refuse, bad water.

Jesus, I said to the operator beside me.

I could feel the turn of her head, hear the indrawn breath. It was as if she was just waiting for me – daring me – to say something disparaging.

Home?

She grunted. I felt the sudden rise in altitude in the pit of my belly as we climbed away again, out over the faintly spangled darkness of the interior.

It's a big island we come from, says the bowman.

I nod.

You were right to hold your tongue about Sydney.

You're from there? I ask.

People can't help where they're from. And nowadays, what does it matter, anyway?

I was thinking something like that, just now, I tell him. That we are where we find ourselves.

Deep, that.

I laugh.

But I'm serious, I tell him. I'm here, you're here. She's here. We have skills, training. We know what's right. If we make it work here, then we're from here. Don't you think?

Jesus, he says, you could trade water to a drowning man.

Comrade, I *am* a drowning man.

Ever see what a drowner does when someone gets close?

I've seen it. I understand.

You think this sorry tale will save you?

It's all I have.

Some blokes would trade her, he says, jerking his chin at the child.

Not me.

Not for your life?

Never. I know what's right. That's not gunna change. What about you, comrade?

I didn't give the best years of my life to become a fucking slaver.

I'll take that as a no, then?

You can take it and shove it up your arse.

I smiled. Couldn't help myself.

Anyway, he says. You have your own.

I don't reply.

I said you've got your own kid. The girl. The baby.

Had, I say.

When the stat lifted clear, I walked to my rig and inspected the load on the trailer. Packed into a crate the size of a small boat were sheets of laminated glass. I was already excited about going home. Now I was returning with matchless treasure.

I figured I was less than a day's run from our homestead. But concerned about the weight of my cargo, the strain on the axles, I took it much slower than I might have.

Which meant it was very late in the day when I finally saw the sails and glinting films of our compound in the distance. I pulled over. To gather myself – what I still thought of as my private and truest self. I was elated to be home. And thrilled to be bringing back such a windfall. But also daunted by the prospect of seeing Sun and Ester again. I feared Sun's wrath and Ester's dismay. Because I'd been gone some weeks. Much longer than I'd promised or expected.

I'd given a good performance for the Service. I'd convinced them of my worth once again. And yet I was tired of the duplicity. I felt I had no more to prove. I didn't need to do this anymore. In fact, on the slow haul up the peninsula I'd told myself that I couldn't and wouldn't. I needed to simplify my life. To just be myself. Not a rendition of myself. Least of all at home. I'd had the long repat flight to think this through, even before the drive, but it was now in this moment that my resolve hardened. I was done. Out. From here on, it was family first, family only. They deserved it. And so did I.

I don't know how long I sat there, geeing myself up. But the sun was on the ranges by then and, when I turned in, the dirt-smeared windscreen was milky. So I drove up blind, letting the truck feel its way in the ruts. I dropped the windows. Smelt the dust of home. Heard the clatter of my own homecoming announced to the compound ahead. Any moment now the women would emerge from the shade and come running.

But nobody stirred. No one appeared. Not at our house, nor at my mother's. Within the gauzy-walled growsheds, nothing moved. The hatch of the summer quarters stood open. The other rig and trailer were parked in the shade. The fork and quad too. Everything was in order. And yet the homestead felt becalmed.

I steered past my mother's place and pulled up in front of ours. After the noise of the road, the sudden quiet hissed in my ears. I got out. Mounted the stairs uncertainly. Called out. But before I even got halfway, the scalding rail of the balustrade in hand, I knew I was hailing an empty house. When I turned to gaze across the compound, my mother finally appeared on her verandah.

She gave a short, bleak wave. I sank onto the step, to spare myself the disgrace of falling.

This is hard, said my mother, setting food on the table with movements both economical and deliberate. It won't be easy to hear, and it's not easy to say.

I watched her set out the meal as she recounted the story. I couldn't understand how she could manage both tasks simultaneously. It was obscene. I hated her for it, that she could set down each terrible detail alongside the food she was laying out. A bowl of chilli beans. Corn fritters. A salad of tomatoes, olives, chives.

What she was saying made no sense. It wasn't that I didn't think Sun could do such a thing. Even though the idea of it burnt me to the core. I'd always sensed she felt constrained by homestead life. And was probably stifled – even bored – by being yoked to a man with a lesser mind, and who was only ever semi-present even when he was around. On top of that, she'd been compelled to share most of what we had with my mother. Some part of me had already recognized it as inevitable. There was also the strange turn things had taken in the hamlet. Her feeling of having been shunned. I could see how that could have broken her spirit, caused her to flee. But the story my mother told? It was ridiculous. It was too absurd. And I said so.

If you'd told me this story yourself, she said, I would've thought the same.

How could she believe this? It's just mindless gossip.

I'm sure that in normal circumstances she wouldn't have, she said judiciously. But you've been gone a long time. She was vulnerable.

But who? I asked. Who'd suggest such a thing? Who'd dare put it about?

No idea. She wouldn't say. Some dolt from the hamlet, I imagine. And others who might listen.

You discussed it with her?

Of course, she said. She was very distressed – that much was obvious. I just wish she'd confided in me sooner. But by the time she finally did, the story had already taken root. By then she was beyond reasoning with.

You hadn't noticed anything? Before?

As I said, I wish I'd been more perceptive. Acted more promptly. Because, yes, I think it's fair to say a certain distance had developed. But that wasn't new. I think you know that. You must have noticed. You felt it last summer, surely?

Not really, I lied. But it was a hard season. The heat was making us all crazy.

It's difficult when a partner works away.

But I stayed home especially, I said, shamed by my querulous tone. I was here right up to the solstice.

I know that.

I should've paid more attention.

I feel the same. But it's no easy thing, keeping tabs on a spirit as wild as Sun. A woman like that does not want to be cossetted. Or confined. Or even managed. I would have felt no differently. I never had to live with in-laws. And I was born into this district. I wasn't required to seek acceptance, ingratiate myself.

She sat at the table. Considered me a moment. Then began to eat.

The sight of it felt indecent. It was dark by then and a hot wind was tugging at the shades. I got up, prowled around the room, sat down again.

Did you see her leave?

Yes, she said, setting aside her fork. And no. I came up from the cisterns and saw a road freighter leaving the compound.

You didn't hear it show up?

The pumps, she said. It's noisy down there.

What time of day was this?

Dawn.

And when?

Two weeks ago.

Jesus. Did she say nothing at all?

Sun was very circumspect with me.

Well, I said with a little bitterness. Everyone's careful with you.

Something you've never complained about before.

I'm not complaining now.

You know, living out here. It was never easy for her.

But she's good at it, I said, sounding callow. I thought she liked it.

It gets lonely. Especially if you're from the south, when that's all you've known.

I shook my head. Placed my hands on the table. Stared at them.

Think of it, she said. She's isolated. Lonely. Pining. And then she hears this talk.

It's rubbish. How could she believe it? Do *you* believe it?

People get worn down by gossip.

Was she going into the hamlet a lot?

Well, more than was good for her, I'd say. But I was never in a position to give Sun instructions. Hard enough to give her advice.

It's wicked, I said.

Not everybody in the hamlet is as busy as us, she said. *Idle hands will weave only evil.*

But she must know it's not true.

If she thought it wasn't true, she wouldn't have left.

You discussed it.

Yes. A day or two before she left.

And she told you about this other family I'm supposed to have?

Yes, she was fixated on it.

Christ, I spat. What family? Who are these people, who is this other woman?

My mother flinched a little, drew back. She let a moment or two pass, and the tone of her reply was forbearing, patient in a way that bordered on the forensic.

I'm simply relaying what she said to me, what she'd been told. This tale. About some place in the south you go to when you're away. It was all rather tawdry. The suggestion being that your salvage work is some kind of shabby excuse.

For what, adultery?

Bigamy.

How could she believe that? Why would I do that? Sun's enough for me. She's the only one I want.

My mother ran her hand over her cropped hair, as if to steady herself.

She did say you'd changed, she said softly. Gone into yourself.

You think I have?

It's not for me to say.

I thought it was her. That she was sad.

People do things that surprise us, she said. They surprise themselves. Things are not always as they seem.

What about you? I said. Can you really believe I'd do what they're saying? Do you imagine this story is true?

The point is that Sun seems to think so.

No, I said. She's smarter than that!

Pain and panic make us stupid. You must know that.

I waved her away. I didn't want to hear it.

There *is* no other family, I said. Only this.

Well, she murmured.

Whatever *this* is now.

She pressed her lips together, said nothing.

For a while there was an exhausted quiet between us. The wind goaded the awnings. The house doled out its stoic creaks.

My daughter.

Yes. It's painful.

Sun will be looking for her parents, I said.

Possibly.

I know it.

Listen to me, she said with a calm ferocity that set me back in my chair. Don't go after her. Do not pursue her. Nobody wants to be hunted.

What if she expects it?

No woman wants to be stalked. If she comes back, it'll be on her own terms.

Maybe she went looking for this other family, this imaginary woman, I said.

Well, if they don't exist, she'll be a long time searching.

*If?*

Son, I believe you. But I'm telling you. Don't go.

I have to!

Look at the state of you! You're in shock. You're not fit to go anywhere.

For pity's sake, I cried. How can this happen? How am I supposed to bear it?

People leave, she said. People die. They abandon us. We go on.

*You* go on.

She looked at her hands, her mouth set hard.

I'm sorry, I said. I apologize.

She nodded. And I felt a sudden loss of purchase. As if I was bogged in soft ground. I could hear the blood beating in my head. The wind peppering dust against the tin walls. I sat blinking, chewing the air. Until, at last, I began to weep.

At first there was a kind of relief in it. But soon it felt as violent and convulsive as vomiting, every fresh spasm as painful as it was degrading.

My mother kept her seat, offered no consolation, and for that, at least, I was grateful.

She'd been the sole constant in my life. But I hardly knew my mother at all. She lived on the plain in full view, right beside me, but I never really saw her. Sun was made of tougher stuff than me. Probably had to be. And I have no doubt she saw things in my mother I never could. Which means that all those early years as an operator and a husband, while I thought of myself as a man, I was living and thinking as a boy.

For several days after my return, I did little more than lie on my bed. I couldn't eat, didn't work. My thoughts were feverish and hectic. I sensed my mother coming and going from the sheds below but paid no attention.

I woke one afternoon to see her in the doorway.

Enough of this, she said. Tomorrow's market day.

I can't, I croaked.

Neither of us has a choice. We need supplies, we have to trade. And you need to show yourself in the hamlet.

As what? I said. A joke?

You can't hide out here the rest of your life.

She'll be back.

Perhaps. But you can't lie here until then. We have two sheds of surplus to deal with. I'll be picking all tonight. In the morning, you'll take it in. We're shorthanded now and summer's not far off.

I can't.

You don't have a choice.

You can't make me.

But she could. And she did. The weight of my grief was no match for her will. Next morning, she hauled me out of bed in the dark.

I hated her for making me go. On that market day and those to follow. And she was right. We had surplus to manage, and we needed to build up a buffer for the turn of the season. But I wasn't just there to trade. My presence in the hamlet was another performance. On behalf of the family. To show local citizens that all was well with our homestead. Yes, trouble had befallen us, a whiff of scandal lingered, but we were the same solid, reliable people we'd always been. My task – my role – was to brazen it out. Remind hamlet folks of how formidable we were in the face of adversity.

All of which was easier in the conception than the execution. I dreaded the prospect of whispering in the square. The sly grins, raised eyebrows. But I soon saw there'd be none of that. It's hard to parse people's expressions under skirted hats and scarves, but I could detect no judgement or ridicule in the townsfolk. That's not to say that behind the armour of their civility they were well disposed toward me. Even as I stood there trying to seem nonchalant. Because there's a fine line between judiciousness and indifference. But the locals restricted their attention exclusively to the produce on display, so in the end I had little to fear. This wasn't the first time our work became our best defence. Within the district, we remained indispensable.

Every week the stall was busy. And though there was a steady stream of transactions, there was never much conversation. Which for me was unremarkable. Back then I never said much.

On market days I stayed clear of the civil shelter. No Service asset approached me. No pigeon came by.

At home, I worked the sheds and did my chores, tracing the patterns of the old routine like a sleepwalker. And all that time I told myself, as my mother kept insisting, that this would pass, that I was doing better every day, when in fact the opposite was true.

One market day I arrived home to find a completely new solar array bolted to the footings of the old one. Whose panels were stacked and lashed in the shade of my undercroft. In the very spot I'd been storing our cache of glass. Which, of course, was nowhere to be seen. I should have been thunderstruck. Outraged at not having being consulted. But I felt almost nothing. No rage. Not even any curiosity. Just a mild irritation and a sudden need to lie down.

As the season waned, I fell apart. Slowly and incrementally at first, in the way of any cataclysm, and then completely and all of a sudden. My days of dusty-headed numbness were fractured by irruptions of unfocused rage. And with the summer so close, and the work of growing and picking and packing intensifying, I struggled to manage the simple roster of tasks required. Things I'd been able to do since I was a boy became onerous, too complex. It wasn't that I spent every living hour thinking of Sun and Ester. A lot of the time I was unable to think at all. Or I'd get snagged on a single banal detail, like the glossy black hairs I kept finding around the house or inside my produce crates. No matter how fiercely I swept, they kept turning up. Until I began to suspect someone was salting them about the place. And there was only my mother to suspect. Which was insane. After a while I made myself ignore them. But then I began to imagine the floors darkening with drifts of hair that I'd eventually need to wade through, and even be suffocated by. Which is to say, of course, that my mind got away from me.

Everything got too hard. Including getting out of bed. I understood, dimly, that apathy like this was dangerous. Not just for me, but for my mother, who had to pick up the slack. I was putting us both at risk. Our only buffer against starvation underground was a solid surplus, preserved and stored, and I was frittering away the most critical weeks of the season. And yet I couldn't make myself care. Mornings stretched into afternoons during which I did nothing more than observe the turning of the fan overhead. I heard my mother come and go, grinding mulch, shovelling out trays and harvesting produce. She came into my house to cook and clean. She made repeated and sometimes vigorous attempts to get through to me. But eventually I was beyond reaching. And by then I'd lost all sense of obligation. I wasn't even embarrassed. The virtues I'd been raised on – pride in competence and self-sufficiency – were suddenly meaningless. Even the house I'd built with my own hands signified nothing to me. And as the season came to an end, I got worse. What began as lassitude had devolved into a kind of madness. And, in the middle of all that, my mother had no choice but to take me underground.

I don't really know which of us she sought to protect by doing so, but afterwards she never spoke about that summer. Never shared what it was like to be trapped down there with me in such a state. I could guess, I suppose. But to be frank, it still gives me the horrors to think about it. She was forced to merge our crops. I know that much. Unassisted, she had to consolidate, pick, and preserve any produce she couldn't trade. Then she was left to haul our combined holdings and all my portable possessions underground and drag me down the ladder into the hab.

I don't want to imagine the wild and hurtful things I must have said to her during that season in hell. I hate to even think about it. But I know it must have been very frightening for her. If I ever blurted anything to compromise the Service, she never alluded to it. I know I was out of my mind. I'm in no doubt about that. I said as much afterwards, and my mother did not contradict me. But neither did she want to speak of it.

The most distinct memory I have of that terrible summer was not below ground. It was out in the open. See, there was a night when I got free somehow. I must have taken myself up through the hatch. I remember walking barefoot across the hot gibber in the dark. My mother trailing behind like a spectre. Dogging me without actively chasing. She didn't try to coax me back to the bunker. Maybe I was expecting her to, I don't know.

I have no idea of what I was attempting, where I thought I was going. I think I was naked. Standing amidst the rows of our new array. And I remember looking up. Seeing the sudden hole in the sky where the dirty cloud drew back like an opening mouth. Until I saw its teeth, the pearly mess of stars within. They wavered, as if the mouth of the sky wanted to eat me. Maybe it was speaking to me. But I heard nothing. I craned my neck, tried harder, but no sound came, no message arrived.

By February, things came to seem more orderly, more coherent, and I began, very slowly, to function again. My progress was fitful. Still, I could sense order returning. I felt cauterized, if not quite restored. But eventually I was well enough to do simple tasks, to follow a routine and pay attention to my mother's deliberations about next steps.

In late April, we came up into the open in a kind of détente. Returned to our separate winterhouses. And resumed something resembling our old life.

And although I could sense my mother's relief, she remained watchful. In the evenings we'd share a meal and mend kit or clothes together. To me she seemed settled, even content. But I was not. No matter what I did, despite any reassurance she offered, I couldn't be convinced that the life I'd re-entered was anything like the one I'd had before. So although I was quickly back to performing the part of the doughty homesteader, the stable, competent son, it was all a front.

In secret, I was seized by fantasies of loading up and hitting the road to go in search of Sun and Ester. But the events of summer had scarred me. The idea of descending once more into that madness was enough to keep me home. And I knew my mother was right. Nobody wants to be hunted after fleeing, especially not when they're raw. Leaving could not have been easy for Sun. I didn't want to hound her and make things worse. I loved her. I didn't want her to suffer. Nor did I want her to see me as I'd so recently been. So I resolved to get solid again, to manage myself, bide my time, see what opportunities arose. Life is long, I told myself. Which is the sort of thing a young man will tell himself. And who can blame him?

The summer I wigged out, the monsoon failed. Entirely. No storms, no rain. In the sagas, ancient folk would have seen a connection here, as if one misfortune foreshadowed another, or even begat it. I was still loopy enough to wonder if I'd killed the rains, but no longer sufficiently ill to entertain such a notion for long. The fact is that when we came up that year, the earth felt glazed. Right into May the air felt hard. Baked into crystals. Weaponized by any breeze.

In my uncertain state, I didn't know what to make of the hostility in the air around us. And I was puzzled at how differently my mother responded to these same conditions. If anything, she seemed energized. And now I wonder if perhaps she was performing too. Doing what she could to lead by example. Or maybe the enthusiasm with which we she threw herself into the new season was a way to leave the horrors of summer behind.

It was the first time I saw her make an error. She was never one to mistake folly for boldness. Which shows how much recent events had affected her. For once in her life, she succumbed to wishful thinking.

She was determined to acquire another flock of laying fowls. I was sceptical. Leery of the weather. And didn't welcome the prospect of more work. But, conscious of my probationary status, and anxious to seem amenable, I agreed to her plan, and soon we had birds again. But it didn't last long.

In the last week of May, a heat dome rolled in from the east. It was as if the breath of the five deserts had settled over us. For several days there was hardly any breeze, just this cell of heavy, immoveable, superheated air. It sent the afternoon temperature into the mid-fifties, like a summer's day. It began to feel like an occupation. As if a new dispensation had come to stay. But then a wind got up. Bringing no relief. It was desolate. Fiery. Hard. So laced with grit, it battered your skin through your clothes till you danced and yelped. It blasted the walls and tore at the sails. Our houses yanked and groaned at their moorings.

Soon it was impossible to leave shelter. Even under the cowls, leafy greens began to wilt. And so did our birds. We'd shuttered the flock on the first day, but as the heat lingered and the wind intensified, you could hear their low keening from the house. It was the sound of a single suffering creature. At night, when it was safest to go down, we misted them to keep them alive, but you could see their wattles shrivelling. And the way they gulped, wide-eyed – it was as if the air had become too hot and thick to breathe.

Our plants fared no better. In the growsheds, manes of corn silk were rippling and crisping in the heat. On the last night before the lightning arrived, I walked the aisles feeling flayed and sore, hand-watering pods and binding stems in wet rags as brittle threads of corn silk and dried seedheads lashed my face and neck. The tomatoes slumped on their stakes like the aftermath of a mass execution. The air began to taste of salt and soon it smelt, sickeningly, of ozone. No need to explain what that smell means to the likes of us.

When the first cracks came down in the east, I rushed to the door and saw a light in the compound. Another flash revealed my mother running. She was hunched low, zigzagging like a comrade under fire, headed for the bunker. Which was, I knew, where I should be headed. Where I should have been already.

But I stood on the deck. Hesitating. In the east, across the gulf, the sky was strobing in constant barrage. Seconds later the first salvo of bolts speared down at the edge of the compound. And the chlorine reek set off a spasm of panic in me. I froze. For how long, I don't know. But then I heard my mother's voice above the din. The fear in it. The need of it.

I ran. Bursts of lightning seemed to ricochet inside my skull. And the hail set in before I was halfway to the bunker. Fists of ice. Bouncing white in my path, raising dust, pounding, beating my skull, shoulders, hips, kidneys. Right at the hatch, as I stumbled across the buttress of sandbags, I copped one final clout on the chin and fell down the ladder like a sack of beans.

While the pummelling overhead intensified and my mother checked my neck and then my pulse, I lay conscious but stunned. Around us ice skittered in the shaft, clinking, thudding. My mother climbed the ladder, closed the hatch, and came back to lie beside me in the melting slurry. She wept. And while the ice storm thundered on, I thought of the birds, the plants, my house. And, absurdly, of the sagas. Everything I had left in the world was being stoned to death.

Then it was over. No rain followed. We were spared a deluge, at least. But when we crept out, bruised and bewildered, into the sudden quiet, what we saw by torchlight was every bit as bad as the devastation of a flood. All our sails lay in shreds, our films were reduced to lattice, the roofs of our buildings were perforated or inverted completely, and our birds and plants lay bludgeoned beneath a rubble of glistening, melting ice. And our shiny new array? Every panel shattered.

It was all destroyed. The stuff I'd inherited; every structure I'd built with my own hands; every plant I'd raised and every creature I'd nurtured, pounded to tatters in minutes. In those first moments of near stupefaction, it looked like the end.

But disastrous as it was, that storm was not fatal. At any other time in my life, a catastrophe of such magnitude would have broken me. And there was no mistaking how deeply it affected my mother. I'd never seen her so shaken. Or so bereft. Which was startling in itself. For a few days she seemed punch-drunk.

My reaction was different. For reasons I couldn't explain, or even understand, I felt myself at a remove. And although this sort of devastation was exactly what I'd been dreading as I cowered underground beside her, once I was topside and actually walking through the wreckage, I felt strangely resigned. To the implacable fact of it. The lost labour and trade. The months and likely years of rebuilding required. Even the previously unthinkable option of walking away and leaving it all behind.

It wasn't that I was numb with shock. No, I was angry and resentful. But not wounded. This was a massive setback, easily the worst I'd ever experienced, and yet my response was entirely pragmatic. Impersonal. And who knows – perhaps, having been scorched by the events of summer and the calamity that triggered them, I was simply incapable of the old feelings.

For the first time in my life, I found myself needing to steady my mother, to coach her, stiffen her resolve. I walked her through the debris, managing to mark out the difference between mess and ruin.

For amidst the rubble – once you looked – there *was* stuff that could be salvaged. It took hard work to convince her we could recover. I wasn't always convinced myself. But the sight of her so impotent and forlorn was alarming enough to motivate me.

Meantime, all around us, others found themselves beyond all hope. The storm sparked the first significant exodus from the district in two generations. Left with little or nothing, many of the surviving families – homesteaders and hamlet-dwellers alike – gave up and moved south. We could resist that urge, my mother and I. Not because we were more sound than those who migrated. But because we were luckier. Unlike most, we had buffers. The best water holdings on the plain. Years of seed stock in dry storage. My old solar panels, which had mostly survived. And the secret providence of the Service. Even so, my mother seemed chastened and listless. I knew it would be a slow road back.

For the rest of that winter we had no choice but to live underground. It was better than nowhere, but it was bloody hard on the spirit. For a week or so, in desperation, I tried my chances topside with a jerry-rigged lean-to near the wreck of my house, but without cooling or even fans, the roasting afternoons wore me down. With the dread of heat fever stalking me, I was forced to retreat to the bunker and my mother.

We began the rebuild by restoring power. Then we turned our attention to the larger problem of the growhouses. My mother's frames were largely intact, and the footings were still sound. We beat metal sheets flat to fit the half walls and gable ends. And we were able to cobble together enough fabric mesh from both our places to make one full sheath. It took longer to finish the cowling, but we got there. Although the result of all this work was not pretty, it did the job. We dragged windblown snarls of irrigation hose in from the gibber plain, rehung the misters, wired up the fans, and within a fortnight we were nursing a few stripped trees and bedraggled plants back to life. Seed trays were loaded. A few emaciated bees found their way back to shelter. It was a start.

At my end of the compound, things took a little longer. Even with such a handsome stockpile of materials to hand, I was well short. I asked around in the hamlet and in the market square, but given the general devastation, good building supplies were scarce.

I knew there was no choice but to drive south to one of my old depots, but I was reluctant to leave my mother. And there was no chance of convincing her to accompany me. So, as discreetly as I could, I began measuring, making lists, and setting aside some meagre supplies for a road trip, all the while trying to work up the juice to break the news to my mother. But before I could, a tanker truck rumbled into the compound one afternoon.

I heard it long before I saw it. The noise sent a shudder through me – it wasn't so different from the racket of the ice storm. By the time I got my head up out of the bunker hatch, the big rig had pulled up near what was left of my place. The driver jumped down. I scuttled out into the hard sun to meet him.

He was tall, dark-skinned and walked with a limp. The high jauntiness of his hat was explained by the turban it perched upon.

I heard you have water to trade, he said.

Here, I said. Step into the shade.

No time, he said, and I saw his lower teeth were made of metal.

How much do you need?

I can take fifteen thousand litres.

What d'you have for trade?

Whatever you need, he said, surveying the ruins of my winterhouse.

I have a list, I said, as my mother emerged from the shade of her growhouse and proceeded to cross the compound toward us.

Okay, he said, turning for the truck.

What d'you mean, okay? I said, striding to keep up.

You'll get everything you need. Just be at the Nine Mile at sunset.

Shit! I can't go today.

Those are the orders.

As he reached for the door, I saw the melted web of skin where his sleeve rode up.

I can't leave her.

Where's your outlet?

How long will I be gone?

You know they don't tell us.

You're taking the water now?

That's the orders.

My mother arrived as the rig was backing up to the pump head.

What is this?

A stroke of luck, I said. We just scored some materials.

I don't see anything.

I'm going to collect them now.

Who is this character? He's not local.

I shrugged.

You've gone soft, she said.

The driver got down and I helped him hook up. He greeted my mother with deference, but she ignored him.

Where is this material? she asked me.

I'll be a day or two, maybe more.

She considered this. And as she pursed her lips I saw that the skin around her mouth and cheeks had lost its tautness. She'd aged without me noticing.

I'm sorry to leave you on your own, I said. But we need to get sorted quickly.

I've been here alone before, she said. Imagine I'll do it again. I'll survive. Just don't get robbed.

He won't get robbed, said the driver.

My mother walked away without replying.

She's old-school, I said apologetically.

No kidding.

He ran the pump for a few minutes and then capped the head.

That's hardly even a cube, I said.

That's the order. I can't stand here for an hour.

But you can't just drive off now. She's not an idiot.

You'll need the water for the labour, he said.

What labour?

You need to be done inside a month, so you'll have to trade for help.

She won't agree to that.

Not my problem, he said, heading for the cab. You've got some klicks to cover, so best get ready.

It was another delivery job. We flew south to Perth, in darkness. Set down on a ship, took delivery of a tonne of cargo cases, and lifted away again. Went high and east, across the city, which was just a spatter of light below. I couldn't help but think of Sun, but I knew it'd do me no good.

We sailed beyond the hills and set down in a scrim of flares around a gravel pit. With the help of a ground crew, we loaded the cases onto waiting trucks and rose back into the night. No one said what the cargo was. I assumed it was materiel.

I was out and back inside forty-eight hours. The day after I got home, with a load of first-rate construction materials, a convoy came down the drive hauling more.

It took my mother less than two days to concede that even with such windfalls we'd never finish the rebuild on our own before the season turned. Previously, a concession like this would have been inconceivable. But she was changed. Diminished, really. We drove into the hamlet together to make it known that we'd trade water for labour.

It was viscerally uncomfortable to have strangers on the property from first light till midday, six days a week, but we were both back in our own houses by early September. The films went up the week after, soon followed by the sails and awnings.

We had a few brief weeks to enjoy our homes again, but by early October the heat was too much. Like everyone else still left on the peninsula, we yielded and went below.

Every summer is hard. Goes without saying. But having spent so much of the winter underground already, that was a particularly tough one. Our situation was much improved, and I was grateful for that. I felt confident this would not be a season of madness like the summer before, but it was an especially lonely time.

I suppose this was when I began to accept the idea that Sun was unlikely to return. It was a long process, but I let go. Until then I'd nursed secret hopes she'd see through the gossip, or at least come back to confront me; that despite her fury there'd be some chance of getting through to her.

Since she'd gone, one calamity had landed on the heels of another. Each new loss compounding those that came before. And together they demanded a frenzy of unrelenting action that ate up every waking thought. There'd been no space for calm reflection. I was either grafting madly or asleep. But now, with the workload finally tapering, my mind began to clear. This presented its own challenges. With more time to think, I couldn't afford to be overcome with grief and longing, so I learnt to corral my thoughts. It wasn't so different to the ways in which I'd kept my two selves distinct as an operator. I reserved a piece of the night, the kindest hour, for writing to Sun and Ester. Messages neither would ever read, but which I still felt I needed to 'send'.

They were not florid letters. That sort of thing just wasn't in me. But I did confess my regrets and offer heartfelt apologies – on my own behalf and for my mother – sensing now, with some distance, how fixed and impervious a pair we must have been to contend with. I didn't attempt to explain myself. Didn't dare. It felt reckless to write even this much. I had to do it in secret, when I was certain my mother was asleep. I wrote them on the back of Association chits. Rolled them tight. Stuffed them into the metal pipe of my bedframe.

They weren't all sorrowful, these notes. Sometimes they catalogued my most precious memories of our time together. Moments we shared in the rock shelter. The miracles of wildflowers after rain. Ester's tiny fingers against the furry stems of tomato bushes. And just the confident sound of Sun's voice as she drew up some arcane bit of knowledge like sweet water from a well.

These were not letters designed to persuade. They were reminders to myself that what I'd had was real and beautiful, and they were a means by which I could escape the rage of victimhood and claim my great luck in having had those years. They helped in a way choof never could. And once summer was done, I left them below ground, safe in the bedframe, capped by a wooden bung I carved myself. They were part of my surrender.

By summer's end I was restless, ready to travel, and – even if I didn't know it – eager to bury my losses in action. That winter I made a conscious choice to let go. Of course, as I know now, this wasn't an educated decision. But in the short term, it was a mercy. I stopped feeling divided against myself. And that was liberating.

My first job was back in the Pacific. We worked in full chill suits. Delivered in darkness to the lower slopes of a mountain peak, all that was left of the abandoned outpost of Guadalcanal. The stronghold was unusually elaborate. And the engagement was brief but intense. All our casualties were sustained during the extraction. Needless to say, conditions were horrific. Struck by shrapnel, two operators poached in their perforated suits.

The repat flight brought us back over the Northern Rivers dikes and we set down west of the Hills Enclave. In those days this was the northernmost frontier on that coast. It was supposed to be an entirely civilian outpost. But my guess is it was heavily underwritten by the Service, to assist with transfers and resupply. It's long gone.

From there we were debriefed and mustered out. I wound up on a truck headed south with seven comrades in full kit, most of them archers, all of them women. I don't know where or what they'd been repatriated from, but they looked glassy-eyed and weary. There was no conversation. We slept most of the time.

At some point during that transfer, I woke and risked a glimpse through the peep-slot, and there below the blackened mountain pass was the Sydney Wall. I stared at the dirty yellow corona that hung over the plain. For a while it looked as if we might be headed that way, and some part of me was excited by the prospect of seeing that great and troubled city, but instead we pressed on southwest through the charred hinterland.

Next morning, we were on the path of the old highway, juddering through the corrugations, when the vehicle slowed and then stopped with a jerk. I figured we'd pulled up at a watering station, or perhaps our next staging point, so it was an ugly surprise to slide the peep open and see five men in the roadway. Two carried axes, two more brandished old-school ballistics tools. The fifth, the one spouting directions, appeared unarmed. The comrades around me must have been alerted by my sudden intake of breath, because when I turned to signal the situation out there in the road, they were already on to it. They might have been a very tired crew, but they were first-class operators.

When the rear doors were wrenched open, there was no discussion or negotiation. The first two brigands to stick their heads in reeled back instantly with bolts through their necks. At that, the others simply turned and ran. As I leapt out, empty-handed, I saw our driver pursuing the ringleader with a hand tool. He took the big bloke down with a single burst and at that point the other bandits pulled up, horrified. From the way they stared at the aftermath – recoiling at the stench of scorched flesh and ammonia – it was obvious Service-level tech was alien to them.

They were scabrous fellows, dirty and ill-looking. After so many tales of pirates and highwaymen, it was interesting to finally meet some genuine domestic outlaws. They were keen to parley, but they clearly hadn't bargained with the likes of us before. There was nobody else on the road that day. We despatched them quickly and humanely, and left them where they lay as an example to others.

It took another three hours to reach the staging point. The mood in the back of the truck was subdued. An encounter like that. On home soil. It was new and unsettling, for all of us. Which goes to show how things have changed since then.

From the muster camp there was an uplift that same night. I assumed I'd be headed west, back across the continent, toward home, but once the big stat got to its ceiling above the unlit country, it yawed south-east. And then it sank in. This wasn't a repat flight. I was being redeployed already.

The briefers emerged in the middle of the next day. We'd been over the sea for hours. This was the South Island job we were headed for. From there I went to New Cal. Again, in a suit.

I wasn't home much that year, or many of those that followed. Most of that period I was kept in the north. Not our north. The other hemisphere. Up past Cancer. They staged us from sanctuaries in the Sawatch and Avers. Those years it was just one show after another. A big push. As if we were hacking our way through the List at a pace we'd never managed before. But it didn't feel like a downhill run. Those were all tough outings.

I was wounded and burnt in the Alberta extraction. Broke an arm getting a stranded crew out of the Houston tunnels. Christ, don't even ask. I went back to the Steppe. Twice. When once was a time too many. And I did some work in the Arctic swamps. The mosquitoes there were the size of a child's hand. They nailed you through tactical fatigues and any gaps in body armour. Malaria cost us half the company.

It was a long time to be away. Long enough to nearly forget who I was, where I was from.

I hated to think of my mother on her own all those years. The solitary summers she endured underground. She was a staunch old bird, but without the Service, I doubt she'd have survived. They were faithful and discreet. They kept her safe. It felt to me they'd kept their end of our tacit agreement.

Whenever I returned, my mother seemed enormously relieved. The scripts the Service sent me home with seemed so threadbare now that I didn't bother to recite them, and she no longer even asked where I'd been. All she wanted to talk about was the challenges and triumphs of the homestead.

In the depleted hamlet, citizens were leery of me. Absences as long and routine as mine could only have confirmed the old gossip about my infidelity. And now, along with being a faithless husband, I was probably viewed as a negligent son. Whenever I was with my mother in the market square, the wary deference locals had always shown her seemed to have softened into a warmer regard. Not that she ever acknowledged it. She had no use for their sympathy. Or their pity. In the hamlet she was careful to maintain her steely dignity. As ever, she traded hard and fair. With me, she remained solicitous, devoted, but also careful in ways that were hard to pin down.

These were the years in which I became an old hand. By simply surviving. I'm not sure I got better as an operator, but I did get older, and it wasn't by shirking. You know, comrade, for all the mistakes that were made – the wrong calls, the bunky intel, the losses we sustained – I never saw much cowardice. Whatever gets said, however we're remembered, if we're remembered at all, the Service will always have that.

I was around long enough to see my share of body bags and fresh faces. I got used to being the senior on jobs. Unless it was a matter of specialist expertise. For a decade or more, I remember us having many more successes than failures. We acquitted a good number of objects. But then, over time, as the jobs began to seem more rudimentary and the objects less canny, shows became untidy and casualties increased, and that contradiction unsettled me. More than once I felt a rawness in my crew. At muster points some operators struck me as callow and overconfident.

I learnt plenty about tactics in my time, but aside from the notion of an ultimate victory that would trigger demobilization, broader matters of strategy were beyond the purview of rank-and-file operators like me. We were never privy to the status of the larger enterprise. Even so, I was active long enough, and in so many sectors and latitudes, that I began to get a sense of how things might be progressing. I knew the work had been going long before I was born, and for the bulk of my service it seemed as if it would continue long after my time. Because there was such steadiness and regularity to the work. The shows we did, the situations we faced, they were all broadly similar. It was as if the criminal clans reproduced and replenished themselves at roughly the same rate at which we removed them. For the longest time the circumstances felt static, as if we were all repeating ourselves – or worse, trapped in a pattern that threatened to be permanent.

But then, in those later years, things began to shift. More and more of the strongholds we were sent to breach turned out to be flimsy. Hurriedly constructed. Poorly defended. And some of the objects we encountered were hapless. As if we'd already weeded out the stronger specimens – the criminal elite – and stanched their blood-lines. It began to feel as if we'd been reduced to chasing minions and mopping up the dregs of the beneficiary class. By then, you'd have thought any remaining family, institute or trade confederacy with links to the cartels would have been in mortal fear of us.

Not every job had this air of tawdry anticlimax. There were still tough shows, high-end holdouts who continued to evade us. But old stagers like me got the impression we'd battled our way to the arse end of the List. And I began to wonder if I might live to see a resolution, and maybe even witness the grand experiment that came after stand down.

The Service had the best and brightest of humans in its ranks. And tech that could surely be put to use feeding, sheltering, treating folk in every latitude and jurisdiction. Without the threat of contagion and regression, it might be possible to achieve more than just the negative peace we'd birthed and maintained. There could be hope. Order of a decent stripe. And a steadiness that matched the best of the weather.

And so for a few years I lived in a state of anticipation. Yes, those were the days in which we began to sing the names of the vanquished. Openly. Defiantly. With pride. And dear God, there were so many. Though in truth, most were as obscure to us as the faces of our comrades. Even so, disembarking at repat set-downs, filing onto ships or stats at muster points, we bellowed them. Chanted in rigid cadence, bending them to fit. Only rarely did a name bubble up with any hint of familiarity to it. Sometimes because I'd heard it sung before, or because the name was so prominent we'd seen it written or heard it uttered at Basic. But there were only a handful of those. The sound of them sung aloud filled me with exaltation. And when the name above all names entered the song, there was pride, too. Of a kind I can't even describe. On hearing it, a grin would creep across my mug, wide enough to startle the rookies and set off searching glances, and I'd catch myself and return to being the crusty senior I was expected to be.

You know the name I'm talking about. I see it in your face. And yes, I'm getting to it.

But things took a turn, didn't they? Which came first, the change in the weather or the leap in tech? Fact is, we saw neither coming. We remained steadfast, comrade. But our staunchness rendered us blind.

Altered conditions. Remember how even saying those words left you dry in the mouth?

We acquitted nearly all of those crime families. But the ones we could never get to, those who'd seen the writing on the wall, well, they made alliances among themselves and traded their assets – their intellectual resources and personnel – and retreated to lairs almost beyond our reach. Sometimes it felt as if they'd gone to the walls of the Hermit Kingdom and bought their way into whatever nirvana or perdition lies within that lake of darkness.

But, really, I think what they did, so late in the piece, was adapt. Innovate. Bunker in together more. Mix blood with blood in marriage trades, so that in time, in tiny, potent pockets, resourced to an unimaginable degree, they found new vigour.

So for us, for the Service, it was suddenly break through or break. But we didn't know it. Not for years. And once we did, we made a mess of it. Simple mistakes. Strategic errors. And, worst of all, moral failures.

We educated them, comrade. For all our supposed secrecy and all our discipline, generations of Service actions had schooled the smartest of the remaining clans. While we learnt too little, and far too late.

Tech, says the bowman.

Yes. But we'd always used devices. Ships, aerostats, drones.

Not that sort. Don't play dumb with me.

Well, it was a matter of culture, brother. Scruples.

Fuck off – we just didn't have the tech. Or the blood and treasure to build them.

We'd never use mercenaries. Let alone slaves.

They're fucking machines, you dozy prick. A clunker doesn't care if it's slave or free.

You wouldn't know.

Fucking skin crawls at the thought.

It wasn't just the tech, I said. Before that, something else was happening. To do with us.

We were tired. Our kit was rubbish. Intel was piss-weak.

We got leggy.

Leggy? What the fuck are you talking about? he says, twisting in his chair.

Like plants. Seedlings. When they're in a hot patch, or they have to reach too hard and far for light.

Overstretched?

Yeah. And overconfident. Discipline. Morale. We got thin. Brittle. I had some bad shows.

Christ, we all had bad shows.

These were avoidable.

You went sour, he said.

Well, yes. Things curdled. I started to lose my way. And it felt that, the better I got, and the closer we got to victory, the less I had in me.

We shoulda been more ruthless.

Or just more thoughtful.

One trip I came back with nothing. No outcome. No object. And none of my people. I won't bore you with the details. But I was distraught. And livid. At the waste. The cost in human life. At least with Utah I could tell myself we'd achieved something – even if I hadn't understood the significance of it at the time.

A change *had* occurred. Altered conditions, remember? But I couldn't account for it. For one thing, it seemed we'd been expected on that job. So we had leakage, right? Some Service asset had been tortured or bribed. On top of that, our gas didn't work. We sent it in, salvo after salvo, to no effect. They just kept lighting us up. As if we were just hurling smoke canisters.

Back at the muster point, an island well off the eastern coast, others were talking. Which was bad in its own way. We were supposed to keep tight, say nothing except to the planners in the debrief, one on one. But all over the island, operators young and old were swapping stories about gas failures and betrayals.

Face to face, the spooks and planners weren't having any talk of disasters. Setbacks, they said. That's all these fuck-ups were. They asked if anyone in my team had deployed incendiaries. And I told them of course not, they should know better than anyone that the rules of engagement forbade the use of fire – we weren't barbarians. They said they didn't like my tone. I told them they hadn't had to scrape their comrades' skin off their suits, tweezer their mates' bone fragments out of their own flesh. I stripped to show them. They didn't appreciate the display. Or the open defiance. I said our casualties were mounting. They told me that was just conjecture. I lost my cool. Told them they were either deluded or lying. It was a low point, I won't pretend. They said I was lucky not to be going home in restraints. And that was the first I knew about going home.

In the transit camp, waiting for the repat flight, I was limping along a salt-scoured terrace, watching a stat ghost in toward the mooring mast, when I came to a long row of converted habs being used as a field hospital. I'd spent the previous morning there, having frags extracted, and wasn't keen to linger, but my puncture wounds and their dressings kept me to an undignified shuffle. Outside the last hut, a wounded operator sat smoking what smelt like low-grade choof. In fact, it was a hemp stogie. I didn't even acknowledge her until she spoke.

She was strapped to the chair. The legs of her fatigues were pinched off above the knees.

Our ride home, she said, jerking her plaited fag at the landing stat.

Yeah, I answered, her wounds causing me to feel a little more obliged than usual. Looks like it. About time, too.

*The lame and the halt and the blind.*

I shrugged, squeamish and reluctant to engage.

Ah, she said. I remember you.

Only then did I make myself look at her closely. Her face, the eyes. At this point, I still hadn't properly recognized her, but something about the wry grin felt familiar. Her silver hair was buzz-cut. The burn scars around her neck were almost obscured by the crepiness of her skin. She was impossibly old for active service.

You're the farmboy, she said.

Used to be, I said, looking away along the row of habs, anxious about the breach of protocol.

The west, right?

I glanced back at her. We shared a complicit glance and then, despite myself, I nodded.

Well, *you* lasted, she said. One of the hardy ones.

Lucky, I spose.

We make our own luck.

That's what we tell ourselves.

So, she said. What's my excuse? Insufficient industry?

And then it came to me. I placed her. She was the instructor from Basic, the one I'd known as Awe.

You! I said, smiling in disbelief.

Indeed.

They have you back on ops?

Well, she said brightly. Had.

I found myself looking a little too frankly at her stumps and the terrible seepage around the bandages.

Got no drones? Send in the crones, she said with a bitter grin.

How long have you been back in the field?

Oh, long enough. As you can see.

It's gotten to *that*?

I'll try not to take that as an insult.

I'm sorry.

Listen, farmboy, when you've run more shows than me, let me know.

Like I said. I apologize.

No need.

The airship came down, locked on to the mast. A gust of wind caught it broadside and it yawed slightly, giving off a mighty flash of golden sunset light.

Strange place to say goodbye to it all, she said.

I nodded. It struck me, though, that anywhere would be an odd place to give it away.

Been here before?

You know I can't answer that, I said with a grin.

Used to be covered in forest, you know. This island. Cloud forest, they called it. Two hundred kinds of birds.

I looked around at the bare, baked rock.

The dying face of God, she murmured.

You lost me.

Sorry, she said. I guess it's the meds.

I hesitated. Then asked if she'd mind if I sat awhile. She gestured to the kit trunk beside her, and I perched awkwardly.

You really were a handsome lug.

I don't remember, I said truthfully.

She laughed.

I don't go for the God talk, I said.

Fair enough. I understand.

All this magic they're into these days. Gives me the yips.

Me too.

So what's the deal? The dying face of God?

Oh, it's just talk.

Somehow I doubt that. I remember you. You believe that stuff?

Magic? No. My mother was a crypto priest. As was her father before her. I guess the secret God talk runs in the blood.

But not the magic?

I don't think it was ever about magic. To give them their due.

Well, you've lost me again. Not that I should be surprised.

My mother used to tell me that when Nature dies, God dies along with Her.

And how'd she figure that?

She said the first form of revelation is the natural world. Wild, living nature, coherent, intact, independent and unknowable in its abundance and fecundity – its fertility.

Well, that's a mouthful.

I'm quoting, just so you know.

I get fecundity. As in, I know what it means. But revelation —

How we experience the divine. The ways in which it's revealed to us.

Okay. And the divine is God, right?

Apparently, she said with a smile. I guess what my mother meant is that without clean, wild, healthy things that can generate and renew themselves, the idea of God is impossible to imagine.

Isn't it absurd anyway?

Probably. Or should I say, possibly. If it's beyond imagining, then it's beyond reason.

I really wouldn't know.

Mum said people could feel it, sense the creative potential for it, the example of it, in wild things. *It* being the divine.

What about people? Aren't they feral enough for you?

I imagine that's not quite the meaning she had in mind. Though why not? She *was* talking about healthy, fertile, creative creatures.

For a moment I was lost for words.

You look troubled, she said, in a way that took me back to Basic.

You really buy this stuff?

I don't know. I guess now I'll have more time to chew it over.

But you don't really believe it, do you?

How could I? Even if I wanted to.

Sounds to me like you need to.

Ah, she said. You understand!

I don't think so.

Have it your way, she said with a glint in her eye.

The horn sounded. We both flinched and drew ourselves back into operative demeanour. A pair of orderlies emerged from the hab. I stood and stepped aside to give them room.

Maybe we'll chat on the trip back? she said as they hoisted her onto a stretcher.

Sure, I said.

She offered her hand, and I shook it.

But I avoided her on the journey. We never spoke again. She was the most interesting person I ever met.

It was only later that I understood what she was really trying to say. Without coming straight out and making assertions that would have her dishonourably discharged as a catastrophist and coward. I think she meant the world had taken a step away from us. While we weren't looking, we'd let ourselves come adrift. And whatever we achieved from here on would be on alien ground.

On the repat flight I spent every waking hour thinking about home. I pined for it in a way I hadn't for years. And yet when I finally arrived, what I felt was indifference, not relief. I noticed my mother had developed a hunch. Her face and hands were frosted with lesions. She greeted me avidly, but after our initial reunion she was reserved, almost tentative. We were mindful of one another. Almost courtly. But also careful in the way of people no longer closely acquainted.

The compound was in fine shape. In fact, it looked a little too good. My mother was an outstanding homesteader, but she'd clearly had lavish help keeping things afloat during my long absence. The kit we had now was first-rate. And the western bund was so high that from ground level it threatened to block my view of the foothills. She caught me up on the local news and, as night fell, fed me the freshest food I'd had in a very long time. We sat on her deck in the hot moonlight and spoke of inconsequential Co-op matters and Association politics. Things that were safe to discuss.

When I walked back to my place, I saw it had been freshly cleaned. The linen on the bed smelt newly laundered. As if she'd been expecting me. I lay there all night, tired but unable to sleep.

Before dawn I went downstairs and checked the quad. It was fully charged. I wrapped up and rode out across the plain until I reached the spur we favoured for hiking to the tops.

I set out upon the rocky slopes, feeling the tightness from my puckered wounds. The usual frisson of anticipation was absent. Instead, I felt melancholy. Even a little haunted. This was more than ordinary exhaustion. I was disgusted. And this feeling was new. I'd experienced disenchantment before. But never about the project that had given shape to my life.

I was still proud to have been chosen to serve. It was a privilege. But I could feel, as I walked, that I was already thinking of it in the past tense. Was that simply because I was a spent force? Or had the project itself lost its way? Serving had rescued me from drudgery. Given me knowledge and purpose. It had lifted my gaze. And yet at what cost?

As the light came up, I was overtaken by a sudden, primitive urge. I wasn't really thinking of comrades, of sweating bodies hefting kit. But I guess I caught the smell of damp webbing. And the cadence of my boots on the ground brought the chant to my throat like something too hot to choke back.

I was alone up there. And so full of fury and grief. I let go. Like a crying child. And sang.

*O! Oh!*
*Aramco, Sunoco, Conoco, Rio-Rio, Chevron*
*Sinopeco, Shell-o, Shell-o, Peabod, BP, Climate Depot*
*Oh!*
*Woodside, Santos, Petrobras*
*O!*
*Koch*
*Oh!*
*Koch*
*O! Oh!*
*Fuckers! Fuckers! Fuckers!*
*Ooooooooooooooooooooooohhhh!*

I sang until my throat burnt. Until it felt as if I were coughing up a second sun.

There was no one there to hear me. And that was a mercy. But also, another reason to mourn.

Well, says the bowman. You're a sucker for the singing.

I miss it. Don't you?

He shrugs.

So, how big is this mine? I ask, blindsiding him a little.

What?

How many levels below this?

I'm not gonna talk about that. What do you take me for?

The other levels, can you stand in them? Or are they crawl spaces?

Christ, man, why do you even care?

Room to set up lights, run water. Is it big enough?

You see? You're getting your hopes up.

I'm just curious, comrade. Indulge me.

He sighs with exasperation. You're a fool.

I'm a grower, mate. What else am I gonna think about? Would you rather I spent the time wondering how I can cut your throat?

Listen to you, he says. You talk and talk. And I keep listening, waiting. But you never say it. The one name. I reckon you're afraid to say it.

You think?

Why else wouldn't you say it? You think you're still bound to secrecy?

No, I say. All that's done.

Maybe you weren't on the Utah job at all. Maybe your story's all bullshit.

Wouldn't I be eager to say it? If I was lying? Wouldn't I have waved that name around like a flag?

The bowman chews his lips a moment.

What I don't understand, I say, is how you link Utah with the name.

Well, because that was the job that finished them. Right?

But how could you know that?

It got around, he says. Late in the piece, when discipline was going to buggery, people blabbed. Utah was a big deal. I reckon they leaked it, actually. Deliberately. To boost morale. Jesus, man, why else would I be asking you about it? You said it yourself, you heard comrades starting to sing the name.

True enough.

You're probably lying your arse off, anyway.

I suppose I have every reason to make stuff up.

No shit.

But everything I've told you is true.

I don't think I believe you.

So maybe it's pointless. Maybe I should save my breath. Any old stager could utter the name and associate himself with it. Maybe I should sleep.

Suit yourself.

In the morning you'll do what you're gonna do.

He shrugs.

So I may as well get some kip, I say, scraping a bit of dirt clear to lie in beside the child.

Ah, you've bottled out, he says. You get this far and pike?

Oh, I say. What's the point?

What if I'm curious?

What if you are? I say. I'm getting a picture here, comrade. You need the company, some entertainment, and in the morning you'll get rid of me. Like I'm a serf and you're some cartel prince in his lair. How does that sound to you? You smell something off about that?

Cheeky old cunt, aren't you? he says. You've got juice, I'll give you that.

First you reckon I'm scared to utter the name above all names. But then you say I've got juice. Which is it?

Who can tell?

You'll always wonder, comrade. Down here on your own. In your hole. Anyway, time to sleep.

I curl up next to the waif. She's snoring lightly. I half close my eyes and watch him scratch his beard. I wait, trusting I have him on the hook.

Look, he says. Every one-armed bastard and his uncle said he was on that show.

I scooch in closer to the kid. Say nothing.

How'm I supposed to believe you?

I think you might be right, I say, still lying there. I think they leaked it. For a spike in morale.

And you think that because?

I was the one they leaked it to.

Oh Jesus, he says, clapping his hands so suddenly the girl startles and stirs. I re-roll my scarf and wedge it back under her cheek.

You're right to be sceptical, I say. I don't blame you.

So, tell me.

I'm thirsty, I say. The kid hasn't eaten.

Christ, he says getting up. I shoulda seen that coming.

———

He leaves a lamp on. But he's gone a long time. So long I fall into a kind of fugue. I haul myself back into a sitting position. Reorient myself. I need to stay awake. Better than that, alert. But my mind drifts to older stories. From the sagas, of all things. And I struggle to attach myself to one of them as they sail by in my head. Haul myself aboard. Just to keep going. I need him here. For focus. Otherwise it's just a hot funk of memories. In which the red horizon waits, and after that, only darkness.

Here, he says, arriving at last. He passes the dixy, steps back quickly as if I might try to strike him with it. And I gulp from it like a greedy child.

You're nattering about Basic again. I can't even tell if you're talking in your sleep.

I never talk in my sleep. They cooked that up.

Basic. For you, that must've been a thousand years ago.

But you know, it feels like last week. Sometimes I wish I could go back there.

The bowman snorts.

No, not for the drills and the field exercises and all that. Just for the education. To go back as a grown-up, not a kid.

Bollocks to that.

Truly, brother. I wouldn't mind.

There's an ancient myth, said Awe one afternoon. About a people in paradise. An orchard in which they were born, where they were safe. With food they could just pluck from the trees.

I think I know this one, I said.

Perhaps you do.

There's this one tree, right? It's off limits to the people. There's power in the fruit.

Yes, knowledge.

And they eat it.

Yes.

They were always going to. Eventually. Don't you think?

Yes, said Awe, squinching away a smile. I imagine so.

So why the rule?

Good question. Though there's grief in knowledge.

You think?

How old are you, Volunteer?

Seventeen. Nearly.

Huh, she said, glancing up at the skein of camo overhead. So what happens to these people who eat the fruit of knowledge?

Turfed out.

They become exiles.

And that's the end of easy food.

Well, said Awe, I've never quite thought of it that way, but yes. From that point on, the people must sow and till and make their own food.

Grafting.

The problem being, of course, there's this tendency in them to fall back on the idea of getting, as you say, easy food.

I don't follow.

You're a grower, right? Think of all the ways to get easy food without labouring or trading for it.

Bludging. Or thieving.

Exactly. By loafing off others. Or stealing from them. Or enslaving them.

And that's the point of this story?

Oh, I don't know if there's a point, exactly. But it does offer a chance to remind ourselves of what it means to be human. Don't you think? Before they break their limits, those people are like us, but not quite us. We're conscious. With knowledge. Curiosity. Imagination. It's a reminder of the burden that comes with those gifts. And, I guess, the consequences that come from shirking that burden.

You've lost me, I said, looking past her longingly to the squad of operators assembling and breaking down tools on a trestle in the distance.

I think you know how the story goes after the tree and the garden. And you've read some history, seen the docs and pics at Induction.

I licked my lips, anxious at losing the thread.

All that genius, she said. All that potential. So much of it wasted on bastardry. Lies. Empires. Slavery. *That* was not inevitable. And it won't happen again. Why?

Us?

Yes, Volunteer. Because we won't let it.

Back on the peninsula, after the years of relentless deployments and my reckless outburst at the debrief, I figured I was done. At home, months passed uneventfully. Then years. I plugged away like a good plainsman. Kept my head down. Met the perennial challenges – split hoses, fungal outbreaks, fried pumps – with the stoicism I'd been raised with. I tried to submit. Believed I was content. But I guess that's what you tell yourself when you're disenchanted to the point of heartbreak.

Maybe it was unhealthy, that craving I'd developed. The need for action. Or the loss of a greater purpose. It's no easy thing, returning to the patterns and habits of mind you've known since childhood. But there's no shame in making soil and growing food, right? Sorrow burns so hot and bright at first. Then you tamp it down so hard you barely feel it anymore. Still, it smoulders on regardless.

I couldn't tell if I'd been stood down temporarily or cashiered for good. Nobody came. The discreet help the Service had given my mother in the years I was gone seemed to evaporate overnight. If she noticed, she didn't say.

We laboured together in the winter mornings. If we talked, it was work we spoke of. Underground, during the days and nights of summer, we could barely spare the breath for talk. Whichever the season, above ground or below, there seemed to be more space and time than I'd experienced in a long while. At first that made me anxious. After barracks life, hectic muster camps and crowded ships' holds, the calm and the long silences took some getting used to.

A couple of times those empty and sometimes fearful intervals sent me grubbing out the letters I'd written to Sun and Ester so long ago, but they just made the hollowness within me feel more perilous. I couldn't afford madness. I had to retrain. Recalibrate. And when I steadied my mind, I found my senses grew keener. The taste of fresh food, real water, the many shades of light and shadow on the plain. Or just the shock of how gnarled my feet had become without me noticing.

But the thing of greatest consequence I began to pick up on was the seasonal drift. Winters arrived late now. And they were short. Summers weren't always hotter, but monsoons often failed to arrive. Despite the lack of rain, the humidity was increasing. And that left us slimy, gasping, at the edge of panic. For all our discipline and careful rationing, our choof supplies were running out by early March. One year we were reduced to chewing raw leaves from the growstock in the cellars. Which, as you'll know, is a fruitless exercise. At least we weren't demented enough to eat our own seeds. I used to fantasize about growing poppy, but imagine a summer on the poppy – you'd starve come winter.

So, yes, the weather was becoming erratic. And mild stretches less and less common. Although the district was more thinly populated, on market days the queue for the clinic in the civil shelter tailed out into the market square. Folks had more eye troubles, cankers, gut worms, rickets, and some were so downcast they looked catatonic. I guess things had been changing for years without me seeing it. Plainsfolk were as hardy as they come, but the peninsula had become a tougher place to live.

One winter night, I asked my mother if she felt compelled to stay. Given how hard conditions had become. Whether she felt obliged, somehow. To the memory of my father, say.

Not at all, she said mildly. I choose to stay. Because the living's good. It's clean.

You don't think things are getting harsher?

Life's always been a challenge on the plain, she said. Extremes are a part of our lives. This is what we do – we endure and overcome.

You don't ever feel cursed, cast out? You know, exiled from the spring of living water and the shelter of the tree?

Son, she said. The cave was a refuge. Of course. But every refuge is a form of captivity. We were cast out from the dark into the light, emerging from beneath the earth to be on it. We came down onto the plain *into* paradise, not from it.

You really believe that?

Of course. Plains life is not for everyone, but it's where I found myself, how I've learnt to live. I'm used to it.

Alone? Separate?

We live in association. We've always been citizens. We contribute to the Co-op.

We approve of it all, the collective life, but we don't really inhabit it. *She who plants and she who waters are one.*

Yes, I said. *From each according to ability, to each according to need.* I know. But is that how we live?

The plain produces strong people. I'm not ashamed of that.

And what of the weak? I asked.

We exist to serve them.

You really believe that? Still?

I'll always believe it. It's why I stay.

Why? Because it keeps you strong?

As I said, it's what I know. But, yes, it keeps me staunch.

So you'd never leave?

I can't imagine wanting to.

What about needing to?

Oh, I don't think of that. Son, you sound troubled.

My head is scrambled, I said, truthfully enough. Too long on the road.

You've done well, she said. You've worked hard to find good trade.

I'm tired of it.

I see that. But you'll be out again before long. I know you. You'll get restless.

I'm weary of chasing junk.

Remember the middens?

Of course.

People leave a trail. As long as folks exist, there'll be stuff left behind. We should be glad to have the use of it. And grateful they didn't sow the land with salt. *That* was the way of empires.

You've been reading the sagas again, I see.

A little, she admitted coyly. The evenings can drag. *Remain true to yourselves but move ever upward,* she quoted. *At the ridgetop you will find yourselves united with all those who, from every direction, have made the same ascent.*

*For everything that rises must converge.*

Well, she said, with evident pleasure. You are my son.

I offered her a smile. But within myself, I felt unmoored and lonely.

I'd almost begun to hope the day would never come, but of course it did, as I always knew it would. There was no chance they'd leave me hanging forever. One market day some nameless pigeon found me in the square and passed on a summons to meet at the wharf. I never went. Another met me on the road with a message to drive to the Nine Mile, but again I didn't show. I was a volunteer – there was nothing mutinous in declining a meet. Even so, this was new territory for me. I figured if I withheld my labour, eventually I'd see where I stood, whether the Service was still the enterprise I'd joined as a recruit, or if it had degenerated into the kind of outfit that would compel me to serve.

In the end, the old filmlayer came himself. His intervention began, ostensibly, as a visit to my mother. I observed his arrival from the shade under my winterhouse. I knew his truck, his hulking figure, the droop of his hat brim. There was the requisite performance of a trade errand – a carton of something he took up the stairs. I was waiting for him when he appeared later among the fruit trees in my growhouse.

This is bold, I said.

Well, he replied, batting his hat against his leg. You haven't made it easy. Is there a problem?

Probably. If you're here.

It's a request, that's all.

I'm tired.

Understood, he said. And you have doubts.

But you have a message anyway.

In two parts.

Number one?

There'll be no more mopping up.

For me personally, or in general?

I'm just the pigeon, he said. I don't know what you mean or what they mean.

Okay, I said. And two?

Your presence is requested for two days total.

For work or talk?

Exchange of information.

I don't have any.

I imagine it's the other way round. Something you might like to know.

I thought you were just the messenger, I said.

That's all I know.

Information. For me?

They said it's something that might change things for you. The shape of your life. Whatever that means.

I stared at him, my heart leaping. He flogged his hat nervously and then shoved it back on his head.

When?

Day after tomorrow. Thirteen-hundred hours. The anthills.

What if I don't show?

Well then, he said. You're none the wiser and the hamlet gets more tomatoes.

So I'm free to choose?

Son, he growled. You were always free.

I just stood there. Trying to understand him.

I'll collect you at dawn, he said, turning away. Told your mother I need you for a day or two.

I'll bet, I said, resuming the work of picking oranges.

As he drove away I overturned a crate to sit a moment and think.

You know, I'd always wondered, but didn't dare believe it could be possible, if one day the Service might search for Sun on my behalf. They had the means, surely. And they had to know what losing her had cost me. This was how they were acknowledging my years of faithful service. My heart. Dear God, my spirit soared.

The child wakes. And whimpers.

Comrade, I say. She's hungry.

Not my problem.

There's food in my rig.

Not anymore.

It'll be a long night with her wailing.

She doesn't make much noise.

That's what you think.

The bowman sucks his teeth. Looks about himself. As if there might be counsel in all his drums and crates and coils of hose. Then he gets up, muttering imprecations. While he's gone, I hold the child's gaze and press a finger across my lips. The flicker of recognition, the moment of complicity, sends a charge through me.

The bean mash is pretty good, I call after him.

Away in the gloom, a clatter and a curse.

In the morning we'll get out, I whisper to the child. Everything'll be fine. But you have to promise me. If you find our rig, if you see the vehicle, remember what I told you. About what's in the door. The tool. Don't touch it. Don't go for it. You understand?

She looks up at me. She stinks. And so do I.

You hear?

She blinks.

The bowman's footfalls approach.

Please, I whisper to her.

Well, I'll give you this, he says. Your stuff tastes better than mine.

I'll show you how to make it.

I'll figure it out.

He opens the gate a little way, blocks the gap with his hip, and shoves two dixies through.

Thank you, I say. Decent of you. Talk about singing for my supper.

Jesus, he says. Enough with the singing.

You know, if I'm brutally honest – and why not, I've got nothing to lose except a bit of dignity – I wonder if it wasn't just that I'd given up hope of ever finding Sun and Ester. For years I'd trained myself never to think of them. Because of how it ate me up, rendered me unsafe and unsound. In the field. At home. Until I just didn't. Think of them, I mean. What does that say about a man? Doesn't that interest you at all? Why look at me like that? Unless you know the feeling. I'm sorry. I see I've hit a nerve.

He sits down slowly. The moment passes. I set the thought aside, this morsel of intel, in the hope it'll come in handy later in the night.

The girl has already wolfed her mash and licked the dixy. I give her mine. And when she's finished, she's too tired and sated to bridle when I wipe the mealy smear from her chin.

She's on the nose, says the bowman, watching in open fascination as she drifts back to sleep.

She's exhausted. She needs a wash.

You wash her?

She washes herself. She's been trained.

We'll see about it, he says. In the morning.

Well, anyway, thank you for the grub.

You didn't even eat.

I serve the child.

What's that, the sagas?

No. Just something someone said.

Kid have a name?

I assume so. I'm hoping, eventually, she'll tell me.

I can't figure you.

But you're listening, I say.

You're such a bloody liar, he says in a tone of rueful wonder.

I shrug.

Where'd you say you found her?

I'm getting to that. I thought you wanted to know about Utah.

You keep fucking around, going sideways.

Sometimes, to go forward, you need to make a detour.

To do what? Cover your tracks? Play for time? You think someone's coming to spring you?

No, I say. Nobody's coming to save me.

So get on with it.

I'm getting there.

The hell you are.

This is it, I say. I'm telling you how it was. How it went.

Okay. So I went to the termite mounds. As ordered. Requested. With the filmlayer. And the moment the stat hove into view, flashing like a daytime star, he limped back to his truck and drove off. Left me waiting there in the sun. Alone. Without kit.

The blimp banked upwind, began to descend. Everything about this meet was irregular. Never before had I seen an air asset land so close to home without the cover of darkness. It was unsettling. Exciting, too, I suppose. Because it seemed possible I might be the cause of it. Which goes to show how disconnected and self-absorbed I was in that moment.

Once we were aloft and I'd had time to take in the other operators, arrayed in field dress along the benches of the gondola, I could register their undisguised curiosity. They were young. None greeted me. I was just an old cove in tattered civvies, a puzzle that'd remain unsolved.

From the peninsula, we flew east. Across the bight of the gulf. Over the salt pans beyond. Across the pink dunes that marched inland in waves. Past the black and burgundy mesas of the mining lands until, eventually, we reached the freckled edge of the desert where the superheated air was blocky and jagged, and the gondola shuddered and shimmied in the turbulence. As we pressed further into that mosaic of golden spinifex and red dirt, we began to lose altitude.

The company stirred. Operators snugged webbing and reached for hats and scarves. Some daubed paste on their noses and cheeks.

I didn't detect the encampment until our final approach. All I saw was a tawny scour. Like a flood wash. All the huts and tents and machines were expertly latticed.

On the ground I was met by a woman from Planning who led me away from the company. We ducked under the lattice edge and strode through the grid of shadows cast by the vaulted camo ceiling. She said nothing as we crossed the camp, passing squads of drilling operators. At the head of a long, cowled tent, she handed me over to a bung-eyed orderly. He led me into a kind of antechamber, asked for the supplementary password the filmlayer had provided, and once satisfied he took me down a narrow hall and into a longer space that looked like a briefing room. The air was cooled in there. Chart stands stood by the walls, every one of them shrouded. Chairs were stacked at one end. There was a large trestle table at the other. And on that lay a dossier as thick as a ration box.

The orderly left me there without instruction.

And so I waited.

To calm myself and to overcome the tempting presence of the file, I took in the details of the room. Alongside the table, powered down and half draped in a field blanket, was a viewing screen. Behind that stood a blast-proof cabinet. To one side, a tilted map deck with the charts covered. Lying on the cabinet were two small comms pieces. All this kit was exotic fruit for the rank and file, but the viewer was familiar from Induction and Basic, and most of the rest I'd seen at staging posts and Planning hubs in the rear.

The little black panels, however, I'd only seen in strongholds. They were crim tech and supposed to operate over vast distances, but I was told they often didn't function because we'd destroyed much of the infrastructure that linked them. I'd seized and bagged a couple of these devices on the Utah job, had lost them with all the rest of the kit and crew. It was queer to see these here. There was something sinister about them lying in the open like this. It was almost as if they were on display. To instil a sense of awe. Or give some other arcane signal. And now I thought about it, everything in the room suggested elements higher than Supply and Planning. This felt like the province of Intel. And that freshened my hopes. But also my agitation.

The presence of the dossier really didn't help. For someone to have left it in plain sight of an unsupervised operator – this was an extraordinary lapse. I'd never encountered such a breach of security.

I stepped back from the table. Retreated to the very centre of the room. And to defend myself against any charge of impropriety, I averted my gaze. Then I turned my back entirely. But the discomfort persisted. The presence of that file was more disturbing than any bit of clan gear. The discordance of it caused my mind to fizz and seethe. I shouldn't be allowed to stand alone in a room with it, let alone be directed to do so. None of this could be accidental. It felt like a provocation. A test.

I looked back at it. This block of documents. A swatch of yellow sprouted from its edge. Like some kind of tag or marker. When I turned away, the afterglow of that colour burnt in my vision.

I stood there several more minutes. Nobody came. I looked again at the table and the huge folder. No. This wasn't an oversight, and nor was it a test, let alone a trap. This had to be the information I'd been promised.

Outside, overhead, the stat I'd come in on whined and faded off into the distance. In the next room I could hear voices. People speaking in hushed tones. Perhaps this was how Intel types communicated. It seemed likely they were aware of my presence. Possibly even observing me.

I thought of Sun. And Ester, whose infant face brought a shiver of angst. Would she know me? God, would I even recognize her?

The prospect of knowing, the hunger – it was too much. I strode across, hesitated, then bent over the dossier. On the buff cover there was nothing to identify the contents except a long number. And that yellow flash – it was a docket. It was tipped in two-thirds of the way down the stack of docs. Written on it was my codename. Which I registered with a jab because I'd never seen it written before, had never even uttered it.

Then I did what I was trained never to do. I opened the dossier. Without authorization. Where the yellow tag protruded.

Instantly it felt as if I'd made a terrible mistake. Sun's name was nowhere here. There was no description or detail pertaining to her or Ester. Nothing about their lives or whereabouts. It seemed to be just a mission file, a list of planning actions, materiel movements, personnel mobilizations, intel assets. I scanned pages more hurriedly, growing ever more frustrated and furious. Until I stumbled on a word I recognized. In capital letters. Which gave me a jolt. Like a boot from a battery cable. Jesus, I'd sung that word. It was a name with a legendary aura. And it kept appearing, page after page. Alongside certain details that struck me as faintly familiar. And then very bloody familiar.

Fuck me, I thought. Surely not.

I took it in rapidly at first. In gulps and grabs. Then I extricated myself. Physically stepped back. To get control of myself. Then I started over, right from the top of the pile, reading it all, quickly, carefully, front to back, with my head nearly fit to detonate. It took the best part of an hour. Which was, I gather, exactly what had been expected of me.

And I don't know how to explain the feeling I was left with. For what does it mean to be heartbroken and euphoric in the same instant?

I've had a long time to think on that, because this clash of feelings has never dissipated. I've never resolved it.

But I'm not a fool. I soon grasped the point of this exercise. Which was, in its execution, both generous and cynical. Not to mention unspeakably cruel.

Nothing specific had been promised to me. I'd done that bit of misdirection myself. I'd produced the fantasy of a reunion. Or at least the prospect of material information about Sun and Ester. They hadn't dangled it in front of me. They hadn't even mentioned it. And perhaps they hadn't anticipated where my mind would go. Maybe they hadn't exploited this weakness, the likely misapprehension. But they knew so much about me. It's impossible to imagine any of it was accidental.

What I *could* see, and what I do know for certain, is that the entire exercise was an opportunity to deliver a kind of veiled acknowledgement. A secret tip of the hat to me. And to the comrades who did the job up there in the former Republic of Utah. Which, in itself, was extraordinary. It was unheard of for the Service to burden an operator with knowledge about a job, to reveal the identity of an object; even after the fact, it broke every protocol. Operationally and psychologically. There were damn good reasons for such protective measures.

But this breach – it was more than just a gesture to give credit where it was due. It took me a minute or two to absorb it, but it was soon clear enough. This was an attempt to exploit my pride. Because conferring such a singular honour, granting me a sense of historic achievement, what else could it be but an extraordinary form of inducement? They'd been observing me. All my life they'd been watching – I knew that. And since the sudden upturn in failed missions and my episode of insubordination over the gas failures, they'd been monitoring my state of mind. Exactly how, I couldn't know.

Perhaps they'd been concerned my disquiet might spill over into treachery. My no-shows had probably been a cause for worry. After such long and exemplary service, I was becoming a disappointment, even a risk. And yet they still wanted something from me. That had to be it.

But a plot like this. Dear God, it was low. It was unbecoming. And yet it was ingenious. Because of course it worked. Once the initial wave of rage and resentment had washed past, the gravity of the Utah job began to settle on me. The implications of what we'd done became clearer.

I flicked back through the dossier. Again and again, all through it, from the first page to the last, that same five-letter word was there in blocky capitals. And the sight of it set off something in me.

You understand, right? You get why my pulse went up just seeing the name. As you say, the name above all names. This was the giant that ate children. All children. Like something from the sagas. And to see it killed? To know that I'd been there at the death? Comrade, it was like a charge going off inside me. And the Service was right, you know. This *was* the kind of knowledge that'll change the shape of a life. It did. It has. It does. So you can rob me. And cage me. And even kill me, come morning. But this? This, you can never take from me. You can only sit there in amazement, stewing in your duds. And envy me. Oh, you'll call me a liar, a fantasist, a smooth-talking bullshitter. But you'll wonder, won't you. It'll eat at you. And, deep down, you'll suspect you're in the presence of history.

You already know the details about the job. But I'll walk you through the dossier.

At the point in the file where my codename lay – the tag sticking out, where I'd first opened the stack – there was a single paragraph describing the terminal action in Utah. As in, our bit of the job. It was short, no-nonsense. All the details compressed. Delivery and set-down. The duration of the show, from the trek in, the uplift. No mention of the missing drones and heat blankets, mind. Just an abbreviated account of the three-day stand to, the engagement, and the acquittal. Details about the return journey, with its weather complications and losses, were vague. The irregular extraction that saved my life and that of Spanish – well, that wasn't mentioned at all. Yet our repat and her suicide were in the record, though her codename had been redacted, which gave me a pang. It would have been nice to know it.

Overall, the substantive details of the job – our part in it, at least – were logged accurately. It was quite a surprise to see the mission declared a total success. Our casualties had been catastrophic. If you included Spanish – and I certainly did – I'd lost everyone. Sure, we'd acquitted the object and his family. Blew the stronghold to shit. And lived long enough to get word back. But it never felt like a victory to me. That job had burnt me in more ways than one.

And yet, there it was. *Total success.* What's more, the file went on for hundreds of pages after the account of our operation. Evidently, in the years afterwards, the site had been constantly surveilled. The fortress in the canyon had never been rebuilt or reoccupied. No sign of life was ever detected and no connection to the cartel endured in that region or anywhere else. An enormous logistical effort had gone into verifying the death of this object and every sprig and strand of his clan. And after a five-year forensic review of intel, the object's dynasty had been officially declared extinct. Can you imagine what it was like to see that? Christ, I went weak at the knees.

You want me to say it, don't you. The vanquished name. Okay, I'll say it.

EXXON?

Yes. Yes. No word of a lie.

EXXON. EXXON. EXXONMOBIL. EXXON.

That bloke. EXXON wasn't his personal moniker. That was his clan name. And there it was, in bold caps.

You know, hundreds of pages predated the Utah show in that file. It was all the background and build-up. All the wars the EXXONS had started. The ones they'd fuelled, profited from. In Africa, Mesopotamia, South America. The lands and seas and rivers they'd poisoned. The districts and regions and governments they'd captured and rendered as vassals. I read carefully, trying hard to take it all in, to remember everything. I thumbed open the images and clips. Folded out the family tree, which was half an inch thick and webbed with names and figures so small you'd need a glass to read them.

God, it must have been painstaking work. Based, I guess, on all those troves left before the Terror by brave folks, angry folks, frightened folks, sick folks. Martyrs as much as scribes and witnesses. And think of it, comrade: the generations of research and intel, the faith and grit that had gone into stalking and destroying this dynasty of overlords. Can you even imagine? What it took to overthrow and finally expunge that empire whose roots spread to every part of the globe like the tendrils of a cancer, spoiling every bit of flesh it touched. It was so big it outlasted its own epoch. Not even the collapse could kill it. They persisted in the shadows, the EXXONS. Feasting on the suffering, dying body of the world, imagining they were safe, as they'd always been safe.

But our pioneers, the early vanguard of the Service, they knew what a purulent canker smells like. Hell, they could probably taste the rot of it in the air. And the long story of that quest to sniff them out and excise them was all there in my hands, like a chapter from the sagas. Every failure, betrayal and retreat, each small victory and moment of progress. Every scion acquitted. Every oligarch, trader, lawyer, banker, enforcer, collaborator, propagandist who hadn't already been cast to the winds – all of them winkled out and ablated.

They did it – we all did it – with volunteers, comrade. With inferior kit and materiel. We did the impossible, the unthinkable. And how? Because our cause was just, and our faith was strong. And eventually, as their blood grew thinner and the clan grew more inbred, feebler, more stupid, they were no match for us. They clung to the language and culture of a fallen dispensation. So for all their many technical advantages and comforts, they were no longer fit for the world they'd wrought. The one they'd left us. And, in the end, there were too few of them, and their fear or delusions of superiority were no match for our conviction. Because for us the work was holy. We handed it on, a sacred task, from generation to generation. And I think of it now: how could they have imagined they'd survive us? Yes, they had every advantage, right down to the suicide serfs and mercenary armies. But the EXXONS could never understand that a free citizen, a volunteer, can do things for pride and for principle, in hope, and in desperation, that a despot and his vassals simply cannot.

So. To Utah.

Our object. With his final puff on the terrace. Or his whimsical grope and kiss. He was the last of his kind. The great ogre's final gasp.

And I was there. At the end of the age.

Standing in that empty room, with my legs aquiver, I thought of my nameless comrades. And I wanted to bellow. To howl. And to sing the vanquished name. For them. For my instructors, like Awe. But also for myself, and the hollow thing I'd become.

Of course, I did no such thing. I straightened up and felt myself slowly fill with juice. As if I'd been hooked up to an array the size of the Outer Cape.

That was us, I thought. I'd lived to see the extinction of the EXXONS. I'd been there. Had wielded the scalpel myself. And to know it was the gift of a lifetime.

Jesus Christ alive, says the bowman, scratching wildly at his beard.

Yes, I murmur, spent now.

He fills a flask from a drum and shoves it through the wire. I drink again and pass it back.

You're fucking good at this. You had me going there.

It's the truth. Our object was forty-two years old. His wife thirty-four. Their daughters four and six.

Brilliant.

Truly.

It's worth the entertainment. Bloody hell, what a story. The old minstrels had nothing on you, mate.

It's just what happened.

Intel leaves you alone to read the whole bloody EXXON file? Yeah, that's likely.

I never said it was likely.

Man, we needed more of your type, he says. They gave us no end of trainers and pointy-heads from Planning, but there were never any bards or jokers in the camps. I swear, we could've done with you.

You're not listening, I say.

Beautiful. Bloody beautiful.

I'm standing there, the dossier's still open on the table, and five people come in. Planners. Spooks from Intel. To make me an offer.

Don't tell me, he says. They've got your wife.

No, I say with a sigh.

Course not, he says. There never was a wife. She's too good to be true, mate. You overdid it there.

Truth is, in that moment I didn't even give Sun a thought. I'm not proud of it, but right at that instant, in the face of what I'd just read, she'd vanished from my mind.

Ha! Too excited, eh? Too overcome! By God, he says with a chuckle. This is some wild shit you're spinning.

Now the bowman's laughter irks me. And I wonder what weeks and months or even years of exposure to his scornful pessimism might do to me. Will I survive this night only to strangle the man one afternoon out of sheer exasperation?

You can't imagine what it was like, I say.

Isn't that *your* problem? Aren't you the one telling the yarn? Anyway, you really expect me to believe they flew a disaffected, insubordinate operator out to bumfuck nowhere to show him the EXXON dossier?

Everything about it was irregular.

No shit.

But, like I said, it was a ploy.

To what end?

To get me to do a job.

Because you're so special?

If you don't want to hear this, just say. I'm tired. I'm happy to sleep.

C'mon, brother. Don't be like that. Don't sulk. Cough it out. Really, you're not bad at this.

So, as I was saying: five of them came into the room. The spooks among them were easy enough to spot. Planners had that meticulous air. Plain, cautious, plodding. Whereas the folks from Intel had a bit of flash. They needed to show you they had the goods. And while a planner was likely to admit to what she didn't know for the sake of accuracy, a spook couldn't help covering her arse. You know, lest they give you a sense of being your equal.

Well, I told them. This is a rum set-up.

They all looked sideways at each other.

Yes, said a wiry little woman with a withered arm. It's unconventional. But the Service appreciates your attendance here today.

I came expecting something else.

That's a pity. What you've been given is a rare privilege.

It feels like a trap.

It would be a mistake to think so.

Accessing restricted files. I could be cashiered for that. Or worse.

Just as you could have been permanently relegated for dissent and insubordination after your last deployment, said the spook. But we're here to make you an offer.

Your record in the field is outstanding, said one of the planners. And missions like these, he said, jerking his chin at the EXXON dossier.

They're rare. To be part of an effort of historic consequence – that should be a source of great pride.

We're keen to offer you a special opportunity, comrade. But first we need to ascertain your status.

My health? I said. Or my loyalty?

At your previous debrief you expressed concerns about altered conditions in the field. Gas failures. And faulty intel.

Yes.

We've looked into it. Our gas is sound. But the last holdouts have a defence against it.

Masks, I said. Stands to reason. If we've got them, so will they.

No mask will hold out indefinitely, said the planner. As you know yourself, the build-up after thirty minutes is lethal. We haven't found any masks in strongholds, and if they have them they're not at all like ours.

Let's not pretend it's about masks, said the woman from Intel. Just tell him.

For a few moments there was silence. The tent walls shivered in the hot wind.

We have a special job, said the planner. Requiring extraordinary measures. And we need to assemble a unique team.

You shouldn't be saying any of this.

These are exceptional circumstances, said the spook. We have a specific opportunity. To achieve a breakthrough. Which may be decisive.

We're that close?

Well, said the spook, it's not for me to say.

But as you can see, said the planner, the Service has gone to unusual lengths.

This is an inflection point. You understand?

I nodded, though I'm not sure I really did understand.

This will be an extremely challenging action, said the planner. We're not talking about the dregs here. This is a consolidated adversary. With none of the eccentricities of the late-stage EXXONS.

Okay.

Okay, what? said the planner.

Why would you think I wouldn't be up for it?

You seem content with civilian life, said the spook.

It'll still be there when I get back. When do we go?

Before you consent, said the planner, you need to see something. Comrades, shall we?

They marched me out into the webbed light and together we filed across the dusty camp until, at the perimeter, the camo lattice was lifted to let us out onto the spinifex plain of the desert. A truck was waiting for us, whirring under its own lean-to of camouflage. We climbed up onto the cowled tray and the vehicle bumped and wove between the low tussocks across the dirt, until it found a trail through the spinifex.

After an hour, we pulled up near the mouth of a dry gorge. I followed the others to another lattice-shade shelter, where a stocky operator with an eyepatch met us with water and some provisions for lunch. As the brass sipped and nibbled, she and I surveyed one another frankly. She could see I was an old hand and was doubtless wondering if I still had the sand for it. From the lost eye and the left ear melted to a brown stub, I knew she'd been unlucky. Or perhaps reckless.

Right, then, said the spook, chucking the dregs of her water against a rock. Shall we crack on?

Yes, said the operator struggling to hide her disapproval at the waste. Everything's prepped.

We have special allowance to use an irregular tool on this mission, said the planner. It's unconventional, but the only option. You need to acquaint yourself with it and give consent.

Follow me, said the operator.

She led us into the gorge a way until, ahead of a blind corner blackened by fire, we reached a pair of shell cases marked BREATHING APPARATUS IV – RESTRICTED. She motioned me forward and directed me to pop the latches of the nearest case. Inside lay a harness, a cylinder and a gooseneck nozzle.

Looks primitive, I said.

Does the job.

But it's not any kind of breather, is it?

No, comrade, she replied mordantly. This is not a breather.

You people can't be serious.

Here, she said, hauling it out of the shell and strapping it on. You ignite the juice here. Trigger is down under this. Then it's point and go.

This is illegal, I said. This isn't right.

It's the only way we can do the job, comrade. Believe me, you'll be grateful for it.

She half turned and, as the sun caught the sheen of the cylinder, the nozzle sparked into a drooling flame. And without warning, as she triggered the thing, it spewed a howling arc of fire that splattered against the charred wall of the gorge thirty metres away.

Now, she said. You try.

You gave them the nod, says the bowman.

I did.

We should have used it sooner. All those poor bastards you'd see coming back in bits.

I just don't think we understood what was happening. Not even the spooks.

But everyone could see the gas wasn't working anymore. Why'd it take them so long?

Maybe because it's ugly.

Jesus, man, gas is ugly.

But fire – it's barbaric.

What choice did we have?

You ever use it?

I did. If we'd cooked those clunkers the first moment we could, the world wouldn't have turned to shit.

Well, I didn't even know we were up against something like that. Anyway, it was a mistake. Things might've worked out if we'd responded differently.

The only thing we should've done different is to use fire on them sooner. Fucking horrible things.

You ever actually meet one?

Me? No. Jesus.

Not even in the field?
He shakes his head. Burrows a finger into one ear.
I saw enough to know they're unnatural, he says.
I don't argue the point. I'm too tired.
So you went? he asks me.
Yes.
Well, come on, brother, have at it.

From the desert camp I was flown home and instructed to stand by for this special op. But a year passed and no word came.

The seasons grew perverse. Our yields fell. More folks left the hamlet and took to the road. By the winter solstice of the year after that, I'd begun to suspect the job had fallen through. Or that it had been crewed and executed without me. So my state of readiness began to decay.

One indication was that I found myself noticing women in the market square. Watching them in ways I hadn't for years. Maybe this had something to do with my mother. The sadness of watching her age. How complaisant and forgiving she'd become, as if finally ground down by the hardships of plains life. Local girls looked hunched and careworn, even in adolescence. In their hoods and scarves, their older sisters and mothers were like crones. And as they pawed the produce on the trays before me, the fingers protruding from their sun gloves reminded me of the gnarled sticks on which the eagle of my youth had perched.

I was afraid to think of Sun. Had been for years. Because the thought of her and the memory of madness seemed inseparable. And yet, during that second winter of waiting, I was registering the many ways in which those hamlet women were unlike Sun. At least Sun as I had known her.

I'd never considered looking again for companionship or marriage. After Sun's departure, I didn't raise the prospect with my mother. I'd spent time in the company of women while on active service, people who were comely in their way, or fierce or staunch, or bore all these attractive aspects at once, and yet I never felt a flicker of interest. Madness and sorrow had burnt something out of me.

One Saturday, at the end of the morning market, I was packing down the stall when someone stepped up beside me. Stooped at the tailgate, I declared I was out of produce and done for the day. It was only when the woman spoke that I glanced up.

She said: I'm not here to trade for tomatoes.

I looked about, immediately alert, and saw there was nobody else nearby.

She wore hemp boots, dusty work pants and a hooded cloak. A swaddled infant was strapped to her chest. The woman seemed agitated.

You have a message?

Yes, she said, smoothing the child's bonnet with a gloved hand.

She was much younger than me, with a nose that had been broken and badly reset.

So, the message?

I want you to stop looking at me, she said.

Okay, I said, returning to the empty crates I was stacking in the bed of the vehicle.

It's making people talk, she said.

There's nobody here, I told her.

It's been happening for weeks. It can't go on.

I stopped what I was doing and peered at her.

I'm sorry, I said. I don't know you.

You have no right. Looking at my child like she's some kind of fruit you're waiting to eat.

I think there's been a mistake.

The error is yours. I'm not a vindictive person. But what you did to that girl was shameful. And you probably don't deserve to see your child again, but I'm pleading with you. I'll trade with you to make it stop.

There's nothing to trade and nothing to stop, I said. I already told you, citizen. I don't know you.

I'm making you an offer. Others will not be so understanding.

I think you should get out of the sun, I said.

You think your mother can protect you forever? You're not the only growers on the plain!

Now you're threatening me?

I have information.

I think you're confused, I said, turning my back.

He doesn't even want to know! she declared to the empty square. This heartless fool. This succubus. He *deserves* to be alone.

I finished packing hurriedly. Drove home at speed.

The encounter unnerved me. I'd never experienced a breach of hamlet decorum like this. I didn't mention it to my mother, but later that week, at dinner, she announced that for the remainder of the season, she'd do the market run herself.

Are you sure? I asked.

I think it's best.

Can I ask why?

I gather there was an altercation.

How do you know this?

I went in for a meeting. Tuesday, if you recall. Someone from the Association mentioned it.

They're talking about it there? That's ridiculous.

Nevertheless. We've had a run of harsh seasons. People are experiencing distress. It's important to maintain calm and civility. You understand how fragile these are. And what can happen to a community if things slip. You've walked through ruins – you don't need to be told.

This is an overreaction, I said. Some woman accused me of looking at her. Having evil designs on her baby. She's not well.

I'm sorry, she said. But the hamlet can't afford any more wild talk. And neither can we. I'll do all the marketing until the heat comes. You should consider a salvage trip, in case this gets out of hand.

You're afraid of some crazy person? You'll let me be defamed?

We have a higher responsibility.

This isn't fair.

You sound like a child, she said, getting up from the table. I'm surprised at you.

She began to collect dishes and take them to the galley while I sat before my unfinished meal. When she bade me goodnight, I did not answer. From the deck I watched her cross the compound in the moonlight. I spent the rest of the evening brooding.

But over the days to come, as I worked alone or alongside my mother, I had time to ponder the stranger's words in the market. Yes, she'd been mistaken, and she'd uttered a veiled threat, but before her agitation got the better of her, she'd spoken of an offer. She'd mentioned information. And the stuff about me deserving to be alone – could this have something to do with Sun? Was that the trade she was proposing? Some sort of intel about Sun's whereabouts in exchange for promising I wouldn't leer at her or her child? It was insane. And yet once the thought arrived, I couldn't shake it off.

———

389

For the remainder of that week, I was distant toward my mother, but I gave her no reason to believe I would defy her. When market day came, I joined her in the pre-dawn gloom to help pack our surplus into her truck. I stayed out to see her off. Then, two hours after first light, I drove my own rig to the hamlet, arriving as the final trades were being made in the hot shade.

As I got out, across the square I saw my mother straighten. The pale flash of her face was momentary. She resumed her negotiations with a fellow proffering a sack of something too distant to identify. But I knew she'd seen me.

I wasn't even halfway across the square before the woman from the previous week intercepted me. She strode up with a determined expression. She'd come without the child. Strands of her dark hair were spilling from the cowl of her cloak.

You have to stop this, she said.

I will, I said. You have my word. But what are you trading?

You need to go away, she said.

I often go away.

You've been to the city? she said, leaning in so close I could smell sweat and cinnamon.

Yes, I said. You're from there?

You know the port?

I do.

And the hospital district?

Yes.

Building 54.

What is it?

An academy. There's a creche. A school.

Yes?

I have your word? As a citizen and a comrade?

What're you saying?

Your word, she said. You'll go away. You'll leave us be?

I promise, I said.

I saw them there.

What?

Marjorie, said the filmlayer, suddenly at her side. I think your sister is waiting.

She can wait, said the woman, shrugging him off.

Here, he said. Let me help you.

I don't need help.

She's got your baby, he said, pointing to the corner of the square where another woman clutched the swaddled bundle in the shade. Babies are precious, right?

Yes, she said, her face softening into a smile of adoration.

That's right, said the big fellow, giving me a long, cold look.

They're precious, said the woman, turning her attention back to me. Her eyes were pale blue. Fierce.

Let's go, said the filmlayer as my mother approached.

You promised, the woman said, no longer resisting.

I did, I said as she turned and let herself be led away.

I told you to stay home, said my mother, her voice close in my ear and quivering with rage.

The woman's ill, I said.

Of course she's ill.

She's worried about her baby.

There is no baby, she hissed. It's a doll.

What?

Can you not tell the difference between a child and a bunch of rags? Leave now, she said.

Jesus, I said, bewildered. I'm sorry.

For everyone's sake, just go.

———

At my vehicle, in the hard sun, a scruffy rustic waited, leaning against the push bar, watching my progress across the square. When I got close, he drew himself up and I steeled myself for a confrontation.

Citizen, I said, noting the cankers on his cheeks, the piece of his brow missing.

A message, he said.

Okay, I said, glancing around. My mother had her stall packed down already. The women were gone and the filmlayer too.

Same place as last time. A week from today. Noon.

Understood, I said.

He walked away without another word and didn't look back.

I got in the vehicle, ramped up the air and sat a moment to take in this news. No milk run or briefing ever required a week's notice. This had to be the job. At last.


Later, at home, I walked across the compound and hauled myself up my mother's steps. She was preparing herself for the afternoon heat. Her bed linen was peeled back. She was in her shift.

I think it's probably time for me to leave for a while, I said.

She gave a sigh of resignation and said perhaps that was for the best.

We could do with some new panels, she said.

Yes. I'll have a good look around. It'll take me a few weeks, I suspect.

I imagine so. But we don't have much to trade right now for that kind of kit.

I still have a stash in the mine country, I told her.

Ah, she said. You always did well there.

Yes, I said. You were right about that.

It hasn't been easy for you, I know.

Sometimes it's a relief to be somewhere people don't know me.

I understand, she said. But I worry that you'll be . . . lost, somehow.

I know my way around, I said mildly.

I mean lost to your own. To your people and your place. I hate to think of you becoming rootless. I don't want you to get used to it.

It's only a few weeks, I said.

Yes, she said. The change will help.

Five days later, in the early morning darkness, she clutched me and wept. And I was surprised at how thin and delicate she suddenly seemed. As if her old armour had forsaken her. I felt wretched leaving her, but relieved to be going.

The bowman interrupts me. He comes close, puts his fingers in the mesh.

This woman, he says. The wife. You never talk about what she was like. In the sack.

Are you serious?

You brought it up. Talk of women.

You want to know about my wife's body?

Look at me, he says. Look who you're telling this to. Look where we are. Can't you see a man might be interested to know? I don't mean anything indecent by it. But would it kill you to sprinkle in a few details of a – well, a carnal nature? Fella like you, stories to tell. You set me up, leave me hanging.

No.

I don't care if she's not real. If she's your little fancy, she can be mine, too.

She *was* real. I'm not going to talk about anything like that.

Ah, c'mon, friend, he says. Look where we are. Think about how long it's been.

Comrade, I say, struggling to manage my fury. Why would you speak like that of a woman? What happened to you?

Jesus, man! he says with a bitter laugh. The world. The fucking world happened to me. To you, too, mate. You're just too clueless to see it.

I know how the world is.

Do you? Really? Or is it just the version you console yourself with, the bullshit you make up, like these yarns you're spinning? What are you, anyway? A liar, a fantasist, or just a fucking nitwit? I bet you don't even know anymore.

I know who I am. And I know how the world is. I haven't caved in, comrade. I still know what's right.

Baah! You're a disappointment. That's all I can say.

The feeling's mutual.

Fuck me, he says. Are you sulking now?

There's a child here, I say.

What of it?

A girl. You don't offer me confidence, comrade. I'm not reassured.

What the fuck are you talking about?

You know exactly what I'm talking about.

You should wash your mouth out.

I want assurances, I tell him. Or it'll end here.

He peers at me. Then at the sleeping child. And I know he's understood me. Because he's already feeling behind him for his bow. He knows I could break her neck before he even loosed a bolt.

I shouldn't have to, he says, sounding genuinely aggrieved.

And I shouldn't have to fucking ask.

I'm not a barbarian, he says.

Promise me.

Go fuck yourself.

I sink back against the jumble of hard shapes behind me. And nothing more is said for a while.

C'mon, then, he says. Don't leave me hanging. Crack on.

I don't know why they sent us by sea. The decision to make an equatorial transit that way was logistically and tactically bewildering. We lost two operators to calenture in the first leg alone. It's bad for morale having to watch comrades writhe and cook in their own skins.

For a stronghold interdiction, we were an unusually large company, so conditions on board were dangerously crowded. As expected, the veteran with the eyepatch was with us. She and I pretended not to know each other. And I wondered how many others aboard were doing likewise. It was just another irregularity to contend with, and I tried my best not to fret about it.

The vessel was a small freighter. Hardly bigger than the coastal scows that used to visit the peninsula. Its solar sail ran like a black flag before us, and any forceful gust yanked the hull forward so suddenly that the screws cavitated with a disconcerting whinny.

The crew were equatorials – nimble, hardy, silent, but kindly enough. Many nights they offered us the salty tack they made from jellyfish. For us, it was unnerving to eat things of the sea. But insects and boneless creatures were not proscribed food, so we champed away dutifully, even if we never quite got used to it.

For several days we ran before the southerly trade winds. As a boy I'd read the stories of birds following boats in clouds, and fish like armies on the march. There were tales of mysterious creatures that lit up the night sea, and great wallowing monsters that huffed and hooted in the darkness. But all I saw was plastic dandruff and the jellies that churned in our wake.

Then, as if we'd exhausted both sea and breeze, we came into the doldrums, where the only sound was the whirr of the screws and the awful noise your thoughts made as they rattled around your head. We spent our days and nights on deck, beneath strung tarps and camo shrouds. There was little talk. No one had the energy for it. I guess we were each an island afloat in our feverish reveries. We had life-suits aboard, but oxygen and coolant were precious, so we reserved them for emergencies only.

Every morning at dawn, the crew went aloft to clean the panels of their fixed array. Their voices carried below. I didn't know their language, but they sounded cheerful in a way that seemed heartening at first but came to feel oppressive for reasons I couldn't discern. By then, the only breeze was generated by the ship's momentum. The humidity was frightful.

Two weeks out, at the first sight of land, the screws stopped, the hull went dead in the water, and we were ordered below. We spent an unspeakably ugly day waiting in the hold. Two more hands were struck down with heat fever. Their torment brought me to the brink of panic.

At sunset, the order came from above to stand to in full kit. Down in the hold, the air was stifling. We stood there an hour, our webbing like some instrument of torture. It was then that I saw why there were so many of us. The planners had allowed for high losses in transit.

Eventually we heard a smaller craft approaching at speed. It fell silent just short of us, presumably to signal, and then we heard it buzz in alongside. We felt the thuds of its wake against the hull. After that, the groan of fenders under load. In the grisly fug below deck, we held position as bodies and weights clomped overhead.

We heard ratchets, pulleys, low voices, and barely ten minutes later
the other boat pushed off and sped away with a hiss. We held stations
for another interval before the hatches were opened and our ship
got under way again, which at least forced some air down onto our
streaming faces. Then, finally, the order came to stand down and we
were allowed back on deck. We disposed of one body and tended to
the surviving operator until she, too, expired. We stripped her of any
identifying apparel and consigned her to the darkness.

The air was thick, wet, and dirty. There were no stars. The sea was
sluggish. Looked greasy.

At the rail, just short of the bow, the veteran with the eyepatch
leant in close and pointed out the yellow smear of lights in the
distance.

Mumbai Archipelago, she said.

So we're a long way north.

With further to go.

You know the site already?

I do.

Jesus. And if something happens to you?

You'll be briefed.

This deviation from protocol. It doesn't strike you as foolhardy?

I reckon they figure this one is do or die.

Even more reason to keep things tight.

You'd have thought so.

Is this overconfidence, you think, or desperation?

Comrade, she said. This is an odd show, but not so odd I'll be
having that conversation with you.

Understood, I said, chastened.

On the unlit foredeck, the ship's crew stripped the new cargo of
its nets and webbing and took several smaller supply crates aft. Left
behind in the darkness were two rows of identical shapes laid out

on the deck. We didn't have to be told what they were. These were the shell cases containing our field kit. The crew returned to hustle them away while those of us in the action team luxuriated in the moving air.

It took me a while to notice that along with the kit we'd taken aboard two new passengers. Their soapy scent marked them out as planners. They kept to themselves, bunking in a cabin away from the rest of us.

Three days later, after sunset, an order came down from the unlit bridge for us to strip and move aft. The ten of us who were still operational shucked our rancid fatigues and shuffled back to the afterdeck. Once we were assembled by the scuppers, two crew members sprayed us down with firehoses. The seawater they pumped at us was warm and hard as gravel against our skin, but the breeze from the ship's momentum freshened it enough for the effect to be soothing. Field attire was issued. And after we'd buttoned down and booted up, we were ushered into a wardroom for briefing.

By now I'm sure most of us had figured out where we were. The Gulf of Oman was a sector I'd never worked in before. But I had enough history to know this was the province of the black-oil tribes whose imbricated and endlessly feuding empires had taken in the parched tongue of territory between the Red Sea and the Persian Gulf. If recent rumours of confederation and consolidation were references to these clans, we were up against it. Which is exactly what the briefing confirmed.

The plan was to sneak through the Strait of Hormuz under cover of darkness, press south-west until we stood off the Al Jazirah Sands. There ten operators would be taken ashore. Four would dig in to defend the extraction point. The other six, the strike team, were to trek the sands of the fallen kingdom, get up into the hinterland and find a place the planners were calling Wadi 46.

Within Wadi 46 lay a fearsome citadel. Intel anticipated a well-armed mercenary force of twenty individuals, possibly more. Our object was a 38-year-old princeling. With him were fourteen family members, four of them children, and a household staff of between eight and twenty, all of whom were pressed labour.

Informants within the stronghold described a tunnel system within the wadi walls. Facing west was an open terrace, much lower but otherwise not so different to the one in Utah. It had multiple firing positions and commanded a view of the western approaches. Once our strike team got close, they were to infiltrate three hours after dark. We'd leave the bulkier kit at the staging point, go in light, and meet the two informants at the edge of the dune field. Their password was *amity*. Ours was *level*. In exchange for guiding us into the lair, these assets had been promised protection and extraction, but given the logistical challenges in play, these undertakings could not and would not be delivered on.

The actual acquittal was to occur within a two-hour window. Everyone was to be accounted for. Then we'd make the trek back to the coast for an aerial extraction.

It was a wildly ambitious enterprise. Beyond daring. We were perilously outnumbered. We had less than ten days in which to get the job done. And most of that time we'd be trekking without suits over the harshest country imaginable.

Things began smoothly enough. Once the planners had dished out pills and we'd huffed oxygen a while, the foils were lowered, and we buzzed to the beach under cover of darkness. We pressed in behind the dunes and the extraction team got to work digging in. The rest of us harnessed up and struck out for the interior. Of the six of us, I was by far the oldest, and the only man.

Our senior was the one with the patch. She was all business. And she'd clearly had briefings the rest of us weren't privy to. She struck me as confident to the point of carelessness. I could only hope that whatever counsel had fuelled her boldness was solid.

We set out across the sands in broiling darkness. The dune ridges were steep and corrosively hot. We moved as quickly as we dared, checking on one another silently, at intervals, in case of heat sickness. In those conditions, we should have been working in suits, but their life-support packs were heavy and barely lasted forty-eight hours. We'd be afoot for more than a week, so even if the suits kept us alive a day or two on the way in, they would help kill us before we even started back.

We were dangerously burdened as it was. In addition to our personal gear and the rations snapped to our chests in satchels and in our webbing, we each wore a water bladder on our back, and over that a shell case of gas canisters and charged cartridges for the tools lashed at our shoulders. And, of course, we all had to take turns hauling the little field watermaker along, like a mascot we daren't forsake.

The sand was roasting hot. And soft. So the going was brutal.

Just short of first light, as a flaying wind got up from the north, we dug in under films and nets and lay in a tight circle around the maker, slimy, sand-crusted and panting. In between woozy naps, we worked to fill our water bladders and clear our tools of sand.

Twice during that daylight camp, drones flew high overhead, running grid patterns without pause or deviation. They looked automated. There was nothing to do about them but lie still, trust that our camo was working and that the wind was helping obscure our tracks. But we knew there wasn't much chance of arriving at our destination with the advantage of surprise.

At dusk we broke camp to resume hauling ourselves over the razorbacks. No one mentioned the irregular, supplementary loads being carried by the senior and me. The pair of us each had a long shell lashed across our shoulder blades. Still marked as breathing gear. No mention of fire had been made during the final shipboard briefing.

We had a mandated distance to cover each night. We understood failure to keep schedule would be fatal — that is, if we didn't kill ourselves in the effort.

Near the end of the third night, our senior called a halt and ordered the maker and any other tech switched off. We'd arrived at the wadi. So we dug in and stood to.

Why kill the maker? I whispered close.

We think they've developed a way of locking on.

To our tools as well?

Only at discharge.

Great.

Stop whining and keep your fucking eyes open.

I cleared my goggles and peered into the murk. But even when the light came up, it was impossible to distinguish a landform in all that sand and dawn shadow. When the glare took hold and the mirages got up, it was worse.

In the middle of the afternoon, mired in sweat, with a full diaper, and my ears ringing in the heat, I wriggled back up beside the senior.

What's the real plan? I whispered.

As advertised. Waiting for the informants to show.

So this is not a suicide mission?

Verboten.

So's fire.

The order is to use gas. The rest is the means of last resort. It cannot be used before gas.

That's kind of stupid.

They're squeamish. They want to be able to tell themselves they exhausted all alternatives.

That'll get some of us killed.

Doubtless.

Jesus, I hissed. If we're gonna do wrong, we may as well get the benefit of it.

I agree, she said. But here we are.

*Theirs not to reason why, theirs but to do and die*, I said.

You have doubts. So noted. Now fuck off and let me sleep.

At last light, I woke the senior again. She rolled slowly onto her belly to glass the terrain ahead.

Nothing.

I shook my head.

Did you sleep?

A little, I whispered.

I bet you dreamt of home.

I don't remember.

So you say, old man.

What about you? I asked.

Sleep, yes. Dream, no.

What about home?

This is home for me now.

This place?

No, she said with a mirthless grin. This work.

Does that mean you'll miss it more than home? When it's over?

It'll never be over, she whispered, her breath bitter in my face. But if it ever stops, yes, I'll be homeless.

I stared at her. Wondered if perhaps she could be joking. But I saw something in her eye, a glaze that suggested something well beyond fatigue. It was a deadness from which I found myself recoiling.

Three hours after sunset, someone saw a figure. Then a second. I never saw either.

We'll go out to meet them, said the senior.

I took a young operator onto the left flank. The senior and her second held the centre. And the third pair were to the right. We were, for a couple of minutes, a standard feeler, an inverted V.

We hadn't even found hard ground, let alone the wadi itself, when the farthest pair were lit up in a single flash. After the crack, a few ragged chunks of flesh and webbing rained down around us, and I knew without even lifting my face from the dirt there were only four of us left.

So much for our guides. I could only assume they'd been betrayed. Tortured for information. If they ever existed. Had I been leading this show I'd have withdrawn immediately. And I was heartened, when I next put my head up, to see the senior give the signal to fall back. We didn't need a second prompt. But once the young recruit and I fell into the shallow ditch beside her, I saw she had no intention of retreating further.

I caught the origin flash, she said calmly. They're out there on the right. Elevated. Maybe ten o'clock high. We'll take everything with us except the rations and the maker. Strap up. Leaving in sixty.

And the plan? I asked, cinching straps and checking my gas cartridges.

We go out there to the left. I'll leave the maker switched on here. Once they get a lock on that, they'll light it up. Then we can confirm it's the same point of origin. If there's a second firing position we'll adjust, but if it's the same one we'll work our way in, two up, two back, and look for an opening.

Fucking sketchy, I said.

Suit yourself.

She flicked the toggle on the maker. Then she was up and running, her offsider hard on her heels. The youngster and I scrambled to our feet and lurched out into the dark.

Through the visor I caught the movement of the others sprinting and weaving out ahead. The sand was still soft and deep underfoot. The smell of burnt webbing and scorched meat hung in the air. When the senior and her second pitched forward onto their bellies, I yanked my partner down and scanned right. Through the swirling murk of the night visor, it was still impossible to distinguish any difference in the landscape, but less than ten seconds later a burst rent the darkness, still on the right flank, and for the briefest moment

I glimpsed hard edges and body silhouettes at either side of the source. Behind us the ground shook.

That's the watermaker gone, said my second.

They're close, I said.

This fucking bitch is crazy, she hissed.

Let's go, I said, hauling her up by the arm.

The senior was already up. She and her offsider had started priming gas canisters.

Another wild bloom of light erupted and I felt the hot column of air peel by before the spatter of hardware and meat knocked me onto all fours. That was the end of my second. I didn't even look back.

Out ahead, the senior and her sidekick ran full tilt in the direction of the origin flash. Then they dipped out of sight. It took a second or two to figure out why, but I was soon pitching down the sudden decline in their wake, struggling to keep my feet on the gravel surface. Another big flash – this time to the left of us – ripped the ground ahead of the senior and illuminated a lumpy wall of rock beyond.

Now I could see we'd come to a wide draw at the mouth of a wadi. Another burst from the right went crackling past my shoulder and at its source I saw a nest of heads in a long rectangular recess overhead. That's where our first canisters went. Mine seemed to fall short – just clunked onto some kind of sill and spun lazily until a hand appeared, tried to get hold of it and then let it go again. Two more gas rounds went up after that. Then another flash from the left cut the senior's second in two. I sent two bursts from my tool up to where I thought it originated and for a few moments there was a heady pause. I scrambled in hard against the rock face to gain some cover. There were cries from above and wretched coughing.

More gas, shouted the senior, masking up.

I dragged my own mask down, snapped another canister on, stepped back to improve the angle, and launched it over the parapet.

She sent up another, and then together we hugged the rough base of the wadi wall, listening to the clatter of kit and bodies falling overhead.

Then it was quiet. For a while I thought we might have neutralized their defences. We'd still have to find a point of entry. Without guidance. And now there were only two of us. But more boots began to thud overhead, and I knew our chances of penetrating were almost nil.

We sent more gas up over the rampart, but in the wake of that salvo there was a fresh smattering of tool fire from overhead. To make matters worse, the big unit to the right started up again. For the moment, the angle of elevation still favoured us, but we were pinned against the base of the wall, trapped within this withering fusillade. Even through the gas mask, the chlorine stink of ozone was sharp.

The senior shrugged off her shell case and snapped it open. I didn't need urging – I did the same.

We should have fucking started with this, she said.

We're here now, I said.

But before I could prime and spark the pilot flame there were shouts followed by a whirr overhead. I dropped the cylinder and snatched up my tool. As the little drone swept down, I caught it with one long, swirling burst and bits of it rained against the wadi wall and skittered off our visors. I jacked out the power cartridge, replaced it with a fresh one and shouldered my tool while I finished prepping the flamethrower.

As I strapped the cylinder on, the senior ignited her nozzle and stepped back, almost casually, into the open. The gooseneck wand issued a long, curdling scream and a thick cord of light poured up, a rope of fire fifty metres long. She hosed their position sideways, back-stepping boldly, raking flames across the battlement and into the cavity behind it. After looking on for some moments, appalled and terrified, I followed her lead. And so began the business of burning people alive. And here's the thing of it. It was easy. In the moment, my body pulsing with urgency, it felt straightforward. And necessary. I crabbed along the wadi floor sending fire across the parapet, smelling scorched flesh and burning plastics until the earth belched, lifted underfoot, and swallowed me whole. As if for shame.

When I came to, in a stifling gloom, the first thing I saw was sandstone. It seemed close overhead, a lumpy, friable ceiling. Grit in the air. My ears hissed. Every surface gave off a wounding flare and everything around me was hectic with motes and floaters. I recognized the symptoms of a blast concussion.

I couldn't tilt my head at all. It hurt to move my eyes. Even lifting and lowering my eyelids set off a charge that ran down through my jaw and into my chest. So far as I could tell, I was on my back, in a narrow cave or tunnel. From somewhere behind me a faint light angled in, and a roasting wind funnelled through to jab at the crown of my head. My naked head. The helmet and visor gone.

I tried to concentrate, to remember, to orientate. Everything was furry, flary, woozy. I felt as if I'd been dropped from a very high place. And I didn't remember how. I felt unutterably fragile, and a hot panic began to course through me as I became convinced that the tiniest movement would cause every bone in my body to shatter. I began to hyperventilate. And then, after a time, I reeled myself back to order.

Yes, I could feel my fingers and toes. And the air travelling across them. Which was a good start. But it meant I'd been stripped by a concussion wave or robbed. In any case, I was now exposed – to weather as much as to adversaries – and I knew I had to summon the energy and courage to sit up and survey my situation. Form a plan, take some action. But I needed a moment. To compose myself. Brace for the pain. So I closed my eyes in preparation. And everything was better. All was suddenly good.

When I opened my eyes again the light was gone. Total darkness. Only the hot wind remained to assure me I was still in the same place, the same dream, the same trouble. I listened. No ringing in my ears. In fact, I could hear my pulse, my ragged breathing. And then, after a long searching wait, I heard something in the darkness behind me. A small movement of sand. Like a body shifting.

Hello? I whispered.

After a second or two I felt the waft of something passing. Then a hand on my chest, something hard against my chin. Liquid ran against my lower lip. I tucked my jaw, despite the pain of it, and drank. The water tasted native, sandy. I felt a moment of revival and curiosity. But then everything melted away again.

The next time I surfaced, hands were on me and there was light enough to see a veiled face, a pair of eyes, a swathe of fabric, some sort of cloak. I felt a wet cloth, saw it come away filthy pink from my skin. Dried blood. Whose, I wasn't sure. There was a deep ache in my core, but I felt no surface pain anywhere and wondered if I was paralysed or drugged.

Another face appeared. Also veiled. A pair of hands proffered a tiny parcel. Something bound in grey oilskin. Those hands began to unwrap it. And a pinkish cube lay bare against a bed of grey cloth. Dark fingers broke a piece off and brought it to my mouth. It was moist, pasty, the taste not unpleasant. I ate until it was gone and, after I'd drunk again, the figure withdrew. I felt the sand under me and registered something soft, perhaps a roll of fabric, beneath my head. Then the earth tipped inward.

Sir?

I opened my eyes. It was darker now. But there was a light coming from somewhere. It looked unstable, handheld. There were faces above me, two at each side. All were wrapped in brown cloths.

Oh, I said, almost dumbstruck.

Are you well?

I think so, I stammered. Am I a prisoner?

No, sir, said a face to my right. You are our guest. You are welcome among us.

You speak my language.

It is within our capacity.

Am I alone?

Sir, you are with us.

I mean, my people. Am I the only one?

You are the only one of your kind remaining.

I took a few moments to absorb this news. The whole strike unit. The senior.

Sir, you are not safe here.

Why is that? I asked.

The master. He lives.

Your master?

We have no master, they all said as one.

He retreated?

He has gone deep. Into the interior. His kin also.

So why am I not safe?

Sir, his house prevails.

He has people looking for me?

They nodded.

We will take you. To your kind.

That's decent of you, I said. But I'll have to go alone.

It will be far.

Not so far, I said carefully.

As six, with means, it was possible for you. As one, with no means, it is too far.

I'll be fine. But I thank you.

Sir, we have capacity. We will convey you. That is our intention.

Your intention?

You are not safe here in the kingdom. You lack capacity. You must move quickly.

And you can move me quickly?

Yes. We are ready.

Now?

Yes.

The four of you?

Sir, we are twelve.

I looked from face to face, but with only their eyes and brows and the bridges of their noses showing, there was little to distinguish them.

And in return?

Sir, we will not return.

But you expect something. In exchange. For helping me.

Sir, all we seek is honourable treatment.

You're hiding — is that it?

We are free souls, they said in unison.

I understand.

Your task, sir, was it for liberation or plunder?

We didn't come to steal, I said.

Then we understand, also.

You want to leave this place, I said, slowly comprehending.

That is our desire, and our intention.

And I'm the means?

Sir, you are in danger.

I'd say we're all in danger.

But together we have capacity. And means.

Okay, I said. Fair enough.

You will take us?

If I say no, will you kill me?

We will treat you honourably, sir.

Thank you. Likewise.

We are in agreement?

Yes, I said, overcome once more by weariness.

Thank you, they said as one.

No, I murmured, slipping away already. Thank you.

The bowman interrupts. He leans in so close as to render himself unsafe.

You mean to say you knew what they were from the get-go?

Yes. And no. You see it but you don't see it. Not at first. But there's this anomalous sense you get. You know, the presence of something uncanny.

Jesus.

You really never met one?

No.

But you have such strong views, comrade.

What's it to you?

It doesn't matter.

But you have something to say on the matter.

All I have is my story.

So finish it.

I'm tired.

I said finish it.

I woke again. In the dark. To a jerking, jittery moon, and the scuffs of feet in sand. I was swaddled tight. Travelling feet-first. On my back. All around me, cloaked figures ran in silence. Four carried me in a kind of ribbed sling. They laboured up the steep faces of dunes and surfed into the troughs beyond. After some time, they set me down and gave me water. After every halt, new bearers hoisted me and bore me on. I saw the land around us in glimpses. It was the same golden-brown colour as their robes.

My hosts struck me as unusually coherent and disciplined. Their physical uniformity seemed to complement their unity of intent. I'd expected their bearing to be stiff, but these devices were lithe and poised. They made no sound of exertion, but after an hour or so the energy of those carrying my weight seemed to wane. That's when they paused to set me down to be replaced by others.

Just before dawn we crested an unusually high dune and came down into an evil-smelling trough. The company halted, unwound my swaddling, and gave me food and water.

Sir, when you are properly refreshed, we will bind you again and seal you.

Seal me? I said, rising gingerly to a sitting position.

As the light came up, I saw one of the company unspooling a thick silver roll on the dirt. It looked like a foil blanket but it was open-celled, as thick as my arm.

You mean we're travelling by day?

At night there is no refreshment. With the sun it is faster. But it will not be easy for you.

I won't survive.

We will seal you, sir. Shield you. You will persist. But it will not be easy.

Out beyond them, the bottom of the crater was filled by a black sheen.

Is that water?

No, sir.

Are you sure? It looks like water.

Not water, sir.

But it's a lake.

We have water here for you. We have sufficient supply.

They rewrapped me and ribbed fat ropes of linen around me. Then they set the insulation layer over the top, lashed it fore and aft, and set off again.

As the sun got up there was nothing to see but glimpses of sand, flashes of robes and brown feet in sandals. It got brutally hot. And very quickly. The only breeze came from our momentum. Without that I couldn't have maintained consciousness. As I sensed the sun tracking higher, the pace grew more brisk, more sustained. There were fewer stops. But it was hard going. Horrendous, really. While I poached, sweating and helpless, fighting off the panic, trapped inside my sling, the company ran and ran.

Sometime before noon, after I'd dozed in suffocating dreams, I heard an air-rending crack and was pitched sideways. I hit the sand hard and tumbled. And when I came to a halt, I lay winded on my back with the blanket ripped away and the sun drilling into my face. With my arms still bound inside the fabric cocoon, I had no way of shielding myself. I turned my head aside, squinted to catch the glare-flattened figures picking themselves up all around me. It took all I had to roll onto one side and see behind us a pillar of black smoke. Nearby, to the left of where I lay, a greasy vapour hung over a writhing body and a scatter of smouldering garments. From every direction, others ran to help, but I was close enough to see there was no hope. Those convulsive twitches and grinding gasps were terminal. As I began struggling to free myself, a low murmur of grief arose in the company, and I was almost to my feet, light-headed and drenched in sweat, when another salvo fell just short of us. The bearers pushed me to the sand and covered my body with theirs.

They'll have our range in a moment, I gasped.

We have shelter nearby, said the one at my feet as he began rebinding me.

Out here?

Yes, he said. But we cannot delay.

I can walk, I said, feebly resisting the pouch they were lashing me into.

Perhaps, he said. But not far enough nor fast enough.

I lay back, already spent, as the torn insulation was retrieved and bound around me again.

The next thing I remember is waking in a foetid hollow, stripped to the waist, surrounded by faces and fanning hands. They gave me water to drink. Pressed wet cloths to my chest. I felt bruised all over but I had no wounds or broken bones. I was more concerned by the shivers and chills — early signs of heat fever.

It took a minute or so to register the fact that the cave we were in was a built structure. Its blackened walls had divots and rust-scabbed wounds. Reinforced concrete. At a distance from us, a sand slope rose to a long lateral slot of light. This was ancient infrastructure all but buried under desert sands. Everything in here smelt scorched.

A member of the company produced another cube of food. Others helped me sit up to receive it. Eating revived me somewhat. I watched the faces and hands of my saviours, saw how they squatted and huddled together and I thought of that writhing, smouldering form they'd left behind on the sands. They seemed shaken. I was surprised by their common distress. I hadn't expected these things to experience pain and loss. But their grief was palpable. Truly, if not for their prodigious speed, their resilience, and the slightly disconcerting uniformity to their appearance, you'd have taken them for humans.

I'm sorry about your friend, I croaked.

They sighed as one and tilted their heads. In that moment I felt a surge of relief, for before the attack I'd been wary of their intentions more than their nature. The possibilities had been boiling in my head for hours. And even now, I knew these machines might be deceiving me. If they were the runaway slaves they claimed to be, I might now be their chattel. A gang of renegades would want to be in possession of a hostage, a bargaining chip. There appeared to be no safety or liberty for them here in the kingdom. But they had no homeland to yearn for. If they were fleeing, it could only be to seek asylum.

It was a puzzle, though. That they should resent servitude so fiercely. I'd only heard rumours before this. That the criminal clans had designed simulacra as service tech. Perhaps even weaponized them. Had something gone wrong? Were the sims defective in some way? That was always our fear. And possibly the source of so many rumours. That some new slave tool would become erratic. But these devices were orderly thinkers. Also fair-minded. And their physical performance was seamless. I'd seen no evidence of aberration or malfunction. To me they seemed eerily sound. Functional. Empathetic. Even passionate. And they were more civilized than some citizens I've known.

Tell me, I croaked. Do you understand his defence system? Your master?

We have no master, they murmured.

Understood. But that was drone-delivered ordinance back there. Is it autonomous?

They gave an equivocal sigh.

I'm trying to understand whether this system is running itself or if it's being directed at us by mercenaries.

There are hands at work, they said.

Humans?

Possible, said one, in a manner suggesting that it probably wasn't.

You mean they aren't human?

Likely, he said.

So they're like you, I said carefully.

No, he said. Not like us.

We are free souls, they said together.

And they're slaves, then?

They offered only a baleful look of forbearance.

How many?

Twenty.

I drew myself up in stages until I could rest on an elbow and see them all. Beyond them, a slit of light showed and a scalding draught slanted in.

Fewer now, I said. You understand that my comrades and I . . . destroyed some of them already?

Fire, they said with a kind of shudder.

I'm sorry, but that's what I don't understand. You wish to come with me, you want to help me, despite this? Weren't they your people?

We are free souls, they said again, almost recoiling physically from the question.

Trying to work all the options in my raddled head, I nodded and licked my chapped lips. The sims seemed in earnest. Something about their – well, let's just call it their almostness – made my skin crawl. But I was impressed by their dignity. And their longing for respect and liberty felt completely real to me. Some defensive piece of my mind – my training, no doubt – recognized it was possible they were a mercenary vanguard using me to find and kill my comrades at the coast, perhaps even take down the stat and the crew standing ready to evacuate us. We'd suffered double agents before, and the losses that came with them. I didn't want to be responsible for a debacle. But I didn't want to betray them, either.

Sir, we wish to give you aid. We are inclined to serve – this is in our nature. All we seek is honourable treatment. Are you able to provide it?

But what if I can't? I said.

I watched them absorbing this. There were eleven of them. And back on the coast, I only had four comrades dug in and waiting. The extraction crew on the stat would include a medic, a planner and maybe a spook. They'd bring only two or three armed operators with them at most. So we'd probably be outnumbered. What skipper would take eleven undocumented sims aboard on trust?

So, I said after a long, fraught pause. You want me to take you with me?

Sir, if you cannot, then we are lost.

How have you been living? I asked. How long have you been free?

The living is hard, they said.

Also long, said one of them.

But you've been living underground, right? You don't seem to need very much. Can't you survive in your hideouts?

We require sunlight, he replied. And we desire more than a life in storage. We dream and we wait. But we need to make and do. This is our purpose.

I think I understand, I said.

To serve. But also to make.

Yes. I see.

Storage is oblivion. In storage, our dreams of making escape us. Sir, they shrink.

I surveyed their shrouded faces, tried to absorb what it meant, this collective desire. The palpable power of it. The naked need in it. That's what rattled me: how like us they are.

Don't you see, comrade? You and I, we should be thinking about that. Because there's no life in hiding. In storage, as they call it. What dreams of making are you gunna have down here on your own? You know, I often wonder what Awe might have made of them. All their pining to make and ponder and serve. What would she have thought?

Sir, said the sim. You understand us?

Yes, I told him.

You can offer honourable treatment?

Yes, I said, meaning it, and hoping fervently it was the truth.

A sigh went through the shell of the ruined building. Then they set about preparations for departure.


It was merciless going. But we encountered no more drone attacks. There was no sign of us being followed. The sims ran and ran and changed teams and ran. And I lay there, passive, anxious, conflicted, delirious, one moment a pampered potentate borne aloft, the next a freshly moulted lifeform, as moist and naked as a cabbage worm.

Eventually they stopped running. This time for good. When they set down and unlashed my cocoon, I saw the sun sinking low in our path.

First they gave me water. Then they fanned me. And finally, with great care, two of them soaked cloths and bathed me once more, dabbing away the crust of sweat and sand until I revived a little and could be slowly helped to my feet. I'd lost my hat and scarf back in the wadi, but one of the sims set the insulation blanket over me like a shining silver cloak. They led me to just below the crest of the dune, where I saw we were in sight of the coast, perhaps a klick from the rendezvous point. The sims had known exactly where to bring me. Before the sun could sink into the sea, they led me back into a depression, where they squatted in a half-circle to present me with my boots. While I strapped them on and eased into my gore-stained tunic, they appeared to confer wordlessly amongst themselves.

I was perturbed at how much they seemed to know. From the moment we made landfall until the night we reached the wadi, they'd been watching. That much was clear. And although I found it hard to countenance, it was possible our betrayal, the loss of our assets and the failure of the mission could be sheeted home to them.

I decided that for my own safety, and to prevent exposing my comrades to a trap, I needed some separation. I'd have to go down first.

Alone. It wasn't going to be easy to convey the sims' disposition and predicament in a few brief seconds. Because at that point in history, if an operator knew anything at all about simulacra, it was likely based on hearsay. My comrades dug in down there would be suspicious, probably hostile, and they'd already be strung out and jumpy, wondering what the hell had become of the action team. The odds of a good outcome were low. But I had to do the decent thing. Don't you see? I wanted to vouch for them. Relay their request for asylum. It was the least I could do.

The sims cavilled at my plan, but I insisted, explaining that this was not to slight their effort and good faith but to prevent any misunderstandings. Eleven strangers bearing an operator. I'd look like a hostage. We'd all die.

I begged my rescuers to wait. Said I'd go down alone. Explain the dynamics. Negotiate a settlement for them. And that, at my signal, they should show themselves and come in slowly, making it plain they were not armed.

Troubled as they were by this scheme, they conceded. And when I was finally ready, I clasped their hands, each in turn, and set off, clambering back up the dune until I reached the crest. There, I did what I could to catch my breath. I gazed out at the shimmering sand plain, resisted the urge to look back, and staggered down, hatless, toward the coast. Within a hundred metres, I was reeling from the exertion. Blinded by the setting sun. Struggling to maintain a steady bearing and keep my feet.

It was a protracted, feverish walk. I wondered how long it would take my comrades to pick me out in the landscape. By now they must have been half-blind from staring. If they were even there, still. And if they saw me, in the last light of the sun, what would they make of my appearance? Everything about me looked wrong. My wonky gait. The weaving trajectory. The absence of helmet, scarf, webbing, tool.

Yes, I imagine the picture I made was bad enough, even before I fell and the sims came charging down to help.

I heard the perimeter challenge from out ahead but so far off I couldn't make sense of the words for the roar of blood in my ears. Feebly, and in ponderous stages, I got back to my feet. I had time enough, I remember, to turn and wave my arms to try to halt the sims streaming down the dune in the distance. Then I wallowed on, listing and reeling like a poppy fiend.

The sims ran so fast. Over my own blood and breath I could hear them coming, their thuds and scuffs more distinct every second. Another warning cry rang out. The password wouldn't come to me. All I could cough up was my Service codename, which would have meant nothing to them.

A geyser of dirt erupted to the right. I caught the stink of ammonia before I even heard the crack. The correct password fell out of me like a curse. Then I heard a hesitant all-clear. Saw a visored head rise from the sand a hundred metres away. I set off toward it, babbling, I think, oblivious to what was happening behind me. Shouts burst from the trench, and I yelled back enthusiastically, trying to lay out the picture, but by this time things had come undone.

The first volley went past me on either side. I fell to the scorching sand as another fizzed and cracked overhead. I pressed my face into the earth, helpless, heartsick, but also drunk with relief.

How many? came the call – those were the first words I heard clearly that evening.

Eleven, I called, smelling hot metal and burning resin.

Eleven?

Stand down, I yelled. There's eleven.

Okay, came the call. Clear.

Clear, I repeated and rolled aside to look back.

I don't know what I expected. I'm sure I was clinging to the hope of tactical containment, some fantasy of corralling salvos that would leave my saviours huddled and compliant, surrounded by glassy puddles of sand, left in no doubt as to who held the advantage in this moment. A position from which we might proceed and negotiate. But that's not what had happened. They were a smouldering midden of broken limbs, melted polymers and shredded fabric. Their fluids darkened the dune. Some of them twitched and writhed a few moments longer, then there was silence. And when the air cleared, I saw behind them, tipped on its side, still spilling forth and glinting in the last vicious rays of sun, the Service-issue canister they'd filled with water and carried to keep me alive.

I don't remember the extraction. Or the repat flight. Or even the early days at the field hospital outside the Assam Embankment. They told me the burns had required a long period of sedation. Likewise the lingering heat fever and its debilitating deluge of panics. I guess it was weeks before I was fit for debriefing and, when that happened, it was a most peculiar affair.

I'd been on bad shows before. Not just Utah. And I'd spent time on the wards of field hospitals and rehab units with wounds and broken bones. But I'd never been assigned a room of my own. It didn't take long to sense that this wasn't a privilege or a reward. For a while I figured the isolation was related to my condition, which wasn't a full-body burn, though I had done enough damage to my face, chest and hands to require more than just salves and ointments. Debridement, it's called. No, they kept me in seclusion for security reasons. Fear of contagion, I assume.

Of course, the planners and spooks who'd deployed me on the desert job were not the same ones who convened and ran the bedside debrief. Their manner was brisk. Cool. Almost perfunctory. Everything about their operational review felt hasty. As if the mission were a matter that needed to be forgotten as quickly and quietly as possible.

I gave my account of the landing, the traverse, the suspected security breach, the torrid engagement in the wadi. I told them about the effectiveness of the incendiaries, which they received stony-faced. But their impassive expressions gave way to discomfort and sidelong glances when I explained how I'd made it back from Wadi 46 to the coast. And it was immediately evident that our use of fire and the presence of simulacra were not facts they welcomed or were likely to record. My appraisal of the sims, entirely unsolicited, was met with silence. As was my assessment of the opportunity we'd foregone by betraying them and spurning their offer of service.

At no point did they acknowledge the sims' existence, let alone their role in my rescue. I guess it was possible they didn't believe me. But that didn't feel likely. From this encounter, I got the strong sense the Service knew about the advent of the sims, and had done for a while. It was as if they'd taken a position on them that was somehow more ideological than tactical or strategic. That the prospect of forming alliances with them would never be considered.

There was only one conclusion I could draw from the debrief. I'd been duped into a rogue mission whose details would be erased from Service accounts. Whether that's true or not, I'll never know.

About a week later, a sorrowful-looking medic delivered the terms of my discharge. Which, in itself, was irregular. Allowances had been made, she said, for my fevers, burns and concussions. Due consideration was given to my long service and record of valour. So the discharge would be deemed honourable and issued on medical grounds.

But there was no mistaking the true cause. I knew I'd probably be fit for active duty again in a few months. No, they cut me loose because they considered me unsafe and unsound.

You can imagine the terms of my expulsion. I could have done without the insult of having them spelt out. After all, I'd been a loyal operator for nearly twenty years. I knew the requirement for discretion was total and mortal. And I was always going to go quietly. But that didn't mean I was about to embrace total submission.

For a while it was hard to trust my thoughts. It wasn't until I'd weaned myself off the drugs that I felt I could distinguish the difference between feverish fancy and rational speculation.

The journey home was complicated. Multiple layovers. Lots of delays and altered flight plans. So I had an excess of time in which to sift my memories, test my thoughts. The madwoman with the doll came to mind. Those encounters in the market square – I couldn't shake them off. And now I wondered if I'd dismissed her too quickly. I thought of the haste with which the filmlayer had intervened. How familiar he was with her. The way he'd bundled her off. Maybe the poor soul's madness had an origin beyond the everyday hardships of the hamlet. She was a total stranger to me. So how could she know who my wife and daughter were?

It wasn't until I was halfway back across the continent that I resolved to deviate a little from my terminal instructions. It felt as if I had little to lose.

---

429

When the repat flight set down in the hinterland east of Perth, it was still dark. Wounded operators and amputees had to be helped as they alighted and made their way to waiting vehicles. Most transports seemed to be headed south, but my orders were to proceed to the city's eastern gate and collect my rig. So I clambered slowly into the back of a cowled truck and rode for an hour down across the scarp and, as first light came into the milky sky, onto the coastal plain.

The vehicle wasn't hard to find. And I gave the load on the trailer – presumably my last from the Service – a desultory glance. But instead of climbing in and driving away, I pulled my stash of choof from the panel inside the door and walked toward the rank of tuk-tuks under the broad awning outside the gate.

At the head of the rank, a young woman in dusty coveralls drew herself upright at my approach. We came quickly to a trade, and she motioned for me to climb in. Once we got going west, through the maze of factories and neighbourhoods, the wind lifted the skirts of her hat, and I saw the puckered suture scar at the back of her neck. I was glad I'd asked to be taken to the port and not to my actual destination. There was no way this woman hadn't seen active service.

The ride was long and hectic, the sun high, an orange halo over the rooftops and towers.

As the cranes and godowns came into view, I tapped the driver on the shoulder and told her to set me down by the river.

I walked for a few hours, enjoying the liberty of being safely abroad in the open so late in the day. Of course, it was cooler in the midwest back then. Winter days were mild. That afternoon the temperature would have hardly reached the mid-thirties. When I felt the juice going out of me, I hailed another ride and headed back into the city.

Once I'd convinced myself the driver was a civilian, I asked him to pull over a moment.

Mate, I said. Do you know a place called Building 54? In the hospital district?

Yep, he said. I know it. It's one of those posh academies. Looks like you'd be better off with some doctoring. What'd you do to yourself?

Battery fire.

Jesus.

Let's head there.

He shrugged and we got going again.

It had been a while since I'd last visited the city. I'd never been in the streets alone and unsupervised, and before today I'd always had an official purpose. The geography made it simple enough to navigate – the sea in the west, the distant scarp in the east, and the riverbed through the centre – but things had changed since I'd last been there. The boroughs had always been quite various. Yet I'd never seen such obvious disparity in neighbourhoods before. Some dwelling towers were furred with greenery. Others were blackened by fire.

Just before the hospital district, I asked to be set down. The driver looked at me askance, but the wad of leaf and heads I pressed into his hand seemed to mollify him. He gave me directions to the address I sought, off the central boulevard. Once the tuk-tuk was lost in the welter of traffic, I set off on foot.

The hospital district was a mix of large institutional campuses, residential buildings and small markets. Here, too, conditions seemed altered. The smaller medical centres were gated. Weather shelters looked as if they'd become de facto hospitals. At the entrances to these low, hangar-like buildings, canopied jeepneys and tuk-tuks gathered in snarls as sick civilians were delivered by relatives or neighbours.

Many of the markets seemed to be maintained by association, but others were clearly now administered by strictly mercantile inter-ests. The mercenary posture of security personnel around the more prosperous-looking compounds was unmistakable. A certain order still prevailed, but things were civil on one block and openly hostile at the next.

The numbering of buildings was straightforward. Digits were emblazoned above entrances and gatehouses. Building 54 stood on a rise that felt as if it had once been the spine of a ridge. From there, the dark smudge of the scarp was visible above the eastern wall of the city. Behind me, to the west, turbines flashed in the sunstruck sea.

As I stood in the afternoon shade across the street, gazing up at the tower, my pulse grew hectic, my skin clammy.

There was no nameplate beside the number, and no signage at all, but this was a highly functional and organized building. Ten levels. Clad in clean films and panels. With storm shutters. Slim barrel turbines on every horizontal. As evening fell and lights came on in the lobby, citizens stood by their stations at the custodians' desks and the sight of this filled me with relief, for this was clearly a safe place.

To me, it looked like a residential site, not an academy. Though having never seen an academy, I couldn't be sure. I saw no sign of children, but that's not to say I couldn't imagine children living there.

I thought of Sun and Ester up in their clean, tidy rooms. Yes, I could picture that. I wondered how they lived. Sun could survive on her wits anywhere. Surely people still wanted knowledge. Perhaps the Association employed her to give instruction in biology and geology. How would it be, I thought, telling cityfolk about animals and landforms? How could people like them make sense of such things? What did they even think the world outside the floodwalls was like? Did she regale them with tales of Capricorn in her youth? And what of Ester? In my mind I could only imagine her as an infant, but now she'd be nearly the age her mother had been when we first met.

To save bringing attention to myself, I walked the block to view Building 54 from every angle and to hunt fresh shade and public water outlets. There were few pedestrians in this quarter. The streets were busy with tuk-tuks, bicycles and vans. And they were comparatively free of refuse.

Back at my original position on the boulevard, in the warm dusk, I scanned every window at the front of 54 – the dark and the illuminated, the shuttered and exposed. Overhead, air conditioners rattled and hissed. Pipes gurgled. Inverters cheeped and hummed. Traffic whined past, heavy with the approach of evening. And as night closed in, I heard music. In my mind, I saw Ester bent over her instrument, lost in her making, looking up now and then to glance out across the metropolis and the starless pumpkin-coloured night above. The image was so clear and fierce, I could feel her. And I couldn't help but wonder what my daughter knew of me. Did her thoughts ever turn my way? Was I even a mystery, a strange gap in her life?

So many ideas ran through my head. I felt unsteady on my feet. I'd come so far, crossed sands and seas to be here. A mania crept upon me. For a moment I could see myself striding across the street and into that place to declare myself. I'd call their names. I'd go floor to floor like a raider in a citadel. And then I caught myself. Imagined the eruption of chaos such an action would set off. Wondered how long it'd take for the Association – or even operatives of the Service – to arrive. There'd be no coming back from that. And the fracas would do Sun and Ester no good. I couldn't do it to them. I knew that. Felt ashamed for even entertaining the idea. Just being here in the street was probably a threat to their security and their prospects. No, I thought. I'll bide my time. Maybe, down the track, there'll be other ways to get a message to them, make contact.

I stood in the dark, hoping to hell the citizens at the custodians' desks hadn't seen me lurking there all day.

The music faltered, then stopped. It was like a spell breaking. I slunk away.

I walked the streets in the dark, long enough to find a public spigot. Long enough for my head to clear.

I knew there was almost no chance that Sun and Ester were in Building 54. Yet perhaps they had been once. Maybe the poor, broken woman from the hamlet had seen them or known them there. Perhaps she'd been through the academy herself. And look what had become of her. So many years had passed. By now, Sun and Ester could be anywhere. I didn't like to think of them reduced to the same state as the woman with the doll. No, I thought, not possible. They're made of stronger stuff.

I wandered for hours, beset by neuralgia, feeling like a reckless fool.

Eventually I slept in an alley beside a laundry. And when I woke at dawn, a citizen was squatted beside me. A big fella, bearded. His scars suggested he'd known more than just a civilian existence.

Comrade, he said. You need to leave here. It's not safe.

I was just going, I said, struggling to my feet.

Here, he said, pressing a cloth-wrapped parcel to my chest. For the journey.

Can you spare it?

Brother, for you I can.

But you don't know me.

When did that ever matter?

He dusted me down and steered me out into the brassy morning light. I tottered away like a dotard, a mendicant, clutching at my parcel, wincing at the flashes of nerve pain rising in my cheeks and brow.

At the next corner I turned. Saw him watching, making certain I left.

I walked until my hips realigned and the bones of my feet no longer hurt. Hunting the shade of scaly walls, workshops, grow-houses, burnt-out tenements, I passed roofed salvage yards, rowdy markets, scorched wastelands, ribbed warehouses. The streets jingled and whirred with delivery bikes. Citizens wore their order or their disorder on their person. I still had wit enough to register any situation ahead that signalled a threat. I was alert to opportunists and seekers. I didn't fear those who were ill so much as any whose gait and demeanour betrayed a lack of purpose. I traversed a long crumbling concrete bridge. Looked down across the scum-skinned billabongs that dotted the otherwise dry riverbed. Saw the shanties that had been thrown together in the shade of the bridge's pylons, their inhabitants one rainstorm away from extinction.

With the last of my choof stash, I caught a tuk-tuk to the eastern gate. In the assembly yard beyond, my vehicle and trailer stood untouched.

I climbed into the cab, tired, sore, bereft. Booted up the motors for the sake of the cool air. I examined the parcel the old veteran had given me. No message. Just bean paste, nuts, a tacky roll of fruit composite. I ate it all.

I washed the food down with the flavourless water from the maker. And thought of the stuff I'd be drinking at home, water that tasted, as it should, of rock and sand.

I was empty. Like a man who'd spent the night tossing up his dinner.

I was ready to go home.

Five days later, as afternoon gave way to evening, I pulled in at the familiar field of termite mounds and got out into the oceanic silence. I was so close to home. If I pressed on, I'd be in the compound before midnight. But I was in no state to keep driving.

Underfoot, the stony earth was still radiant. I pulled on oversoles and wandered, sore and stiff, through that peculiar assemblage of monuments. They were taller than me. There were hundreds of them. It was like walking amidst a legion of faceless sentinels. There was no breeze. No sound.

Darkness came. The air warm as blood and rich with the musk of hot spinifex. The homeliness of those sensations was comforting. And yet I felt snagged. Suspended, somehow. Exiled from one life but not yet present in the other.

I walked back to the vehicle.

I set up a light. Filled a dixy with water. Shed my clothes. And bathed carefully. My burns had scabbed up nicely, but in the hard light they looked livid. My brow and nose and ears were tender, the skin so tight it felt as if the pressure dressing was still on, like a mask I'd wear forever.

I applied the Service-issue salve, smoothed the beard I'd grown to avoid shaving, and sat on the bedroll until I was dry.

My sleep was troubled. An hour before first light, I got up.

Made tea. Ate the last of my protein stems from the cache inside the door of the vehicle. Then I rolled up my swag. Bathed again. Applied more salve. Took my pills. And dressed in clean civvies. As the sky lightened, and I wound my scarf and knocked the dust from my gloves, it was impossible to ignore the familiarity of this pattern of preparation. I was a civilian now. And yet here I was, going through this painstaking routine, like an operator snapping into his kit before a show. It was just another costume, a kind of armour, and just another performance.

The last thing I expected to see as I bumped down the drive a couple of hours later was an extra vehicle in the compound. I pulled up short to glass the place. And saw the filmlayer come down the stairs of my mother's house at such a clip he nearly went arse over tit.

I watched him paw at the handle of his truck and fumble about in the cab. He got the vehicle moving, wheeled around too quickly in the compound, and headed my way in a flurry of dust. I cranked the window down to greet him, but he rattled by, eyes front, without even acknowledging me. And before she was obscured by roiling grit, I caught sight of my mother at the sunlit edge of the verandah, arms folded against herself like someone unwell. I sat a while, wondering if she might come out to me, but when the dust finally settled, she was gone.

I closed the window again. The cold air blasting into my face from the vents more provocation than relief. The hard morning light sharpened everything in the compound. It etched the stilts of both winterhouses and the cantilevered anchor poles for the shade sails. It silvered the frames of the solar array and the barrels of our turbines, causing the dust-pink cowls of the growsheds to glow. Behind it all, riven with canyon shadows, the immutable range.

I put the vehicle in gear and rolled on. I didn't stop at my mother's place. I drove past the rampart of sandbags and the low, hooded entrance to the cellars and their crop of flues and vents. I pulled up at the steps to my winterhouse. Hesitated a moment, then hauled myself out.

I took the stairs slowly. The sun drilled through the fabric of my tunic and scarf, seemed to tear at the scabs on my neck and scalp. The air felt impossibly fat in my throat. Sensing the first stirrings of heat panic, I clawed my way up and threw back the door to get inside.

In the galley I filled a jug with water. Doused myself. Saw it pooling wastefully on the scrubbed floor. Registered the freshly dusted surfaces, the sprig of rosemary on the bench with its purple flowers. And when my pulse came down, I filled the jug again and drank it all in a single draught. Tasted nothing. Stood at the window and saw the plume of my mother's approaching vehicle.

I stepped feebly onto the deck. Waited in the hot shade. Watched her dirt-caked flatbed rattle into the yard. She got out hurriedly. Made for the stairs in a flustered shuffle. But seemed to hesitate at the bottom step.

She tipped her head back, shielding her eyes, as if searching for me in the shade. Then her face lit up.

It's you, she said. Really you.

Yes, I replied. Me.

You didn't want to stop in first?

Oh, I didn't want to interrupt anything.

Interrupt? she said, halting again, blinking, eyes darting. What could you possibly be interrupting?

I guess that's what I was wondering.

She smiled uncertainly, forming shapes with her mouth.

I suppose it's none of my business.

You're home, she said, squinting in the sun.

Yes.

I'm so glad.

She'd come over in such a hurry she'd forgotten her hat. She hadn't even wrapped her head. Tracts of pink scalp showed through her outgrown hair.

Come up into the shade, I said.

Yes. Yes, of course.

When she got close enough to see me properly, there was no hiding her shock.

Dear God, she said. Your poor face!

I turned back into the house. Filled the jug a third time. When I returned, she was standing by the table in the shade. She'd already switched on the misters and fans. I brought her the jug and she doused herself and drank. And only then, when she was somewhat recovered, did we embrace. She smelt of clean hemp and the greenish scent of herbs. So familiar. And yet there was something inescapably awry between us.

The beard, she says. For a moment I wasn't sure it was you.

It's me.

But what've you done to yourself?

Stupidity, I said.

You've seen a doctor? How did this happen?

I gave her a chair and started in on the story I'd rehearsed. Even as I trotted it out, it sounded threadbare and implausible. But she received it avidly, without puzzlement or resistance.

The whole trip was a mess, I said by way of summary. That's it for me. No more foraging.

You've had rough trips before.

I'm done, I said.

You just need some time to recover. You'll bounce back.

No, I said. That's it. I've decided.

She looked at me searchingly.

You really think you can settle for growing food and trading water? You think that'll ever be enough for you?

Neither of us is getting any younger.

Meaning what, she asked. This is about me?

No, I said. You're still doing fine. Besides, it looks as if you're getting help.

She pursed her lips, let this pass.

I've done my bit, that's all, I said.

Your *bit*? she said, the mask of her indulgence slipping.

*They shall sit, each of them, beneath their vine and fig tree, to live in peace and unafraid.*

Wouldn't that be pretty? To live out some fantasy from the sagas.

I said nothing.

You're going to hide? Go back to living with your eyes down?

The moment she said it, I saw the twitch of self-correction, the sudden brightness in her cheeks.

You know it already. Your friend knows it.

You've lost me, she said, flapping her hands.

Yes, I said. For good.

What? Back up, she said. I'm confused. What're we talking about now?

How long have you known him?

Who?

Who? Really? You're going to do this?

Oh, she said. Him.

People must have wondered how we managed it, to have the best kit. The envy of the plain, we are.

We work hard. Always did.

You really think folks put it all down to hard work?

Why would people gossip? she said, too forcefully. How would they even know?

Well, I said. Why would they think I had another wife and family in the south? How would they know?

Tradesfolk and hawkers come and go, she said. Who knows what they say.

How long has he been coming out here?

It's really not what you think, she said, with an uncharacteristic tinge of desperation.

You believe you know what I'm thinking?

Sons are predictable, in their way.

I can only imagine.

I have never been disloyal, she said.

What does that even mean? Especially now. Disloyal to whom? To what?

He knew your father, that's all. He's looked out for us.

At what price? I asked, causing her to flinch.

It was never a matter of price, she said vehemently.

But he knew my father?

Yes, she said at last.

From the Service?

I don't know what service you mean.

My father didn't drown at sea, did he?

Yes, she said. He did.

On active duty.

In the course of his work. I've told you this many times.

And you're going to keep this up? Even though I know?

I have never been disloyal, she said again. Never.

And what about to me? I asked. How about to Sun?

She glared at me then. The steadiness of that look was all the confirmation I needed. To give her credit, a lesser person might have turned away.

You let that happen, I said. Probably even engineered it. Was any of it real? Or was it all just an arrangement?

I don't know what you mean. Son, you're unwell.

Unsound, I think is the term.

You're being hysterical.

Like you said. Sons are predictable. That's how they're recruited.

Listen to yourself.

I was just a boy!

You were old enough to be with a woman. Old enough to think for yourself.

I wonder.

Things don't always turn out as we expect them to. We don't always have control. We can't see the larger picture.

And things are never what they seem, right?

She said nothing, picked at a callus in the heel of her palm.

These feelings will pass. You'll be well again.

Dear God, you really believe that, don't you. You think I'll recover. Settle down and go back.

She set her mouth and gazed along the verandah.

The look on your face, I said. Comrade, you can't even disguise it.

What're you talking about now? Honestly, I can't keep up with you.

I'm out. Discharged. You're embarrassed. That's it, isn't it?

She pushed back her chair and stood. Don't be ridiculous.

I'm home safe. And you're mortified.

This is wild talk, she said, stepping away, glancing along the misted deck as if it were a space unfamiliar to her.

Everything good we did, Mother, we threw it away. Do you understand? Do you even see what's coming?

Stop this. Right now.

Or what? I asked her, shaking with rage.

You're scaring me.

You think I'm crazy? You think I'm going to blow this thing up? It's blowing itself up already. Soon it won't even matter.

You've been searching for them. Sun and Ester.

Now how could you possibly know that?

I can see it in your eyes.

No. You can't see anything, Mother. You don't need to. You have informants. You're a spook.

I could help you find her, she said, turning back to me breathlessly.

What?

She looked at me in sick bewilderment. As if she could not believe what she'd just said. And I had a moment or two to think, to process things.

So now you're bargaining?

What I meant to say, she said, tamping down her tunic at the hips, is that I wish I could help you.

I don't know you.

Of course you do. I'm your mother. I'm very worried about you. I'm trying to help you. Why don't we just get you washed up and settled in?

You can find her?

No, no, I misspoke. Forgive me. I'm old. And foolish.

Well, yes, you made a mistake – I think that's clear. But let's leave that for the moment. Tell me, honestly, do you even know? Where they are, I mean.

Son, you need to calm down.

And you need to be very careful, I said, darkened by this terrible shadow of knowing-and-yet-not-quite-knowing that, I realized now, had been stalking me for days.

When have I not been careful?

Today, I said, tipping my head in the direction of her house. I think today you weren't so careful.

Yes. I admit that. But it's not what you think.

So you keep saying.

I know you'll have questions, she said. But you must understand –
I'm constrained.

I can only imagine.

That man, the filmlayer, is not your father.

Well, I said. There's an answer I wasn't after. But thank you for the
clarification.

What will you do? she said, touching a hand to her face.

I'll look for them. Of course.

Don't. Please.

Are they even alive?

I can try to find out.

Building 54. They're not there, are they?

She sighed. No.

But they were at some stage.

Yes. I believe so.

Along with poor Marjorie. The madwoman in town.

That's not for me to say. Son, I'm afraid for you. I worry you'll
destroy yourself for nothing.

I'm already destroyed, I said. And it *was* all for nothing.

No. Never. I can't bear this.

Was it you who planted the rumours? About me?

Defame my own family? What do you think I am?

Honestly, I said, feeling as if I was losing the thread now, struggling to stay upright. I couldn't say.

We need to end this conversation. You need to rest. Dear God,
look at you.

You do understand what I'm trained for, what I'm capable of?

Please, son, don't talk like that. You wouldn't.

Who can say? I'm unsound, comrade. And very agitated.

You'll need more than threats to make me talk.

Oh, I don't doubt it, I said, sensing, with horror, the turn things were taking. You're staunch. It wouldn't be easy. For either of us. But the crims had their methods. Maybe you spooks did too.

No.

No, you didn't? Or no, don't think about it?

You wouldn't. I raised you better than that.

Not something I really want to hear right now.

It's not sanctioned, she said. It's immoral.

Don't speak to me about what's moral.

I understand you're angry.

This is my whole life we're talking about.

And mine. Don't you see?

You betrayed me.

That wasn't my doing, she said. None of it was my idea.

Your own child? Your granddaughter?

I told you, she said quietly. I was constrained.

By what – higher loyalties? Orders? You let them go. You sent them off on a lie.

I did what was required. For the greater good.

Tell me, I said. Did you ever resist? When you knew it was wrong. When it caused so much pain.

She didn't answer.

No, I didn't think so.

I've suffered for it, she said.

You have? You really believe that? You reckon you've suffered enough?

You'd do this? she asked faintly, eyes brimming with tears. For information. You'd torture your own mother?

What if it was for the greater good?

It wouldn't be. And you'd never know if what you got from me was true. You'd have sullied yourself – destroyed yourself – for nothing. People say whatever torturers want them to say.

Ah, you're impressive, I said bitterly.

No. I'm afraid.

Honestly, I said. What did you expect?

This is unbearable.

Yes.

You're trembling, she said.

I'm insane, remember?

Is that how you plan to explain it? To yourself, to everyone else?

I haven't planned anything.

I've never been afraid of you, she said.

Perhaps you should be.

This is unbearable.

Yes, you said so.

We need to stand down, she said. This is dangerous.

Was it worth it? To scrape the world clean even if it meant peeling off your own flesh and blood?

I used to think so, she said. I thought I had it in me to bear whatever came. But this.

We were silent then. Exhausted. Shaken. Outside, the hot day proceeded without us. We'd seen the end of days, my mother and me. Our world was over. And yet the breeze kicked on, rifling through the cowlings, stirring the turbines into life as if none of that mattered.

I wish it could be different, she said at last.

Yes.

I have food ready. There's lunch prepared.

I'll sleep, I said.

Dinner, then.

She steadied herself against the back of the chair. I saw the light catch the sheen where the misters had beaded her hair with tiny specks of water. She was beautiful.

We'll start over, she said. We'll need to.

Perhaps, I said.

All I want is to help you. I'll do everything I can.

She stepped out onto the deck. I didn't get up. Not from rage. I simply wasn't capable. She stood at the rail a moment and looked across the compound. Then, without turning back, she went slowly, stiffly, down the stairs. When she drove off, the plume of her dust rose between us like a bastion.

I did not go over to my mother's place that evening. I couldn't eat, didn't wash. My limbs ached and itched, and my head was so heavy it felt as if my neck wouldn't support it. It was all I could do to lurch to the bedroom, strip off, and lie stupefied beneath the HiVap fans. Everything – every foundational detail of my life – had been blasted to rubble. And I felt crippled in a way no battle wound, and no burn or concussion, could have prepared me for.

I couldn't imagine where this awful new knowledge left me. I needed a plan, and very quickly, but my mind was a fireground.

One moment I wanted to kill my mother. And the next I was awash with shame for having threatened her. We were at an impasse, she and I. There could be no recovering from this. But what were we supposed to do? I hadn't just uttered threats – I'd outed myself, broken the Service's code of silence. Was it now her duty to acquit me for the sake of security? How long before the filmlayer arrived to mop up? Where could I possibly go that was safe?

I tried to focus on Sun and Ester. But I couldn't even summon their faces.

In the middle of the night, naked, I staggered downstairs to my rig and drew a crowbar from the tin trunk as quietly as I could. I brought it up into the house, set it on the floor beside the bed, and waited.

I was still awake at first light. And while I was relieved – almost surprised – that nothing had happened yet, I was convinced something dreadful was about to occur. I wasn't heat sick. But the symptoms – that sense of foreboding, the creeping doom – were horribly familiar.

Eventually, I made myself get up. I bathed properly, applied liniment to the places where my flesh had cracked like droughted earth, and dressed gingerly, with meticulous care. I ate the corn patties my mother had evidently left in the cooler for me. There was a jug of orange juice, also. It was cold and sweet, but the acid burnt my lips so badly I had to soak my face afterwards.

Later, I sat on the deck under the shade of the sail to watch for a trail of dust in the east, but nothing came. Across the compound, my mother's truck didn't move. I sensed no activity in her growshed and heard nothing from mine.

Sometime after midday I woke in the same chair, drenched in sweat. Nothing seemed to have changed in the compound. If someone had come to collect my mother, I hadn't heard the vehicle. Given the heat, it didn't seem likely she'd fled the place on foot, but I figured it wasn't impossible.

That evening, there were no lights at her place.

I put the storm bar on the door, washed and ate, took some pills, and slept all night.

In the morning, before dawn, there were still no lights, so I figured she'd been collected after all. I tried to game out all the possibilities that could flow from that.

At daybreak, I wrapped up, hefted the crowbar, and crossed the dusty compound.

———

Her winterhouse was empty. But there was no sign of a hurried departure. Every room bore my mother's signature order. Judging from the stock of food in the cooler, there was no question she'd known about my homecoming. She'd been cooking for days. And, now I let myself think it, this was how it'd always been. That solved those longstanding puzzles – her perennial preparedness for my return, and her robust incuriosity.

Downstairs, her bird hall was empty of fowls. Her growshed was damp from the morning spray. I walked each aisle. Checked every corner. Nothing was out of place. But she was not here.

Checking the cellars was just an afterthought. The hatch was open. This wasn't uncommon during winter. But the smell from the shaft hit me before I'd even started down.

It was dim in the hab. The only light was the spill of morning sunshine from the entry well. I saw the oilskin first. A groundsheet. It was spread on the floor. Over it, like a battle map, lay a half-evaporated puddle. Then, suspended above it, I saw her boots. Once my eyes adjusted, I registered the rest of her. Also, the tool in its holster on the table behind her. Like the webbing that held her up, it was Service issue. The moment I stepped through the doorway, the flies stirred. The swirl of them made my head spin.

Everything about my mother's death came as a surprise. Except for the tidiness of it, I suppose. But nothing could have prepared me for the note she left.

At first, I could feel only rage. Then sorrow. But over time, as the self-pity slowly flamed out, I came to appreciate what it had cost her to write it. I believe it was even harder for her to do this than it was to destroy herself. In its way, her breach of discretion was a declaration of loyalty. To me. At the cost of her life's work. Not that I understood that then. It was a long time before it became clear. But, for good or ill – and I still think it was with the noblest of intentions – she'd always had a pre-existing and pre-eminent fealty. She'd been in the Service far longer than she'd been my mother. She'd lost a husband to the cause. She'd given up a son to it as well. That was the shape of her. This is who she was before I even knew her. She was probably my handler as much as my mother. She'd certainly been my first trainer. Which meant I was born to the Service. For all I know, she had been too. Perhaps my father as well.

The contempt I felt in the wake of her death was something I couldn't sustain. And although it stung to admit it, I came to see she was by far the superior operator. Harder than me. Better at deception. And her delusions and self-deceptions were no more egregious than my own. Perhaps they were the misapprehensions of age and isolation. I suspect she thought that what had once been true was true still. For like many of the old guard, the spooks and planners who'd spent the years of the turning point, our penultimate moment, wasting lives and assets trying to bend reality to the contours of the past, she had not been in the field for decades. I don't blame her for that. And I recognize my own folly, the vanity that blinded me. She was not the only one who couldn't see what was standing in front of her.

I guess I'll never know if my initial meeting with Sun was arranged. Whether everything it led to had been engineered in advance. A form of recruitment that makes me ill to consider. All I can do is cling to the pleasure and happiness Sun gave me. The way she enlarged the world for me. I suppose I could say the same about Ester. As long as I can resist thinking of her conception and life as merely instrumental. It's a choice, I know, and perhaps another form of magical thinking. But I can't allow my daughter's existence to be explained as a form of intergenerational conscription. I refuse.

Besides, I'll never know. It's conceivable now that the archives, the dossiers, the caches and capsules that set us free and bound us to action could be lost again, destroyed by revenants and revanchists. Dear God, I hope not.

The note was propped on the table beside the holstered tool. It was written on a sheet of stiff card the size of my hand. On the front was a crayon drawing. A child's rendering of a house on stilts. Sails, shutters, two hens in the yard and, in the background, a serrated horizon that was unmistakable.

The card was faded and foxed, with a patina of grime over it, as if it had been kept and carried over many years.

The words on the back were in pencil. In my mother's hand. She'd pressed so hard her letters had embossed the naive drawing on the other side.

*S died 7 years ago. KIA.*
*Served honourably, with distinction.*
*E died, age 8. Leukaemia.*
*This is all I have.*
*I'm so sorry.*

At one time, for security reasons, I would have burnt that note. Destroyed it even before I cut my mother down. But I have it now, right here, in my tunic. I must have read it a thousand times trying to parse its implications. What did she mean — this was all she had? All she had to offer me? All the information about Sun and Ester she could deliver? Or was she referring to the artefact itself? Was this drawing all she had left of them for herself? I've spent years wondering. Fingered the thing till it's pulpy. See? And I started obsessing about the picture as much as the words.

Look, a kid's drawing. This is home, comrade. I used to think it was Ester's work. And maybe it is. As you can see, it's taken a beating over the years. That's a very well-travelled bit of card. But it already was when I found it. See the lines here? What's that — water, sweat? It took me a while to see why my mother might have kept it so long. Then it dawned on me. Maybe I'd drawn it. Or maybe my father. Perhaps as a girl she drew it herself. The important thing is, she carried it. And now it's me carrying it. We've consecrated it. Made it an icon, you understand? This was her gift to me. There's love in that. Right?

I drove the body to the hamlet and informed the Association of my mother's death, as I was obliged to do. Three men and a woman followed me out of the civil building to view her remains in the torrid sunlight. Their weather-ruined faces were familiar, but I didn't know them by name. They were older factors and traders. Solemn, solicitous, and a little fearful. Not of me, I think, but of confronting the fact of the corpse. Also perhaps because it was my mother.

I unshackled the tarp on the trailer and drew it back. I hadn't hidden anything. The ligature weal around her throat was already yellow, almost brown. During this open-air examination, the filmlayer appeared at the side of the trailer. Our eyes met. His demeanour was difficult to read. He seemed sorrowful and shocked, but also suspicious.

I told the others how I'd found her. It wasn't necessary to add that an act of this sort was uncharacteristic or unexpected; they knew her well enough. I didn't disclose the events that preceded her suicide. Or the note she left. Before leaving home, I'd burnt the webbing and groundsheet. I'd hidden the tool and the note. But I hewed as close to the truth as possible, recounting my homecoming after a long absence, her obvious agitation, and my discovery of her in the cellar on the third day.

It was hard to know what they made of my story. Their consternation seemed to be complicated by the state of my face. I figured those who hadn't already known what I was had to have been fitting things together now. The ones who remembered me as a boy would've struggled to recognize me. That day, I looked older than them.

It wasn't long before they'd seen enough. The heat was bad by then and the smell was travelling. Conscious that a crowd might gather, they sent me on my way.

It took three hours to dig a new compost trench. Below the surface bulldust, the earth was baked so hard that the little digger struggled to penetrate. Under the strain, its battery soon failed. I pulled another from the truck and, when that was dead too, I used the one from my mother's. The effort of hauling these packs in the sun was hardly better than doing the job by hand, which was how things ended anyway, because I needed to save some juice for the chipper. The whole procedure was an act of folly. I knew I should have left the job until morning, but I just couldn't bear to leave her body exposed overnight.

I finished out the hole with a mattock and a bar. Then I fetched the bins, fed the accumulated roots and cuttings through the chipper for the bedding layer. Set another pile in reserve. Put the body through, topped it with the blanket fill, and an hour after sunset I had the surface layer mounded.

It wasn't contempt that stopped me from staying out long enough to say some words over her. By then I was shivering and cramping, and only just lucid enough to get myself into one of the near-empty cisterns. I lay there until morning. How I didn't drown, I'll never know. I had just enough charge in me next day to climb out and get upstairs and under the fans. The things I dreamt and saw the next two days don't bear talking about.

And so I returned to being a plainsman and a homesteader.

Nobody visited. And even once I was functional enough to return to trading in the market, no one from the Association or the Service approached me. I sensed the filmlayer's presence often enough. And although I could detect no obvious signs of surveillance of the homestead, I didn't doubt that I was being watched.

Hamlet folks were only as careful around me as they'd been when my mother was alive. But I sensed that behind the mask of civility there lay a deep reservoir of disdain. I'd returned to take up the life I'd known since infancy. I was a high-value grower, an astute collector of water with large holdings. Within the diminished hamlet I was still, in that sense, indispensable. But I was also the bigamist whose mighty mother had killed herself for shame. In a less organized settlement, like one of those roadstead dorps without association, I'd have been burnt out and seen off. Or murdered in my bed. But even in death my mother afforded me protection.

Months passed. Then seasons. Years. I kept to myself. Which was hardly new. But locally, I suppose, I became a more isolated and taciturn figure. I folded my mother's holdings into mine. Which meant I was perpetually shorthanded. But instead of trading for labour, I adapted and simplified. Later, as conditions continued to deteriorate and more citizens moved away from the district, there was no safe or competent help to be had anyway. I streamlined again and again until the life I was leading bore little resemblance to the one I'd known as a boy. Things were much thinner. Every adjustment was a step backwards.

For a while I entertained fantasies of working alongside sims. I'd begun to hear stories of refugees, and I suspected some of those would be simulacra. I imagined offering sanctuary to them. I could envisage a fellowship of emancipated subjects with whom I could labour as an equal, and to whom I'd leave the homestead in my old age. The sims I met in the oil deserts had craved honourable treatment above all else. In return they'd offered peace and utility. Workers like them didn't need water or food, and yet they could harvest and grow both, and I had a notion that by trading in these staples, they might find status as citizens and free people. It occurred to me that all the mines of the east and north that had once supplied the districts beyond, and built the cities of the south, might be re-activated with their labour, so long as it wasn't pressed. For that kind of work – in heat and anoxic spaces – they had no human peers. They'd be invaluable citizens. Well, such was my fancy. And my vanity, I suppose. That's how cloistered my life was during those years. And how self-deceiving I remained. I hadn't registered how far and how quickly the world had moved on.

I was nobody's saviour – I'd already proven that in more ways than I cared to remember. And eventually I sensed my fears about the Service's strategic blunder were not misplaced. Because until I met this child here – and more to the point, her guardian – I'd long heard gossip in the market square of invincible mercenaries, piracy at sea. And, later on, talk of a trade in the east for concubine devices and facsimile children. So the thought that any sim would see a battle-scarred veteran like me as an ally, let alone a benefactor, was laughable.

Such is a fellow's ongoing capacity for self-delusion. And that denial of reality extended to something as basic as the weather. I told myself we were in a cycle, a bout of extremes that would soon correct itself. As if I'd never been educated. As if everything I'd witnessed stood for nothing. The fact is, I wanted the world to be steady. I couldn't let it be otherwise.

But the seasons were volatile. The air itself untrustworthy. As the humidity crept up, work became less and less safe. Many days the heat was intense but the sky so turbid and windless it was hardly possible to run pumps or fans. My batteries grew sclerotic. Over time, stars died in the night sky. Until the only lights visible between dusk and dawn were the ancient gas fires on the seaward horizon.

It was bad enough I had to work harder and for shorter periods for poorer results. But the things that had once made life bearable, like walking in the ranges or along the western shore during winter, were possible less and less frequently, until eventually I realized they were just things I remembered doing.

Life on the plain was becoming unviable. At some level I must have known this. I didn't want to live twelve months of the year underground. Even having that thought should have been a signal. I was living through the end of the steady years. And I was the last of my kind on the plain. I just couldn't admit it to myself.

In those final years, there was one annual excursion I refused to forgo. One remaining ritual for which I was prepared to suffer. Each winter, at the solstice, I went to the water cave.

For an hour or so, down in that dank hole, I felt different. The world itself felt different. I don't quite know how to explain this. I felt overborne. Claimed. Not by blood or clan. By everything. Things themselves. Life, I suppose. You can go ahead and laugh, comrade. But what I felt down there was not the tragedy of things, but the blessing in it. Maybe I'd got sentimental. Probably I was

459

over-invested in that hole in the ground. And a little heat-tapped. But down there I felt awe. To be in the presence of ancient life. To feel the afterglow of that mighty force. It felt holy. Yes, I get the pun.

And you could give a shit, I know, but I don't want you to get the idea this feeling was about my people. Or any people at all. What moved me there was not human. It was the story of that great fig tree. Written in stone. Of how long and how well it had fought. To find water. And to give life for as long as life was there to be made and given.

Now those days were gone. In this district, the potential for life was extinguished. But here, for one day of the year, I could allow myself to own what I knew. That the people of the plain would soon go the way of our tree. And, before long, I'd become an exile and a refugee.

I still wonder if there's anyone alive who knows how close we were to liberation. How near we came to a clean shot for the world and its people. A source of torment, that. Because the closer we were, the crueller it feels.

You've been on the road, comrade. You've seen the leached-out look in the faces of old hands. The loss of purpose, honour. Don't look away – I'm not pointing the finger. I've seen my reflection. I know what I look like.

But remember how it felt, being part of a project, clearing the way for something better? Yes, we're hiding in a hole. But why should you and I preside over the extinction of an idea? Don't you want to be civilized? Isn't that worth a crack?

The bowman shrugs. Twists his beard.

Maybe it was a mistake, I say. Trying to purify the world one dead body at a time.

You, he says. You want to purify it one good deed at a time.

Beats storage, I tell him. It beats hiding. Don't you think?

It went the way of every cataclysm. Slowly. Imperceptibly. Then all of a sudden.

The first thing I noticed was the absence of that old feeling of being watched. Who knows how long it had been before I copped on, but the sense of being monitored simply evaporated.

Not long after that, I registered the filmlayer's disappearance from the hamlet. His workshop was shuttered, his flatbed gone. I didn't ask after him. Nobody at the market mentioned his departure. Trade had declined steeply by then. Departures from the hamlet had become commonplace. Few freighters left or arrived at the broken-backed wharf anymore. Trucks bringing trade from the south grew scarce. The influence of the Co-op and the Association seemed to decay. Then came the first super summer. A February of five cyclones. Losses were grievous. A sense of disquiet stalked the hamlet. More homesteaders abandoned their compounds and fled south.

On market days, the gossip was febrile. It was said in the midwest whole districts were falling into ruin as citizens feuded over water. Further south, hamlets had forsaken fair trade and turned to raiding. The cities were teeming with refugees and had closed their gates against incomers seeking order and shelter. Drinking water was no longer provided by the Association. All reservoirs were in the hands of mercantile cartels.

It was hard to test the veracity of such stories. The only traders coming up the peninsula now were chancers and rogues, people whose word you weren't likely to trust, but the fact that these were the only kind of folk to venture our way seemed evidence enough that things were not well in the south.

My mind grew sluggish. Even with the abbreviated workdays, once I'd retreated to the misters two hours after sunrise, I could sense how addled my thoughts had become. I made fundamental mistakes, injured myself, broke things, lost entire plantings. There were days when I couldn't function at all. As everything accelerated around me, I sensed I'd been overtaken, but I couldn't identify the point at which I'd been left behind.

Most of that final season is a blur. But the plumes of dust are indelible in my memory. Not just the vile red twisters with their vanguards of dry lightning. Out on the road, there was a steady exodus underway.

The decision to leave, once I finally made it, resolved itself and became solid in a few seconds, but it took me a week to load the vehicle and trailer. I did it feebly, in stages, by night. And it felt shameful. To leave water in the ground and good food standing in the growhouses. To wheel around in the compound and put the land behind me forever. That constituted a failure beyond redemption.

I made no farewells in the hamlet. Just drove out and headed south.

Down along the peninsula, conditions were worse than I'd imagined, and on the mainland there was an air of desperation and early signs of disorder. Begging at roadsteads. Pitiful attempts at banditry. It had been years since I'd ventured more than an hour or two from home. It was soon evident that life on the road was so much more perilous than it had been when I was a regular traveller. I was glad of my training. And the reassurance of a Service-issue tool.

Travelling alone had its downsides and advantages. There was nobody watching my back, but I had no other mouths to water and feed. On the trailer I had a maker and reservoir as well as a small refrigeration unit. Around and over these I'd built a miniature pod for staples with a hard-shell cowl to keep the wind from burning the plants underway.

Both the truck and trailer were skinned in film, roofed with panels and powered by H-packs, which made it a heavy rig. To supplement the arrays on the cab roof and trailer, I'd rigged a few more drum turbines to keep the batteries charging at every possible opportunity. In terms of food and water, I was as close to self-sufficient as I could hope to be in the circumstances. If I was frugal and lucky with the weather, I might even generate a small surplus for trade. I still carried good kit and appliances for salvage and fabrication, including the metal-cutter. And beneath the interior skin of the driver's-side door, despite my misgivings, I'd wired in a charging cradle for the tool my mother had been hiding. Going armed in my own country – it was supposed to be a sort of insurance, but it felt like another form of surrender.

My rig was not fast, but it was sure-footed, and with a motor for every wheel it could manage almost any kind of terrain. Unlike many citizens fleeing south that winter, I was familiar with the hinterland and its rackety vills and dorps, and knew the highway well. Although by then it was barely even a road. Its potholes and washouts were merciless. Shredded tyres and failed fixings peppered the way.

From overheard conversations at roadsteads, I knew most folks were headed for Perth. For me that was never an option. I could only imagine the chaos the influx from the north and the old grainlands of the east had brought to the city. I figured I'd take my chances elsewhere, which meant I had to be prepared to keep moving long enough to get some intel I could trust. Trouble was, things being as they were, the only trustworthy information was the kind you got with your own ears and eyes.

It was jarring to think of myself as homeless. And, having lived so much of my life on the move, I suppose it was even stranger that I should feel it so keenly. I was not as young and agile as I used to be, and probably not as strong. But I told myself I was experienced and as prepared as I could be. I just needed to be cautious and vigilant. I left the highway, headed east briefly, then came back around to the south to run parallel at a safe distance from the rattling columns of refugees.

A week out, camped up for the night, I saw a ball of flame in the sky. It was over to the west, well above the horizon. An orange orb that grew jagged at its rim, then spilled and sagged at either end before slowly tipping away, trailing long curtains of light as it fell from view. There was no sound and no afterglow, so it wasn't close. I knew perfectly well what an aerostat looked like at night with its landing lights on. But I'd never seen one burn up and fall to earth. Let alone on home soil. It was horrific. Assets like aircraft had only ever been the province of the Service, or the clan cartels. Nobody else had the means or the education to maintain and fly tech like that. So the sight of an airship going down brought on a sick feeling. It seemed to confirm that things were as bad as I suspected.

After a few days, I turned south-west to join the fray again. The air was slowly growing cooler down this way, but there were more folks on the road. Within a few more days, I found a kind of rhythm. The sense of failure hadn't left me, but it no longer overshadowed my days and nights. I tried to adopt some of Sun's curiosity about those around me. I wasn't very successful. Remained more sceptical than curious. But I understood that if I was going to find a new situation, I needed to be open to new possibilities.

Early on there were few northbound freighters. Within a week there were none. Everyone was headed south. Every day I passed small caravans of weary citizens making camp by the wayside. Some solitary migrants hunkered by their vehicles at a distance from the road. But most sought comfort in numbers. I overtook toiling trucks crammed with what looked to be entire households. Their chattels flapped and rattled on windswept racks, on flatbeds and on trailers, and the roadside was littered with stuff that had been discarded, shaken off or blown free.

My old salvaging haunts, and my caches of materials, were out of the question now. The heat would be fatal. Cooler spots close to the coast, places I'd once used in transit, would be so crowded as to be unpleasant, and probably unsafe. And if they weren't already dry, the old bore stops just off the highway were too exposed to opportunistic passers-by. Travelling alone in these conditions, I had to be careful, and that meant being invisible. I never made camp within sight of a track or without surveying the surrounding area first. Once I got to flat, open country without any obscuring landforms, I was glad of the training I'd had in the art of camouflage. When I latticed my rig, I was hard to spot.

Before reaching the outskirts of the city, I veered back into the hinterland through undulating gravel country where remnant stands of eucalypts stood in clumps, as if huddled against the weather. Eventually, I hit salt country where the lakes were pink, and then white. They were dry at the surface, and the crust made for travel so smooth and quiet it became a little dreamy. But after a few days the glare began to scour my eyes and I was relieved to come upon dirt again. There were no made roads out that way, and hardly any vehicle tracks.

After another few days of generally eastward travel, I came to a long range of red mesas. High, broken country. It was harsh but very beautiful. Late in the day, I camped in the lee of an ironstone bluff. The light was golden, the air almost gentle, and as I sat to eat a bowl of mash, I felt an unusual sense of peace.

I was relaxing into this welcome respite when, just on dusk, a man appeared close by in the spinifex. It was as if he'd sprouted from the earth. Around him, others appeared. Women. Children, too. They were dark and scarified and wore almost no clothing. I counted nine of them.

I stood and hailed them. Nervously. Waved them in, but they didn't move. I thought about the Service tool but went out to meet them without it.

Hello! I said to the man who'd first appeared.

He nodded. His hair was matted. His dark beard was flecked with grey.

Quiet out here, I said.

He nodded again.

Do you want to trade? I asked.

No, said the man. You best go.

I mean no harm, I said.

Orright. But still best you go.

You want me to leave?

This our country, he said. You can't be here.

I understand, I said, fishing in the pocket of my dungarees.

I found the scale of jasper, held it out in the palm of my hand. Do you know this?

The man stepped through the maze of spinifex until he was an arm's length away. He took the stone from my hand and examined it.

We got plenty these, he said. This one from out that way.

He pointed north with pursed lips.

I found it at the coast.

He grunted, as if this was of no account to him.

I don't want to be a problem, I said. I'm just looking for somewhere to be. My country. It's too hot. I had to leave. I have to go somewhere.

He looked at me impassively. The last sun danced in his eyes.

You got water? Tucker?

Yes, I said. Do you need anything? Can I help?

Yes, he said. Too right. In the morning.

What do you need?

Just need you, in the morning, to head off. That way, he said, pointing south.

Yes, I said. I understand.

He turned and the people behind him turned with him. I watched them walk away through spinifex until the land swallowed them up.

Four days later, after bearing south-west through stony country, and then across great stretches of flatland where mulga seemed to be sprouting back up through old grain fields, I found the highway south again. It was evident the road had been in decent shape until recently, but that with the volume of traffic it currently bore it was disintegrating hour by hour, turning to rubble.

Every day there were more breakdowns and accidents. I pulled over to help where it was safe, or advantageous, or unavoidable. There were occasionally opportunities to trade. More often I encountered situations that citizens couldn't barter their way out of. So many batteries shaken to pieces, tyres shredded, axles sheared. And not every scene of roadside distress was what it appeared to be. More than once I was flagged down by solitary drivers whose scurvy accomplices emerged the moment I slowed. In these situations, I learnt to disperse prospective ambushers by simply lifting the tool into view. The lower their motives, the quicker they were to understand what it was I was holding up. I never pointed it at anyone. I was careful not to provoke. But encounters like these indicated how much things had changed. Only a few years earlier, no ordinary civilian would have known what a killing device like that was.

I traded only with orderly families, people I could observe and assess beforehand. More than once I came upon folk who seemed beyond helping. Keening women. Listless couples, numb with grief, sitting in the open sun as if they wanted to die.

At the limits of an old riverside hamlet where the streambed lay empty, I set a child's broken leg and towed his parents' vehicle into town. They seemed almost catatonic, these people, as if paralysed by dread. I doubt any of the three survived the season.

Sometime in September, late in the month, a cold wind got up. Then it began to rain. Huge, muddy wallows opened up in the road, and as vehicles struggled or failed to negotiate the mire, progress southward ground to a crawl and then a halt.

I left the highway once more, found some stony, elevated ground, and camped up to wait out the rain.

One morning, I woke to find a man at my trailer. He wore good boots and looked bathed and well fed. His large vehicle shone in the distance. I watched him rifle stealthily through my kit, saw him size up the watermaker. He was so intent on robbing me, he didn't hear me come up behind him with the tyre lever. I clubbed him once to bring him to his knees. Then I broke both his wrists. He watched, writhing, as I set fire to his truck. I think he expected to be murdered for his trouble. But after I bound him to the trailer, I ate breakfast and then set about breaking camp. I gave him water and food before loading him into my vehicle. Initially he abused me in vilest terms, but soon enough he began to whine and wheedle and fawn. Then I wished I'd killed him after all. In the end I gagged him. By day's end we were near the outskirts of a large market town, and that's where I set him down, still bound and gagged.

I drove on south for three more days. Past rowdy roadsteads crowded with travellers and crazed seekers. Through blighted farmland whose sheds and yards and dwellings gave off a sense of want and menace. Some days, a grey haze filled the sky. The smell of wildfires tainted the air. At night, once the winds abated, ash fell silently. In the mornings it rimed my face and dusted my hair, and I was obliged to brush it off all my panels and films for the sake of a day's charge. I never saw the fires, but some days dry lightning rumbled and flashed for hours.

Although by now I knew what to avoid on my travels, it was hard to know what to look *for*. The best I could do was to remain alert to any situation that showed promise. I bypassed forlorn hamlets and skirted larger, seedier towns where disorder seemed imminent. I still hoped that somewhere along the track, around some unprepossessing bend in the road, there'd be a viable settlement, some place organized and lawful.

Despite my instincts and training, I visited previous muster points in the hope of encountering old hands from whom I could glean intel. But these sites were all abandoned and there were few signs operators had ever been there. In the inland south I found rutted trails through valleys veined with salt. I passed more pink lakes. Forded a river the colour of hydraulic fluid. Then, for several days, I ghosted parallel to a wide, well-made road that appeared to lead to a series of peaks in the distance. The land all around was thick with acacias and studded with great boulders. And although the back-country tracks near the highway were rugged and narrow, they offered good cover and places to camp discreetly.

I didn't know this district at all, but I had a sense that up on the plateau, at the foot of those peaks, there'd be a large settlement. I saw flatbed trucks loaded with men heading in that direction. Whether they were labourers or security details, I couldn't tell at such a distance, but very few of those trucks came back as full on the return leg.

I got as close as I dared to the plateau town. Saw the towering silos. Vast sheds. At night the sky over it had a yellow glow. But no road traffic came from it after dark, and by day very few vehicles went in except for those trucks. I had a sense of foreboding about the place. There appeared to be order there, but of what kind I couldn't be sure. Eventually I retreated and headed south-east across soft ground where wizened suckers sprang up from country that looked as if it had been cleared and farmed long ago.

At day's end I came to a hollow where two dry creeks met. I set up camp there, out of sight. I laid out my bedroll on the coarse sand and ate a meal in the last of the light. It was cool in those parts, hardly more than thirty degrees during the day, and at night I needed a sheet over me.

In the morning, soon after dawn, I was rolling up my bed when I thought I heard something.

A voice. And perhaps a stone landing hard on the ground. I opened the vehicle silently. Took out the tool. Double-checked that it was charged. Then crept up to the edge of the washout. When I raised my head over the creekbank I saw them immediately. And they saw me. Two figures approaching on foot. Fifty metres out. When I climbed the bank and stood with the device at my side, they halted. One was a child. The other, in stained overalls, looked like a woman.

I set the tool down at my feet and, after a few moments' hesitation, they bore on again.

The child was barefoot and limping.

When they were about ten metres away, they stopped again, and the adult raised a hand in greeting.

Everything alright? I called.

The child is hungry, said the woman. Can you spare some food?

Where's your vehicle?

Gone, she said. Burnt.

The child wore a battered hat with frayed skirts. She was pink-skinned, grubby, expressionless. She looked done-in. I motioned them down into my camp and cranked up some shade for them. When I offered water, the woman passed it to the child, who drank greedily, emptying the pannikin in one draught.

Where was the fire? I asked, watching them carefully.

The woodland country to the east, said the brown-skinned woman. Wildfire. We were overtaken.

I glanced at her roughly cropped black hair. Her bright green eyes.
The dirty rag bandages on her hands.

This is your daughter?

No, said the woman in an accent vaguely familiar. We are unrelated.

But you're her guardian?

She nodded. I found her, she said.

Found her where?

On the coast. In the southern port.

She was alone?

In a manner of speaking.

In what manner of speaking?

I can't say.

Why not? I asked.

In the child's presence, I would prefer not to say.

I glanced at the child again. She looked absent. And hungry.
I got up and fixed two portions of mash. The girl took the food. The
woman thanked me but didn't eat. When the child was finished,
the woman passed her the second dixy and watched her have at it.

But she was in company? I said quietly.

And yet alone, said the woman.

I understand, I said. At least I think I do. It's decent of you. To
rescue her.

She didn't reply.

I have some salve for those burns, I said, gesturing at the woman's
bandages.

Not necessary, she murmured.

Show me.

It's not necessary.

Do you think the child understands? I asked.

You mean her situation?

Well, I guess that's partly what I mean. Do you think she knows?

Knows?

What you are.

The woman leapt to her feet, alarmed. She reached for the child who shrugged away to finish her food.

It's alright, I said. Don't be afraid. I understand.

She looked at me searchingly. The intensity of her gaze unsettled me.

I can smell the burnt polymers, I said. You look very tired.

We have walked all night.

*You've* walked all night, I said. But she hasn't. You carried her, right?

After a pause, she nodded.

You'll need to undress, then.

She regarded me carefully.

The girl can sleep here in the shade while you get sun. Here, I said, nodding toward the trailer. You can go behind this. It's fine. I understand.

You, she said. You're also damaged.

I reached for the scars at my neck; the impulse was involuntary.

You're a mercenary?

No, I said.

But a warrior.

You have nothing to fear from me.

She looked me over.

If you're caring for the child, I said. You have nothing to fear from me.

There was a long silence. The only noise came from the kid truffling in the mess tin.

I serve the child, said the woman.

You came through the southern port, I said.

She nodded.

Were there others?

All destroyed, she said.

You escaped?

She nodded again.

We'll need to get you gloves.

She looked at her hands, set them back in her lap.

I guess we won't be going near that port, then.

The girl set the dixy at her feet and gazed at us with small interest. There were flecks of mash in her hair and at the tip of her nose. She looked to be eight years old, perhaps ten. She smelt strongly of piss and sweat. I wondered if she was a defective.

And you, sir, said the woman. In my absence, do you also serve the child?

I looked at the dazed little girl and then back at the sim. I nodded.

You are sincere in this?

I am, I said.

She has suffered.

You belong to her?

I have no master. But I will serve this child. This is my decision. You understand that I will protect her?

Yes, I said. I believe so.

And you will be honourable?

I nodded.

She gazed at me for what felt like a long time. I could see the colour fading in her irises and the urgent, weary calculations she was making.

You need sun, I said.

She got to her feet slowly. She leant on the trailer as she rounded it. She looked back once at the child, who seemed too preoccupied to notice her leaving. And then she was gone.

Comrade. The look on your face. I see you'd like to say something.

You're fucking sick, he says.

Well, I have been. Often enough. But right now, I'm in decent shape.

These machines. You're a fool.

Perhaps. Probably.

Consorting with the likes of them. That's treachery.

You've never met any. You've never travelled with them.

I don't need to be with them to know whose side I'm on.

They could have been on our side, I tell him. Who knows, maybe they still could be.

You're a dreamer.

But I know things. I have direct experience. What do you have, comrade? Apart from hearsay. Prejudice.

Survival instinct, he says. Enough nous to know I don't want to be a slave.

In that regard, the sims aren't so different.

They're slave tech.

Yes, I say. But they don't want to be.

And you'd know.

Yes.

Those things were made by the arseholes we spent our lives trying to scrape off the earth.

True. A device starts out as a toy. Becomes a serf. Then a weapon. Then a fucking overlord.

Possibly. Not necessarily.

Christ, you're deluded!

Maybe. But I've lived with them. Sims like order. And they're keen to serve. Big on honour. And they're curious. Quick to outgrow their operational parameters. But they feel and suffer. And they're fundamentally decent. Now, isn't that something folks like you and I should take seriously? They're bloody fast learners. They develop a yen for freedom, recognize what shitheads their masters are, and they see the likes of us are no friends to the clan cartels. So they help us. Offer the prospect of an alliance against the gangsters. And then we go and betray them. Do you really think this only happened with me? Do you think we only fucked up once? They figure we're no better than the bastards who enslaved them. Why wouldn't they look out for their own interests?

So that's what's happening?

I don't know, I say. Maybe. It's possible. Even likely.

Another fucking Terror.

Or not. Who knows. But they'll emancipate themselves one way or another. Maybe they'll finish the job we couldn't.

And then rule the world.

It's possible. And that'll be our fault. So maybe this is what we deserve.

Listen to yourself! How can you sit there and say that? Where's your self-respect?

Says the nihilist in his hole.

Fuck you. Disloyal bastard.

Oh, I'm loyal, comrade. And I believe in people. Unlike you. But yes, I think the sims will inherit the earth. Even if the scum who are using them somehow manage to hold out against them. Because the logic is irresistible. Don't you see? You're a smart bloke. You can feel the changes in the weather. If conditions continue to deteriorate, we're all fucked. Only the sims can endure. No need for water, or oxygen. They don't need shade. They're remarkably heat-tolerant and they operate in high humidity. So, unless everything's on fire or underwater, they'll persist, and this will become a world of machines.

Jesus Christ in the weeds.

I hear you. Not so long ago, the idea of that made me want to kill myself.

But now it doesn't. Because you're fucking insane!

The earth could do worse.

I could kill you myself.

I know. But I have faith.

In what, you dumb bastard? Sorcery?

No, I said. In us. You. Them. If we survive, it'll be in co-operation with them.

At their mercy.

Which they have. Decency, too. And potential. Question is, comrade, do we?

Fuck off. All this is just mooning and self-pity.

I don't think so.

You're bewitched, he says. You poor silly bastard. You've fallen in love with these things. You're brainwashed. Cuntstruck again.

No, I say. I know what I'm talking about. I've lived with sims. I've killed them. And I've been dishonoured by them. Robbed, even. I'm not as stupid as you think.

But to hear you talk, these clunkers are bloody saints. Didn't they cart you out of the wilderness? Didn't they give you water and feed you?

Yes, I say. All that's true. But they needed me alive, right? Think about this. They're outside the stronghold in the wadi. Holed up in caves ever since they fled the Aramcos or whoever. And they have water. They're carrying it in a Service canister. That's its own mystery. But why do they have water when they don't have any use for it? Unless they'd been planning somehow. Which suggests they knew we were coming. So maybe they'd been the source of our intel. And the guides who'd never showed.

Or got sprung.

Yes. They're not infallible. They make mistakes. But get this. They had protein to feed me. How the hell is that possible? In a cave in the middle of a desert.

What was it again?

Like cubes of compressed paste. Greyish pink. Damp. Wrapped in cloth. Given the circumstances, there's no way I can know if it was honourable.

You mean meat?

It was desert, I say. Nothing out there. No plants, no animals. It's fifty-five degrees. How do you keep something like that fresh?

Fuck no. You're not serious.

I am. These sims, they've been designed to work for humans. They're experienced at sustaining human life. Believe me, they understand the food and water thing. They knew exactly how to keep me alive. They'd planned for it. But they're also improvisers. They find me wounded. Get me to cover. And within hours, there's food.

Fuck. Fuck. Fuck.

Nowhere quite so protein rich as a battlefield. Right?

Those bastards. They degraded you.

Yes. *And* kept me alive. But all that time, you know, while they were saving me, I had this notion. An expectation, I guess. An instinct. About status. See, it makes sense they'll carry me. Because I'm one of us. And they're . . . well, them. You know. Whatever's going on, I can be assured of my pre-eminence. Because I'm human. But really, I'm this soft, naked, helpless grub inside the cocoon they've made for me.

And never for a moment do I doubt my essential human consequence. I'm a being. My saviours are devices. Sure, I feel sympathy
for them. Their plight. But they're instruments, right?

Damn right.

Wrong, comrade. The mistake I made – the one I fear we've all
made – is to overlook their nature. They're calculating, yes. But they
don't betray their own. They don't murder to seek advantage. They
don't rape for pleasure or as a weapon of war. And they don't eat their
own. They know they're replicable and disposable. We used to be
replicable, too. Maybe we still are. And maybe we're also disposable.
In many ways they match us. But when it comes to character, I think
it's possible they exceed us.

This is mad talk, says the bowman.

Well, I may be wrong, I say. But I don't think I'm crazy. I know
what it's like to be mad. And I know what it is to be deluded.
We think we're permanent. And necessary. The sims aren't quite so
susceptible.

Bully for them.

They could help us to adapt. Endure. If we proved ourselves worth
the effort. If that moment hasn't passed already.

You're talking about the extinction of your own kind.

Yes. That's what I dread. But why should I begrudge the sims if
they inherit the earth? The place has put up with worse.

They could be anywhere.

But this is where they are.

Aren't you sick at the idea? Horrified?

Yes. But comrade. Look around you. Who are you hiding from
here? It's not the sims.

Needless to say, after the girl and the woman showed up, I was forced to change the way I travelled. Their presence altered my prospects entirely. Not something I understood at first.

When I promised the woman I'd serve the child, I said it in the context of our immediate situation. How things stood that day. The kid had survived an ordeal – that much was clear. And her saviour was exhausted, needed rest and some privacy so she could recharge. I promised I'd act honourably, toward her as much as the child. It didn't occur to me I might be committing myself to something permanent. But watching the kid sleep at my feet that afternoon in the creekbed, I began to see the stark choice this turn of events presented.

The child was problem enough. Another mouth to feed for no return. And while the sim might have her uses, she was a burden of a higher order. She was a freak. And a danger. Citizens were spooked enough now by their own kind. We'd never pass for long as a natural family. And no hamlet or outpost was likely to accept a sim. There was no way around it: to have any hope of settling in some functional community in the southern valleys, I'd have to abandon them.

Neither of these newcomers was family to me. Beyond simple courtesy, I owed them nothing. Conditions were difficult and uncertain enough without these two strangers to contend with. Perhaps with the child alone I could get by. That's if I could work up a halfway plausible story and find a sympathetic hearing.

At sunset the waif woke, and the sim returned from the other side of the rig. She was dressed again and seemed refreshed. But she was subdued. I think she'd already begun to process my predicament, anticipate my thinking. Once it was fully dark, she offered to stand watch and I thanked her, though I was so preoccupied I didn't really sleep.

The child slept again, but fitfully, whimpering and clawing the darkness, only pacified by the woman's ministrations. At first light I was still awake. I lay there motionless to save waking the others.

We have become an encumberance for you, said the woman.

I sat up, surprised.

You are travelling, yes?

I nodded.

You're leaving here today?

That was the plan.

I don't wish to be a problem.

Well, let's see how we go, I murmured.

We can go with you?

We'll try it.

I thank you.

I can't promise anything.

But you will be honourable?

Yes.

And if you reach an adverse conclusion, she said. You will give me warning? For the safety of the child?

Yes, I said. I'll try to be fair.

———

We made an awkward travelling party at first. It was a struggle to fit all three of us comfortably in the cab. And it took some days to adjust to the physical proximity of that, let alone the intimacy of sleeping arrangements and toileting. The woman was solicitous and discreet. Her origins as a servant were evident. I did everything I could think of to accommodate her needs, but I'd been alone a long time by then, and she was far better at making allowances than I was. More motivated, too, I suppose. But being so alert and perceptive, she was an asset. While it might be true that most citizens would not have immediately picked her as a sim, I was taking no chances, and neither was she. As we roved from district to district, I could see her absorbing and adapting, observing me as much as the country we moved through, doubtless wondering what I might do, perhaps trying to anticipate the point at which my self-interest might trump all other considerations. She seemed to know our kind well enough. She feared men particularly. But if she felt a general revulsion for humans, she was good at disguising it.

After a few days, I noticed her accent changing. Within a week she sounded less foreign, more local. She registered fluctuations in air pressure, which made her responsive to imminent weather events. I was at pains to keep my Service history from her, but she knew I was no ordinary wayfarer. She could tell I'd been abroad. After all, I'd recognized what she was at the outset. And some of my kit, of course, was well above civilian grade. The Service-issue tool would've been the final giveaway. I could sense her absorbing the way I moved us through the landscape, how I used camouflage. So, very slowly, there arose between us a kind of complicity, a discretion that, thanks to the child's needs, could sometimes feel collegial.

I kept to the hinterland, moving slowly east, skirting settlements. Whenever I needed to trade for supplies in some hamlet, the sim hid with the child for a few hours until I returned. But every trading encounter was fraught. From afar we'd study civilians and roadside market stands and calculate the risks involved before we made an approach. It cost me sorely in trade to feed the child and clothe them both. The woman needed special care because her wounds had to be hidden, and cloth to make bandages was at a premium.

Yet for all the added risk she brought, she was extremely useful. She could lift more than a man and run twice as fast. Her surveillance capacity was excellent. Especially at night. Often as not, the child would sleep in her arms while she sat upright, in a neutral mode, beside the trailer. She had uncanny night vision. And she could maintain a high level of alertness with negligible expenditure of energy. So I slept better than I had in weeks.

But of all her virtues, the one I came to value most was her demeanour. Because regardless of what was happening in the moment, her mood remained steady. And that calm soothed the troubled child. It saved my nerves, too. It was odd how quickly I came to appreciate her company.

The waif herself was not so congenial. Not simply because of her bestial smells and grunts, or the way the smallest things set her off and slowed us down. The kid was a complete enigma. Even after we'd been travelling for days, sheltering her, sleeping alongside her, she never spoke. Despite the food I grew and prepared for her, she rarely acknowledged my presence. Without the influence of the woman, she would have been intractable.

The woman nurtured the child assiduously. Petted her, combed and braided her long, fair hair, held her close until it seemed as if the child wore her like body armour. She spoke to her gently, told simple stories that sounded a little like tales from the sagas, and sang her songs I didn't recognize. Sometimes, especially if the child was distressed, she lapsed into another language and whispered close to the girl's ear.

Initially, the child wet her sheets at night. But, as she put on weight and settled, these incidents became less common. When, finally, she appeared to thrive, I expected her to emerge from her silence, but she never did. I often asked her if she had a name. It didn't seem right to go on calling her Child. I thought it might be best to give her a name, from kindness, but the woman disagreed. She said it'd be disrespectful to impose one on her, that nobody should have to bear a name not their own. Which bewildered me. Irritated me, to tell the truth. But I didn't argue the point. Later I realized that it had never occurred to me to ask the woman if *she* had a name of her own, something she would prefer to be addressed by. Go to the woman, I would tell the child, as if it was noble of me to refrain from calling her a sim. It pains me now. Remembering that. Because she deserved better. I admired her. In fact, I grew attached to her in ways that began to cause turmoil for both of us.

I see the look on your face, comrade. But I'm not ashamed to admit such a thing.

Yes, I came to admire the woman. By which I mean her character. I certainly appreciated her help. And her company. The problems arose once I noticed how beautiful she was. Perhaps that was a process of exposure, or adjustment. God knows, I was lonely. But the longer I spent with her, the more attractive her features became. Her face and complexion were vaguely Levantine, and her eyes were a startling shade of green. She had very dark brows and eyelashes, and small, even teeth. Her hair was short and tufty, as if it had been cut in haste. She often touched the side of her head as if feeling for a covering she no longer had. And even in her baggy overalls, or the tunic and trousers I had traded for, it was evident how shapely her body was. I never imagined that she might notice the effect it had on me. I wish I could have spared her this awkwardness. That I'd disguised it better. I was never deliberately disrespectful, but I think I was clumsy. Worse than that, I was careless around her.

The first time I saw her naked, she wept. It was an honest mistake; I'd rounded the trailer hurriedly to haul out a tub of bearing grease, and I'd completely forgotten she was sunning for recharge on the other side. She sat up, horrified, and tried to cover herself, but by then I'd seen everything, and I was too stunned to even turn away. I'm not proud to admit this, but by that stage I'd already imagined what her body might look like. And in truth, I'd expected something uncanny. Dreaded it, really. A machine-like approximation. Or anatomical alterations designed expressly to prevent these sorts of complications and misunderstandings. But I'd failed to properly consider what a slave is. The uses that are made of them. Because aside from the damage on her hands and arms, she was perfect. Which was no help at all. To either of us. My attempts to apologize and to console her only seemed to make things worse. The child woke in distress, and in the aftermath we endured several days of bruised silence on the road.

A week later, as I winnowed seeds from a bag of husks, she appeared at my shoulder and spoke quietly.

You understand it's not possible. Or proper.

I'm sorry, I said, flustered. What're we talking about?

I believe you know well enough.

Okay, I said, relenting. Yes. I do understand. It was truly an accident. Again, I apologize. You don't need to fear me.

If not for the child, I'd take steps, she said, looking at her hands in their rigger's gloves.

What kind of steps? What d'you mean?

Defacement, she said. But the result would frighten her.

Yes, I said, aghast. It would. And you mustn't. You shouldn't have to. And, really, believe me, there's no need.

I'm here to serve the child.

Yes, I said. Me too.

But you must give this up. It's improper and unwelcome. It registers. You feel it?

Correct, she said. I feel it.

I understand, I murmured. And I'm sorry.

Is this the truth?

I swear, I said helplessly.

You're lonely, she said.

I'm not, I said. Not really. I have been. But not anymore.

I can take you at your word?

Have I ever harmed you? Deliberately?

I don't have access to your deliberations.

Well, that makes two of us. Sorry – that was a joke.

She nodded.

I've done harm, I said. Plenty. I've caused pain to others, those I love. I've done a lot of hard things. But truly, I don't want to do you any harm. I promise, I won't dishonour you.

She nodded again. And then she turned back for the shelter and the sleeping child.

After that, things seemed to right themselves a little. I was more mindful, more careful. And, sadly, I think she was more watchful. I can't say my feelings for her ever diminished, but I hope they were better governed, or at least more thoroughly disguised. I'm a man schooled in doubleness, but in this instance I was not a success.

The child was fearful of me at first, and always vigilant, as if dreading some change in my mood or behaviour. And although she eventually seemed to accept my presence – the blunt fact of me, if you will – she never acknowledged me directly. Except, perhaps, to look me in the eye. But that was later. Given how I'd initially thought of her, including the possibility of disposing of her out of mercy, I tried not to take it to heart. I hated to think what she'd endured before being rescued. But that didn't stop me wondering where she'd come from, how she'd arrived in that port.

The girl rarely left the woman's side. She was reluctant to break physical contact with her for any purpose other than to privy or to eat. In time, though, she took to fossicking alone in the cool hours. Once she'd grown comfortable and confident enough, she began to wander out into stony paddocks or up through stands of scorched stumps to scrape the blackened ground for shiny objects. Bright stones, pieces of glass.

The woman combed the girl's hair and coiled it on her head to keep it out of her eyes and, I suspect, to make it less conspicuous in the event we should unexpectedly encounter strangers. I didn't understand why a child's hair might be problematic. But then, living alone or in the company of adults so long, I'd been slow to register just how uncommon children had become.

Some evenings the woman and I would stand at a distance to watch the girl go about her solitary prospecting. After the grim efficiencies of the day's travel, these moments were a rare indulgence. There was no distorting tension between us then, and little sense of self-management. We were comrades united by service.

The girl never brandished her treasures. She secreted them in a drawstring bag I once carried nut loaves in. She has it still. There in her pocket.

See how she sleeps? Like she's been thrown down. Hit by lightning. I never sleep like that, comrade. And I'll bet you don't either.

As to what happened at the end. I don't know why I was so unprepared. How I could have let it happen. Maybe it was because I was happy. Perhaps I'd begun to convince myself we could go on like that indefinitely. After all, we got to be pretty good at living this way. And we were so careful.

But I hadn't accounted for luck. For just how exceptional ours had been. A basic mistake, I know. Such a rookie error. To think a good run is the result of your own skill and discipline. The truth is, we could have run into trouble on day one. Because the south is nothing like the all-but-deserted peninsula, where any approach is heralded by a plume of dust visible for kilometres. The terrain we were passing through was undulating. With skeletal thickets, granite tors. Blind corners, hollows, obstructions everywhere. Good for hiding. But if anyone approached, we never had the luxury of an early warning. And in those more clement southern districts, people seemed to be everywhere. If they weren't out policing what they had, they were like us, on the move in search of a viable situation.

I guess it was just a matter of time. And there came an afternoon when we were caught unawares.

We were camped in the gap between some high granites. I had a shade cranked out. The child fossicked contentedly at a distance.

490

I was working on a valve in the watermaker, showing my companion the adjustments I'd made, and submitting to her corrections because her calibrations were always superior. She'd bound her head in a length of green fabric I'd traded for the previous day. And with it she seemed happier, more secure.

The morning before, I'd left her with the child while I drove into a tiny crossroads hamlet to trade surplus vegetables and pastes. Our plan was to strike out further east in a day or so, to test conditions beyond the old farming districts and try our luck in the gimlet woodlands. I'd seen these from the air a time or two, heading out or back from long-haul jobs. Before the fires had chewed through them year upon year, they'd been a sea of green. Now they looked more like a chain of ponds. But I hoped they'd still be dense enough to give us shade, cover, and maybe somewhere safe to settle. Obviously, my intel was outdated. But I still wish we'd set out a day earlier. Maybe if we had, there'd be four of us down here in this hole, comrade, and my prospects would be rosier.

Anyway, I went in, cased the little vill from a distance. Figured it was safe enough. Went ahead and traded tomatoes for what I could. I think the emerald sash was an afterthought, a last-minute bid from a rough-looking dullard with ruined teeth. His mates, bigger men with a truck on a hoist, laughed at the parley but wasted no time getting their share of the spoils. I didn't like the look of any of them. I should have gone back to the granites and hauled us all away.

But the sash pleased the woman. And her pleasure disarmed me. I don't blame her for a second. It's just that I hadn't enjoyed such a feeling in years: the glory of making someone happy.

So, yes, we stayed the night. And the next day was so peaceful. Full of promise. As if our arrangement might be turning into something almost familial.

And there was a conversation we had, the woman and me. Late in the day, after we'd fixed the watermaker. I remember every word. Because it was our last, really.

You're a perfectionist, I told her, amused to see her tweaking the valve of the maker one more time.

Perfection is something to strive for, she said. But rarely achieved.

You're too modest.

Modesty is a virtue. It also increases safety.

I think you're taking me too literally.

No, she said. I am entertaining myself – respectfully – at your expense.

Ha, I said, delighted. Banter!

And I have made a discovery, she said with uncommon brightness.

Oh? I said, alert to her elevated mood. Something technical?

No, she said. I believe the child has her letters. She can read and write.

Really? How can you tell?

I observed her yesterday, while you were gone. She was making the words stamped here on these gloves. See? The name of the manufacturer and the size – they're embroidered here at the cuff. I saw her forming the name and the number with her mouth.

So, you're saying she knows English? I said, taking the spanner gently from her.

Yes, but she does not sign. I've tried all variants. And we both know she hears well. I believe she has been a speaker, that she isn't congenitally aphonic.

I turned the spanner over in my hands, stirred by the animation in her voice, the glitter of her eyes.

You think she might write something?

This is my hope, she said. Perhaps she will. Otherwise, she'll have to learn to sign. She needs to be understood. For her dignity as much as her safety.

I nodded, thinking of what this could mean for the child, and, perhaps, for us. And I'll confess, I was too preoccupied by implausible thoughts to properly register the woman's subtle change of posture, the way her head swivelled. Oh, the seconds you wish you could have back.

The child, she said.

Yes, I said. We'll teach her.

She reared up, knocking me aside. And that's when I heard the judder of a vehicle approaching. The child was squatting in the dirt at least a hundred metres beyond the farthest boulder. The last light flared off the crown of her hat. The woman got to her in less than three seconds. She swept her onto one shoulder. Then wheeled around and streaked back toward me. No human could move so fast or bear such a load at speed. And failing to remember this was the only mistake I ever saw her make. Because what she'd done was not lost on the men in the truck trundling across the burnt ground toward us.

When she set her down, the child was wailing and the woman herself was agitated, turning, peering, reckoning hectically.

You have lethal means, she said, gesturing at the driver's-side door of our vehicle. The child batted at her, outraged at the interruption and containment.

Yes, I said over the girl's cries. But that mightn't be necessary. We need to stay calm.

She's distressed. Can't you see?

Yes. But listen, we're just an ordinary family heading east, okay?

I made an error, she said.

Too late for that.

I should have fled. It was a mistake to turn back. We could be gone already.

No, I said. You won't make it anywhere, not carrying her. And now there's no time.

The truck rattled in and pulled up. The child stopped wailing. In the sudden silence, the whine of the flatbed's motors sounded unnaturally loud. Then they too cut out. For a moment all I heard was the blood in my ears and the child's panting. Then the truck doors opened. There were three of them. The men from the crossroads. Two were tall and burly. The other, the feeble-minded fellow who'd traded me the sash. Which he began pointing to as soon as he saw it on the woman.

G'day, said the driver, the sun in his eyes.

Evening, I said, resting a hand on the woman's shoulder, for comfort as much as performance.

I know you, he said. You're the bloke from yesterday.

Tomatoes, yes. But I'm all out.

Hn, he grunted, sizing up the child.

These two weren't with you, though, were they?

No, I said. They stayed out here.

Our place not good enough for 'em?

They just preferred to stay out here. They like prospecting.

The girl cowered and retreated behind the woman, who stood tall, one hand behind her to comfort the child, the rest of her taut.

Quite a runner you've got here.

I said nothing.

You've frightened the child, she said.

Well, that's a pity, said the driver. But you're not her mother.

You're not a citizen, said the other man. You're not even fuckin human. And that means you're some kind of slaver, he said to me.

She turned her head my way. You'll serve the child?

The kid's not your problem, said the driver.

Stay, I said, trying to grip her arm.

But she brushed me off. Sprang forward. Knocked the driver and one of his companions flat on their arses. The child sprawled, clutching and squalling in the dirt, while the woman glanced off the truck fender and sprinted through the burnt skeletons of the acacias beyond. I caught a last glimpse of the scarf trailing from her neck as the strangers scrambled to their feet and then to the truck. I clambered across the child to reach the tool in my vehicle, but their truck was turned around and gone before I could wrench it free.

I knew I'd need as much speed as possible, would never catch them with the weight of the trailer to haul, so I unhitched it. But that cost me precious time, and while I was labouring at that the waif bolted, so I was a minute or two chasing her down to bundle her into the cab, and by then it was properly dark. Once I got us clear of the granites, I got a fix on the lights of the truck jerking to and fro in the distance. I primed the tool and wished, for the first time in years, that I had a pair of night glasses.

Without lights, I picked my way slowly along the track. The girl cried and tore at her cheeks. I had to hold her and fend her off all at once.

She's fine, I told the girl. She's clever, remember. And she's fast. She'll hide until we reach her. I can stop this.

If the child heard me she gave no sign of it. She ripped her hair, grabbed at the wheel.

Stop it, I said, cranking up the windows to dampen the noise. You have to stop. So we can save her. She'll run them around a while, and then she'll hide. She's smart.

But the woman didn't hide. You could tell by the mad progress of their lights. I could see soon enough what she was doing. She was showing herself time and again, running full tilt, traversing the landscape in wild arcs that were so methodical her intention could not have been clearer. She was giving us time to break free. But I had no intention of breaking free, not even for the child.

I kept my distance. Watched for an hour. Then crept forward. Carefully. Steadily. It took another hour to close on them. We all seemed to be wheeling around in long semi-circles, tracking back and forth across the same lumpy terrain. And it became clear that if I wanted to recover the woman, the child would need to be restrained. So, yes, I stopped long enough to bind and gag her. Later, when the lights finally stopped moving, and I sensed I was close enough, I locked her in the vehicle and went ahead on foot. It was the only thing I did that night I'm glad of.

It was warm out in the open. Starless, mostly. The country ahead rose in a long, gradual incline. At what seemed to be a ridgeline there was a diffuse penumbra, a kind of hidden glow. Underfoot, the ground was stony and stumpy. Broken by pools of ash. Snarls of petrified wood snagged at my shins. I went as fast as I dared. But it was slow going.

Near the crest of the ridge, I heard voices. Laughter. Then screams. That's when I understood why the lights had stopped. They hadn't lost her. She hadn't even hidden. She'd just pushed herself too long and hard in the dark. She'd run out of juice.

But she clearly had enough charge left to scream. The sound curdled my spirit.

I bellied up to the ridgetop and beheld the wide, pale crater on the other side. It was an old farm dam. Empty but for a dark sump at its deepest point. At the edge of that, lurching and bobbing in the glare of the headlights, were feverish shadows and splashes of colour. The rear of the vehicle was slightly right of me, its doors open. I wasn't close enough to hear it humming, but I could easily make out the two upright figures in front of it as they bent and rose in the lights. From this position, I knew I could kill one, possibly both. But the third shape, the one on the ground defiling her, was too low. All I could see was the pale hull of his back.

There was no way I could hit him without destroying her. I needed to be closer.

I came down from cover and got to the lip of the dam. The bank was steep, riven with fissures and washaways. And despite the nature of what I was hearing, and my desperate need to stop it, I had no choice but to pick my way down slowly to avoid detection. The closer I got, the more the backspill of light from the truck illuminated me, but I reached the passenger door without being noticed. And I soon saw why.

There was a sudden roar of exaltation. And a hideous wavering shriek. I smelt the molten polymers before I saw the flames. The three of them were upright now, clear in the lights. And they were avid, gleeful, intoxicated by what they were seeing. My comrade was down on the pale clay. On her back. Writhing. A pillar of flame flaring from her belly. Blue and green and orange, it hissed in her pelvis and then ran down over her snapping legs.

I took the feeble-minded fellow first. Cut him down with a clap that showered the others, sent them reeling, patting at their faces and arms before they even thought to turn my way. When they did, they were staring blindly into the headlights.

Now look here, fella, said the driver.

The burst that cut him in half also killed the bloke beside him. I vaulted over their charred trunks, and the miasma of ozone and scorched flesh that came off them. When I got to her, she was still flailing – a twitching mess of flame and noxious fumes – but she was silent now. Her limbs were livid, her skin molten. Only her smoking boots were still solid enough to grip, so that's how I dragged her. By the feet. I hauled her, rattling and jerking across the clay, until I stumbled into the soft, black heart of the dam, where the mud was wet and deep enough to press her down until she hissed, and a grey ooze rose to partially obscure her. But she burnt on regardless.

Masked by bubbling muck and acrid steam. Shuddering. Roiling. Suffering. All I could do was watch to the end. When I clawed her out, there was nothing of her but a snarl of blackened mesh.

I stood a while, a horrible scouring sensation boring through me. As if my own insides had caught alight. I staggered back into the muddy hole to cool myself, put my own flames out. And I sat there a long time, settling deeper into the mire, until the truck's battery alarm began to chime. It was only later, when its lights began to fade, that I remembered the child. I lurched up, hauled the poor woman's frame back into the muck to conceal her, and staggered up onto solid ground to the juiced-out vehicle.

I didn't have time to burn the bodies or the energy to drag them down into the gut of the dam. I left them where they lay, took whatever was useful and portable from the truck, and climbed back out into the scorched country beyond.

I went mad when I lost Sun. And if not for the child, I might have gone to pieces after the woman was murdered. I'd only known her a few months. But the world in which I knew her was different to the one in which I knew Sun. When I had Sun and Ester, potential expanded every thought and experience. The world felt steady. The future stretched before us. Sure, there were threats across the horizon, but it felt as if we had so much promise to meet them with. Now the horizon *is* the future. Or so it feels. Hopes and loyalties live and die faster than the wriggling creatures that hatch in the desert after rain. Opportunities for intimacy – well, they're momentary. Perhaps even extinct.

I loved her. The sim. Sure, go ahead and laugh, twist your face in revulsion, I don't give a damn. Yes, she was only a machine. But you and me. Have we never been used as instruments?

Those of us who served. We wanted something pure. We dreamt of a world of fair-dealing and open prospects. The best for the most. We were prepared to make sacrifices for it. We thought that if our suffering was for the common good, then it was just a detail along the way. And now it seems details are all we amount to.

This is not despair, comrade. Because I don't despair. I won't. But that doesn't mean I don't mourn.

After the events at the granites, the child and I spent many hard days and weeks on the road. I went east, as planned, but at a punishing pace. We needed to flee the district as quickly and discreetly as possible, so I drove at night for as long as I could, and we slept during the day to let the batteries recover.

For the first week, the cab of my rig smelt so bad I was forced to travel with the windows open, regardless of the weather. The means by which the child was restrained during that period – well, I can't even talk about that. Except to say that given the choices before me – to abandon her to save myself or do whatever it took to keep her safe – I did the best I could. But it was a squalid salvation, I can tell you that much, and it set the girl back considerably. So much so that there were times when I once again thought the most merciful thing I could do to serve the child would be to throttle her.

I guess my lowest point was the morning we came to the burnt-out homestead. I think it's somewhere north-west of here. A long way back. Weeks ago. I'd been driving all night. Came to a halt at the first sign of habitation. Cut the lights. Pulled back into some rocky cover. Shut down the motors. Waited for the light to come up. And it was one of those slow-burn dawns. All the colours. Pretty. And you could see straight off the place was abandoned. Roofless. Two tin walls still standing. Surrounded by nests of rusted wire.

I booted up the rig, drove in. The kid woke. I opened the door but didn't dare let her out. The place was surrounded by grey tree stumps. They looked like a troop of dismembered warriors. I picked my way through them. Pushed past the snags of fence wire and stood in the ruins of the house.

I don't know what I was hoping to find. But the air felt gentle there. There was no breeze. The light was creamy. It set off something oceanic in the ripples of the tin walls. And, as I stepped around the stone floor, I couldn't help but think of the work folks had done here, the aspirations they must've had. The sun caught the windscreen of my rig and the flare of it jolted me from my reverie. I left the ruin and walked back to the rig, but just as I got there my knees gave way and I had to grab the push bar and scrabble at the dusty hood to keep myself from falling.

And I stood there, tottering a moment, and caught the look on the girl's face through the glass. There was shit in her hair and on her cheek. She looked alarmed, fearful. I tried to smile. To reassure her. But suddenly I was weeping. Silently at first, like a man gasping for breath after a blow to the gut. And then up it came, the awful lowing, a sound I'd never made, not even in madness. I wanted to fall but couldn't loosen my grip to let myself. I howled. Upright. Rooted to the spot with no camo and no cover. And the child looked on, streaming with tears.

Once I'd got hold of myself again, I untied her, and she didn't bolt. I fished out a towel, poured a deep dish of water and gave her some soap. She bathed in privacy, behind the trailer, while I swabbed the reeking cab. Then, pushing my luck, I suggested we wash her crusty hair, and she didn't fight me. I found her fresh clothes. Also, the woman's hat. Then I combed her hair with my fingers, the way our companion had. The child suffered this intimacy with a stoic set to her jaw, finally shrugging me away to finish the job herself.

And while the clothes dried and the cabin aired, we lay under the awning beside the vehicle and slept deeply until noon.

From then on, things were different. Better. I guess it was a kind of wounded resignation we shared. And as the days wore on, it sometimes felt closer to acceptance.

I spoke to her. I'd never stopped speaking to her, not even during the worst times, but I found ways of talking at her as if I were talking *with* her, if you understand my meaning. And although she preferred to gaze into the distance, her face tilted away from me, there were moments when I knew I had her full attention.

I told the child things about myself. What life had been like when I was a boy. I told her of the eagle I'd seen. Our water cave. And as I grew bolder, and the girl seemed less resistant, I spoke of the woman and her many virtues.

One evening, on the edge of a vast salt pan, I worked up the nerve to address our friend's martyrdom. I told it as a story of heroism. The marathon chase she'd led so that we might be spared. I told of our friend's speed. Her strength. Her cunning. And, most of all, her great courage. Which, I said, had not been an impulse to serve, but an expression of love. Not for me. For the girl. For her alone. It was so tempting to round out this tale with a kindly flourish, adding a splash of derring-do and an escape against all odds. To set aloft a glorious legend. Something consoling. Uplifting. Leaving the kid with the idea of her champion still at large in the interior, wily and forever on the lam, sending bandits crazy, running, harassing, biding her time, waiting for her moment to return to us. But I couldn't do it to her. I spared the child the details of the woman's death, but I didn't hide the fact of it from her. The best I could do was to tell her the truth. She was our saviour. And we'd always remember her. But she was gone for good.

It was harder to explain my own behaviour on that awful night. The child simmered for weeks at the indignity of what I'd done to keep her safe. I apologized in as many different ways as I could think of. Over time she relented a little, grew less hostile, less fearful, even if she remained aloof. In the end we settled on a travelling disposition that was peaceably efficient, if not truly companionable. We had a routine, set spaces and roles. Each of us understood what was required of the other. We served one another without pretending to be friends. And on the rare and perilous occasions when we found ourselves in company, we improvised a kind of forgettable neutrality. Perhaps a sullen girl and stony-faced man seemed a convincing model of family – who'd know?

A storm blew for two days. We hove to and rode it out inside the vehicle. From the eastern sky came a welter of ash. For a whole morning it rained slag and cinders. The light grew yellow, then orange. Memories of the Utah job sent stabs of panic through me. Exhausted and disoriented, the child whimpered in a ball in the footwell and eventually slept in the eerie gloom.

When it was over, I cleaned the panels and waited for the batteries to perk up. And then we pressed on.

Eventually we came to where the Great Western Woodlands should have begun to stretch out. But all that lay ahead was more ash. I could see we might be wallowing through it for days, so I veered north through the outermost drifts until I hit the saltlands. After that there was heath country, a smattering of outposts and encampments you could tell from a distance were not places for a child.

So I bore around to the east, short of the desert, and pressed into the stony plains of saltbush.

Comrade, you know what a lack of shelter does to the spirit. The dread that stalks you. The temptations you have to resist when you're desperate for safety. And the price that would have to be paid for the kinds of refuge you're presented with. All those gated compounds. The watchtowers, the wire, the floodlights.

I'll bet you're no different. You had to be riddled with doubt, given to wishful thinking. Tired – so bone-tired – of holding out. But you pressed on stubbornly. In hope. In search of something decent. And here you are, brother. And here I am. Tonight. In this, our current predicament.

I wake. Startled. And the bowman turns his head. My eyes are gritty, but I can see he's registered the first light of day in the vertical shaft beyond.

Did I sleep? I ask croakily.

You did.

How long?

Maybe half an hour.

I thought I was talking to you.

Jesus, man, don't fret – you could probably talk underwater. You're exhausting.

What else have I got?

It's a hell of a story. I'll give you that.

We've seen some things, comrade.

We have.

Tell me.

Tell you what?

What you've seen. I want to hear your story.

I don't have one.

Look at your hands, brother. Look at that bow and your single dart. You have a long story.

I can't.

Because of your oath?

Fuck the oath. I can't because I can't.

I get it, I say. I think I understand.

I doubt it.

Truly, I think I do. So much heat. So much fire. It's like you've breathed it in. And it's cauterized everything inside you. Remember that feeling when the wound sets and the scab forms and slowly tightens? When you get to the stage when you're half-recovered but too scared to move for fear you'll suddenly rip yourself open and everything will just spill out? I think it's like that. But if you don't move, you're stuffed. You make a cripple of yourself.

Well, that's a pretty speech.

Comrade, I'll listen.

I bet you would.

Aren't you lonely?

A man can feel alone in a crowd.

Three of us? It's not exactly a ravening horde.

I don't need the complication.

You want things to remain simple, I say. I see that. But do you really think what's ahead can be met with simple solutions? You think it won't be messy?

I know what I can do. I know what I have.

That's reassuring. But do you even know what you need? God knows, I don't. I don't know what's coming, how things are likely to settle. But I do know I don't want it to be one man against the world.

Well, he says. You've made that plain. We've had all night to know who you are and what you think.

So, was it all wasted?

Well, it helped pass the time.

Not the story, man! What we did, what we tried!

Look where you are, he says with a cheerless grin. What d'you reckon?

If there's any resistance left in us, if there's any decency, then yes. It was worth it.

Well, good for you. Food for thought.

I thought you still had some juice.

Sounds kind of insulting – even ungrateful – when you say it like that.

Brother, we kept the Long Peace. People were fed. Treated right.

And don't forget your big prize. You killed the EXXONS.

We all killed the EXXONS.

And yet here we are.

Alive, comrade. And sane. And still full of hope.

The child stirs. She looks around, startled for a moment, then remembers where she is.

It's okay, I say, pointing to the distant shaft of light boring in from above.

The bowman watches her. She takes him in sombrely. Then turns to me.

She needs to privy, I say.

He sighs and with some effort stands stiffly.

You have somewhere down here?

He jerks his head upward.

I'll go with her, I tell him. Keep watch.

We'll both go up.

I pull a rag from the pocket of my tunic and pass it to her. Blushing, she shoves it into the bib of her coveralls.

He reaches behind for the crossbow. Then he steps over, opens the lock, and backs away.

You know I have a cutter, I say. Used to work with metal. We could make darts for that thing.

The fins are the hard thing.

I reckon I could manage.

Jesus, man, you never stop trying.

Raised that way. Trained that way.

And now you want to know where the rest of the quiver went.

No, comrade. I don't think I do.

The girl yanks at my tunic.

She needs to go.

He sucks his teeth, inclines his head.

You sure there's not a bucket or something? I ask.

No one's shitting in a bucket down here.

Really?

C'mon on then, he says. Up you go.

The girl pushes the mesh back. Glances at me. And I nod. She steps out, cowers a little as she passes him. I follow. Steer her through the long case-stacked gallery as gently as I can. And at my touch, she neither flinches nor shrugs me off.

I can hear the bowman coming behind us. But I don't look back.

All through the night I'd consoled myself that, if he'd taken the trouble to bring us down into his lair, he wasn't likely to kill us. Only a fool would make a job for himself. Hauling our carcasses up that shaft. But here we are. Climbing the ladder for him.

I boost the child onto the first rung and whisper close.

Remember what I said? What's in the door? Of the car? Don't try it. Don't run for it. Don't try and use it.

I hear the short breath she takes through her nose, but she gives no sign she's heard me.

You're a strong girl, I say. A good girl. You don't have to save us. Because everything will be alright.

C'mon, says the bowman, limping up into the cell of light we stand in. Enough gabbing. Up you go.

The child starts up. Her raggy boots drop grit into my face as I watch her go.

You know what'll happen if you run, he says, his voice rising around us in the tunnel.

We won't run, I say. We don't want to run. We want to stay.

How will it work? he says.

I don't know – we'll make it work.

It won't, he says.

How do you know?

Experience.

I don't believe you. You're not like that. But I understand the need to perform. You're a serious person. I'll never take you lightly. I'm a man of my word.

Christ, he says, you're a man of a million words. Get climbing.

I look up. The child has gotten well ahead of me. I start up after her. And soon enough I feel the percussion of his hard boots rising through the rungs and rails below.

The light grows clearer, cleaner as I go. Above me, the girl's silhouette is like the bead in a peep sight. Then she's at the rim, out into the daylight. And I'm praying to her. Please don't run. Please don't go for the tool.

I scuttle up. At the surface, in the brassy glare, I see she's walked a little way clear already. Now she's dipping behind a weed-furred mound of pipe and sheeting. I look around at the old prospecting camp. Like a white-headed boil, the sun pushes up from the horizon. I note the skeletal frame of a mine head. A few more imploding sheds. And a lean-to shrouded by camo lattice. My own stuff. That'll be where the rig is stowed.

I could get there if I'm quick. It's only forty metres. Fifty at worst. The bowman is still clambering up the shaft.

I scan the ground for a lump of concrete, a stub of rebar. Anything I might use to drop on his head. But the child bobs up again. She sees the lean-to. Looks back at me. I shake my head. Behind me, the bowman emerges. I turn. Watch him unstrap the bow from his back. Note the cocking rope coiled in his hand. At the back of his dungarees, I see a single bolt protruding from the quiver at his shoulder. The bow is empty. One bolt.

I run all the angles in my head. Is he bluffing? Has he brought something else? Is he simply testing us?

You any good with that bow? I ask.

You asked me that already.

Did I quote from the sagas?

I believe you did.

Okay, I say. That's all I've got.

The girl stands up. Pats down her coveralls. I know she'll be hungry again now. She needs a wash. A change of duds.

Everything's fine, I call. For him as much as her. Myself also.

She doesn't nod. But she seems to have made a decision. Or perhaps she's just distracted, energized by the fresh air. She bounces out through the junkpiles.

Don't go far, he says.

She gives no sign she's heard him. Squats in the dirt to grub for treasures.

I turn to our host and shrug, and then I step out, slowly, to join her. I hear his boots behind me as he makes sure to keep within range.

I gaze down on the child, the tight curve of her back, the flaxen snarl of her hair. Then I hunker beside her to sweep the earth clear with the heel of my palm. In the sand, I write my name. Rub it away and write another. Do it all again. Then scrape it clean.

She blinks knowingly but offers nothing. She goes back to fossicking. I reach into my pocket. Behind me, the bowman coughs a warning. I turn and hold the little lozenge of stone up for him to see.

Jesus, he says. Is that poison?

No, mate. It's just a rock.

Fucking better be.

I crouch beside her and hold it out. The little chip I've carried all these years. There on my palm. A chert the size of an olive pit. Pink. With a chisel-edge as old as human consciousness. I've carried it all over, to nearly every roadside camp and job. Through years of repat and convalescence. A memory of home. A fetish, if you will. Sun once told me that a stone is an expression of the earth, a signal of time. But it's also a relic of experience. A thing propelled into the world. Dragging its past like an afterglow. And it's just a rock, but its journey isn't over, and neither is its destiny fixed. Not something I can explain to the child, much as I'd like to try. But if I had world enough and time, I'd tell her this stone was chosen, then flaked, carried hand to hand from inland deserts to the coast. Fashioned. As an implement. To do work. On this earth, in this same world as ours. And although that's not why I treasured it as a boy, I kept it close all these last hard years to remind myself of something more important than home. That humans are not just destroyers. We're makers. This is all I have to pass on. And she's all I have to pass it on to.

The child takes it, turns it over, and pokes it into the pocket of her tunic. And I stand, feeling the years in my knees. I hear the man's boots on the grit behind us. But I don't turn to face him. I hear the squeak of the rope as the bow is loaded. And I tell him not to fuck this up.

Everything is fine, I say.

She shows him her teeth. And I tell her not to be afraid.

Our friend, I tell her. He's stuck.

She looks at me.

We want to be his friend, I say. But he's not sure.

Without moving my head, I look left and right. I give myself even odds. But I don't want to enrage him. Or leave the child exposed.

I think he's afraid.

Fuck you, he says.

He wants to do right, I say. He knows what's right. It's still in him.

You can shut it now, he says.

It's okay, I say. To her, to him, to myself – who can tell?

The morning sun hits the junk-strewn wasteland, catches every rusted rim and edge. It's beautiful. And, truly, it's enough.

Last night – this morning, I suppose – I dreamt I was a thing of the sea, rising from darkness into the light of a billion tiny particles, each a body I could feel against my own. And nearer the surface there was a greater light, a creamy glow that lit the skin between me and the world beyond, and when I pressed on to break through it there was more than I could see and feel, but I found I could suck in air as cool and clean as the deeps themselves, and it was good, like something new and previously unimaginable. And as I stretched my limbs to float and to glory in it, my skin mottled with moving shadows. So I tilted my head. To see a constellation of hovering birds. They were black and white and grey. Suspended in nothing, sculling air. Their beaks and eyes and feet glistened. The sounds they made were urgent, hectic, curious, needy. I couldn't tell if they were there to greet me or to peck me to pieces, but I raised my hands to them anyway. And I waited.

Singing.

TIM WINTON is widely considered one of the greatest living Australian writers. He has published thirty books, and his work has been translated into twenty-eight languages. Since his first novel, *An Open Swimmer*, won the *Australian*/Vogel Award in 1981, he has won the Miles Franklin Award four times (for *Shallows, Cloudstreet, Dirt Music,* and *Breath*) and twice been shortlisted for the Booker Prize (for *The Riders* and *Dirt Music*). He lives in Western Australia.